KEEPER OF THE KEYS

a novel
by
Rosemarie Sheperd

Keeper of the Keys is dedicated

To my children, Sally and David, for their technical assistance and expertise and for their astute observations and guidance that made *Keeper of the Keys* evolve into all it was meant to be.

To Joe, my husband and steadfast proofreader, whose advice and vision for the cover inspired the story's unique conclusion and for his constant love and faith in me.

I thank my family for their encouragement and support, and I am deeply humbled by the level of their commitment to me and to my work.

ABOUT THE COVER ...

The tree featured on the front cover is a photograph of the 300 plus year old elm, known as "Hangman's Elm," that still thrives in the northwest quadrant of Washington Square Park in Greenwich Village in NYC. Individuals featured on the cover are deceased family members of the author, who were immigrants from Italy. The story bears no resemblance to their actual lives in either NYC or Italy.

BOOK ONE
ANA

Chapter 1

Ana Luisa Testadura
Villa Franca Sicula, Sicily
1902

"Epilogue. All that remained of the proud, beautiful, powerful beings that had once roamed heaven and earth were the keys to their kingdom, a thirst for their former glory and a maddening belief that one day they would return to reclaim them."

Ana closed the book, sighed and leaned back against the elm. One tear squeezed through her lashes and rolled down her cheek onto the page. She sniffled and wiped her cheek with the heel of her hand. A gentle breeze caressed her face, stirred a few strands of hair and fluttered the book's pages. She closed her eyes and hugged *Tales of Greek Gods & Men* to her heart. It was her newest, most favorite book, and she'd already read it so many times she could recite it by heart. Papa said books planted seeds in fertile minds, but in her mind books planted little explosives. Papa was right, but there was something he didn't know, and she did not have the heart to tell him. When the dust cleared, she was left with two choices: To remain here by the elm and brook, or to flee as soon as she could and venture into the world. She opened her eyes and frowned at the stream, feeling jealous. How it sluiced past anything in its way! If water could run as free as it pleased, why couldn't she?

The back door squeaked open. "Ana!"

Ana looked at her mother and scowled.

"Put the book down, and come in and wash up now," Mama shouted. "We're sick and tired of having to wait for you every time we sit down to eat. Do you hear me?"

Bristling at the razor-sharp edge of Mama's tongue, Ana felt the breeze stiffen and nudge the hem of her skirt. "The whole world can hear you," she whispered through clenched teeth.

"If you don't put that book down and come in right, now, I'll—"

Ana's eyes narrowed, and the wind picked up. It shouldered past her, devoured the rest of her mother's words and slammed the door shut. It swept leaves and twigs from bushes and trees and danced them into the stream. Startled, she watched the stream rage, foaming against rocks, ripping soil and twigs from its banks and rushing them downstream. The stream whipped up stones. One hit her cheek, and she flinched and jumped to her feet. The book slid off her lap, but she grabbed it before it slipped over the bank and into the stream. Thankful, she breathed a sigh of relief and—

The wind died. And the stream shrank to a babbling brook.

Ana looked around her, trying to grasp what had happened, when the back door squeaked open and Mama yelled, "Ana, for goodness sake. Did you hear anything I said?"

Ana sat down to dinner deep in thought.

"Young lady."

She looked up at Mama, who looked down her nose at a pitcher of milk next to the platter of sausage and pasta. "It's your turn," she said, her voice pinched with impatience. "Stop daydreaming and pour."

"Sorry, Mama," Ana said, and her sisters and brother giggled. She shot them a wait-until-later look, got to her feet, bypassed garlic bread, bowls of salad and grated cheese and grabbed the pitcher. To the din of her siblings' chatter, she walked the pitcher around the table and filled their glasses while the craziest thought drifted through her mind, a thought she dared not speak because no one would believe her. Was it possible that the change in her mood had whipped up the wind and riled the stream? She frowned and retraced her steps. She'd finished her book. She heard the door open. She heard Mama yell and—

Anger welled behind her eyes in a wave of heat that weakened her grip on the pitcher.

She tightened her grip on the pitcher and set it down on the table. She held her breath and darted a nervous glance around the table. To her relief, it seemed that no one had noticed. Next to Papa's plate was a jug of his homemade red wine. She exhaled slowly, gripped the jug with both hands, filled his glass and set the jug down. She slid into her seat, frowning harder. She'd been outside alone. Had she done it? Had she really whipped up the wind and the water?

She glanced at her Papa who had told her how special she was for as long as she could remember. Mama used to tuck her in, kiss her goodnight and say, 'You are the seventh daughter of a seventh daughter, and someday you'll understand exactly what that means.' That was before Ana grew up, and everything changed between them. She never believed Mama then, but after what just happened outside is this what they meant? This 'power' or gift, or whatever it was, had it come to her and not to the others because she was the special one?

On one hand, it sounded like a story from *Tales of Greek Gods & Men*, but on the other, Mama had said it, repeatedly, and Mama never lied. Ana longed to ask Mama, but her instinct warned that for now she must keep whatever this was a secret. Ana knew, that unlike her sisters and brother, there were times her behavior embarrassed her mother, badly. If word of this 'power' got out … Her eyes darkened, and suddenly she was afraid. What if she was mistaken? What if it wasn't a gift? What if it was a curse?

She gazed at the pitcher and despite her fear, she smiled, thinking whatever this was its possibilities were endless. What if she just *willed* the pitcher into the air and *willed* it to fill their glasses? And after dinner, what if she looked at the dirty dishes and thought, *clear yourselves!* And oh the pranks she could play on her siblings! She could spill their drinks, muss their papers and hide their toys. These thoughts made her want to laugh out loud. What fun and how much easier life would be if beds made themselves, and plants pulled their own weeds, and sheep herded each other. Then she could sit by her beautiful elm with her charming book and read till her eyes fell out.

A chilly finger grazed her cheek, and the smile slipped from her face. Gift or curse, whichever it was, Ana sensed it had just changed her life forever.

Chapter 2

Ana, Luisa and Giani

Ana saw her empty plate as a metaphor for her future, waiting to be filled with delicious possibilities. Papa always said that if she looked at the past and the present with open eyes, she could almost predict her future. Ana decided that now was the time.

Ana Luisa Testadura, the seventh daughter of Luisa and Giani Testadura, was born in Villa Franca Sicula on the island of Sicily in 1888. Discounting Chiara, Maria and Carmela, her three married sisters who no longer lived at home, she glanced at Francesca and Gina, and her younger brother, Tonio, and smiled. There was no doubt in her mind that *she* had been gifted with the superior intellect. A tiny frown creased her brow. Her theory would be flawless if not for a tiny blemish. Her oldest sister, Lucia, might have been the brightest had she not died the day she was born. Weary of letting a sister she never knew mar her self-image, Ana erased the phantom Lucia from the equation once and for all.

A voracious reader and a quick study, Ana knew that her superior intellect would be of little or no use to her in turn-of-the-twentieth-century Italy. To her knowledge, few Italian families educated their daughters beyond the basics. To her misfortune, Italian parents believed that when a woman became a wife, she was her husband's property, and he would take care of her for the rest of her life. Ana openly scoffed at such ignorant traditions. She'd rather die than wear the straitjacket of provincial beliefs because mothers in Villa Franca Sicula expected it. Unlike her five older sisters and her younger brother, Ana craved to taste the wide, robust world that existed beyond her narrow, malnourished one. In preparation for the glorious day she would leave Villa Franca forever, she sharpened her wits on anyone who had the misfortune to cross her path. If a boy said the sky was blue, she would argue until he walked away convinced it was red.

As a realist with perfect eyesight, Ana knew she was not pretty, but she was not unpleasant to look at either, especially when she smiled, so she'd been told. And, having seen each of her sisters naked on more than one occasion, it was obvious that the characteristics her mother resented were housed in the most perfect female body the good Lord had ever created. It was as if He had handcrafted Ana as a prototype in whose image He would henceforth create all women.

She was dishearteningly aware that she lived in a time where women were overprotected, and handsome young men were not likely to court girls whose looks did not match their brilliant minds. With her marital prospects slim to nonexistent, it appeared that her flowering loveliness was destined to stay a well-kept secret, indefinitely.

Ana knew everyone believed that Mama, a tall, reserved woman, suffered from crippling migraines caused by Ana's incorrigible behavior. To the contrary, it was clear that the father she adored, seemed pleased, perhaps proud, of everything Ana did.

The harsher Mama frowned at Ana's perceived transgressions, the wider Papa smiled. Ana saw how her papa delighted in her confidence, wallowed in her irrepressible wit, and respected her astute perceptions and her indomitable spirit.

Ana trusted that Papa, her greatest ally, would never see her in the same light that her mother and the rest of their tiny world had. They were deaf, dumb and blind not to see how her papa adored her. She knew by the gleam in his eye that she was refreshing, a welcomed change from her annoying little brother and her five boring sisters. When she behaved in a way that incurred Mama's wrath, Papa would laugh and remind Mama that Ana was the seventh daughter of a seventh daughter, and that the fig doesn't fall far from the tree. But instead of laughing with him, Mama would scowl and turn away.

Ana basked in her papa's admiration. She loved that he loved the way her mind worked. He clearly relished her outrageous sense of humor. Hadn't she heard him explaining to Mama how she, Ana, had a gift for identifying the absurdly comedic in everyone and everything around them? Ana closed her eyes and smiled. If she truly was as irreverent and unmanageable as Mama believed, Papa was to blame. Hadn't the twinkle in his eye emboldened her to behave in that very way every chance she got?

"Ana!"

Ana flinched, opened her eyes and looked around the table. The twins, Francesca and Gina giggled.

"Stop daydreaming and fold your hands," Mama said. She swept her skirt beneath her and slid into her seat. "Papa is ready to say grace."

"Yes, Mama," Ana said, scowling at the twins, who stuck out their tongues and giggled harder. She smiled thinking of all the "powerful" ways she would get even.

Giani tapped his dish with the handle of his fork, and the fidgets and giggles stopped. His stern expression melted into a smile, he folded his hands on the table and closed his eyes. While others bowed their heads and closed their eyes, Ana glanced at her mother. Mama frowned deeply. She lowered her chin to her chest, unclasped her hands and massaged her temples, a signal that a terrible headache was brewing. Mama could rid herself of her headaches. All she needed to do was shed the straight jacket that *her* mama had forced her to wear.

"In the name of the Father, the Son and the Holy Ghost, amen." Papa opened his eyes.

"Amen," they said and opened their eyes.

The air was thick with flavor. Giani inhaled. "Ahhhhh," he said, and his children giggled. He licked his lips, passed his plate to Mama and rubbed his hands in anticipation. Luisa filled the plate and handed it to her husband.

Knock! Knock! Knock!

Luisa looked at the door and said, *"Who is it?"*

"Dio," a man answered.

"Ah, *Dio.*" Luisa said.

Hearing his name, Ana suddenly smiled. She raised her glass of milk to her lips.

Luisa stood the spoon in the pasta, wiped her palms on her apron and opened the door.

"Ven aca, Dio." Come in, *God,* Luisa said.

And *God,* a dwarfish balding man with bad skin, a snub nose and small black eyes, whose personal hygiene matched his physical appearance, walked through the door, clutching his cap in his hands.

Meeting 'God's' eyes, Ana felt a ripple of laughter begin in her toes and rise in a wave that broke at the back of her throat. She coughed, and milk shot from her mouth across the table, missed Francesca and hit Gina. Her face dripping in milk, Gina looked down and wailed at the stain on her dress, and then she looked up and scowled at Ana, who was laughing so hard she howled.

"Ana!" Luisa said, pounding the table, and the dishes and glasses danced.

Ana jumped up and grabbed her napkin. "Sorry, I—" She stuffed her napkin into her mouth, and stifling her laughter, she hurried out of the kitchen.

Her skull splitting with rage, Luisa's face tightened. The rage crested and broke in droplets of sweat along the lines in her forehead. Her knees weakening, she steadied her gaze and met *Dio's* eyes. *"Dio. Please."* Motioning their neighbor in, she looked at Giani with eyes that said, "Fix what your daughter has broken!"

Giani cleared his throat and got to his feet. *"Dio."* He hurried around the table. "I apologize," he said, "I'll deal with Ana later, but first things first, my friend." He took his neighbor's arm. "Please, sit and break bread with us."

Not good enough, Luisa thought. See the way he averts his eyes and shifts from foot to foot? See the way his fingers clench and unclench his cap. Luisa felt her armpits dampen her dress with crescent moons of sweat.

"No. Grazie." Dio said. He shook his head and squeezed his cap harder.

"Please. Do us the honor." Luisa said. She heard her voice crack and she felt her color deepen.

"Thank you but my business can wait for a more convenient time."

Looking embarrassed, *Dio* bowed his head, backed out of the room and closed the door behind him.

Three pair of wide, anxious eyes stared at their mother. Luisa scowled and said, "Go to bed."

"But, Mama," Gina cried, trying to wipe the milk from her dress with her napkin.

"Do as I say!" Luisa snapped. *"Now!"* She grabbed a broom she kept near the door and swatted the legs of her children's chairs. Francesca and Gina scurried away like two terrified mice. Luisa dropped the broom and glared at her son. "Go to bed!" she screamed. She grabbed a fistful of hair and yanked him out of his seat. Chest heaving, Luisa let go.

"It's not fair. Ana is bad, and we have to go to bed without supper," Tonio sobbed. He ran out of the room.

"You know he's right," Giani said softly. He picked up his fork and toyed with his food.

Her headache worsening, Luisa sat and exhaled a tired breath. Her eyes welling with tears, she pounded her fist on the table again, and the place settings jumped. Sauce spattered napkins with tiny red stars.

"You must punish Ana. Now!" she whispered harshly. She picked up her napkin and blotted her eyes.

"Luisa, please, calm down. You're behaving like a madwoman." He licked his lips and moved chunks of sausages back and forth in the sauce.

"This time Ana has gone too far." Luisa threw down her napkin and stood. She snatched Giani's plate away. "Did you see *Dio's* face? Behind that face seethes a cauldron of treachery," she said, scraping his uneaten food into the trash. She set his plate in the sink. She collected her children's unused plates and shoved them onto shelves in the cupboard. She crammed the pasta, bread, salad and cheese on the counter next to the sink.

"My God, Luisa—"

"Stop!" she said, wild-eyed and clenching her jaw. She took her seat, folded her arms on the table and leaned toward him. "Let me tell you exactly how your precious Ana's latest outrage and lack of respect will unfold.

"Armed with juicy morsels, our little rat of a neighbor will hurry to town before the cock crows. The other rats will sniff the air and crawl out of their holes."

"Why do you insist on telling tales?" Giani shook his head and reached for his wine, the only sustenance left on the table.

"I don't tell tall tales. I know him. I know how he thinks. I know how the rats in the village think. You of all people must know by now that when I sense things strongly, they usually come true. As my mother's—"

"Seventh daughter, I know that you feel things," Giani said. He stood, lifted his wife to her feet and tried to hug her. She stiffened, pulled back and looked into his eyes.

"You know that the things I sense are more than feelings. They're premonitions."

"Of course, I know. I've seen first-hand how your premonitions come true."

She frowned at him. Did he mean it this time, or was he trying to smooth her ruffled feelings as usual? Gazing into the distance she stared blankly and said, "First the village will sympathize with us over our little Lucia having died the day she was born, and how God has blessed us, because we've married off Chiara, Maria and Carmela. Then," she smiled coldly, "they'll slither like the snakes they are and hiss that unless we learn to control Ana's unacceptable behavior, we'll be saddled with her for the rest of our natural lives!"

"Luisa," Giani said, tightening his hold.

"They'll wonder aloud why Ana cannot behave like Francesca and Gina, like a genteel woman should."

Sensing his protest, she squirmed out of his arms, looked him in the eyes and pressed her finger to his lips. Her eyes stung. Her hand tightened into a fist.

"Don't you see, Giani? When the village learns what Ana did tonight, her fate will be sealed. I know it, here," she said, laying her hand over her heart. "Even the most desperate family would never choose a rude, arrogant, headstrong girl for their son to marry." She lowered her arm, unclenched her fist and pressed her cheek to his chest. "Because God help me, Giani, I would never choose a girl like Ana for Tonio." She pulled away again and looked into his eyes. "Unless we tame Ana and force her to change her ways," her eyes grew wider and more distant, "I sense she is destined to suffer a horrible fate."

Her doorknob turned, and her door creaked open. Ana shut her eyes. Someone stood by her bed. Inhaling the scents of wool and tobacco, Ana thanked God it was Papa. He sat on her bed, and she felt her heart sink with her mattress.

"Young lady, I know you're awake."

Dio's face flashed before her eyes. Her lips were a dam. She pressed them together before they burst with her laughter. She mustered her self-control, raised herself up and reached for the gas lamp that stood on her nightstand. She turned up the flame and looked at father.

He simply said, "Why did you do that to *Dio?*"

The dam broke, and Ana drowned in a flood laughter.

"Ana!" he whispered harshly, sounding far more indignant than he looked. She stopped laughing and sniffled. She watched him dart a worried glance at her bedroom door. He rose up and softly closed it. "Ana," he said, quietly moving toward her. His voice matched his calm, but his face could not hide his anger. She watched him closely. It seemed like he wanted to shake her. She scooted back against her headboard.

"Surely you of all people saw what happened in there, Papa," she said, sniffling and wiping her eyes.

"I saw an ill-mannered, arrogant brat, whom I've indulged most of her life, embarrass her entire family, especially her mother. Not to mention poor *Dio.*"

Ana smiled. Giani glared, and the smile slipped from her face.

"I'm waiting." He folded his arms across his chest, trying hard to look stern, she thought.

Eyes downcast she said, "We finished saying grace," she paused. She brushed her bedsheet free of imaginary lint. "We started to eat, when *Dio,*" she said, her lips twitched into a smile. Papa cleared his throat along with her smile. "When Mama asked who was at the door, he said, 'God,'" she paused and looked at her father, who looked puzzled.

"But, *Dio* is his name."

"I know. I've heard his name my entire life, but in that instant, perhaps because we had just finished thanking God for our blessings, images of our Heavenly Father and *Dio* got all mixed up in my mind. I mean, *think*, Papa, who in their right mind would name their child, *God?*"

Suddenly, his stern-mask-of-a-face shattered, and they laughed until their eyes and noses ran.

The bedroom door he had closed softly burst open and banged against her dresser. Father and daughter stopped laughing as abruptly as they had started.

Her hair long and flowing, her eyes sizzling, Luisa said, "How could you embarrass *God* like that?"

And Giani and Ana burst into peals of laughter. Luisa stormed out, slamming the door behind her. Giani stopped laughing. He jumped to his feet and opened the door, but before leaving her room, he turned and faced Ana. "We're not finished, young lady."

Knowing he'd failed again in his wife's eyes, Giani opened the door and crept into their bedroom and closed the door behind him.

Luisa sat at her dressing table. Glaring at him through the mirror, she picked up her hairbrush. "How could you betray me like that?" She grunted, accompanying each word with punishing strokes that made him wince at the obvious depth of her anger. She stopped, twisted around in her seat and faced him. "I sent you to Ana's room to discipline her, and what do I find? The two of you laughing as if what she had done was a great joke."

"Getting angry and yelling at Ana won't solve a thing, Luisa."

"You're right." She jumped up and slammed her brush to the floor, cracking its mother of pearl handle. "Where Ana and you are concerned there is no solution. She's bewitched you from the day she was born."

"Bewitched? That's a strange word to use," he smiled. "I'll admit I tend to be a bit more lenient with Ana than—"

"Lenient?" Luisa touched his nose with hers. "You spoil her rotten."

"That isn't true."

"It is." She backed away, sat on the bed, clenched her fists, and pounded the mattress, "and *you* know it!"

Giani slid next to his wife. "Please, let's not argue, Luisa. You're her mother, and you're a good mother."

"How can you say that, when you know as well as I that no matter how hard I try, I can't get through to her."

"Nonsense. Ana is lucky to have you. She's young. You must be patient. She has a lot to learn from you."

"Like what?" she said, staring into his eyes.

"Like how you've managed to survive life in our tiny, complicated village." He took her hands in his. "You must talk to her. How else will she learn that skill, if not from you?"

"I've talked my tongue limp. I lie awake nights thinking of ways to reach her before her shameless defiance makes it impossible for us to hold our heads high. I'm at my wits' end."

"Don't say that." Giani squeezed his wife's hands. "Don't even think it. Keep talking. She'll hear your words."

"Words!" She pulled away and threw up her hands in disgust. "Yours. Hers. Mine. I'm sick of words."

"A mother must keep talking until her daughter hears her."

Giani stood. "I know mothering Ana is hard at times." Despite his sympathy for Luisa, he felt his pride in his Ana glow in his eyes like candles in darkness.

"My God," Luisa said, looking astonished. "Even now, though her behavior tonight may have added the lethal blow to her sparse marital prospects, you continue to delight in her. Her eyes flashed. "And it's obvious you feel the same way she does."

Giani frowned. "What way is that?"

"That I, who chose being a wife and mother over being educated, that I'm too ignorant to understand my husband and my own daughter."

"Ana would never think such a thing let alone say it, Luisa, and you know that." Luisa's nostrils flared. Her chest rose and fell. A storm brewed in her eyes. Hoping to deflect the inevitable, Giani smiled and said, "Besides, if you can read my mind, I must watch what I think."

Luisa closed her eyes. "How many times must I tell you, this is not a joke, Giani." Tears oozed past the tight knit of her lashes and rolled slowly down her cheeks.

"You're right," he sighed. "It's not a joke, but it is our duty and our responsibility as parents to understand her. If we don't, who will?"

Luisa opened her eyes. "We have a duty and a responsibility to Gina, Francesca and Tonio, who get so little of our attention because Ana soaks most of it up like a giant sponge. We also have a duty to uphold our honor and our good name."

"You're making too much of this."

Luisa sniffled and wiped her tears. "No matter how I try, Giani, I can't seem to enter the world you and Ana share. How can my husband and my daughter understand each other more than I can understand either of them? The older she gets, and the closer the two of you become, the more you exclude everyone from your world. Especially me."

"Of course," he sighed. "Now I see that this product of your imagination concerning Ana and I is the real reason you resent your own flesh and blood. Tell me I'm wrong."

Luisa felt her face flush with shame. He was right. She was jealous of Ana, but what she sensed and felt went beyond jealousy. Luisa knew that her seventh-daughter intuition had never held sway with Giani. But it was her intuition that made her see Ana in ways Giani could not.

Besides being unnervingly smart and different to a flaw in her thinking, Ana had crawled, stood, walked and talked more quickly than her sisters, her brother and every other child they knew in Villa Franca Sicula. But the power Luisa knew Ana possessed had yet to manifest itself. And that scared Luisa to death.

She must admit, as Giani had pointed out strongly on more occasions than she cared to remember, that as an *impressionable* child growing up, Luisa had soaked in her mother's and aunts' riveting tales about how those who'd lived before them were gifted with second sight. Riveting or not, they were not tales. Luisa possessed the power of *knowing.*

"Luisa!" he said.

She gasped. His words shattered her silence like stones against fragile glass.

She wished she could swear to Giani that he was wrong, that she was not jealous. If she whined, he'd stop listening. And then whom would she confide in? Her pride was a fierce master. She'd rip out her tongue before letting it wag to strangers about private matters. Luisa would rather die before conveying less than domestic perfection to the outside world. And life truly had been perfect, until Ana grew up.

"Ana rejects and resents me," she said.

"I don't believe that."

"As you wish. But it's true." Luisa stared blankly. "At her age I sat enthralled while my mother taught me to stitch the delicate buds that border our linens." She smiled at the memory. "I remember my mother's face beaming with pride when I mastered the skill, and how we talked and planned and laughed while we packed the linens away in the chest that my father had built especially for me."

Luisa snapped out of her reverie and looked into her husband's eyes. "The chest you built for Ana is empty. Why? Because Ana wants nothing to do with embroidery. To her it's a waste of time. She wants more out of life than to marry a boy from Villa Franca Sicula, bear his children, and then spend the rest of her life in a house like this, leading *my* life." Luisa's lips trembled. "Go ahead. Deny it. Defend her."

Giani grasped his wife's arms. "How can I make you see that Ana says these things as a defense to cover the hurt she feels when families in the village came and asked for her sisters' hands in marriage and not hers? Oh, Luisa. Sometimes your anger blinds your love and your judgment."

Luisa frowned. When she opened her mouth to protest, he took her hand and kissed it. "But this time, you're right. Ana was rude to *Dio*. And if she does not apologize soon, I will punish her. I promise."

Her eyes brimmed with tears of joy. Could it be that the husband she so desperately adored finally understood her dilemma? She hugged and kissed him and thanked God for answering her prayers.

Giani stroked her hair. My poor Luisa. What crouching demon twists your thinking and makes you think that by loving Ana I'm turning away from you? God knows the harder I try to explain how absurd your thinking is, the less you understand me. You are my wife. I love you and nothing can change or replace that. And Ana, she is this

19

wonderful gift you gave me. A gift I never expected, but one for which I will always be grateful.

Luisa looked up and smiled, and Giani kissed her forehead. On one hand, she was a caring, loving, wife and mother who handled the concrete duties of their world with remarkable efficiency. On the other, she lacked imagination. The abstract eluded her. The implied or inferred confused, unnerved and angered her. How could he make his wife understand that their daughter comes to him because her mother has made it impossible for her to do otherwise?

Chapter 3

Giani, Ana and Luisa
Villa Franca Sicula, Sicily
1902

Giani stood in the parlor watching Ana place the Three Wise Men, the Virgin Mother and St. Joseph near baby Jesus in the manger. He'd kept his promise to Luisa. After Ana apologized to *Dio,* the tension between his wife and daughter had eased up a bit, before growing steadily worse.

He handed Ana an ornament, a little angel with golden hair and sparkling wings that she'd made in school years ago. "Your mother loves you," he said, realizing how quickly time had passed, making what Ana must do for him and for herself more urgent. Her eyes glistening, Ana smiled and placed the golden-haired angel on the roof of the stable.

"I know you love your mother," he said. He saw Ana's body grow tense. Her fingers froze in mid-air. He reached out and touched her shoulder, "You need your mother, and she needs you."

Ana sighed, "Papa—"

"Please, let me finish," he said, taking her hands in his. "I want you to make a sincere effort to move closer to her. She worries about you. A daughter should not cause her mother to worry, especially on Christmas Eve."

"I've tried, Papa, but—"

"You must try harder, Ana. Please, for me."

Giani belched softly into his napkin dabbed his lips and sighed contentedly. He leaned back in his chair and smiled. Basking in his family's lively chatter, he picked up his fork.

Hearing its tines tap twice against his glass, his children's chatter faded, and their gazes slowly drifted his way. Smiling more broadly, he caressed his wife's cheek and lifted a glass, half-filled with his homemade wine. The others followed suit.

"I believe I speak for everyone when I say, thank you, *cara mia,* for *La Vigilia di Natale* that you labored long and hard to prepare. We tasted your love in every bite."

"Cin! Cin!" the others cheered. Following Giani's example, they drained their glasses.

"I'll brew a pot of *demitasse* and cut the *buccellato,"* Luisa smiled, gathering the dinner plates and blushing, obviously pleased by her husband's words. As if on cue, his daughters put their glasses down, rose, and began helping their mother clear the table.

Giani got to his feet and patted his stomach. "In the meanwhile, I think I'll step outside and walk around a bit. Give my stomach a chance to make room for dessert.

"Children," he motioned at Chiara, Maria, Carmela and their families. He slid his chair under the table, "come join me. You, as well," he said looking at Tonio, Francesca and Gina.

They looked at their father and then at each other and frowned. "But, Papa," Gina said, "we always help Mama clean up."

"Can you grant your papa his wish and give him ten minutes of your time on Christmas Eve?" he said, softly, corralling them toward the door. Locking eyes with Ana, he nodded solemnly toward the kitchen where Luisa had begun rinsing plates.

Dreading this moment, Ana walked into the kitchen. She wrung her hands, and not knowing how or where to begin she took a deep breath and said, "Mama?"

Luisa turned. Noticing only Ana, she frowned. She picked up her favorite serving dish, scratched at baked-on tomato and rinsed. Placing it in a pan of hot, soapy water, she said, "Where are the others?"

"Outside with Papa. I need to talk to you, Mama."

"Is something wrong? Are you all right?" Luisa wiped her soapy hands on her apron.

"Yes and no," Ana stammered, sensing that this talk Papa wanted her to have with Mama was going to end badly. Not knowing how to begin, she clumsily blurted, "You and I, we have very different views on life, Mama and—"

"Ana, what are you talking about?" Luisa's frown deepened. She reached for and rinsed a wine glass.

"Papa and I, we were talking, and—"

"Of course," Luisa scoffed. "That's why we find ourselves alone in the kitchen." She washed the wine glass, rinsed it and stood it on the counter.

Ana let her mother's comment slide. "Papa said you're worried about me."

"He's right, I am." Luisa reached into the soapy water for the serving dish.

"Please don't worry, Mama. Please let me try to explain my feelings. Perhaps I haven't done it well enough in the past. You see," she spoke quickly before she lost her nerve, "I'm different from my sisters and the other girls in the village."

Holding the plate in her soapy hands, Luisa turned and gaped at her daughter.

Desperate to please Papa, Ana dismissed her mother's widening eyes and ignored the soapy water dripping on the floor. The thoughts she had locked away breached the door in her heart that she had so carefully bolted shut. "I don't want what they want," she frowned, distracted, "well, at least I don't want it now.

"First, I want to travel the world and see the places I've read and learned about. I want to stand on Mt. Olympus where Apollo, the Greek god of healing and medicine stood." There, I did it, Ana thought, cautiously optimistic.

"Look out the window, Mama," she said. She felt her eyes sparkle with the promises the window framed. "There's a whole world beyond this farm and our village. I want to see it. Meet its people. Eat their food. Dance to their music." Her eyes shone, and her heart's desire fueled her courage. She clasped her hands and closed her eyes. "Perhaps I'll write about my travels. After all, I get excellent grades in language. Aren't my teachers always telling you and Papa that I have a wonderful imagination and a gift for writing?"

The sound of porcelain hitting the floor and smashing to bits snapped open Ana's eyes. She turned away from the window. "Mama," she said, stunned. "You dropped your favorite dish. Thank goodness you have another," Ana darted her gaze to the shelf where it stood.

Kneeling, Luisa carefully gathered each shard and placed it into her upturned apron, "What a pity you were not born a boy," she mumbled. She shook the shards from her apron into a trash can near the back door and made her way back to the sink.

Crushed by her mother's words, Ana felt tears well in her eyes. She trembled in stunned incredulity. "How can you say such a thing to me?"

"Because, my naïve little Ana, only boys can dare to dream of leaving home to see the world. And as far as this notion of writing is concerned," she snarled, "it's frivolous and impractical. You need to learn how to cook and clean and keep house for your husband and children. Words heaped on their plates won't fill hungry bellies."

"She wants to do *what?*" Giani got to his feet. Drained of color, his face looked weary, strained. He paced the kitchen floor, rubbing his hand across his mouth. He stopped and frowned, shook his head and rubbed his eyes. Was he hiding tears?

Luisa's scalp tingled. She'd never seen Giani so angry, but with whom? Her? Ana? Both? If repeating her conversation with Ana backfired, being able to undo the harm would be like trying to un-ring a bell. Her heart racing, Luisa watched Giani pace. Each time he passed her, his face seemed to sprout a new worry line.

"And to add insult to injury," he said indignantly, "her foolishness angered you so, that you dropped and broke your favorite dish. Thank goodness you have another."

Broke my favorite dish? *Gesu Cristo,* Luisa thought, trying hard to control her racing heart. Her underlying fear of Ana's words, the fire in Ana's eyes and how such unbridled anger might trigger the power Luisa sensed Ana had, distressed Luisa beyond a concern as mundane as a broken dish.

Don't you see, Giani? Unless we control Ana and force her to change her ways ... she is destined to suffer a horrible fate.

Then, without warning, her heart slowed, as though it had beaten her mind to a life-altering conclusion. Watching Ana's foolishness send Giani into shock, Luisa suddenly realized that this same foolishness was affecting her differently. Clearly, Ana's words had opened his eyes wide enough to see that dreaming was one thing. But to hear that Ana was bound and determined to make her dreams come true was very much another.

A smile played at her lips. Ironically, Ana's assessment of her mother had been right all along, but not in the way Ana or Giani thought. It was true that Luisa's perceptions and wisdom did not extend beyond knowing how to survive in their provincial little village. But the blinding fear in her husband's eyes, had given her insight into her problems. The patience and persistence Giani had invested in trying to teach her to grasp reality on levels other than those of stone and mortar had finally yielded one very narrow, very deep dividend.

With crystal clear vision, Luisa Testadura knew she must cement Giani's fear of losing Ana to her foolish dreams with his instinct to protect. This would be the perfect way to neutralize Ana's behavior. It would also lessen Luisa's fear of whatever power she believed Ana possessed. And as a bonus, Luisa would reclaim her rightful place in her husband's life.

Luisa smiled broadly with her new insight. Timing was everything. Now, she would just sit back and wait.

Her smile melted. Her eyes glistening, she said, "Giani, look at me." He turned, and she gasped. His eyes seemed to swim with fear. Before they could weaken her resolve, she said, "We've indulged Ana far beyond what is safe. Now, we must tighten the reins and discourage her from such foolish ambitions."

"But how can we do this, Luisa?" His words sounded thick with desperation.

Luisa gathered him into her arms, and pressing her cheek to his, she fixed her eyes on a bright horizon. "Don't worry, Giani. When the time comes, I'll know exactly what we must do."

Chapter 4

Ana and Giani
Seeds of Migration
1905

Sniffing a handful of basil, Ana opened the back door. Before setting foot in the kitchen, she kicked each boot against the back step. Soil fell away. She kicked the clumps aside and closed the kitchen door behind her.

Mama stood at the sink, wringing out delicate laundry, glancing at Papa and looking worried. Seeing Papa frowning and staring blankly, Ana dropped her hands to her sides. Her fingers loosened. Basil leaves fell to the floor in a green flutter. The look in her papa's eyes, a look she had seen only once before, made her want to run out the door and into the hills until she dropped.

She rushed to his side, knelt, and clutching his arm, she stared at his unblinking eyes suddenly realizing, that the last time she'd seen Papa laugh so hard he cried, was the night *Dio* had come to call. The very next day, when Papa had walked her to *Dio's* to make her apologize, she was so angry she'd fumed for days. Living up to the Testadura name, the hard-headed Ana had refused to speak, especially if spoken to. That happened in 1902.

In 1903 their world had collapsed. It seemed as if Lucifer had opened the gates of hell, unleashing a demonic plague whose destruction was still fresh in their minds. A sixth cholera pandemic had broken out in North Africa. Despite the extreme measures Europe had taken, cholera hit Sicily, and tales of the way it occurred had spread faster than the disease. A band of infected Tunisians fleeing the plague had managed to stow away aboard a Sicilian steamboat that was anchored near the North African coast.

Fearing an outbreak, some friends and neighbors had barred their doors, covered their windows, and huddled in fear and darkness. Others had crammed into churches where the hum of their prayers, begging God to spare their villages, buzzed in the air like a plague of locusts.

In the fifth pandemic, God had seen fit to spare Villa Franca Sicula. In the sixth, for reasons of His own, He had not. Lucca Sicula and Burgio, the villages where her sisters and their families lived had not been spared either. In addition to placing them under quarantine with questionable security, Rome had ordered the people to burn their clothes, bedding, towels, linens and to the dismay of all, their livestock. Just when the people thought life couldn't get worse, Rome had issued a final decree to burn the dead before burying them.

Day and night dead bodies twisted in purifying flames, until the suffocating stench had reached Palermo. Besides shattering lives and ruining families, cholera had taken her sister Gina, and *Dio,* their strange little neighbor.

With grim determination and a deep faith in God and family, Giani, Luisa, Ana, Tonio and Francesca had worked day and night in the struggle to start over. Amid the nightmare one bright spot emerged. Francesca had married Paolo, and last week they announced they expected their first baby. Life would never return to what it had been, but by 1905 it had slowly gotten better. At least, that's what Ana had thought until now.

"Papa? Ana closed her eyes, terrified of the question she had to ask. "Is it cholera?"

He shook his head. Weak with relief, she opened her eyes, and a soft gasp escaped her lips. His eyes were sunken pockets ringed in grayish blue. When had the flesh shrunk from his skull and left his cheeks looking hollow? When had his black lustrous hair become limp and tinged with gray? Ana reached out, but he grabbed her fingers before they touched his face.

"mPlease leave me, Ana, I must think."

She squeezed his fingers. Her eyes never wavered. "No, Papa. You can't chase me away this time." She sat opposite him. "If it's not cholera, then what is it?"

Cut from the same stubborn cloth as her father, Ana tugged on the thread and weakened its seam. She held his rough hands in hers and looked into his eyes.

"You haven't confided in me since—"

"For goodness sake, Ana!" Luisa said, cutting her off.

Nostrils flaring and eyes glistening, Ana glared at her mother.

"For once in your life do what your father asks. If you really want to help," she said, gathering a bundle of wet clothes in her arms, "take these and hang them on the line while the sun is still strong." She set the clothes in a basket on the floor and waited. The moment life had resembled normalcy, the relationship between Ana and her mother had returned to 'normal' as well.

Ignoring her mother, Ana turned to her father and squeezed his hands.

"Papa, I'm not leaving until you talk to me."

"Ana." Luisa said, in a harsher voice.

"Not now, please, Luisa." Giani looked at his daughter. "Perhaps Ana's right."

Luisa drew in a sharp breath as if she'd been slapped. Ana saw her mother's eyes turn hard and flat. Her jaw tightening, Luisa hoisted the basket of wash against her hip, opened the kitchen door and let it slam behind her.

Ana watched her father stare at the table of his childhood and his father's and grandfather's childhoods. He ran his hands over its strong, hard surface. "Do you realize if these scratches and cuts could talk, they could tell you our family history?"

"And what a story it would be, Papa."

"Look at the questions they raise. Take for instance, this one." He slid his thumbnail into a crack. "How many onions and cloves of garlic had been cut here?" He put his hand in the table's center and rubbed it in a circle. "How many loaves of bread had been kneaded on this very spot?" He pointed to where Ana had folded her hands.

"How many lessons had been learned, meals eaten, wounds dressed, birthdays celebrated? How many deaths—"

He lowered his head on his forearms and wept, most likely for Gina, she thought. "Papa." She leaned over and smoothed his hair.

He lifted his head, wiped his eyes and took her hands. "When I was a boy, I'd sit at this table for hours with my father and uncles, who doused hot words in cold wine, dreaming of the day Italy would be free of Austrian rule.

"Do you realize, Ana, that sixty short years ago under Giuseppi Mansini, Sicily rebelled against King Ferdinand of Austria and actually succeeded in getting a representative constitution?"

"Yes! I learned it in school," she cried, thrilled that Papa was talking to her like he used to! She started to go for her textbook, when she realized it had burned by mistake in the mandated fire. Closing her eyes, she added what she could remember. "Ferdinand moved his armies through Italy into Sicily, and in eighteen forty-nine Palermo surrendered."

"Ferdinand punished the rebels," Papa said. "Ten years later the British stepped in. By eighteen-sixty, Giuseppe Garibaldi marched into Sicily with one thousand men. A year later Sicily became part of the mainland."

Ana smiled, but hearing Papa scoff, she frowned. "The people soon realized they had traded one tyranny for another as usual," he sighed, "which made an already intolerable situation worse. Martial law was declared, causing a deeper schism in north-south relations that had already been badly eroded by mutual hatred and mistrust."

Papa stopped talking as suddenly as he had begun and stared. The silence got awkward. Ana shifted uncomfortably. "But that was ten years ago, Papa. It can't be the reason you pace the kitchen floor night after night."

Under a deep frown, his features turned grayer and more ragged. Her heart pounded wildly. "Papa, I go to the village and I hear words like *cosche nostra.*" There, she panted, she said it. "And terrified whispers about the state of things. What things, Papa?"

His eyes blazed. "Ana—" His voice trailed off. His eyes suddenly clouded.

Frightened he would stop talking, she said, "Sometimes in the middle of the night I hear such loud pounding on the door it wakes me." He stared at her, looking too dumbfounded to speak. "I hear your bed creak and your feet shuffle across the bedroom and kitchen floors." Her eyes widened. Staring blankly, she said, "I creep along the hall, peek into the kitchen, and when you open the door, I see two men. Even though I hear them speak, I can't understand their words, and I don't recognize their voices. They scare me so much I dip into the shadows, hold my breath and flatten my back to the wall. I hear you mumble. I hear the door close and the legs of the table scrape across the floor. When I hear the floorboards creak open, I know that you are taking your hard-earned money and giving it to these men. Why, Papa?" Ana blinked and faced her father, surprised at the sweat that shone on his pale face. Terrified, she said, "Who are they, Papa?"

"Ana, there are forces," he said, his voice cracked and trailed off.

"What forces, Papa?" Her heart sank at the fright she saw in his eyes.

His eyes suddenly dulled. He ran his hand across his lips and said, "Go help your mother, and leave me to think. There are decisions I must make," he said in his this-conversation-is-over voice she knew well.

She pushed her chair back and got to her feet. Her shoulders slumped, she squeezed his hand and walked toward the door.

"Ana?"

"Yes, Papa?" Hopeful, she stopped and turned.

"Thank you."

Later that night Giani Testadura stared at his grim-faced friends and neighbors at a meeting he'd called in his barn.

"We're all painfully aware that some decisions some of our families made have created the state of things in *Sicilia* today."

"What choice did my family and other families have?" Federico Assante jumped to his feet, clearly indignant. "The whole island was disgusted and ashamed with having to live for centuries under the crushing heels of occupying forces. At least some families had the guts to protect themselves and others." His glance swept slowly over them. "If we hadn't joined together to protect ourselves none of us would be sitting here today."

"True," Giani said, "but you know as well as I do, that no matter how good their intentions, some groups began 'protecting' themselves from friends and neighbors. They carried out their own system of justice and retribution, and their vendettas in secret. And in the absence of law and order, they began extorting 'protection' money from landowners. By the time your family and others realized they had spawned the Mafia, it was too late."

Enrico Panini cleared his throat and all eyes turned toward him. "Forty-four years ago, when Sicily became a province of Italy, law-abiding families thought all that would change. It did. It got worse." Clearly agitated, Enrico said, "I still can't believe Rome allowed Sicilian mafia clans to go after other Sicilian criminal gangs," he scoffed. "The worst part was that Rome succeeded in turning our own against us!" Heads nodded. Enrico had had the courage to speak the truth.

"Yes," Salvatore Ricci stood next to Enrico. "In return, Rome turned a blind eye while the mafia extorted honest landowners, like all of us in this room.

"How could the government expect us to believe that this deal they made with the devil was temporary?" Salvatore said. Angry voices rose to a crescendo.

Giani raised his hand and the crowd quieted down. "The Mafia is so strong now, it scares us into voting for the candidates it favors. It's destroying our economy." He looked directly into each pair of eyes. "Even if there were policemen we could trust, we are bound by *omerta*. The Mafia has threatened to kill us or our families if we contact authorities for justice or cooperate with any investigations! That was bad enough, my friends," Giani removed his cap.

"But when I learned that Holy Mother Church had asked the Mafia to watch its properties and keep its tenant farmers in line," he whispered, squeezing his cap in hands that shook with rage. "That was the ultimate betrayal. I have made my decision. I suffer with leaving my three older daughters and their families behind, but for Luisa, Ana, Tonio and me, the future is clear. I cannot live under a government or a church in a country I no longer recognize."

Chapter 5

Ana's Betrothal

Luisa set her cup of tea on the table. "You told our friends and neighbors we are going to America?" she cried. She clapped her hand over her mouth and listened for a moment. Hearing nothing beyond the kitchen, she silently thanked God that Ana and Tonio were asleep. Despite the fire crackling in the hearth and warming the room, Luisa shivered and rubbed her arms. Round-eyed with concern she said, "Do you really want to uproot two children and cross an ocean?" She brought her cup to her lips. Watching Giani stoke the fire, she sipped and waited for his answer.

"You sound like you're having second thoughts."

No matter the issue, his voice remained soft and indulgent. That's what she loved most about him, she thought, until now. Gazing into her teacup, she traced its rim with her finger and frowned. "When would Ana and Antonio ever see their sisters and their families again? They'll be strangers to their nieces and nephews, and baby Mariana will grow up not knowing them, or us," she sighed. "And how will I keep Gina's memory alive in my children's minds and hearts if we're in America and she is buried in Sicily?" She put the cup down.

Giani stood the poker by the hearth, took his seat, reached across the table for her hand and squeezed it. "And Americans speak English," he teased.

"Yes!" She pulled her hands away from his and raised her eyes in exasperation. "A hard language that makes no sense! How would we communicate?"

"Luisa." He reached for her hands again. "Of all those who went before us, how many have returned to Sicily and stayed?" She shrugged. "From what I hear, few to none." He raised her hands to his lips.

"What about money?"

He read the concern in her eyes. "We'll have enough for a while."

"And when it's gone," she said, pulling her hands away again, "how will we support ourselves in a city? We are country people. Farmers."

"You've heard the stories people tell. America is the land of opportunity. If our money runs out, I'll do what men must do to feed their families." She watched him rub his hand over the table's pitted wood. "This may sound foolish," his voice wavered. "But of all the things we own, I can't bear to leave this table behind."

"You shouldn't have to," she said, getting to her feet. "Why," she clenched her fists. "Why are we forced to break up our home and family and go to America?" Her voice cracked, and her eyes pooled with tears.

The sound of her mother's wailing plea startled Ana awake. She rubbed her eyes, slipped out of bed, tiptoed past Tonio's room and crept toward the kitchen, praying her parents' voices would drown out the creaks in the floorboards. Inching as close as she dared, she pressed herself to the wall and listened.

"We have no choice, Luisa."

Her father's voice sounded heavy and sad, and Ana frowned, wondering why.

"We either go to America now while we can still get out with the means to start a new life," he said, "or we live here and risk a dangerous and uncertain future. The life we once knew no longer exists."

Go to America? When? Now? Not believing her ears, Ana pressed her lips together to keep from screaming with joy. If she were dreaming she never wanted to wake up! This was better than she could have ever imagined. America! The opportunities that awaited! She could barely keep still.

Suddenly, she stopped smiling. What was wrong with her? How could she feel happy when her parents and everyone else could anguish over this decision? But on the other hand? Ana closed her eyes, dear God up in heaven, thank you for the chance of a lifetime! She clasped her hands and opened her eyes. Her face upturned, she could not stop grinning, thinking that her dream of seeing the world would begin with America!

"You do see what I mean, Luisa, don't you?" Giani said.

The underlying urgency in her papa's soft voice caught her attention. The grin faded. She craned her neck straining to hear him.

"What?" Luisa said.

Ana frowned at the odd, distracted inflection in her mother's voice.

"That we'd be better off taking our chances—"

"Moving to America will force us to take one chance that concerns me more than any other," Mama said, cutting him off. The sharp edge to Mama's voice surprised her. Ana inched closer to the parlor.

"What chance?" he asked, sounding bewildered.

"Ana."

Ana's skin prickled at the sharp, curt way her mother spat out her name.

"Ana?" Papa sounded more confused than Ana felt.

"Yes." Her mother answered, sounding calmer, clearer and more determined. "I will board that ship under one condition," she said. Ana pictured her mother, arms folded across her chest, staring into her father's eyes.

"And that is?"

"Ana must be married before we leave."

Stunned, Ana gasped. She slid slowly down the wall. Tears rolled down her cheeks and trickled onto her fingers.

"Do you realize what you're saying?" Papa said.

The distraught sound of his voice was unprecedented. Ana sat as rigid as stone. Papa. Oh, my darling Papa. Please, don't listen to this.

"You … you're talking crazy, Luisa," Papa sputtered.

"Very well. Perhaps I am. Let me say this, then. Ana must be betrothed before we leave. The sooner the better."

This is all wrong, Ana thought. Shaking violently, she tried to make sense of her mother's desire to seal her fate.

A chair scraped the floor. The footfalls that followed sounded as heavy-hearted as she felt. Ana pictured her father pacing while her mother watched. She saw Luisa's hands in her lap laid one upon the other; the left palm turned upward, gently supporting the back of the right hand in a kind of noble supplication. The gesture always struck Ana as absurd and out of place even for a well-to-do, gentleman farmer's wife. It was as if someone had *told* her mother that this was the pose a lady would strike to add a touch of feminine nuance to a delicate situation.

The pacing stopped. "You'll have to forgive me," her father said. Ana heard a chair being pushed back under the table. "But with everything we have to consider now, how can you even begin to make proper wedding plans, or even a proper choice for Ana?"

"You're right, Giani."

Mama sounded subdued. Conciliatory. Ana stopped shaking. Something was wrong. Mama never agreed with Papa quickly with problems involving her.

"We'll wait until we get to America to have the wedding," she said, as if the decision were final.

Ana shuddered

"*Gesu Cristo*, Luisa. That's not what I meant!"

"Giani, please—"

"No!" he said, harshly. Ana heard a fist pound the table, rattling cups on their saucers. "Wedding plans? Now? And to whom? This was not the way I envisioned Ana's future."

Ana held her breath.

"Giani, I've just had a thought," Mama said.

Ana gasped. She heard nothing random in her mother's voice.

"Perhaps you could speak to Alberto Petruzzi. I hear they plan to migrate to America as well."

The finality in her mother's voice confirmed Ana's suspicion. This thought had not just occurred to Mama. She'd been planning this for God knows how long! A chair scraped the floor again. Ana heard the lighter click of her mother's shoes on the wooden floor.

"We could make some mutually beneficial arrangement and announce Ana and young Alberto's betrothal before we leave."

Her father didn't answer. Ana imagined Papa's eyes filled with the same acidic revulsion that burned her stomach and throat.

"He's a good boy, and he'll make a good husband. Our families have known and liked each other for years." Her mother spoke quickly. "He carries the skills he learned at his father's knee. There are many Catholics in America for whom fish is an important food."

"Think of it, Giani," Luisa said. Her voice sounded light, almost joyful. "A fisherman would be worth his weight in gold. The sea's bounty is plentiful and eternal. Ana and her children will never starve."

Dizzy with anger, Ana panted.

"But, Luisa," It was a plea. "Alberto Petruzzi is a—"

"Fine young man," her mother finished his sentence.

"But—"

"Giani! Open your mind for once and look at Ana the way she really is. Headstrong with too many dangerous ideas."

"Nonsense! Ana is a child with a vivid imagination."

"She's a woman who needs to be settled and off in the right direction. If we don't do that before we leave, something terrible will happen. I feel it, Giani, here."

Ana pictured her mother's hand, curled into a fist, pounding her breast over her heart. The vision tamped down Ana's anger, and she frowned. As the seventh daughter, Mama had always claimed to *know* things. And yes, her feelings had come true often, but to Mama's great annoyance, Papa could always point to concrete reasons why.

"Giani," Luisa said, "I'm begging you to believe me," Mama said.

Her voice cracked, and Ana winced.

"I sense terrible darkness, a thick impenetrable blanket that will smother us if we do not heed my feeling."

Ana trembled uncontrollably at the tone of finality in Mama's voice. Was Mama so determined to get her way, she would stop at nothing, not even play acting?

Oh my God. Ana dug her fingernails into her palms. That must be it! Hotter tears scalded her cheeks. This was not a premonition. This was bold-faced, flagrant deception! Shy, obedient Mama was manipulating Papa! Her kind, sweet Papa was blind to such manipulation, because Mama had never used such tactics. Ana frowned. Or had she?

Ana's heart pounded with savage fury, pounding beats out in head-throbbing force.

Glasses and dishes rattled on kitchen shelves, stunning Luisa and stopping their conversation.

"Giani," Luisa stammered, jumping up. Her wide-with-shock eyes were riveted to the shelves. She was terrified, but she had to keep talking or she would lose the ground she'd gained. "Ana is as precious to me as she is to you, but you know as well as I, that Ana is not—"

"A great beauty," Ana whispered, mouthing her mother's words. Ana's heart shattered, deflating her fury. Tears of shame and embarrassment ran down her cheeks. Nauseous and blind with disgust, she groped her way back to her room and her bed.

Ana spent the night sobbing and drifting in and out of sleep. She shivered despite the eiderdown quilt she'd burrowed under. Hours later she glared at the bright sunny eye peeping through her window. So what if she was the ugliest creature in all of Sicily or in the universe? Alberto Petruzzi was fat, and he stunk like fish.

Premonitions be damned. She would die before marrying Alberto Petruzzi.

Ana's eyes narrowed. She hated him as much if not more than she hated her mother.

Luisa screamed. Her second serving dish flew off the shelf. Narrowly missing her, it hit the floor and smashed into dozens of pieces.

Chapter 6

The Testaduras
1905

"Is there some way we can go to America without selling our home?" Luisa stirred the bubbling pasta sauce, lifted the spoon to her lips, tasted it, frowned and reached for the basil.

Giani sat at the table, making a list of supplies he needed from town. Shaking his head, he glanced at Luisa. Even though she'd agreed to leave *Sicilia,* if and only if he agreed to Ana's betrothal, her question implied that she could not or would not accept the move as final. Very well then, he would simply give her something new to worry about.

"Rumor has it that the government may stop people from taking large sums of money out of the country," he said casually, adding twine to his long list.

"My God. How can we go to America without money?" Luisa turned quickly, the spoon slipped from her hand, hit the stove and fell to the floor.

As she looked past the red splotch on her white apron, he saw her eyes widen. The spoon lay on the floor in a puddle of sauce, next to a porcelain shard she had missed when she swept up her broken dish. She picked up the shard and stared at her husband.

"Luisa," he said. "I told you last night. Those dishes rattling on the shelves were due to Mount Etna showing us her displeasure at our leaving. Today when I ask around town, those who decided to leave will say that Etna had rattled their shelves too." He got up. "So far the talk about money not leaving the country is just talk," he said, trying to relax her worried frown. "But if it happens, I'll merely arrange for our money to meet us in America," he said confidently. He picked up the spoon she'd left on the floor.

She took the spoon, handed the shard to him and frowned harder. "How?" She left the spoon in the sink, wet a rag and wiped the sauce from the floor. She rinsed the rag, took a sponge, scrubbed and rinsed the spoon and returned to stirring the sauce.

He threw the shard in the trashcan by the door. "There are ways. We'll work through the Italian consulate in America." He took his seat at the table. "In the meanwhile, we must go through our things. We'll sell or give away what we can't take." He folded his shopping list and slipped it into his shirt pocket. "I hear the journey will take quite a bit longer than usual. The ship has to make stops at several ports of call before heading into the Atlantic."

Luisa stopped stirring and looked at him again.

"Don't worry." He held out his hand. She sat opposite him at the table. "This is good news. An extended ocean voyage will give us perspective, time to leave the old behind and anticipate the new." Staring blankly, he slid his hand across the table.

"Giani, what is it?"

"Nothing," he sighed "I was just remembering the last time I sat here with ..." He rapped his knuckles on the table. "Ana," he sighed, "who should be brimming with joy preparing for this voyage. Instead she mopes around the house like the end of the world is coming. She's slow to finish her chores." He drew in a sharp breath and looked at Luisa. "My God, Luisa," he said. searching her eyes. "You don't think she's depressed because of the betrothal, do you?"

"Of course not," Luisa said, sincerely, he thought. "Ana knows that in *Sicilia* fathers have been helping to arrange their daughters' marriages for centuries. Didn't she watch you help to arrange her three sisters' marriages with her own eyes?"

He sighed. "You're right, but even so, every night her face creeps into my dreams. Every day I watch her become thinner and more withdrawn. The closer we come to departure, the less her eyes sparkle. She breaks my heart, but I am her father, and I had to take steps to protect her." He rubbed his eyes.

Luisa pulled him to his feet, hugged him and pressed her cheek to his "You did what every father in this village would do." She took his face in her hands and looked him directly in the eyes. "I know Ana seems a bit distracted, but the idea of marriage, a new husband and children is heart-stopping enough, even if we remained in Villa Franca, but to have it happen in a foreign country must be overwhelming." She kissed his cheek. "We mustn't worry, Giani. Ana is smart, young and resilient. She'll adjust better than you or I."

"Thank you for understanding, Luisa," Giani kissed her forehead, picked up his list and opened the door.

Luisa stood at the window. She watched him pet the horse, climb into the wagon head and head down the road. When he was no bigger than a speck on the glass, she stepped away from the window, went to the stove and put out the flame under the pot of sauce. She shuddered, overcome with guilt for deceiving him about Ana, but she had no choice. He had indulged Ana so that he'd forced Luisa to be practical, the disciplinarian. Of course, Ana was depressed because of the betrothal to Alberto Petruzzi, she scoffed. How could he not see that?

In retrospect, Luisa admitted that part of her was relieved, that instead of waging a world war, her headstrong daughter had responded sedately to the betrothal. Ana and Alberto would be married as soon as possible after reaching America, and that was that!

On the other hand, Luisa had to admit that part of her was sad for another reason. She tried to love Ana the way she used to when Ana was little, but every day the bond between Giani and Ana grew stronger. And as much as she denied it, it sickened her with envy.

"This new development knocks you down a step or two, doesn't it, Ana?" she muttered, staring blankly. "That's what you get for competing with me for my husband's attention, and for being so arrogant. Now maybe you'll believe Father DeGrazia when he says pride always goes before the fall. I must say you are a lucky girl. You will benefit from the large dose of humility this experience will force you to swallow."

Suddenly, Luisa closed her eyes and rubbed her temples. Giani was right. Ana was subdued. Too subdued. Ana had *changed*. There was a look in her eyes that Luisa had never seen before. She picked the porcelain shard out of the trash and realization, like forked lightning, illuminated what she'd dismissed as nonsense. Long before the cholera pandemics all her children except Ana had come to her swearing their house was haunted. How else, they'd complained, could objects move by themselves day and night or go missing and then show up?

My God. Now Luisa knew the real reason the dishes had rattled on the shelves that night. She knew why her serving dish had flown off the shelf, hit the floor and smashed into a hundred pieces. She stared at the shard, desperately wanting to interpret Ana's mood as a mixture of resentment and acceptance, but as Ana's mother she knew the broken shard had nothing to do with Mount Etna and everything to do with Ana and her power. Shivering uncontrollably, Luisa realized the first shoe had fallen.

Chapter 7

The Christening
Ana

The Testaduras were due at a christening at the Petruzzi home. Luisa was godmother to Elena Petruzzi Belmondo, Alberto's sister, who had just given birth to a baby boy.

Ana watched Tonio hug the stallion that Ana had christened Rocinante and then climb into the back seat of the wagon behind his father. Seeing Ana, Rocinante nickered and nuzzled her hair. She closed her eyes and smiled.

"Ana, climb in now," Luisa said.

Ana frowned, opened her eyes, kissed Rocinante's face and climbed into the wagon.

"Tonio," Mama said. She handed him a large dish of ziti and meatballs and gestured toward Ana. After Tonio passed the dish to Ana, Mama handed him two loaves of bread and said, "You hold these until we get there." Mama climbed into her seat, adjusted her bonnet, smiled at Papa and said, "Hurry, Giani, we mustn't be late."

The lighter and more cheerful Mama's voice sounded, the tighter a fist squeezed Ana's heart. The wagon bumped along the rippled road, jostling them like four sacks of potatoes. The day looming before her, Ana bit her lip and choked off a sob. Tears stung her eyes, blurring the brown seam of road binding the green quilt of fields. Bushes and trees moving slowly by seemed to lash out. Dead flowers and weed-choked grass signaled that they were near *Dio's* abandoned house. As they drove by, its dark, dirty windows peered at her like accusing eyes.

Anger tingled behind her eyes, narrowing her vision. Why must she go to this stupid christening when all she wanted to do was to jump in the stream and hold her head underwater?

Dio's house suddenly shook. The windows rattled wildly in their rotting frames. Her eyes round with astonishment, Ana tightened her grip on the dish in her lap. She looked at Mama and Papa, who were busy talking and hadn't seemed to hear or see a thing. She glanced at Tonio and froze. He was watching the house. After what seemed like forever he turned and faced her.

The look in his eyes said that he knew it was she who'd rattled the windows. He knew it was she, whose pranks had scared them into believing their farmhouse was haunted. The looks on their faces! She'd laughed till she couldn't breathe. If he told Mama and Papa, would they be angry enough to force her to marry Alberto Petruzzi today at the christening?

Tonio twisted around in his seat and stared at *Dio's* house. At the next bend in the road when the house was out of sight, he frowned at her and said, "I think our ghost has moved to *Dio's*."

And Ana sighed, relieved.

The road dissolved at Petruzzis house along with her fear, but her eyes stung with grief for her future. If she burst into tears at every turn, how could she get through this day? How could she get through the rest of her life?

Tonio set the bread on top of the ziti on Ana's lap and then he jumped to the ground, He circled around the wagon, grabbed Papa's reins, patted Rocinante and then hitched him to a crowded fence. Papa helped Mama step down. Nodding and smiling at friends and neighbors, she lifted the ziti from Ana's lap. "You carry the bread."

Ana followed her mother and a murmur rippled through the crowd. Did everyone know about the betrothal? Mama, how could you! She felt her face burn with humiliation. And suddenly people talking, dishes clanking, dogs barking, birds chirping went as silent as the picture shows in Palermo.

"Ana," Mama said.

Ana blinked, and her ears swelled with sound. She watched Mama rearrange platters of meat, fruit, cheeses and pastries on Petruzzi's banquet table to make room for her ziti.

"Put the bread near the ziti and follow me."

Her lips drawn into a pout, Ana followed Mama onto the porch and into the front hall.

"It's so good to see both of you," *Signora* Petruzzi said, smiling warmly. She held out her hands. "Welcome, Ana."

As Ana took the *signora's* hand, her eye strayed to Alberto, standing next to his mother. She cringed at the empty grin on his wheezing face. The thought of marrying Alberto made the large, airy hall shrink into a small stuffy room. No longer able to breathe, she backed away.

"Ana," Luisa whispered harshly.

"I'm sorry, *Signora* Petruzzi," Ana backed further away. "I feel faint. I need fresh air."

Before her mother could stop her, Ana barged her way through the line forming behind them. Bursting through the door, she stumbled onto the porch, down the steps and into her father's arms.

"Ana." He cradled her.

"Papa," she whispered. She spotted the outhouse on the far side of the large yard, squirmed free and ran toward it. She felt Papa's eyes burn holes in her back. Perhaps she would explain herself later, perhaps not. He didn't deserve an explanation any more than Mama.

Ana knocked on the outhouse door. Thanking God no one answered, she let herself in, bolted the door, and flattened herself against it. She panted in fetid air but compared to Petruzzi's hallway the air in the outhouse smelled fresher than country meadows. A small window framing the sun bathed the commode in a shaft of light. She hiked her dress up and slid down her panties and squatted to pee. A shadow moved slowly across the window, eclipsing the sun. Ana looked up. The eclipse wheezed. Scrambling for cover, she sputtered, "Alberto! You filthy pig! What-what are you do-doing?"

Alberto laughed his braying-mule laugh, and Ana knew she would kill herself before raising a brood of braying mules. "How dare you, Alberto Petruzzi!" Her cheeks twitched. Her hands shook with rage. The outhouse rocked on its footing. The wooden-mouth of a door banged open and closed.

Ana jumped up and looked out the window. Hot urine streamed down her thighs. With hard-as-coal eyes she aimed. Vowing to die before marrying Alberto Petruzzi, she fired her rage. Alberto fell, held his ankle and yowled in pain.

"*Goooooood!*" she shouted, laughing and shaking her fist in the window. "God punished you! I hope He broke your leg!" She saw Alberto get to his feet and hobble away like the Quasimodo of Villa Franca that he was. "Damn you to hell, you pig-dog, Alberto!"

Moving away from the window, Ana plopped down on the seat. She wiped herself as best she could and burst into tears, hating Alberto more with each tear that fell. "Don't let that fat coward make you cry," she shouted. Sniffling, she stood up and ran her hands down her dress, smoothing the wrinkles as best she could. She looked at the window and pictured his leering eyes. The thought that he saw so private a moment made her cry harder. The last place she wanted to be was here at this stupid party. She clenched her fists and stomped both feet hard on the ground. The outhouse shook with her rage. She took a calming breath and the outhouse stopped shaking.

Alberto Petruzzi. The sound of his name made her thick hair go limp. How could she face him? Refusing to let him win, she held her head high, threw back her shoulders and opened the door. Wiping her last tear away and willing no more tears to fall, she made her way to the house deep in thought.

Mama said that Rosa Damiani, Ana's best and only friend, would be at the party. Ana knew that no matter how often or how hard Mama denied it, she hated Rosa, and Ana knew why. One night she overheard Mama telling Papa that she'd caught Rosa brazenly flirting with Tonio. Mama was such a … what did Americans say? Stick in the mud. She giggled. That was it. Ever since Mama had convinced Papa to betroth her to Alberto, Ana could care less how her stick-in-the-mud mother felt.

Rosa was the only one in the world with whom Ana would dare talk about Alberto. Rosa would know how to handle that pig. Feeling lighter of heart, she smiled at some neighbors she passed on her way into the house despite the wet panties chafing her thighs.

Ana spotted Rosa, standing on the far end of the parlor, talking to Marco Bellini. Girls flocked to Marco like magnets to the North Pole. Right now, Rosa had Marco all to herself, which was what Rosa told Ana she'd planned to do. Rosa was small with generous bosoms that filled out her pink and white dress, accentuating her tiny waist. Marco Bellini must have thought so too. Why else would he keep staring at them? Rosa had long wavy blond hair that shimmered like the morning sun on the Mediterranean Sea, and mischievous brown eyes. She was worldly with a naughty confidence that Ana secretly envied. Rosa leaned over and whispered something in Marco's ear. Suddenly, Marco burst out laughing and Ana smiled, wondering what Rosa had said to make him laugh so hard.

Some guests wandered by and stopped in front of Ana, blocking her view. She moved to the side, stood on her toes, craned her neck and waved her arms to get Rosa's attention. Rosa saw her. Ana smiled. Rosa turned away, clearly choosing to ignore her. Ana made her way through the crowd, despite her wet panties and tapped Rosa on the shoulder. "I need to talk to you."

"Excuse me a moment, Marco." Rosa smiled sweetly. She faced Ana and glared. "Are you blind or mad or both?" she whispered, harshly. "I'm *busy*." She faced Marco and smiled.

"I'm sorry, but I must talk to you now!" She grabbed Rosa's arm and pulled her away.

"Ana! Stop!" Rosa whispered through clenched teeth.

"No!" Ana pulled her through the crowd. Marco stood alone and stared after them, clearly shocked that two girls had dared to desert him. Rosa tugged in resistance, but Ana would not let go.

"Do you realize what you just did?" Rosa jerked her arm free.

"Rosa, I'm sorry. I—"

"You should be." Rosa looked across the parlor. "You see that! Maria Spagna, that little tramp, was itching to lure Marco away from me, and you helped her."

"Rosa!" Ana said, dragging Rosa out the door, down the steps and into the yard near a clump of deserted bushes.

"This better be very good or—"

Bursting at the seams, Ana rained down a torrent of lurid details from the horrid betrothal to the outhouse outrage and burst into tears.

"Your betrothal to Alberto doesn't surprise me in the least. It has your mother's fine touch all over it," Rosa curved her lips in a smile. "But what happened in the outhouse," Rosa giggled, and then burst out laughing.

Ana's mouth dropped. Rosa grabbed Ana's hand and pulled her behind some bushes. She wiped the tears of laughter from her eyes with the hem of her dress.

"I'm sorry, Ana. But—" Her words got tangled in a skein of giggles.

"I'm glad my humiliation at the hands of that pig is so amusing."

"You don't understand." She stopped giggling and gazed in the distance. "Don't worry. You'll never have to marry Alberto, that is, unless you really want to!"

"How can you think I would want such a vile thing? And how can you make such a promise to me?"

"Oh, very easily. I know all about his dirty little habit."

"You? What? How?"

"I caught him peeping at me."

"And you said nothing to your parents? To anyone?"

Rosa sat on the ground, pulled her knees up, and wrapped her arms around them. Horrified and intrigued, Ana scrunched down next to her friend.

"I'll admit at first I got angry enough to kill him." She pulled a fistful of grass out by the roots. "I swore I'd make him sorry he was ever born. Then I calmed down and started thinking that keeping his dirty habit a secret might be of value someday. And now," Rosa smiled at Ana, "I can see I was right!" She pitched the grass aside and pulled up more.

Ana stared wide-eyed. "Right? How? I don't understand."

"Shhh. Be quiet, listen to me and you will."

Ana obeyed, grateful that Rosa knew of her hateful betrothal. It was a burden she'd carried alone for far too long. Rosa frowned at Ana, clearly misreading the look in her eyes. "On second thought, I don't know whether I should tell you the rest of my story."

"What story? Of course, you should. I'm your best friend, or have you forgotten?"

"Well, perhaps. After all best friends are supposed to share everything, aren't they?" Rosa stroked her friend's face. "And besides, I can't remember the last time I've had such fun!"

Fun? "Please, tell me, Rosa, I need to know."

"Alberto Petruzzi. Ugh." Rosa pushed Ana's hair out of her eyes. "Your father must be insane. What kind of a choice is Alberto for the daughter your father cherishes?"

Ana looked at her friend with huge round eyes.

"Now your mother is a different story," Rosa smirked. "I can see why she picked Alberto for you."

Rosa was right. Ana lowered her eyes and pulled threads from her dress. "Let's not waste time talking about my parents. Tell me the rest of your story."

"I don't know. I don't think you're ready."

"Of course, I'm ready. What a silly thing to say," Ana blushed.

"Well," Rosa hesitated, "okay. The last time he peeped was into my bedroom window."

"No!"

"It made me so mad that I had to get even."

"How? Did you tell your parents?"

Rosa sighed impatiently. "Of course not. Have you heard a word I said? Never mind. God, in all the books you've read, have you ever come across the saying, *sapere e potere?"*

"Knowledge is power? Of course. Who hasn't?"

"Good. Now be quiet."

"But what has that saying got to do with—"

"Did I tell you to be quiet and listen?" Rosa said. "Now, where was I? Oh yes. Alberto. I decided to taunt him by showing him what he could never have, except in his dirty little dreams, or over my dead body."

"What did you do?" Ana was almost afraid to ask.

"I let him have a long, hard look."

"This was your solution? I–I've never heard of such a solution in my entire life!"

"How can you be so smart and so naïve? Honest to God, Ana, you're too serious. I'm finding it hard not to laugh at you. You *know* that I hate him so much, I wouldn't be caught dead talking to him in public, except in front of our parents and only because they expect it."

"You hate him, yet you allowed him to see you … naked?" Blushing hard, Ana yanked out more thread from her dress.

Rosa slapped the thread out of Ana's hand. "If you keep pulling on your dress, *you'll* be the one going back to the party naked." Rosa sighed. "Honest to God, Ana, if Alberto Petruzzi were the last boy on earth, every girl on the planet would enter the convent." She made the sign of the cross and kissed her fingers to heaven and then she shook her head "I don't know why I did what I did. It was just a crazy impulse. Anyhow, after that he was peeping into my window all the time."

"Of course, he was. Because you encouraged—"

"I didn't know you were studying to be a nun." Rosa made the sign of the cross again. "Forgive me my sin, Sister Ana, and I'll stop talking right now."

"No. Please, Rosa. I'm sorry." Her teeth held her tongue between them to keep it still.

"Well, one night while I was changing into my nightgown, I heard the sound of leaves and twigs being crunched outside my open window. I turned and there was Alberto, leering at me and panting like a wild animal. I ran to the window and guess what I saw?

Streams of sweat ran down Ana's back. She opened her mouth, her teeth released her tongue, but it did not wag.

"I saw Alberto naked from the waist down, rubbing—"

Ana screamed and jumped up, but before she could run, Rosa grabbed her arm, and howling with laughter, she yanked Ana to the ground.

"After I laughed as hard as I could at what I saw, he never peeped in my window again."

"My God," Ana said, fanning her face with her hand.

Rosa grabbed Ana's hands, squeezed them hard and said, "For once in your life, get your head out of your books and think! Knowledge is power." Rosa got to her feet, brushed herself off, smiled and said, "Would your prim and proper mama consider a boy who did such a filthy thing to be a *respectable husband* for her daughter?"

Dumbfounded, Ana sat on the grass and watched Rosa saunter toward the house. On one hand the thought of Alberto seeing Rosa naked reviled her. But on the other? Ana frowned. Maybe Rosa was right. Knowing Alberto's dirty secret was a powerful weapon; one she must have the guts to use when the time came.

"Knowledge is power."

Hearing the magical words, Ana felt the Villa Franca straitjacket her mother had forced her to wear loosen and fall away. Her heart felt free. Her dreams for her future would come true after all! Feeling less anxious and oh my God, *hungry,* she got to her feet and brushed off the grass. Hopeful for the first time in days, she made her way to the house, grinning like a fool, until she saw Alberto Petruzzi.

Ana stopped short. Watching that filthy pig fill his plate with her mother's ziti and meatballs, she remembered how he'd wheezed in the outhouse window. Hearing his braying laugh and imagining his pig-dog eyes seeing her naked turned her heart hot with rage.

Staring at him coldly, she narrowed her eyes. His plate flew out of his hands, across the lawn, missed the porch, and smashed into a rose bed.

Voices fell silent. Movement stopped. A graveyard hush fell on the yard.

She saw Alberto's eyes bulge at the sight of his hands digging into the serving dish. She watched his eyes grow round with terror as his hands shoved the food into his mouth until tears streamed down his face, snot ran from his nose and the meatballs and ziti were gone.

Mouths contorted in horror. Tongues remained silent. Eyes bulged with disbelief.

Wheezing and shaking his head, Alberto lumbered across the yard to the porch. He hung onto the railing and retched, vomiting on the rose bed. His face bluish purple, he sank to his knees and collapsed in his own vomit. Confused fright showed on every face but one.

Mama glared at Ana, and Ana froze.

At that moment, realizing full-well the enormity of her new-found power, Ana turned her back on her mother and walked down the road that led to home.

Tears streaked the film of road dust on Ana's face. She licked the dust from her lips, scowled, spat out the grit and wiped the back of her hand over her mouth. The closer the wagon rolled up behind her, the louder the wheels groaned on their axles. The wagon stopped. Ana blew out a breath and stopped walking. Turning, she stood face-to-face with Rocinante, who shook his head, nickered and rubbed his nose against her shoulder. Silence, taut as a rubber band, stretched to snapping.

"Get in," Mama said. And the silence snapped.

Her eyes downcast, Ana gripped the back of Papa's seat, hoisted herself up and climbed in behind him. Papa tugged on the reins, clicked his tongue and Rocinante pulled the wagon forward. Her heart ticked like a time bomb about to explode.

"I know you blame me for what happened," she blurted, looking at Mama whose eyes seemed to accuse. "But I was the only one there who was nowhere near him." If Mama knew what Alberto had done! She lowered her head and smothered a giggle, *sapere e potere.* Knowledge really is power. She silently thanked Rosa. What would she do without her best and most worldly friend? Thank God Rosa's family had decided to go to America, too.

"Arresto!" Papa said. Rocinante stopped and Ana and Tonio lurched forward. Papa held the reins and swiveled around. "What makes you say that, Ana?" he pleaded. "How could anyone blame you?" Ana looked at Mama, whose eyes clearly blazed with suspicion. "Whatever the reason poor Alberto behaved like that, and only God knows what it was, it had nothing to do with you."

Chapter 8

The Voyage
1905

Standing at the dock in Palermo, Ana inhaled deeply and smiled. Any lingering thoughts of Alberto Petruzzi had blown away with the Mediterranean breeze.

Thank goodness preparing for the voyage had been so unforgiving a task that no one, especially Mama, had time to think about anything else. Before setting sail, they rose with the sun and worked like slaves packing, finishing chores, wrapping up loose ends, saying goodbye to her sisters and their families. They worked till their clothes were too heavy to wear, their eyes were too tired to cry and their mouths too tired to complain. Aching to the roots of their hair, after eating a hearty supper, they collapsed into bed. This became routine until the day of departure had arrived.

Their voyage seemed like a dream until this very moment. Seeing the *SS Sicilian Princess*, the ship that would take her family and friends to America, made her heart airborne with joy. She opened her pink parasol, the one with the white polka dots, a gift from Papa for her thirteenth birthday. Shading her eyes from the sun, she tilted her head back and followed the ship's bow, which was so tall it disappeared into the clouds and probably touched the hem of God's robes. So dazed were Tonio and she, that Papa had to herd them along like two sheep. And if merely glimpsing at the *Sicilian Princess* had mesmerized them, boarding it had struck them dumb. And to Ana's utter joy, Papa had purchased second class accommodations, a sign that this voyage would be *the* defining moment of her life! Agreeing to meet after settling in, Ana, Tonio and Rosa stood on deck. The sparkle in their eyes made them join hands and shout out the same thought, "First class."

Putting their heads together, they crept, crawled, slid and giggled their way to first class. Eyes wide and mouths open, they gawked at a staircase fit for royal feet. Its solid oak panels rose from the lower landing to the skylight.

Giggling and clapping her hands Rosa shouted, "Come on!"

They skipped down halls and scurried up staircases past a swimming pool, Turkish baths, and veranda cafes. There were staterooms with parlor suites, reading and writing rooms, lounges, and a dining room. Before getting caught and shooed back to second class, they had stumbled across a smoking room at the end of a promenade deck. "For men who want an after-dinner drink," Ana said, lifting her nose in the air and fluttering her eyelashes.

"I heard that in third class they separate single men and women," Tonio said, his lips turned up in a mischievous grin. "I know what we could do next," he said. "Let's find steerage."

"Maybe tomorrow," Ana sighed. "I promised Mama I'd come back to my room to unpack."

"Oh, Ana, you're such a killjoy." Rosa smiled at Tonio and grabbed his hand. "We can unpack later." She ran down the hall and Tonio ran after her.

The hustle and bustle had occupied her completely, but now that they'd been onboard ship a few days, the loathsome betrothal loomed above Ana, making her anxious.

Ana and Rosa were walking the fresh air deck. "I'm worried about how Mama will feel and what she'll do when she finds out I refuse to marry Alberto."

True to form, Rosa shrugged, emphasizing the fact that she had little love and even less patience where Mama was concerned. Feeling her face flush Ana said, "For once in your life could you be a little sympathetic to my problems?"

"What are you talking about?" Rosa stopped and pulled Ana's arm. "I care more about you than your prim and proper mother! Have you forgotten who it was that solved your betrothal problem?"

Ana lowered her eyes. "I'm sorry, Rosa."

"Forget it," Rosa waved Ana's apology down, and she started walking away. Suddenly, she stopped. "Honest to God, Ana. I'll never understand how you can be worried about your mother, when only a few days ago she made your father ask Alberto's father—"

"She cries a lot," Ana said, cutting Rosa off. She knew Rosa was right, but Mama was still her mother. "She's worried she'll never see my sisters and their families again. I guess being a grandmother has changed things in ways she never realized."

Rosa turned toward the ocean, clearly ignoring what Ana was saying. Refusing to let her win, Ana said, "Mama thinks that bringing Tonio and me to America—"

"Can we stop talking about your mother?" Rosa said. "I'm bored. I'm hungry. It's getting late. Let's head for the dining room."

Rosa walked fast, but Ana knew it wasn't hunger or the fresh sea air that had put the glow in Rosa's cheeks. She watched Rosa's eyes sparkle whenever she saw Tonio. Maybe Mama was right. Maybe Rosa was flirting with Tonio after all.

"Speaking of dinner, I notice that every time you take your seat, your handsome waiter can't take his eyes off of you."

I think not, Ana thought, but said, "Which one?"

"The dark Spanish one. His nametag says Carlos," Rosa giggled.

"No, Rosa. I think you're mistaken."

Ana is as precious to me as she is to you, but you know as well as I, that Ana is not...a great beauty.

Mama's words still stung.

"Yes," Rosa giggled. "Wait until dinner. You'll see."

Ana hadn't noticed him, until now, but when he poured her water and handed her a menu, she glanced up. Rosa was right. His nametag said Carlos. Rosa sat two tables away. They glanced at each other and giggled.

"Ana! You're forgetting your manners," Luisa said.

"Sorry, Mama." Ana blushed. She didn't dare look at Carlos now. How could Mama embarrass her in front of strangers! Rosa was right. Why should she care about Mama when Mama didn't care about her?

"Luisa, let the girl be!" Giani said. "She's only having fun with a friend." Giani smiled at Ana. He followed Ana's gaze to Rosa, and when he smiled at her too, Ana could not love her papa more. Blinded by the sparkle in his eyes, Papa seemed not to notice that he'd just embarrassed Mama. Ana smiled. Grateful for having the best Papa ever, she turned her attention to her menu.

Luisa squinted over her menu at Ana, thinking. Enjoy yourself while you still can. This voyage merely postpones the marriage that awaits you in America. She gazed at her menu and smiled.

While her family frowned at their menus, Rosa looked at Ana's table. She winked at Tonio, flashed him a slow, broad smile and ...

…Tonio blushed. He wiped his clammy palms on his trousers and glanced at his parents who were focused on Ana as usual. But this time, instead of feeling resentful, he was grateful to Ana for soaking up their attention. Staring distractedly, he remembered when Rosa …

… giggled, grabbed his hand and pulled him down the hallway to a door. She pushed it open and giggled harder. He followed her down two flights of stairs to a second door. It opened into an empty hallway. They tiptoed to the end and peeked around the corner. At the sound of voices and footsteps, they doubled back, slipped through the door and closed it behind them. They stood stone still and listened. The voices and footsteps grew louder, and then softer before fading completely. Suddenly, Rosa coughed and gagged, pointing toward steerage.

She looked in his eyes and something … changed. Her lips parted. She slipped her arms around his neck and pressed her body against him. She kissed him, and something happened that until that moment, had only happened in dreams. The taste of her lips, the scent of her skin. He wanted more, and he knew she did, too.

Tonio picked up his menu. He tried to read, but with his heart pounding so hard behind his eyes he had trouble seeing.

Carlos Rodriguez, twenty-two and a Spanish national, had worked hard waiting tables. Soon he would have enough money for himself and his beautiful wife to start a new life in America. One more journey across the Atlantic and he could afford Elena's ticket. He stood at the table, watching this family frown at their menus. When the rest of the family had placed their orders, Carlos smiled at the daughter. "Would the *signorina* care to order?"

The girl looked up from her menu. She blushed, and Carlos tried not to smile. He wouldn't call her pretty, but he found her obvious innocence, her inquisitive eyes and her hesitant smile quite alluring. A challenge. Challenges excited Carlos, but he must take care. He glanced at her father who clearly adored her. If Carlos rose to the challenge and things went wrong, he could lose his job and his future in America. Acutely aware of the danger, but unable to resist, Carlos smiled, waiting.

Suddenly the mother frowned and said, "Ana, for goodness sake. The young man doesn't have all day."

Ana. So that was her name.

Ana's color deepened. She averted her eyes and cleared her throat. "I'll have the Clams Bianco, Calamari Marinara, and Spumoni for dessert."

"Excellent choices, *Signorina*," he bowed, smiled and collected her menu.

Carlos served his brightest smile with each course. Carlos sized his Ana up, flirting subtly so as not to attract her father's attention. Naïve. Impressionable. Perfect. He planned to make this a voyage that neither of them, especially his Ana, would ever forget.

The father smiled and patted his stomach. "Superb. Our compliments to the chef."

"Grazie, *Signore*. I'll tell him." Carlos stacked the plates and silverware.

"Luisa?" Giani rose and extended his arm. "Would you care to join me in a walk around the deck?"

Luisa smiled, slipped out of her chair and took her husband's arm.

"Ana," Giani said, "care to join us?"

"No thank you, Papa. I think I'll wait for Rosa."

"Very well." Giani guided his wife through the tables of diners to the door.

Carlos collected Ana's goblet, making sure that his hand brushed hers gently. "Did you enjoy your meal, *Signorina?*" She gasped, and he wondered which had surprised her more, his touch or his words?

"Yes, it was delicious. You speak Italian very well."

He thanked God for the foresight to learn Italian, and then he frowned. His Ana seemed ill at ease. Nothing had happened between them, so it could not be something he'd said or done.

"Thank you, *Signorina*. Can I get you anything else?"

"Oh. No, thank you."

She dabbed her lips with a napkin and stood, preparing to leave. Without reacting to his advances? He had misjudged her. The heavens had smiled. Luck was on his side. Her naiveté ensured that the rest of the voyage truly would be unforgettable. When the ship arrived in New York, he'd slip away, and no one would be the wiser. Shame and guilt would seal her lips and lock their secret inside her. But he had to sow the seeds now to reap his delicious harvest.

"Pardon me, *Signorina,* but you are stunning in that dress."

"Thank you," she blushed and began walking away, surprising him, again. Her parents must keep her stricter than he realized. He found her lack of experience refreshingly frustrating, a stumbling block he would enjoy removing. He'd lost track of the women who claimed that they couldn't resist him.

"*Signorina!*"

"Yes?"

He'd be modest. Direct. Sincere. "I was wondering," he said, wringing his hand towel humbly, "If perhaps I could see you sometime?" By the way she gasped, it was clear that this time he'd surprised her. He talked fast. "I don't quite know how to say this, but you see although the crew is not allowed to fraternize with the passengers, I really would like to see you. Alone." She hesitated and frowned, clearly unsure how to respond. He moved closer. Whispering, he decided to spell it out. "I'm a crewmember, you are a passenger. Regulations forbid us to see one another." Her face turned white. She stumbled into her seat.

"*Signorina,* are you all right?"

"Yes," she said. "I'm fine. Could you get me a glass of water, please?"

"Of course." He smiled. She was stalling for time.

Ana watched him walk through the kitchen door. She wasn't sure she'd heard him correctly. Meetings like this never happened to her. The closest she'd come was to read about them in novels. The moment Carlos was out of sight Rosa slid into the chair beside her.

"I saw what happened. What did I tell you?" Rosa giggled. She pushed a lock of hair behind her ear.

"My God, Rosa." She raised her fingers to her mouth. "How did you know?" Suddenly, Ana was back in Sicily. Back in the Petruzzi's outhouse. But this time when she looked at the window, Carlos looked back. Heat rose in her body, making her tremble. Of course, she would meet him. And she would begin her memoirs with their encounter. Carlos emerged from the kitchen with Ana's glass of water.

"Here he comes," Rosa whispered. "I'll talk to you later."

Her eyes fixed on Carlos, Ana barely noticed Rosa slip away. Carlos was all that mattered. He was handsome. He wanted her, and for the first time in her life Ana felt pretty!

Her shoulders suddenly slumped. The moment she opened her mouth, he would know she was a child in a woman's body. She played with her napkin, begging God to help her convince him otherwise.

Carlos set the glass in front of her.

"Thank you." She lifted the glass, and the movement caused tiny waves. She took a sip to stop her hand from shaking.

"Have you reached a decision?"

"I don't know what to say, or how to reply, *Signor*. I'm not a woman of the world. I know nothing of such matters." She was telling the truth, but where had such sophisticated words and phrases come from just when she needed them?

"That is one of the most charming things about you," he smiled and said, "May I make a suggestion?"

"Of course."

"I want to see you. Tonight. If you agree, that is," he said, looking into her eyes. "*Por favor.*"

She saw him lick his lips and glance around the dining room. A few stragglers were deep in conversation. He covered her hand with his and squeezed. "Say you will."

Ana froze.

Clearly anxious, he said, "I apologize, but the meeting must be kept secret."

As her mind processed the meaning of his words, her heart thundered. "*Signor,*" she said.

"Call me Carlos," he said.

"Carlos," she said. The truth worked once so she opted to try it again. "I can't go out tonight or any night. My parents would forbid it." She refused to say she was betrothed, because as of this moment her betrothal was nothing but a figment of Mama's imagination.

"Then perhaps we could meet during the day."

Yes! She surrendered to his Spanish eyes. "But people will see us. Every place on the ship is public." Ana raised the glass to her lips and took a sip to keep her mouth from blurting out something embarrassingly immature.

Would the *signorina* have any objections, to a room?"

"Do you know of one?" Her heart thundered harder. She must stay calm.

"Yes." Carlos leaned close.

"Whose?"

"Mine."

His breath felt warm and moist against her cheek. She tingled. "I see." She took a sip of water. "Well, I—"

"Say yes, Ana."

Her skin erupted in gooseflesh. She stared at him, incredulous. "How did you know my—"

"I heard your parents call you."

Her heart pummeled against her chest. He knelt as if to pick something up. His fingers brushed her ankle, sending chills up her calf. He pressed a slip of paper into her hand.

"Day after tomorrow at three o'clock." He walked away.

She glanced at the paper on which he had written number 302. Bursting with pride, she reviewed her clever words over again. They must have come from every book she had ever read. Ana smiled, thanking God for her desire to read. What a pity Mama had traded her education for marriage. How many times had Mama begrudged her lessons, demanding she put the book aside and learn common sense from her elders? Mama was jealous, God forgive her, but Mama was ignorant, too. Her thinking was provincial. Why couldn't Mama see that the books she scorned preserved not only our elders' words, but every human voice that had ever spoken?

Ana worshipped her tiny parchment worlds, perennial as the words that filled them. There were no guards at their leather borders forbidding her to enter. She needed no passport to cross into each land, stand among its people and share in the most intimate details of their lives. She lived their joys, suffered their sorrows and learned from their mistakes.

Ana congratulated herself for her profound and mature insight. She applauded herself for covering her inexperience with finesse. She used the intellect God had given her to keep from appearing a fool in front of the first man who'd ever looked at her as more than a prop in his landscape. She feasted on rich, creamy pride. She noticed the fruits of caution and prudence off to the side, but she was too bloated to take another bite.

Bursting to find Rosa, she rushed through the dining room door. On deck, her heart pounding, she wended her way through a sea of faces, bumping into men and women and colliding with Mama and Papa. Feeling her cheeks burn, she muttered, "Sorry," and pushed on.

Where could Rosa be? Tonio's face swam into view. She'd bet her last *lire* that Rosa was with Tonio. Spotting a door mid-ship, she sideswiped a woman, begged her forgiveness, and then bounded up the steps into the hall to Rosa's room which was directly above Mama's and Papa's.

She put her ear to the door and listened. It was quiet, but certain they were inside, she made a fist and knuckles up, she frowned and lowered her hand. Deciding not to knock, she curled her fingers around the knob. Curiosity holding her hostage, she turned the knob, cracked the door open and peeked inside.

Her eye followed the muted glow from a nightstand to a mound of clothes on the bed. Rosa hadn't unpacked, she thought, smiling, until the hill *trembled*, exposing a slender arm and a small, delicate shoulder. An undercurrent of rumbling unearthed a strong arm and a sprawling leg. Rosa and Tonio.

Torn between wanting to stay and wanting to go, she felt her heart flutter. Bedsprings groaned with deep-throated moans and cries of pleasure. Her head felt as light as a hot air balloon. No longer able to breathe, she slammed the door shut and ran.

Before she reached the end of the hall, Rosa screamed, "Ana!" She stopped, turned. Rosa was draped in a sheet, leaning out of the doorway.

"Please, Ana. Let me explain."

Her stomach churning, she opened the hall door and charged down the stairs, out a second door and onto the deck. Petrified, she grabbed the railing. A cool ocean breeze moved across her cheek. She squeezed until her knuckles were white and then burst into tears.

A hand grabbed her shoulder, and Ana stiffened.

"All I can say is it … just … happened, Ana, but even if I could take it back, I wouldn't."

Ana shrugged Rosa's hand off her shoulder.

"Suddenly, we were in my room, kissing. We fell on the bed, he kissed me. Then he …" Rosa stopped. Ana turned and saw her friend blushing. "Then there was this … feeling. Oh Ana," she shook her head. "I can't explain. You must feel it for yourself. But that wasn't all."

Ana ran her hand over her lips. "That wasn't all?" *Gesu Cristo,* how could there be more?

Ana had never seen Rosa's eyes sparkle like this. "All I know is this feeling must be one of the seven deadly sins." Her eyes widened as if she'd stumbled upon a treasure. "Lust!" She looked at Ana. And a teeny smile twitched at her lips. "That's what it is."

"Lust?" The forbidden word lay hot and sweet on Ana's tongue.

"Yes! And then I realized that lust is the very thing that feeds the great passion that fuels your precious literature. Lust is what Romeo and Juliet died for. Lust is what men and women risk honor, glory and their reputations to satisfy."

Dumbstruck, Ana stared.

"After I lust for the man I marry, we will lie together, racked with pleasure, making baby after baby!"

"But you're not marrying Tonio, are you?"

"Oh my God, Ana. You're so smart, but you keep missing the point."

"That's not the point?"

"Of course not! The point is that lust is the reason why courtships are kept so strict. Why our parents, the church, and the Pope feed us the Bible from birth. What else but the fear of God, and eternal damnation would keep people from wanting to make each other always feel this way?"

Rosa's eyes seemed to shine with a strange enlightenment. "And oh my God, Ana, can you picture your mother and father doing and feeling these things!"

Ana, to whom this blasphemy had not occurred, rebelled body and soul. "Mama and Papa would never do such a thing!"

"You silly goose! Of course, they would and they did. Look at all the babies they had."

Ana broke free and ran, leaving Rosa doubled over in a fit of raucous laughter.

Rosa's words enticed and repelled her. Images of men and women she knew lying together, thrashing in pleasure chilled and thrilled her. By day they flashed through her mind. At night they invaded her dreams. Warring body and soul, her body won, and Ana let the images linger.

Chapter 9

Carlos
1905

As Carlos finished his second glass of wine, his mind drifted beyond the confines of his tiny cabin. Ana was due at three as usual. He checked his clock and groaned. Two more hours.

Each time he took her was better than the last. Carlos filled a third glass and sipped, remembering the thrill of their first conversation and how his Ana had described herself as not being a woman of the world. Code for being a virgin.

God had blessed him again.

Carlos was adept at being *first,* and Ana, like the others, had been clay in his hands. As mentor-creator, he'd kneaded and shaped her. His expert touch had fired her passion, driven her to a fevered pitch and launched her on several blissful voyages. And just like the others before her, Ana returned, begging for more.

Ana was addicted.

Soon she would be the perfect lover. He looked at the clock and groaned. He imagined his face between her breasts, aching to enter her soft folds, to feel her shudder against him. He stared at his cabin door, remembering the first time his Ana had walked through.

Locking the door behind her, Carlos held a glass of red wine to her lips. She shook her head. He kissed her and tipped the glass to her lips. She swallowed the wine quickly. A tiny tear of garnet pooled on her lip. He licked it away. She drew in a breath and gazed into his eyes. He set the glass on his nightstand and eased her onto his bed. He kissed her and slid his hands over her breasts.

Ana shivered. Her innocence excited him so, he fumbled undoing her blouse. She opened her mouth. His kiss swallowed her protest. She moaned and pulled back. Her eyes mirrored her heart which pounded with desire. Carlos knew what was coming. Before giving in, her honor demanded she fight.

"I don't know what's gotten into me." She blushed, and Carlos smiled. "I've never done anything like this before." She hugged her blouse to her. Carlos caressed her cheek. "What must you think of me?" Ana's eyes begged for an answer.

"I think you are beautiful," he whispered, sensing they were the words she'd longed to hear all her life. He eased her hands from her blouse. She didn't slap him and she did not run away screaming.

Good Christ! He took off his shirt, loosened his pants and lifted her to her feet. His lips brushing hers, he slipped her blouse off her shoulders. Throbbing with desire, he controlled his urge and took his time. He slid her dress down around her.

Trembling and blushing, his Ana stood before him, naked.

Taut nipples on olive breasts. Her chest and ribs tapered at her waist and broadened again at her hips, the classic hourglass. Her legs curved where God had intended, leaving perfect spaces between her thighs and calves that narrowed toward delicate ankles and tiny feet. This girl, this gift from God, had surpassed even his perfect Elena. Carlos seared each luscious inch of her into his mind. Aching to preserve her forever, he would trade his immortal soul for one week inside the mind and hands of Michaelangelo.

"I disappoint you," she said, shocking him.

"Oh, Ana, No!" She mistook his shock for displeasure. The sincerity in his voice surprised him. His exquisite Ana. He promised to help her green fruit mature and have his fill till he burst. But he must be patient. If the animal inside him took control, it could cost him the prize of his life! For the first time ever Carlos Rodriguez dreaded the end of a voyage with only a memory to store away. But not with the others. Ana would dwell in the most special place in his heart. Feeling as powerless as a love-struck slave, Carlos moved close to Ana. "Your beauty takes my breath away." He fumbled through his words. His blood surged. His loins were on fire. He lifted her into his arms and lowered her onto his bed Sweet Ana, he thought, sweet as a peach in summer. He'd taste her again. Patience. Carlos closed his eyes.

He straddled her and when timid, shy Ana wrapped her arms around his neck he slipped in between her thighs. She stiffened. He slowed his advance. He kissed her and breathed in her ear. "I won't hurt you. I promise. You excite me like no other woman I've known." He whispered against her skin.

Knock! Knock! Knock! Yanked from his reverie, Carlos looked at the clock. Too early. It couldn't be Ana. His temples and groin throbbing, he set down his glass and opened the door.

Chapter 10

Ana

Bursting with love, Ana raced her heart down the steps to the decks below. She was early as usual, because lately, time, that impudent little snail, barely moved at all.

She hid on the steps down the hall from Carlos's cabin, hugged her legs and squirmed with impatience. Every time she closed her eyes she was in his room, his hands and mouth exploring her body in places that made her blush. At his command she soared, peaked and landed, craving to soar again. She pictured Carlos serving her meals and blushed. The same strong hands that cupped her breasts, lifted her hips and impaled her had seasoned her mother's salad and poured her father's wine.

Last night she had dropped her napkin. Stooping to pick it up, Carlos had slid his fingers gently up her calf, making the delicate bud between her legs tingle. Ana had grabbed her glass and gulped down her water to drown the groan in her throat.

Ana frowned. A tiny insidious worm poisoned love's apple. Why would someone as handsome and worldly as Carlos choose her when the ship was filled with beautiful girls who shamelessly flirted with him? If he only had eyes for her, why did jealousy eat at her heart?

She closed her eyes. She must be careful. She dropped out of sight so often. It was becoming difficult not to arouse suspicion. Her love for Carlos filled every crevice and pore. She needed release before she exploded.

Tonio worried her. When he wasn't occupied with his new shipboard friend, Vincenzo Sciorri, or his girlfriend Rosa, he picked up on her moods. She was convinced he was part snake. He'd catch a scent in the air and grin and stare, making her squirm. His look questioned the sparkle in her eyes, when to his knowledge there was no apparent reason, or was there? She remembered that dreadful night Rosa had stood in on deck draped in a sheet pleading to let her explain.

Speaking of Rosa, thank God she was keeping Tonio busy. He stammered and blushed whenever he saw her, and Ana had caught them together – yesterday morning. After breakfast Rosa was nowhere in sight. Ana had roamed the decks and peeked in every doorway and corner twice. On her way back to her cabin she saw Rosa sneak out of a closet, two doors down from the dining hall. Her clothes and hair were a mess. Ana had squirreled into a corner, looking out only when she thought it was safe. Tonio had stepped out of the closet, tucking his shirttails into his trousers. The old, provincial Ana would have been appalled but the new, worldly Ana smiled. Having loved Carlos, how could she judge her friend and her brother?

Speaking of Tonio's friends, Ana wondered why her brother befriended Vincenzo Sciorri. He was a strange one. He was a little older and dazzlingly handsome, with dark, piercing eyes. But he seemed distant and brooding. He walked the deck and the crowd parted or people stepped back to give him room. One morning when Tonio had been dangerously close to uncovering her romance with Carlos, she tried diverting him by asking about Vincenzo. She remembered his answer and how it had surprised her.

"Vincenzo's traveling with his mother, Bianca. His father left them in the old country at Vincenzo's grandfather's, so that he could travel ahead and set things up before he sent for Vincenzo and his mother," Tonio said, buttoning his shirt.

Ana frowned at her brother.

"Why the frown?" Tonio said. "His situation is common enough. Lots of men do it." He picked up the comb and looked in the mirror.

"Living without his father must have been hard for Vincenzo and his mother. My God, Tonio, if Papa had left us, no matter the reason, I would've wanted to die."

Tonio shrugged and combed his hair. "Vincenzo said his father went back and forth many times before he was born and while he was very young. But for some reason the older Vincenzo got," Tonio paused, licked his finger and glued an errant hair into place, "the less his father came home, and then he stopped coming home altogether."

"With no reason and without a word? So now after all these years," Ana said, staring at Tonio, trying to understand, "Vincenzo and his mother will arrive on his father's doorstep?"

"I guess. Who knows?" Tonio said, putting the comb down.

"Time has a way of changing people's lives. What if they get there and things are different?"

Tonio rarely took her into his confidence. But to her pleasant surprise, this conversation or perhaps his feelings for Rosa had softened him.

"Actually, Ana," he said, facing her. "Vincenzo has some ideas of his own. The truth is he doesn't really know his father, so he'd rather make his own way in America. He claims he has 'friends', contacts, in America. As a matter of fact, people in the old country have already referred him to their associates in New York."

"I guess," Ana said, hesitantly. "Vincenzo is a man, and I understand his not wanting to live with another man, one he hardly knows, even if that man is his father," she frowned more deeply. "But on the other hand, if I put myself in his place, I can't imagine Mama and me migrating to a new country, and then moving away from her as soon as we got there. As far as those contacts his friends had in America, I—"

"Ana!" Rosa whispered, bringing her back to the present.

Ana opened her eyes wide and jumped up. "Rosa?" she said, pulling Rosa out of the hallway and onto the steps where she sat. "What are you doing here?"

"I followed you. What are *you* doing here?"

Ana's heart pounded. Torn between wanting to share her feelings for Carlos and terrified to do so, she whispered, "I'll tell you, but if you breathe a word to anyone and I mean *anyone*, our friendship is over."

Rosa's large blue eyes grew larger with every delicious detail Ana divulged. Ana laughed as Rosa swept the blonde ringlets from her forehead and fanned the heat from her face.

"Oh, my God Ana. You're so lucky," Rosa said breathlessly. "Carlos is so handsome!"

"Our time together excites me so, I can't sleep, and I can't eat." Ana clasped her hands. "But, I'm never tired or hungry. I have to tell you something else, Rosa," she grasped Rosa's hands and squeezed. "I'm in love!" Giggling and blushing, she let Rosa go and buried her face in her hands.

"Love? No, Ana, you can't be in love. You must be mistaken." Ana stared at Rosa, stunned at her best friend's reaction. "You barely know him. What if he's married?"

"What? What makes you say such a thing? What did you hear?" Ana said, horrified.

"Nothing. I," Rosa averted her eyes. "I mean this trip will be over. After we land in America, what if you never see him again?"

Ana pressed her palm to her mouth, as a wave of gut wrenching nausea crashed inside her. To never taste his kiss? Or feel him inside her? Life without Carlos? Rosa was the mistaken one. Ana had bewitched him as he'd bewitched her. He loved her. She felt it in his touch. Saw it in his eyes. But Rosa's words ate at her heart like acid.

"It's love, Rosa. I know it! I've never felt anything like it before. And, Rosa, he loves me too."

"Did he say, Ana, 'I love you?'"

"Not in so many words. But he shows it." Heat warmed Ana's cheeks. Embarrassed, she bowed her head.

"Oh, Ana, even if Carlos says he loves you, what about," Rosa stammered, "Alberto Petruzzi and your betrothal. Surely you haven't forgotten!"

Of course, she'd forgotten, or had she barred Alberto Petruzzi from her mind because after loving a man like Carlos, a pig like Alberto no longer existed? *Sapere e potere*. Knowledge is power. Carlos and she would deal with Papa, Mama and her so-called betrothal when the time came.

"Rosa, you need to leave. It's time for me to go."

"Don't, Ana, please." Rosa's eyes glistened. She stood. "This isn't love. It's a terrible mistake. You must stop meeting him before it's too late."

No. You are the one who's mistaken, Ana thought, watching Rosa climb the steps and slip out of sight.

The only world Ana wanted was here and now aboard this ship. If only she could stay here forever with Carlos! Had they been lovers for only a few glorious weeks?

Lovers. The most delicious word her tongue had ever tasted. Luckily, due to some mix-up with some passengers' papers, the ship was late heading into the Atlantic. After having made several overnight ports of call, before heading out into the Atlantic, the engine had broken down, thank goodness. Forced to veer off course, they set sail for Cagliari in Southern Sardinia where they spent several days waiting for a replacement part. If not for that 'divine' intervention, her time with Carlos would have been even shorter.

And, what about her big plans to travel and write her memoirs? That did not have to change. She would write about the sacred love of a wife for her husband so glowingly, Holy Mother Church and The

Holy Father would approve! Her future had seemed so dark when her journey began, but now, Ana smiled, it was blindingly bright.

The voyage would be over in a week or less. She and Carlos would have to make plans for their future. Should she marry him and live in Spain, or should she live in America with Mama and Papa while he continued to work aboard ship? Perhaps they should start their new life in America right away. He was bright. Ambitious. He could work any job. So could she! America was the land of opportunity. They'd be together always! Yes, that would be the best, the most wonderful solution!

Would their love shock her parents? How would Mama and Papa react to Carlos's and her plans? Papa seemed pleased that the voyage agreed with her. He neither suspected nor questioned a thing. Mama had seemed slightly less convinced.

She seemed to have reverted to her role as dutiful wife. Mama had always obeyed Papa to keep the peace. Surely, they would cancel her betrothal arrangements when they realized how in love she and Carlos were!

A noise in the corridor interrupted Ana's reverie. She stood up and flattened herself against the wall. A wave of nausea tipped her stomach. She couldn't keep food down. She was getting thin and feeling faint all the time. Her liaisons with Carlos excited her so, they took her appetite away. She must be living on love. Ana took deep, slow, breaths. Her nausea subsided. Hearing noises, she frowned, peeked down the hallway, listened closely and smiled. The sound came from Carlos's cabin. He seemed to be fumbling with the door from inside.

The door opened. A young, pretty girl stepped into the hallway. Ana recognized her, Graziela, the maid who tidied her parents' room. She slipped her arms around Carlos's neck and kissed him full on the mouth.

"Santa Maria, Graziela. No, no more. I told you, you must go now. Ana will be here any moment. I cannot risk—"

Their words ricocheted off the walls, exploding into disjointed, incomprehensible sounds. Bits and pieces fused into a meaningless hum. A thin sheen of sweat moistened Ana's forehead.as she slumped to the floor.

Chapter 11

Ana's Betrayal

Ana woke up in her cabin in her bed with no memory of how she had gotten there. She remembered Rosa had found her sitting on the steps down the hall from Carlos's room. Bursting with love for Carlos, she remembered telling Rosa everything. She burrowed under the covers, praying she wouldn't regret that moment of weakness. She frowned deeply, trying hard to remember what had happened after that. Had she seen Carlos? She couldn't remember. An image flashed through her mind, an image that made her shudder, but it was gone before she could grasp it. She burped up an acrid bubble, grimaced, pulled the covers up to her chin and stared into the dark, wide-eyed with confusion.

She heard muffled voices coming from the hallway. She looked over her shoulder and noticed her door was slightly ajar. Mama and Papa were talking to someone, a man, in the hallway. The man's voice was subdued. When he spoke, her parents, Mama especially, sounded alarmed. Hearing her name, Ana kicked back the covers, tiptoed to the doorway and listened.

"Pregnant?" Tears streamed down Luisa's face. She leaned against the door feeling as haggard as she must look. "But, Doctor, there's no one in whom she's shown the slightest interest!" Luisa leaned heavily on Giani's arm.

"Pregnant! Mother of God," Giani steadied his wife. Luisa watched the color drain from his face. He stared at the doctor and then at Luisa. "My wife is right. Ana has no one in her life …" His voice trailed off, and his eyes lost focus.

"I'm sorry," the doctor said.

"My God!" Luisa turned her tear-stained face to her husband. "The shame. The disgrace. Our good name!"

"Please, Luisa. We must remain calm." He squeezed her arm.

"They'll know, Giani," she sobbed. "Everyone aboard ship will know that our Ana is damaged and not even in the name of love!"

"That's the very thing I can't understand. At least if she were in love, perhaps in time, all would be forgiven," Luisa's eyes narrowed, "but never forgotten. What's the use?" she said, dabbing her eyes with her sleeve. "Nothing can help us now. Dear Lord, Giani, when the Petruzzi's find out—"

"The Petruzzi's?" Giani said. Luisa watched his eyes suddenly sparkle as if he'd discovered the culprit. His eyes dulled and deflated, he exhaled. "No not," he shook his head. "Not Alberto. Ana hated him."

"You realize of course that as of this moment our daughter's betrothal is off."

He grasped Luisa's arms and squeezed. "Perhaps we arrive at the wrong conclusions."

"What are you talking about?"

"Perhaps we are so upset that we're overlooking the obvious." He raised his eyebrows.

"Luisa, you were right when you said Ana has no one. Therefore, someone must have," he said, as his eyes darkened. He swallowed and winced at the obvious lump in his throat. "Someone must have violated my Ana, and she didn't tell because she feared what I might do."

"Oh my God. That thought never crossed my mind!"

Luisa knew her husband. Even in her state of shock she could see his mind working hard on a rationale. The doctor, a stranger, was the first on whom he would test the rationale he must create to fit their unspeakable situation. If a doctor, a man of prestige and respect accepted it, then others would follow.

"Doctor, my Ana knows me. She didn't tell me who did this, this terrible thing because she knows I would find him and kill him before we reach America. I'm telling you the truth!" The doctor nodded, preparing to leave. "Doctor?" Giani said. The plea for the doctor's support in his eyes and voice was humiliatingly obvious.

"Pregnant!" Luisa touched the doctor's arm, directing attention to her. "Are you certain?" she asked, with genuine desperation.

"I'm afraid so, *Signora*. The symptoms you described," he sighed. "I've brought too many babies into the world to be wrong. If I can be of any further assistance, you know where to find me." The doctor snapped his bag closed, nodded and took his leave.

"This ship is a hotbed of rumors. A tiny floating village. God only knows if the doctor will respect our privacy and keep our shame to himself." She joined her hands as if in prayer. "Who made our daughter pregnant?" Her lips trembled. "Who?"

Giani grasped her hands and looked into her eyes. "You and Ana have had your moments. I sided with her in the past, because I believed there were times you were too rigid with her."

"And now?"

He let go of her hands, closed his eyes and rubbed the bridge of his nose. "If my Ana disgraced us on purpose," he opened his eyes, "I cannot defend or forgive her."

Luisa blurted, "She must tell us who he is."

"She will, and we will deal with him. The bastard can't escape. We're all on this ship until we land in America."

He grasped Luisa's hands. "We must wait. Alerting Ana prematurely will make things worse. And above all, we must think."

Giani opened the door wider and peeked into her stateroom. When he saw Ana in bed asleep, he closed the door. "Come, Luisa. We'll talk on deck in the fresh air."

Ana lay statue-still until their footsteps faded.

"Pregnant? I'm pregnant?" she whispered. Eyes wide, she put her hand on her stomach gently. Pregnant with Carlos's child?

An army of feelings battled to conquer her heart. Shame and humiliation joined forces and won. Now Mama, Papa, and everyone onboard ship would know what she and Carlos had done. But what they thought they knew couldn't be further from what had really happened. Her heart pounded. After she told Carlos she was carrying his child, they would stand before Mama and Papa and tell them not to worry. Everything would be fine. She loved Carlos. He loved her, and they loved their child. They would marry and raise their child together.

Ana crept out from under the covers and gasped. She was fully clothed. She looked at the clock on the nightstand. It was late afternoon. How did she lose all that time? Shivering, she grabbed her wrap, opened her cabin door a crack, peeked out and tiptoed down the hall to the steps and bumped into Rosa.

"Ana, are you okay? Where are you going?"

Ana lowered her head, brushed past Rosa and took the hall to the stairwell, with Rosa trailing behind her.

Carlos's cabin door was open. They heard voices, moved closer and held their breath.

"Tell me what happened again, Graziela." Carlos sounded nervous.

Carlos and Graziela? Ana turned white and drew in a ragged breath.

"Calm down, Carlos. Save your tantrums for Ana! I can't tell you what I don't know!" Graziela snapped.

"Damn you!" Carlos said. "Tell me what happened."

Ana heard them scuffle. Her head swam. She leaned against the wall praying she would not faint.

"Ouch! Let go of my arm. I told you a hundred times," Graziela said.

Silence, and then, "Ouch! All right. Let me go. After Ana fainted and you ducked into your room, I called a steward. He helped me get her back to her cabin."

"Did the steward connect her with me?"

"Of course not. You hid in your room so quickly, how could he?" Graziela said, sounding annoyed. "Anyway, when I couldn't wake her, I left her on the bed and went to look for her parents. I told them I'd found her passed out in the corridor and that was all."

"You didn't mention my name?" Carlos said, sounding distraught.

"Of course not! Do you take me for a fool?"

"Very good. You did the right thing, Graziela." Carlos said, sounding relieved, almost happy.

Ana held onto the wall. Carlos and a maid! She pictured them naked and sweating. She pictured Graziela moaning and arching her body in pleasure.

Ana felt the ship roll. She felt the floor move in waves under her feet like the sea moved under the ship. Her stomach churned. Doubling over, Ana fought to keep from retching. A wave of disgust swelled in her heart. She refused to sink down against the wall and sob.

Carlos revolted her. Suddenly, she hated him more than she'd hated Alberto Petruzzi. Her eyes burned with anger that turned to rage. Rage burned through her like acid.

The hallway lights flickered. Looking stunned, Rosa gasped.

No longer able to stem her rage, Ana barged through the doorway.

"No, Ana! No," Rosa yelled, following Ana into the room.

"Damn both of you to hell!"

The cabin and hallway lights dimmed. The wine bottle and glasses on Carlos's nightstand clinked and danced wildly.

Rosa, Carlos and Graziela froze, stared at her, at each other and at the bottle and glasses. Her head lighter than air and her stomach wanting to purge, Ana fought to stay conscious. She'd rather die than faint.

"How could you betray me?" Ana's tears streamed down her cheeks.

The cabin and hall lights went out. On. Out. On.

Carlos darted his eyes and licked his lips, looking terrified. "Ana." His face as white as the cabin walls, Carlos walked toward her.

"Stay where you are," she sobbed. "What a fool I was."

"I can explain. Please," Carlos said.

"There's nothing to explain," Ana said, "except that I'm pregnant."

The color drained from his face.

"I came to you all these weeks because I loved you." She looked at him with red, swollen eyes. "I see you here with her, and I still can't believe my eyes."

"Ana," Carlos said, moving toward her again.

"No!" Ana screamed. Tears rolled off her chin. "You used me!"

Closet doors and bureau drawers creaked open and groaned closed. Carlos and Graziela gasped. The bottle wobbled and hit the glasses. The glasses hit the floor and shattered. Graziela backed toward the door. Rosa stood in the door blocking her exit. She stared at Ana. Ana rushed at Carlos and pummeled his chest with her fists. The bathroom door blew open and slammed shut. Open. Shut. Open. Shut. Bottles, brushes and combs flew and hit the walls. Glass shattered. Rosa gasped. Graziela screamed.

Barely noticing, Ana whispered, "I thought that because we were in love, being with you was pleasing in the eyes of God." Carlos moved closer. He attempted to take her hand, hesitated and then seemed to change his mind. "I was so happy." She forced a laugh through her tears. "I believed that when I told you about our baby, we would face Mama and Papa together," she sniffled. "I thought you would want the same thing I do. To marry and turn the nightmare I made for my parents into a dream that would last a lifetime."

Carlos stroked her cheek. "My darling, beautiful Ana, that was never possible."

"Why not?" she stammered.

His eyes shone with pity. "Because I'm already married."

Ana frowned, wondering how so soft a voice could utter such brute-force words. Married. Pregnant. He was married. She was single and pregnant with his child. The weight of her shame was a vise that squeezed her heart and lungs making it hard to breathe.

Married. Pregnant. The words and their ramifications suddenly terrified her. The lights stayed on. Brushes, glasses, bottles stopped throwing themselves against the wall. Drawers and doors stayed open or closed.

Ana turned away from Carlos and stared at Graziela. Did she know Carlos had a wife? The answer to her question shone in Graziela's eyes. Ana's legs gave way. She stumbled against the wall and inched her way to the bathroom. As she bent over the bowl and groaned, she saw Carlos rush toward her.

"Get back." Heaving, she waved him off. Her eyes and nose ran. "Leave me alone!" The bile on her tongue tasted bitter. "I'll take care of myself and my child." She glared at Carlos, swearing that somehow, she'd find a way.

Ana, Carlos thought, his poor, exquisite Ana! *Gesu Cristo in cielo, come avrebbe mancato.* How he would miss her! She meant more to him than all other women. He had loved her in his own way. Carlos cursed his weakness for women, and for Ana most of all.

Pregnant! He'd escaped that fate most of his life. He took comfort in knowing that his Ana was as smart as she was strong. She'd get through it all right. But he could lose his job! He'd be put ashore the moment Ana told the captain. He'd slaved on this ship for months. If his plans for Elena to join him in America were destroyed, he would have no one to blame but himself. Knowing a sharp clean break worked best, Carlos clasped his hands behind his back hating himself for what he had to say.

Ana! If only...How I wish...Feeling emptier than he thought possible, he said, "Under the circumstances, Ana," he paused, struggling to push the words past the lump in his throat. "I'm afraid there is nothing left but to say goodbye."

At that moment Carlos knew that the hate he saw in her eyes would haunt him forever. He saw something else in her eyes. Lack of doubt. Ana knew this dilemma was hers. They couldn't run into each other again, and to make certain of that, he'd start by getting transferred to another dinner shift.

Rosa sat on Ana's bed, watching Ana sob into her pillow. Rosa knew that *she* wasn't pregnant, and *she* never would be. Ana always thought she was so smart. Now who was the smart one? So much for Ana's belief in education. And what about all that strange, hair-raising business that had happened inside and outside of Carlos's room? What made the hallway and cabin lights go on and off? And the wine bottle and glasses smash into each other and the doors and bang open and slam shut? Rosa shivered and rubbed her arms. It was almost as if his room had been possessed by Satan.

Well, she'd heard from the staff and a few other passengers that the captain had posted an explanation. Hearing the word, 'weather' she was so grateful for a rational explanation that she immediately closed the door on the distasteful subject.

Rosa pictured Tonio's handsome face, the way his deep dark eyes devoured her and the way he shuddered and moaned when they made love. She planned to see more and more of Tonio from now on. And if he failed to amuse her to her satisfaction, she could always watch Ana deal with her mother and father. The door opened. Rosa looked up. Speak of the devil. *"Signor e Signora Testadura,"* she said. Sensing she was not welcome, Rosa got up and left.

Papa and Mama sat with her. His eyes begged for an explanation. She drew herself inward and cringed at his disappointment.

"Ana," he whispered.

"Papa, not now please. I need to sleep." She tried not to cry harder.

"You'll do nothing of the kind, *Signorina.*" Mama's spine seemed to stiffen with her expression. "You owe us an explanation. And we won't leave you alone until—"

"Just a moment, Luisa," he said. He stood up and squeezed his wife's arm. "Can't you see that Ana's in—"

"I can't believe what I'm hearing! Even now you defend her? Can she do no wrong in your eyes? What must she do before you—"

"Enough!" he said. "I've had enough from you! Your child writhes in her own private hell, and you make it a weapon to influence me against her?" Giani clenched his fist, jumped up and punched the wall.

Luisa sneered. "Your precious Ana committed the gravest offense against a family a daughter could," she said, "and she still holds the highest regard in your heart! I dare you to be so gallant and forceful when the tide of public opinion drowns us in shame."

Her piece said, she glared at her husband. Once tall and proud, he seemed shrunken and old before her eyes. Ana must have noticed it too, Luisa thought distractedly. Perhaps that's why she was sobbing.

Chapter 12

Ana

Her eyes glazed over, Ana sat in her room on her bed watching the milk in the glass on her nightstand. She tried to obey Mama and drink it, but her stomach rebelled. Feeling the ship roll, she watched the milk slosh back and forth, leaving a film on the sides of the glass. She picked the glass up, sniffed, gagged, and then set it down on her nightstand. Knowing her shame was grist for the dinner mill, she refused to leave her cabin.

The two days that passed since her parents and she found out she was pregnant seemed like two years. No matter how her parents insisted, pleaded, or yelled, Ana refused to name her baby's father. Knowing it was Carlos would make the rest of the voyage worse for everyone. He was married. They were both Catholic, and the church hadn't budged on divorce for centuries. She couldn't marry anyone else, because there was no one else. Besides, if she told Mama and Papa about Carlos, she'd never succeed in putting time and distance between him and herself. Ana knew that to survive, that's exactly what she must do. For as long as she lived she'd never forget how Carlos had used her. None of this was her baby's fault. She raised the glass to her lips and forced a swallow.

When she thought she could sink no lower, Mama told her that Alberto Petruzzi had broken their engagement. As if she'd disgraced him, he was telling anyone who would listen, how glad he was to find out exactly what Ana Luisa Testadura was before he married her. Perhaps she had disgraced him. If she'd given a damn about him at all, her broken engagement would have been the blow that destroyed her. Thank God for little favors. She pulled the covers up to her neck. She needed sleep. She turned out the light, but the darkness could not blind her to the disappointment she saw in Papa's eyes.

Alberto's brash declaration had humiliated Luisa, but Giani, to Luisa's amazement, had simply shook his head. Luisa was a practical woman. Nothing made her come to her senses faster than the need to protect her family. They were in the corridor and before they went out on the fresh air deck, she grasped his arm and Giani stopped walking.

"If we don't unite as a family, we'll never find our way out of this," she said.

"I couldn't agree more," he sighed, placing his hand on hers. "What do you have in mind?"

"I think Ana should start showing her face in public."

"I'm surprised. I thought for sure you would agree with Ana when she said she wanted to stay indoors," he said. "It's a brave and good idea, but I doubt Ana will—"

"Nonsense," she said, holding onto the rail and looking at the horizon. "Ana's been locked up in a dark room for the last week. It's bad for her health. And bad for the..." Luisa could not bring herself to say the word. "Perhaps I'll speak to her now," she said, "you wait here."

"I'll come with you and wait outside in case you need help."

Luisa grasped the few remaining threads of compassion she could muster and opened Ana's door. "Ana?" she said and walked in. Squinting at the light, Ana held her arm up. "Good. You're awake." She sat on Ana's bed. "Your father and I are worried about you. You haven't come out of this room in days." Ana shook her head. "Listen to me. In a few days we'll be landing at Ellis Island in New York City. Everyone will be out on deck to see the Statue of Liberty. You mustn't deny yourself that. I'm told it's a tradition among immigrants."

"Mama, how can I—"

"I won't take no for an answer. If you start showing your face now," Luisa's tone softened, "it will make you stronger for what lies ahead." Luisa touched her and said, "Please, Ana. Am I asking so much?"

"No," Ana sighed.

"Good," she said. "Perhaps the fresh air will give you back your appetite."

Chapter 13

Tonio and Vincenzo

Tonio stepped out of the tiny supply closet in the corridor near the ship's dining room. He was straightening his hair and buttoning his shirt, when his friend Vincenzo Sciorri caught up with him.

"Rosa?" Vincenzo smiled, thumbing his hand at the closed door. Tonio did up his trousers, smiling, and Vincenzo smacked his friend's face and laughed. They started to walk.

"Being on this ship was okay, but now that we're close to Ellis Island I'm getting edgy," Vincenzo said, running his hands through his hair.

"Not me," Tonio smiled, and Vincenzo friend-slapped Tonio's face and laughed harder.

"Hey! There's your family," Vincenzo pointed to his parents and Ana climbing the steps. "What's going on with your sister?"

"What do you mean?" Tonio frowned and stopped walking.

"How come I never see her at dinner anymore?"

"She's pregnant," Tonio said in a neutral voice.

Tonio saw his sister in primary colors. She was smart, sometimes flighty and funny. She'd see things in ways that sometimes made them laugh so hard they couldn't breathe. If Mama lived for a thousand years, she would never understand Ana or her sense of humor. Papa indulged Ana, and Mama resented him for it. But regardless of how they felt about Ana, she still sopped up most of their attention. When they boarded the ship, Tonio thought all that would change. It had. Now Ana had *all* their attention. But he was in love with Rosa, and he no longer cared. He looked at Vincenzo and a shiny new thought glimmered in his eye. When he got to America maybe he'd follow Vincenzo's example and strike out on his own. He and Rosa.

Vincenzo slipped his thumbs into his belt buckle and squared his shoulders. "So, who's been playing hide the sausage with your sister?" he laughed.

"She won't say. You know how it is. Ana's shame is driving my parents crazy."

"Yeah?"

"Look, I don't want to talk about that. It's family business, which means it's none of yours," he said. The look in his eye showed he meant business.

"All right." Vincenzo backed off. "Calm down. I'm not looking for trouble," he said, dusting imaginary lint from Tonio's shoulder and good-naturedly slapping his face, again.

Tonio punched his friend's arm, acknowledging he understood. After spilling Ana's beans to Vincenzo, the last thing he wanted was to chat with his family. Tonio backed up. Vincenzo followed Tonio down the hall to another staircase.

Vincenzo climbed the steps listening to Tonio, but his mind was on Ana. The answer to her 'shame' could be profitable for him and a way out for her. Not that he gave a damn what happened to her or to most women he'd met. Ana, like all the rest, including his mother, had created her own trouble. When he got to America, he planned to go his own way. But now, Ana's foolishness may have come along in time to change his life for the better.

He needed money. Sure, he could read and write, but he was unskilled. Prior to Ana's problem he'd had two choices. He could work at hard labor or call some friends. The second was a more dangerous choice, but thanks to Ana, he might have a third, safer choice.

She wasn't bad, and although she wasn't his type, for the right amount of money he could be persuaded to give her child his name. He could not get this opportunity out of his mind, but Vincenzo knew that when he spoke to her father, the old man would see him as a godsend. For Vincenzo Sciorri, Ana's shame was *his* godsend.

He pictured Ana and smirked. He'd known a few girls like her in his town in the north. They were high and mighty. As far back as he could remember, because they were born to a better class than he, they looked down on him or through him or acted as if he were invisible. His mother had been one of them, until she fell in love with his father and slid too far into hell to have a life at all. And from where Vincenzo stood, his mother's marriage had turned out not to be worth the price she continued paying.

Marrying Ana would end his chances with someone else, because like his own parents, for better or worse, you lived with your lot. And that was fine with him. He never wanted to marry anyone, but if he should want or need another woman, he'd have one or as many women as he wanted.

His square jaw, large black eyes, and dark skin fit the timeless standard of Latin beauty. He knew he was handsome. He saw it in the eyes of women who'd fancied him. But thanks to his parents there was a darkness in him that frightened most women away shortly after meeting him. He buried his secret deep inside in what passed for his heart. If Giani Testadura discovered what that secret was, he would never allow his naïve Ana, pregnant or not, to become Vincenzo's wife.

Chapter 14

Ana
1905

In less than a few days the ship would dock at Ellis Island in New York City, and Ana would step onto American soil—pregnant. Her little problem weighed on her like a ton of granite. Despite it being summer, the brisk ocean breeze chilled her. She pulled the light deckchair blanket more tightly around her shoulders and over her stomach.

Mama and Papa were right, Ana thought, sitting next to them and staring at the horizon from a deck chair – a horizon as bleak and flat as her future. The ocean air refreshed her and smelled good despite her depression. She looked down past the deckchairs, smoke stacks and lifeboats, and caught sight of Tonio walking with Vincenzo Sciorri. They were headed in her direction, but apparently, something had changed their minds, because for no apparent reason, they turned in mid-stride and headed in the opposite direction.

Adrift on her emotional ocean, Ana sensed tiny waves of pity emanating from Mama, but disappointment stormed in Papa's eyes. No matter what had happened in the past, he'd been her rock. Her safe harbor. How could she bear losing him now when she needed him most? But how could she blame him when she'd violated every ethic he held dear? Their special relationship was over. Her sins had changed it irrevocably. She had never felt lonelier. Loving Carlos had cost her Papa's love and respect. Demoralized by reality, her determination to handle her situation alone was disintegrating bit by bit. Why had she not realized before how strange America would be? She didn't speak the language. She was smart and quick, but under her insurmountable circumstances—

"We're going below, Ana. It's getting chilly."

"You go below, Luisa. I want to speak to Ana a little while."

"Very well, but don't be too long. You didn't sleep well last night. You need to rest," she said, bending to kiss his cheek.

"I'll be along soon," he said. He stayed in his deck chair, tucked the blankets under his thighs and stared at the ocean. "In a few days we'll be landing New York City. You must tell me—"

"Papa, please." Ana kept her eyes on the horizon. "We've been through this." Tears rolled down her face. She wiped them away.

"You're not thinking clearly."

"Forgive me, Papa," she said, swallowing hard, "but it is you who are not thinking clearly." She looked into her father's eyes. He seemed so forlorn. "I know you think I refuse to name the father of my child because I want to protect him, but it's you I want to protect. Identifying him won't do any good." Ana averted her eyes and bit her lip.

"That's not so. He'll pay for hurting all of us. He'll marry—"

"He won't marry me, Papa."

"He'd goddamned better or I'll—"

"He's already married."

The look on his face made her bury her face in her hands and sob.

Jaw clenched, he stared at the ocean. "My God, Ana! I don't know who you are anymore!"

"Papa, I swear to you on God's Holy Mother that I didn't know that until, I just didn't know."

The blood drained from his face. "That bastard! Tell me who he is, Ana! I'll ... kill him with my bare hands!"

"That's exactly why I can't tell you. Facing reality is the only thing that's going to get me through. Pregnant or not, women don't have futures with married men. Only foolish, stupid women believe married men will leave their wives."

She pictured Carlos and Graziela laughing at her expense, and put her hand over her belly, wondering what would become of her and her baby.

"But, Ana," Papa said, "I can't stand to see you suffer like this. We must do something. I know what I said to your mother before, but this time she's right. If I knew—"

Ana closed her eyes. "No, Papa, you're wrong. *I* must live with it. Please, I don't want to hurt you any more than I already have. Can you let me be alone for a while?"

He sighed and grasping the arm of the faded striped deck chair, he grunted and pushed himself up. She felt him pause and stare at her, but she wouldn't open her eyes. She heard him bump into someone.

"Hi," Rosa said.

Ana opened her eyes and looked at her father, who seemed not to hear Rosa. Seeing Rosa frown and then shrug Papa off, Ana suddenly gasped.

No Ana, you can't be in love. You must be mistaken ... You barely know him ... What if he's married?

My God, Rosa. You knew!

"Hi, Ana," Rosa said, and Ana stiffened. Clearly unaware, Rosa sighed and played with the fringes of the white and gold shawl draping her shoulders "It's good to finally see you on deck."

Ana's eyes narrowed, watching the audacious Rosa slip into Papa's deck chair and tighten her shawl around her.

"Ana, please. I know you're angry with me for ignoring you since you found out you're—"

Ana stared at Rosa who stammered, "I don't know what to say except that I'm sorry. I was selfish, and I miss talking to you. Ana, please say something. Don't ignore me. I can't bear it. You're the only friend in the world that I have."

"No wonder!" Ana spat.

Her heart thumped against her ribs with anger.

"You should've thought of that when you found out Carlos was married and never bothered to tell me. Why?"

Her face turned white. "Ana, I ... how did you—"

"Never mind how I know. How could you do that to me? You say you're my friend. You're not. Friends are loyal. Friends protect each other. You kept your mouth shut and helped Carlos betray me. You're as guilty as he."

Anger pulsated in her throat, behind her eyes.

"No, Ana, please don't say that. I didn't betray you, I swear," she pleaded, "I didn't betray you."

... choking anger ... blinding anger ...

"What would you call it then? What made you do it?"

... burning a hole where her heart used to be.

"I don't know. When you told me about you and Carlos, you sounded so...so excited. Your skin, your eyes, they glowed. You seemed so happy, I hated to spoil it!"

"*Liar!* You are a liar!" Ana screamed, not giving a damn who heard. She leaned over. Her nose touched Rosa's. "You've known me all of my life. I told you I loved him. Would I give myself to someone I didn't love? And you were the only one in the universe who knew I loved him!"

"But I thought you were just—"

Her temples pounded, her mouth trembled. As her fingers flexed with wanting to choke Rosa to death, the shawl began tightening around Rosa's neck.

Eyes bulging with surprise, Rosa jumped up. Red-faced, her mouth soundless and frozen open, she gagged. Her frantic fingers tore at her shawl!

"Ana!" Luisa shouted.

Ana jerked her head toward the sound of her mother's voice, and Rosa's shawl loosened. Rosa slumped onto the deck chair, coughing and gasping. Her nose ran. Her terror-filled eyes darted from Luisa to Ana.

"What happened?" Luisa frowned at Ana, looking worried.

"Nothing, Mama. We were just talking and—"

Luisa's eyes narrowed at Ana. "What did you do?"

"Nothing! I swear. We were talking and—"

The look in Mama's eyes stopped Ana—dead. She followed Mama's gaze to the bright red bruise encircling Rosa's neck, and the day at Petruzzi's flashed through her mind. How her rage had rocked the outhouse.

How its door had banged open. How she'd fired her rage at Alberto. How he'd stuffed his mouth until he vomited. How every face had reflected confusion and fright except one.

Mama glared at Ana now in the same way she had glared then. The message could not have been clearer. Mama had known all along what Ana was capable of. If Mama hadn't shouted, breaking her concentration, she could have strangled Rosa to death. Ana shivered and shut her eyes tight. In her right mind, she would never kill a soul. What made her come so close?

Rage.

She must take care to never unleash such rage again. Ana opened her eyes.

"It's okay, *Signora*," Rosa sniffled, holding her shawl up. She pushed three fingers through a gaping hole. "My shawl got caught on the deck chair. When I jumped up, it choked me."

Luisa gazed at Rosa with a look in her eye that said she knew Rosa was lying too.

"Really, *Signora*," Rosa said, looking worried. "We were just talking, and my shawl, it—"

"Why are you here, Mama?" Ana said, anxious to draw Mama's attention away from the shawl.

"It's almost time for dinner. You need to get changed, both of you," Mama said. The look in her eyes began fading. "Don't be late," she said. She turned and headed toward the dining room.

Watching Luisa walk away, Rosa sighed and said, "She looked angrier than usual."

"Can you blame her?" Ana said.

"Oh God, Ana. I'm sorry for insulting your mother. Can you ever forgive me? I have no excuse. I meant no harm. I never thought you could fall in love with someone onboard ship, someone you'd never see again. That wasn't sensible at all. And you're always so sensible and so good.

"You're right, Ana," Rosa said. "I should've told you Carlos was married."

Ana trembled thinking how close she had come to killing Rosa.

Clearly misreading Ana, Rosa squirmed, touched Ana's shoulder and said, "Can you ever forgive me. Please?"

Imagining what could have happened, Ana stared at Rosa, unable to speak. Ana looked into Rosa's eyes, and her heart churned with desperately wanting to make things right. Whatever Rosa had done, she didn't deserve to … Ana shivered.

"Ana, please. I'm so sorry."

Suddenly she took Rosa in her arms. She knew Rosa well enough to know she was sincere about being sorry. It was on her face and in her voice. Rosa was lucky that Ana understood her, and Ana was lucky Mama had come by and had broken the spell in time.

Blaming Rosa was wrong. Ana cursed her sense of fairness. She and Carlos were to blame. *She* was at fault because *she* disobeyed God's commandment and committed adultery. And Carlos was to blame because he was married. Instead of sinning, she should've walked out of his life. It was as simple as that. Punishing Rosa wouldn't even feel good, because such anger was misguided and displaced. It would drain her energy at a time she needed every bit for what lay ahead. And, if she didn't forgive Rosa, she'd be punishing herself, because right now, Rosa was the only person in the whole wide world she could talk to.

She needed to ask Rosa a question. Irrespective of everything that had happened, the survival of their friendship hung on Rosa's answer.

"Rosa, I want you to tell me the truth about something."

"Anything."

Ana stared into her friend's eyes. "Did you know Carlos was married *before* you told me about him and pointed him out to me for the first time?"

"No. I swear as *Gesu Cristo* is my judge, my jury and my executioner, and may He condemn me to hell this instant for all eternity, I swear to you on every book, chapter and verse of the Holy Bible, I didn't know Carlos was married until you were," she said, lowering her eyes. "Until it was too late."

"Rosa, you must promise me something."

"I promise, I swear to God, before I even hear what it is that you want."

"You must never tell anyone who the father of my baby is," she said, emphasizing each word to underscore its importance. "Promise me that much, or our friendship is over now and for all of eternity!"

"I promise, Ana. I swear it on all that is good and holy."

"I believe you," Ana said, relieved she could put this part of the mess behind her.

Carrying Ana's secret to her grave was the only promise Rosa had ever kept. She'd overheard Graziela talking with the other maids, so she knew Carlos was married before Ana had met him. But she had to lie. If Ana knew the truth, she would never speak to her again, and Rosa would die if she lost Ana. She did answer one question truthfully. She truly believed that Ana was too sensible to fall in love onboard ship. How could Ana be so smart and so naïve at the same time?

Oh well. She leaned her head on Ana's shoulder. When Ana gave her a comforting hug, her tension evaporated. Rosa closed her eyes and sighed. She smiled, content with knowing that this was the first step toward life returning to what it was before all this Carlos foolishness happened.

Suddenly, Rosa wondered where Tonio was. The moment Ana went to her room to change for dinner, Rosa would scour the decks and find him.

Chapter 15

Giani and Vincenzo
1905

A wind whipped the sea, slapping tufts of foam from cresting waves. Giani stood on deck and shivered. The wind chilled, but no matter how tightly he wrapped his sweater around him, nothing could warm the chill in his heart. His hopes and dreams for a start in a new land had all been destroyed, and he blamed himself for Ana's dilemma. He pictured his family table and squeezed his eyes shut. Perhaps if they'd stayed in Villa Franca, he wiped a tear from his eye, this would never have happened. How could Ana and he succeed at grasping and dealing with life and political turmoil and fail at grasping and dealing with the turmoil in their own lives?

He contemplated the surface of the Atlantic and perceived it to be much like their future, big and empty with a choppy uncertainty on the horizon. He laughed with tears welling in his eyes, realizing that of all the people he knew, only his Ana would understand and appreciate what he meant. He missed her. As close as they were physically, emotionally they were oceans apart.

"Sir?"

Giani turned and saw Vincenzo Sciorri, Tonio's friend.

"I don't mean to intrude. And I don't know quite how to say this but—"

Giani sniffled and wiped his moist cheeks. He wanted to be alone, but the young man appeared to have something on his mind. The consummate father, he pushed his troubles aside. Perhaps hearing someone else's would do him and Vincenzo some good.

"Vincenzo, my boy," he said, patting Vincenzo's shoulder. "We're no longer in the old country. This voyage has drastically changed the old ways for us. Please don't worry about standing on ceremony. Just tell me what you have on your mind."

"Thank you, sir. Forgive me, but I don't know where to begin."

Vincenzo Sciorri was pleased with his success at coating his words in humility. The subject he needed to discuss was sensitive, and one wrong word could destroy any chance he might have of making his plan work. Vincenzo studied Ana's father, suspecting that by now, he must be insane with needing a respectable solution to Ana's problem. He smiled to himself. The expression in Giani's eyes confirmed two things: not only would he, Vincenzo, be a godsend to the Testaduras exactly as he'd predicted, but the Testaduras would be a godsend to him.

"Tonio and I have become good friends on this voyage," Vincenzo began. "Forgive me for being blunt, but I know about your family … trouble." Vincenzo sighed. "When I arrive in America, I will have trouble too."

"But, Tonio said that you and your mother are joining your father."

"My mother is joining my father. I'm not."

"I don't understand, my boy."

Vincenzo chose his words carefully. "Well, I don't know my father the way I should, the way Tonio knows you. I haven't seen him in years. And to be truthful I don't think I can live by the rules of a man who is a stranger to me." He stared into Giani's eyes, adding the finishing touches. "All these years growing up without a father I kept thinking that if my father really loved me, the way you and your wife love Tonio and Ana, he would've come back for me, or written, or tried to send for me."

"What do you intend to do then?" Giani asked, clearly moved.

Heart thudding, Vincenzo set the trap. He lowered his eyes. "I want to be independent in America. But I need financial help while I look for work," he said, knowing he'd just stepped onto shaky ground. He lifted his eyes, relieved that Giani appeared to be listening intently.

"Vincenzo, forgive me. But what does this have to do with me and my family's trouble?"

Heart pounding harder, Vincenzo baited the trap.

"I would like to ask you for Ana's hand in marriage."

Giani's jaw slackened. His eyes darted right and left, appearing to attempt to process what his ears had heard.

"And sir," he added quickly, "if we start off with a lump sum, I know I can make my own way in my own time, Ana will set foot on American soil as my wife, your family's good name will be saved, and no one need know any different."

He watched Giani reach for the bait.

"But you don't even know my Ana. I don't believe I've ever seen you speak to her."

"True, *Signor*. But if you think about it, there's very little difference between what I propose here and now and the old way. In the old country my family would've proposed the offer, subject to your approval of course. In the old country Ana would have no choice. If you beg my pardon, *Signor,* there is very little difference between the two situations.

"It would solve everything for you and your family, and especially for Ana. She could hold her head high. She would have a husband, and her baby would have a name."

"Suppose I agree," he paused.

Vincenzo flinched and licked his lips. Giani had taken the bait!

"I don't have all my money with me. Most is still in Sicily. Channels must be cleared before the authorities will release it. I don't know how long that will take," Giani said, pulling his sweater tighter around him.

"Others on board say you're an honorable man." The wind messed Vincenzo's hair, and he patted it into place. "If we agree, your word will be good enough."

"I must speak to my wife."

"I understand, *Signor,* but keep in mind that we land at Ellis Island soon. I don't know what American laws say about people who wish to marry. Especially people who are not citizens. And with respect to Ana's condition, the longer we wait—"

Giani's eyes darkened. "I can see you've not taken this lightly."

"I admit I've given it a great deal of thought."

"Allow me to do the same. I will give you my answer tomorrow," he said, and extended his hand.

Vincenzo smiled, shook Giani's hand, and the trap sprang shut.

As Giani watched his son's friend walk away, his head swam with cautious relief. For the first time since learning Ana was pregnant, there seemed to be a solution in sight. Vincenzo's plan showed Giani that he was a survivor. If Ana married Vincenzo, she and her child would survive, too. But Vincenzo and Ana had not yet met and that worried him.

Vincenzo was very handsome. Giani noticed the way he could turn girls' heads. That should appeal to Ana. And Vincenzo was right. In the old country, this is very close to the way marriages were arranged.

Giani perspired despite the chill in the air. What should he do? Ana's trouble couldn't be worse, and although he'd never really talked to Vincenzo before, the young man seemed intelligent and rational enough. But there was something strange about the way both he and his mother had kept their distance, observing life onboard ship rather than participating in it. The few times he'd tipped his cap to the *Signora* Sciorri, the coldness in her eyes made him shiver.

Leaving the familiar for the unknown, weeks spent on the ocean in the ship's confines, most passengers had appeared to forge friendships and genuine affection for one another. Vincenzo and his mother seemed to isolate themselves from the others. They even seemed distant even from one another. Tonio was the only one Giani had seen Vincenzo talk to. Perhaps because they were close in age? He hurried below to find Luisa.

"Giani!" Luisa said. "This is wonderful news! A godsend. A sign that the Lord does not hold our daughter's sin against us."

Giani sank into a chair angry at Luisa's predictable reaction. He breathed slow, deliberate breaths to calm himself. Luisa was who she was, and her myopic way of viewing herself in relation to the world and those around her, especially where Ana was concerned, would never change. This was not the time to fight over what Ana might feel about what they were proposing she commit herself to for the rest of her life. No. That line of reasoning was a trap. They'd go around and around and end up at the same place: Luisa crying and saying that he always took Ana's side against her. Truthfully though, and for the sake of her child, Ana had no other option. She had to marry Vincenzo Sciorri.

His heart writhed in anguish. He could not bear to think that he knew nothing about the man to whom he would give his precious Ana. His stomach twisted in turmoil, and not having the luxury of time, he chose to forego the fight with Luisa and give in to the inevitable.

"Yes, Luisa, perhaps you are right. Perhaps it is a sign."

"So, are we agreed? Ana will marry Vincenzo Sciorri?" she said.

The tears welled in Giani's eyes, and he let out a sigh.

"And may God help us all."

Chapter 16

Ana's Wedding
1905

"Ana! It's me and Rosa," Tonio cried, after several frantic raps on her cabin door.

Behind the door feet shuffled. The knob jiggled, turned, and the door opened. Her face pale and gaunt, Ana peered at them through red-rimmed eyes. Rosa gasped and squeezed Tonio's arm. Tonio heard Mama ask who was at the door.

Ana looked back over her shoulder and said, "It's Tonio and Rosa, Mama."

Tonio took Ana's hand, squeezed it in his and whispered, "Can you step into the hall, Ana, please? I don't want Mama or Papa to hear what I have to say."

She nodded. "I'll be right back, Mama," she said and closed the door softly behind her.

Midway down the hall he stopped and frowned at his sister, whose face looked more pinched and drawn, as if the few steps she took had taken a mountain-climbing toll.

"Ana," Tonio held her shoulders and looked deep into her eyes. "Don't marry Vincenzo. Please." He squeezed her shoulders. "Reconsider."

"Tonio—"

"You don't know him, Ana." His eyes clouded. "We barely know him ourselves."

"Please, Ana. Don't do it," Rosa said, her eyes brimming.

Ana stared at Tonio, stunned. His face seemed sculpted in worry. His eyes welled with tears. She sunk her teeth into her trembling lip. They shared the same blood, but she'd never felt close to Tonio or to her sisters. They seemed to resent her almost as much as Mama had. Papa was the only one to whom she felt—

Her pulse quickened as the reasons for their resentment became clear: Papa was the only one to whom she felt close. Because he was good and kind and understanding, she'd gobbled the lion's share of his love, leaving scraps for the others. My God. How could she have been so selfish? Her pulse slowed. Her throat cleared, and she swallowed hard. A tiny spring of hope welled up. If nourished, this closeness she felt for Tonio could blossom, she touched her stomach. Perhaps it would be the second miracle to grow from her foolish mistake.

Touched beyond words she stroked his face. "What choice do I have, Tonio?"

Ana tugged Rosa's arm, surprised anew at the glimmer in her eyes. Did Rosa sense the depth of her dilemma? Had she actually put someone else's worries before her own?

Rosa said, "I know you are angry with me."

Ana saw the confusion in Tonio's eyes. Apparently, Rosa had kept her word and hadn't told Tonio about their conversation or that Carlos was her baby's father. Would miracles never cease? Then again, how could Rosa tell Tonio anything without revealing her part in Ana's problem?

"Ana, please." Rosa took her hand. "You were always much better with words than I. I don't know how to say this in a way that will convince you. But if you do this, if you marry Vincenzo," she looked at Tonio and back at Ana, "we will be afraid for you. There's something about him. We both feel it," she said. "As handsome as he is, there's a deep, dark coldness about him."

"Thank you both for caring enough to tell me this," Ana said. Her lip trembled. Tears spilled. Emotion choked her. "But I've made up my mind."

Even though they'd never formally met, when Giani personally extended an invitation to Vincenzo's mother, *Signora* Bianca Sciorri, her white, tight-lipped silence and the shock he'd read in her eyes had chilled him beyond his fear of *la mafia*. Cap in his shaking hands, he watched the *signora* back away. He took a step forward and then stopped, terrified to ask why she'd refused to attend the marriage of her only son to his precious daughter.

The Testaduras, Vincenzo and Rosa gathered in their tiny cabin. The shipboard marriage was a quick formality performed by Captain Gianbatiste Volpe.

Giani's eyes welled as he looked at his Ana. Despite Luisa's expert alterations, her pale blue gown hung on Ana's delicate frame, making her seem more like a child playing dress-up than a woman about to be married. Lacking fresh flowers, Luisa had worked her magic again. She'd fashioned her mother's beige, antique lace scarf into a single cream-colored rose. When she placed it in Ana's hands, Giani's heart shattered like fragile, Venetian glass.

Captain Volpe cleared his throat, signaling they were about to begin, and Giani took Ana's arm. Vincenzo Sciorri, wearing a dark suit and a blank expression, took his place near the captain and stared straight ahead.

"Dearly beloved in Our Lord Jesus Christ. I am not a priest, but by the authority vested in me on this ship I am ordained by God, Holy Mother Church, and my country to call upon you to bear witness to the joining of Vincenzo Domenico Sciorri and Ana Luisa Testadura, in the holy sacrament of matrimony."

Lips trembling, Ana smiled and Giani choked back a sob at his daughter's attempt to be brave. She glanced at him, for what? Guidance? Had there been another way, he would never have arranged this marriage for her. He stared at Vincenzo and thought, *Gesu Cristo!* How could something that had felt so right moments ago feel so wrong now?

The captain looked at Giani. "Who gives this woman to this man?"

"Papa?" At the sound of Ana's voice, a tear fell from Giani's eye. He cleared his throat and choked out, "I do." He wiped the tear away realizing that with those two words he had given the light of his life to a stranger.

Captain Volpe looked at Ana and Vincenzo and said, "Place your hands on the Bible and repeat after me."

After the ceremony Giani opened a bottle of wine and everyone toasted to the health and happiness of the bride and groom. He'd arranged for an urn of coffee and a tray of delicate Italian pastries to be sent to his cabin. The attempt to create a light, pleasant atmosphere only served to expose the dark charade that had taken place.

"Whatever his feelings Vincenzo appeared to mask them," Tonio whispered to Rosa. He poured three glasses of wine, handed one to Rosa and carried the others across the room. He handed Vincenzo a glass. The three of them huddled together and chatted.

Ana seemed subdued. Giani stood beside her. He put his arm around her shoulders and kissed the top of her head.

"Vincenzo seems quiet and reserved, but he's very handsome. And you know, Ana, what happened here is not too different from what would have happened in Italy sooner or later."

Ana nodded and hugged her father, as he cringed using Vincenzo's logic to soothe his own flesh and blood. He kept his voice neutral.

"And the success of every marriage, regardless of how man and wife come together, depends on the patience and understanding they give to each other. In time happiness and even love might follow. Didn't we see that happen time and again in the old country?"

"Papa—" Ana stopped, and he frowned. "Yes of course you're right. Things will work out. I know they will. I promise you I will do my best to see that they do, especially for my baby's sake."

Giani held her closer. The icy apprehension gripping him when he first talked to Vincenzo thawed a bit. He looked into her eyes, and his fragile illusion shattered. The happiness he saw was as artificial as the cream colored rose that shook in her young, slender hands.

Captain Volpe, a self-proclaimed romantic, cleared his throat. He smiled and raised his glass of champagne. "As you know," he smiled, "after leaving *Sicilia,* the *Princess* was forced to make several stops before heading out. As a result, we are overcrowded. But," he said, puffing his chest up, "as your captain and priest," he paused, and as if on cue, his audience tittered, "I've performed a miracle. I moved heaven and earth and managed to secure a cabin for the newlyweds for their honeymoon night."

The groom's eyes widening, he barked out a raucous laugh, raised his glass to the captain and drank while the bride and her family stared at him in awkward silence. The captain appeared astonished at the groom's strange show of gratitude for his generosity.

Giani shook the captain's hand. "Captain Volpe, we are humbled. My wife and my family deeply appreciate your efforts."

Captain Volpe's eyes twinkled with obvious skepticism. "You're welcome I'm sure, *Signor* Testadura."

After a few pastries and a respectable amount of time, the captain informed the young couple he had to leave, but he'd be happy to take them to their quarters now, if they were ready to go.

Reluctantly, Ana kissed her family goodnight and followed the captain and her husband to a small stateroom on the deck below. After the captain wished the newlyweds well and bid them goodnight, Vincenzo closed the door behind him.

Chapter 17

The Wedding Night

Vincenzo grinned at his wife trying to decide whether he wanted or even needed a honeymoon night. Why not? This marriage had been bought and paid for with his freedom. He watched Ana take in the tiny stateroom. She stared at the bed on the opposite wall between the two portholes as if she sensed his intentions. She headed for the bathroom door which was open.

"Stop right there." His voice was gravelly. Its whisper appeared to send shivers through her. Good. Best to establish dominance early.

"I have to go," she said, nodding toward the bathroom.

"Get undressed, now. I want to see what my wife looks like."

"You can't be serious!" The haughty old Ana spoke up.

"What do you think?" he said, whispering more harshly. "As my wife you'll do what I say."

"But I can't undress in front of you. I hardly know you. And besides I'm pregnant."

"I know you're pregnant." Vincenzo took her arm. "Take your clothes off."

"Why?"

"This is our honeymoon."

"Our honey—" She jerked her arm free and shook her head. Tears sprung up in her eyes. "I can't let you...what if you hurt my baby? I can't let you hurt my—"

He grabbed her wrist. "Do as I say, and your baby won't get hurt."

"No," she said. He grinned and twisted her wrist until she whimpered. "That was the first and last time you will ever defy your husband, Ana Luisa *Sciorri!*" He pulled her close and whispered softly. "Now take off your clothes!"

Ana choked back tears. Vincenzo ignored her. Was she frightened? What a joke! It's not like he was her first. Even though her father had tried to keep it secret, by now everyone knew they had married because she was pregnant.

Her shaking fingers fumbled with the ties. She let the dress fall. She stepped out of the pale blue hillock at her feet and wriggled free of her foundation garments

Eyes wide, Vincenzo gaped at his wife's naked body. If he hadn't locked his knees in time, they would have buckled. *Gesu Cristo!* The angry bruises that braceleted her wrist where he'd grabbed her were the only flaws in her perfection. He wanted to fall before her and worship. Lacking the words to process his feelings or her beauty, Vincenzo's reaction was primal. He unbuckled his pants and reached for his wife

Recoiling, Ana tripped, but Vincenzo caught her and eased her onto the bed. He could feel her tense under his hands as he explored the angles and planes of her perfection. He palmed the curve of her hip and caressed the swell of her buttocks, traced the circle of her navel and cupped her warm breasts. Feeling her shudder, he smiled. Perhaps marriage might not be so bad after all. He'd wait and see. Right now, he would make her forgive and forget their tiny marital mishap.

A frenzy of terror slammed through her. She squeezed her eyes shut. Carlos's face swam into view. She flew out of hell and into his arms. Holding him close, she breathed him in. Tasting his wine-soaked kisses, she felt him hungrily straining against her.

No! She squeezed her eyes shut. Carlos was gone. For the sake of their child she had to survive. Surviving meant keeping her vow, and keeping her vow meant being a wife to Vincenzo. Gasping, she drew in a breath. Vincenzo nibbled his way down her throat. His lips brushed her breast. Her pulse quickening, she moaned.

Her pleasure excited him, making him grin. Compared to the women he'd known, pregnant or not, she was a virgin. Suddenly, Vincenzo dared to hope. Perhaps, or because unlike the others, she was his wife in the eyes of God, maybe this time God would have mercy. He begged God to cast out the devil that took him each time he took a woman. Believing God would listen, he pinned her between his thighs and …

… fire raged. She raised her hips. Arching her body against him, she balled the sheets in her fists. How could she carry the child of one man yet thrill to the touch of another? Could miracles happen? Was

Papa, dear Papa, right? In time, could she grow to love her husband, Vincenzo?

As thunder claps in the swamp of a grown man's mind, a small boy wakes to the sound of muffled cries. He creeps out of bed. His tiny hand parts the curtain dividing his space from theirs. Pale arms and legs flail in a tangle of moonlit sheets. His mother whimpers. The small, powerless boy begs God to bring his father home and take them far away from this place and the monster they live with. When God fails to answer his prayers, the boy grows into a man who hates the mother who let another abuse them. And when she responds, the man hates the woman beneath him. A sobbing woman rears up and bucks against him. The ocean rolling beneath them, Vincenzo cries out and collapses.

Ana lay as still as a corpse until his breathing slowed, and his chest rose and fell in a steady rhythm. Barely breathing herself, she crept out of bed. Muscle and bones screaming with pain, she hobbled to the bathroom. She closed the door softly behind her, turned on the light and drew in a ragged breath. Her eyes welled with hot, unshed tears. She raised her arm. Her fingers feathered the purple bruise on her breasts, then stopped inches from the bruise on her cheek. Her face hardened. Her dizzy-with-anger head spun into rage and gurgled up behind split, trembling lips. And ...

... lights dimmed and flickered. Faucets gushed. Glasses rattled. Towels tied into knots. Drawers banged open and crashed on the floor. The medicine cabinet flew open. Bottles rattled on shelves, sailed into the room. Some hung in thin air, some smashed in the sink, others flew across the room and slammed against walls, their contents streaming down walls like tears of rage.

"Wiiiittttccchhhh," he growled, winding her hair around his fist. Seeing Vincenzo showed no fear, Ana collapsed in terror. Faucets stopped gushing. Hovering bottles hit the sink and the floor and shattered. Flickering lights glared to a steady burn. He bent her head back. "Clean it up, witch," he spat and banged her head against the wall.

Chapter 18

Bianca Sciorri
New York Harbor
1905

Bianca listened to the passengers scurrying down the hallway to gather on deck to see *la statua della Liberta* in New York Harbor but instead of doing the same she decided to stay in her room and prepare to meet Domenico, her husband and the only man she would ever love.

The dream she had dreamed every night since Domenico left *Sicilia* to make a new life for her and Vincenzo in America, the dream that had helped her survive years of unspeakable degradation would come true the moment she stepped onto American soil and into his arms. Months before setting sail, Bianca had sent him information pertinent to their arrival. Much to her relief, days before they'd boarded, Domenico had sent word that he would be there on the dock in New York Harbor to meet them.

Bianca stood before the mirror in the long black skirt, white blouse and light shawl she had carefully packed away years ago. She smiled, pleased to be as trim now as the last time Domenico had seen her wearing them. She closed her eyes and hugged herself as she pictured Domenico running along the dock, neck craned, eyes frantically searching the passengers disembarking the ferry to catch sight of her. When their eyes locked, without averting his gaze, he would push his way through the crowd to the foot of the gangplank, eyes brimming with love, throat too choked up to talk, trembling arms outstretched, aching to hold her. They hadn't been man and wife for more than a decade, but the months they'd spent making love in the early years of their marriage were as fresh in her mind as if they'd happened this morning.

Bianca opened her eyes and glanced in the mirror. Spotting her suitcase on the bed, she turned around, dug through it and pulled out a packet of letters she'd received from him. She closed her eyes, pressed the packet to her lips and silently begged him for the last time to forgive her for barely answering. But the terrible truth she must tell him must be told in person.

She opened her eyes, put the packet on her dresser, pulled out her hairpins, and shook her hair loose. She watched it tumble and her heart pounded, remembering how he would run his hands through it, tilt her head back and cover her throat with kisses. Confident that Domenico would see the girl he'd promised to love forever, she smiled. Raising her hand, she looked in the mirror. Her arm froze in mid-air while the smile slipped from her face.

The once thick, black, lustrous mane framing her face seemed dull. Dusted with gray, it hung limply on her shoulders. Frowning, she combed it back from her temples and away from a face that looked gaunt and exhausted. She leaned forward and relaxed her frown, but telltale lines remained. She dropped the brush and frowned harder. When had her big, black eyes gotten smaller, and when had they lost their luster? Sweat beading at her temples, forehead and armpit, rolled down her cheeks and dampened her sides and back.

With shaky hands and shakier confidence, she reached for a fan next to a bottle of lotion on her dresser. Panting, she spread the fan and fanned frantically. Her cheeks and forehead began to dry. Feeling calmer she took stock, realizing that time spared no one. If she'd aged, Domenico had aged, too. "When there is love nothing else matters." The words, passing through lips whose smile failed to return the sparkle to her eyes, seemed hollow and offered no comfort. Her head ached. Suddenly, she dropped the fan, covered her ears and shut her eyes.

"Shut up!" she screamed at the non-stop voices taunting her from her village across the sea, "I won't let you spoil this. You're wrong," she shook her head. "Domenico loves me, and he always will. He's on the dock waiting for me. You're jealous because I'll have a life in America with the man I love, while you rot in Sicily!"

The voices stopped. Bianca exhaled a sigh of uneasy relief. She opened her eyes. Looking in the mirror again, she pulled her hair taut and knotted it at the top of her head. She licked her fingers and shaped her brows.

Perhaps some makeup? She almost laughed. She hadn't stepped onto American soil and already she was thinking like an American woman. She was a good Italian woman who needed no makeup. Whores and tramps wore makeup, and besides, hadn't Domenico told her hundreds of times how her natural beauty had captured his heart from the moment he saw her?

Bianca picked up the bottle of lotion. Dropping a silky pearl onto her fingers she massaged until she saw her age lines vanish. Wetting her finger, she fixed each errant hair firmly in place. Grabbing her flesh between thumb and forefingers she pinched color into her cheeks.

Beaming with confidence, she smiled broadly, bent her head back, and raised her arms to the ceiling. She hadn't felt this good in years. God bless America! And God bless the ocean that separated her from the filth she'd left on the other side. Standing tall and proud, she lifted her chin, tightened her shawl around her, scooped up her fan and purse, opened the cabin door and stepped into her new life.

Bianca arrived on deck next to Vincenzo in time to see the ship move north through the Narrows, leading to Upper New York Bay and into the harbor. First, the tip of Manhattan came into view, then the Statue of Liberty. Last would be Ellis Island.

Overwhelmed, Bianca lowered her fan, attracting Vincenzo's attention. His jaws dropped. She watched him stare as if he was seeing her for the first time.

"You are lovely, Mama," he said, looking astonished and extended his arm. Bianca's eyes shone. She parted her lips in surprise. Flustered, she bowed her head to hide the blush on her cheeks.

She'd taken great pains to prepare for this moment. If Vincenzo noticed, then surely Domenico, would. She smiled as the thought sailed through the air over the bay. She smoothed the few strands of hair the harbor breeze had mussed and took her son's arm.

"Stories about Ellis Island are running rampant," Giani said. He stood on the deck next to Luisa, sweating and folding and unfolding his handkerchief. The sun beat down on his throbbing head. "We're blessed. If we'd traveled third class, we'd have to go through Ellis Island. And God forbid if it was overcrowded, we'd need to stay on board until the crowd thinned."

"My God," Luisa said, dabbing her cheeks with a white lace hankie. "That could take days."

Giani nodded and wiped the sweat from his mouth. "I hear if a doctor on Ellis Island suspects illness, he places a chalk mark, a code on a lapel and ..." He closed his eyes.

"Code? What code?" Luisa clasped her hand around his arm.

"H for heart, P for physical and lungs." He opened his eyes. "S for senility, X for mental retardation, a K circled for insanity and so many others," he said, half-sighing, half-sobbing. "I can't remember." He unfolded his handkerchief and frowned, looking for a dry spot. "The worst is Ct, the code for trachoma. The doctors turn up eyelids with a buttonhook or a hairpin, searching for trachoma, a contagious disease that, if left untreated may cause blindness." He looked in her eyes. "And then, after spending days or weeks in quarantine for whatever reason, if passengers still don't pass inspection they are sent back."

"How could such a cruel thing happen?" she whispered, staring blankly.

"You haven't heard the worst, Luisa. Last night after dinner Gerardo Spicci told stories that made the strongest among us cringe. Ah," he waved his hand and shook his head. "Never mind."

"Tell me, Giani, please, the least I can do for those less fortunate than us is listen."

"The ventilation in steerage is so bad it may as well be nonexistent. The air stinks of vomit, body odors and waste from toilets and washrooms. The air is so foul it dizzies them. The sight of food sickens them. Not only is the open-air space on deck small, it's subject to the most violent rolling of the ship. The air there is polluted from smoke stacks and smells of the hold and the galleys."

Her eyes welling up, Luisa pressed her hankie to her lips and turned her head away.

"The poor souls who sold the clothes off their backs to raise money for tickets and food for the voyage travel half-naked or covered in rags. Remember the stops the ship made before setting out to sea?" Sniffling, she nodded. "The delay caused some to run out of food. They had to beg or dig whatever bones and scraps of fat they could from the garbage."

Luisa shuddered. "My God, Giani, if their food and clothes are already gone, what will they eat and wear on the way back?"

Covering her hand with his, Giani squeezed it and said, "On the way back to what?"

Clutching her bundle, her bright pink parasol with white polka dots, and *Tales of Greek Gods & Men* her most prized possessions, Ana joined Vincenzo and Bianca on deck. People pressed past them. Some stopped, penning them in at the railings. In addition to hair-raising tales of quarantine and deportation running through her mind, Ana heard chilling tales of how swindlers preyed on the unsuspecting immigrants landing on Ellis Island by overcharging them for food and cheating on money exchanges. They offered fake housing, fake railroad tickets and forged citizenship papers. Some were so bold, they hinted at bribery.

She closed her eyes. Thank God Papa and most of their friends could afford second class accommodations. Spared the humiliating ordeal at Ellis Island that the lower classes were forced to endure, second class patrons would pass directly into New York Harbor and then into New York City.

Doctors had already inspected Vincenzo and her in the health suite earlier for contagious diseases like cholera, smallpox, measles. The list went on and on ending with mental illness. The doctors who saw her bruises had exchanged glances that had paralyzed her with fear. After immeasurable seconds, the doctors had shrugged her off. She breathed a sigh of horrified relief as her shaky legs walked her out the door. She felt her skirts for the entry papers she thought she had tucked safely in its folds and gasped. Her heart thumped wildly until she remembered. Vincenzo had snatched them away, for safekeeping he said, the moment the doctors had left.

Desperate to replace her wedding-night nightmare with a show of good faith, she decided to disembark with her husband and her mother-in-law, but first she had to find her parents to let them know, or they would worry. She left Vincenzo's side. She stood on her toes and stretched her neck. Looking past the half-starved and bleary-eyed clogging the decks and lining the handrails, she noticed that most of the women carried small children and infants, while the men carried their meager belongings in battered, broken bags and bundles fastened with twine.

When the crowd saw *la statua della Liberta* some cheered. Some cried. Some faces seemed to reflect fear, some relief, and some outright exhilaration. Husbands and wives clung to each other and stared through tearful eyes. Parents pulled children close as if fearing that seeing the statue might cause a stampede that would drag their children away.

At the sight of Ellis Island, the door to America, the immigrants seemed dazed, yet Ana felt the ripple of their enormous collective excitement pass through her. As the ship docked, the crowd lumbered hypnotically toward the clang of the lowering gangplanks. From there, they would sluice onto a dock where they would wait to board the ferry to Ellis Island.

Seeing Mama and Papa, she waved and slipped away from Vincenzo to join them. Heart pounding, she talked quickly, explaining what she planned to do. Her parents stood by her side, but she looked straight ahead, careful to keep her bruised cheek hidden.

"No, Ana!" Giani pleaded as they inched toward the gangway to watch the people. "There are hundreds of people getting off in New York City. What if the crowd swallows you up?" Her father stopped walking, grasped her chin and turned her face toward him. "Look at me when I speak to you." Luisa gasped hard and clamped her hands over her mouth. Jaw clenched and cheek muscle quivering Giani gaped at his daughter's bruised face.

"My God, Ana," he choked, "what..." he raised his hand and touched her face gently.

"Please, Papa, don't." She turned her cheek to hide the sadness in her eyes. She grasped his fingers and tightened her lips, fighting to keep them from trembling. "I'm fine. Please trust me. This," she waved off her bruises, "was a misunderstanding. An accident."

"An acci—?" he rasped. "I'll kill him!" His jowls puffed. His face turned purple. "I—"

"Please," she cried. "Try to understand why I must get off the ship with my ... with them." She kissed his fingers again. "I promise I won't leave the dock without you and Mama."

Her throat choked closed, Ana left her parents behind. Fighting the impulse to run back to the safety of Papa's arms, she placed her hand on her stomach and snaked her way through the crowd, searching for the Sciorris.

Chapter 19

Ana
Ellis Island
1905

"Papers!" A big, burly inspector said, stopping Ana as she tried to bypass the gangplank.

"Papers?" Ana frowned hard, repeating the word in heavily accented English.

"*Carte!*" he said, impatiently, ushering people past her down the gangplank to the wharf.

"*Oh. Si,*" she smiled, relieved she understood. "*Mio marito he le mie carte.*"

"Jesus Christ, lady." He jerked his head right and left. Clearly seeing no one belonging to her, he took her arm and said, "*Andare,*" nudging her down the gangplank.

"*No!*" she cried. "*Mi scusi, per favore. Non si capisce. Mio marito he le mie carte.*" Her plea drowned in the flow of the crowd cascading her down the gangplank.

Hundreds from the *Sicilian Princess* merged with hundreds from other ships into waves of immigrants that flooded the wharf toward the ferry to Ellis Island. Swept up with the diseased, the filthy, the starving, Ana clung to her bundle, her bright pink parasol and her book while disjointed thoughts sailed through her head.

...America? ...Ana pressed her lips together to keep from screaming with joy. If she were dreaming she never wanted to wake up...She could barely keep still...her dream of seeing the world would begin with America...

Her head throbbed. Her eyes shimmered with tears. Were those thoughts ever real or were they echoes of thwarted dreams doomed to haunt her? Instead of a symbol of freedom and hope, America loomed before her—a prison. Ana knew that the moment she set foot on American soil, an iron door would clang shut and Vincenzo, her jailer, would lock it behind her.

It was August. It was hot. Humidity's fingers grabbed her neck in a chokehold. Sweat, urine and feces-smelling air filled her nostrils. Her stomach rolled. Perspiration soaked her back and sides and plastered her dress to her body. Her head swam. Daylight dimmed. Sounds faded. Smells dulled. Just as her legs gave way, an arm shored her up and anchored her to a body.

Her eyes fluttered open. "Tonio," she panted. "Thank God."

"I've got you," Rosa said, linking her other arm.

"How …?" Her lips quivered. Grateful tears rolled down her cheeks.

"We saw you and the others being herded down the gangplank like sheep," Rosa said as she and Tonio guided Ana through the crowds on the dock and off to the side.

Ana felt her cheeks flush with color. The day brightened, and sounds hummed to life.

"We've got you now, and we won't let—" Tonio's smile faded. "Ana!" He pushed her hair away from her cheek. "What the …"

"Please, Tonio." Her bruise burned under his stare.

"Ana. My God," Rosa whispered. "What did that monster do to you?"

"I can't explain now. Please." Hot tears spilled down her cheeks.

"Okay," he stuttered, clearly flustered. "We'll wait until later, but now we need to go." Tonio took her arm and started nudging her back through the crowd toward the gangplank.

"No. I can't, Tonio." She pulled away and cried harder. "Vin. Cen. Zo," she cried trying to speak, but her sobs cut off her words. "Has my papers. I don't think they'll let me back on *la princessa* without them. I may have to go through Ellis Island."

"The hell you will," he said. "Rosa, you wait here with Ana. I'll go and get Vincenzo."

"Hurry, Tonio. Don't let the ship leave without us."

The crowd had devoured Tonio so quickly and completely, if it wasn't for Rosa standing by her side, Ana would have doubted that her brother had ever been there.

"All right, ladies," a bigger, burlier inspector said, taking Rosa and Ana gently by their arms, "move along."

"No. per favore. Non si capisce," Ana cried.

"Yeah. Yeah," he said. "I heard it all. Come on. Come on. Move." He stopped talking and frowned. "Where's your name tag and number?"

Ana and Rosa stared blankly at him and each other.

"God damn, you people. You're supposed to have, shit. What's da use? Move!" he said, shoving them.

Clinging to each other, Ana and Rosa reluctantly followed the crowd through a building, the size of which they had never seen, into a giant hall, where dozens of strange languages roared in their ears. Ana watched a man by a cordoned off space, motioning people to drop off their bundles. Hugging her bundle, parasol and book tightly, she took in the hall. Against one wall were men behind caged-in counters, exchanging money. On the wall behind another counter were pictures of trains and people buying tickets to places with names she couldn't pronounce.

Pointing, Ana yelled, "Oh my God, Rosa, look!" Across the hall was a staircase jammed with people. "I heard about this onboard ship, Doctors watch the way people climb to see if they're lame or deformed."

"And if they are, are they sent back?"

"I don't know." Staring blankly, Ana shivered as if the vaporous idea had hardened into reality.

"Ana!" Rosa said, shaking her.

Ana blinked, "What?" she said, focused.

"Where do the stairs go?"

"To the second floor. People follow a maze of lanes that lead to an examining room."

"But we've already been examined!" Rosa cried, turning a lighter shade of pale, as if the shock of their reality had just drained the blood from her face.

"Where's Tonio, Ana? What's taking him so long?" Her face screwed up in panic, Rosa stood on her toes, stretching to see above the crowd. She grabbed Ana by the shoulders. "The more time goes by, the lesser the chance Tonio will have of finding us. We don't look any different from anyone else. How will he know where we are?" She burst into tears.

As Rosa's words gelled, Ana set down her bundle and book. Raising her pink parasol with the white polka dots into the air, she opened it up, and it waved above the crowd.

Chapter 20

Vincenzo and Bianca

With Ana by his side, Vincenzo helped his mother off the gangway onto the New York Harbor dock. He glanced at his new wife. Rankled at having to rescue her, he had to grudgingly admit that waving her parasol above the crowd showed brains, and Vincenzo respected brains even more than he respected money. A rare ghost-of-a-smile touched his lips. Perhaps there might be some hope for this marriage. Still, none of the parasol-spectacle would've happened, if he'd forbidden her to look for her parents. For that infraction she would pay. After that, what happened with their marriage remained to be seen.

Tonio and Rosa joined them on deck. Ignoring Tonio and his tramp, Vincenzo watched his mother peer into the crowd, searching each face. Following her gaze, he stopped and drew in a breath. He never would've recognized his father were it not for the woman standing beside him. As the first American woman he'd ever seen, Vincenzo could not take his eyes from her.

She removed her gloves and grasped the black veil that covered her face with pale, slender fingers. Lifting it over the brim of her hat, she smiled at his father. Her dress, a shiny mysterious fabric his fingers itched to touch, bustled at the small of her back. Tall blonde and slender with fine features and creamy white skin, the woman was a delicate, porcelain doll with pale blue eyes and full, red lips. A doll that someone had wrapped in shimmering black to accentuate her strikingly pale beauty. The ruby broach on her black lace collar matched the red rouge on her lips. She'd linked her arm through his father's. Her delicate white hand rested on his forearm. The polish on her nails matched the shade of her lip rouge and the red of the gem in her broach. When she noticed Vincenzo staring, she parted her ruby lips, revealing bright white teeth.

She nudged his father's arm and nodded in their direction. Looking slightly embarrassed, his father took the woman's hand and guided her through the crowd toward Bianca. Seconds before the fates collided, Vincenzo digested the truth. There were no words to describe the contrast between his mother and the *other* woman. Compared to the American woman, Bianca Sciorri was ugly. Plain. Diminished. For the first time he could remember, Vincenzo pitied his mother.

Bianca followed Vincenzo's gaze to a strikingly beautiful woman dressed in black. No wonder the woman had caught her son's eye. Absorbed with the American woman, Bianca did not notice Domenico at the woman's side until he said, "Bianca," obliterating the façade Bianca had mistakenly thought was her life.

As her jaw slackened, Bianca's gaze drifted from the woman whose arm linked Domenico's, to Domenico's face. And his eyes told her all she needed to know.

The dock suddenly wavered. Bianca's disembodied feet took two steps then her knees wobbled. Vincenzo grabbed her arm. He stopped her fall, but nothing could stop her from spiraling so deep into hell she might never return. Tension thickened the air. Crowds passing by sensed it and clustered around them.

Unshed tears scalded her eyes. She closed them and braced for the merciless voices from across the sea. Instead their silence bit like a snake. Infected with truth, Bianca sank to the ground. Domenico knelt. His eyes met hers with what? Fear? Incredulity? Contrition?

With her last shred of sanity, Bianca Sciorri realized that no one deserved to know the truth more than the stranger kneeling before her. With shining eyes and a smile frozen on her lips, Bianca said, "Do you remember the little girl we conceived on your first visit home? She never drew a breath, because instead of protecting her, I chose to protect you from the truth: Your father, the man in whose care you left me and your son, raped me until I miscarried."

The thickening crowd gasped and rumbled. Sandwiched between Rosa and Tonio, Ana turned white.

Suddenly freed from the crushing weight, Bianca got to her feet. She looked at her husband's confused face and laughed until she sobbed, until the staggering weight of another truth had filled the vacuum. She'd sacrificed her child and her life for him, and in return he'd betrayed her.

Bianca opened her purse, pulled out a handkerchief and dabbed the last tears she vowed she would ever shed. "I'm going back to Sicily to kneel at our daughter's grave and beg her forgiveness." She stared into space. Beneath her blank eyes, the shadow of a vacant smile crossed her lips. "Back to your mute, invalid father, where I will spend what's left of my life repaying him for crimes he committed against me."

The giant beast of a crowd shifted, reacting as one.

"There's something else you must know," she said. "Something I should have told you long ago." Bianca squeezed her fingers around the fan.

He reached for her. "Bianca—"

"*Sta 'zitto!*" she spat. "You have nothing to say that I want to hear!"

She grabbed Vincenzo and shoved him at Domenico. She sneered as the man and boy stared in each other's eyes. Domenico extended his hand. Vincenzo frowned as if he'd never seen a hand in his life. After a silent, awkward moment, Domenico pulled the boy to his chest and hugged him tightly.

"Domenico," Bianca said, "Meet Vincenzo Sciorri, your father's son and *your half-brother.*"

Clearly stunned to his bone marrow, Vincenzo stared at his mother. The crowd rumbled before all noise and movement stopped. Ana shook her head. Tonio and Rosa clasped each other's hands.

The crowd began murmuring, but no one spoke. Bianca looked at her husband and son, swearing that this time after the dust cleared, she'd be the one standing.

"My father's son? I don't understand!" He reached out to grab her. Her stony glare stopped him.

"Have you lost the ability to understand your first language?"

"I understand now why each time I came home to see you, you seemed so ..." His eyes widened as the impact of her declaration struck. He grabbed her shoulders. "My God! Why in God's name didn't you tell me? Why?"

"Would you have believed me? Would anyone? Would you have given up your new American life with your new American woman?"

The crowd grumbled, some nodding, some shaking their heads.

"I knew your trouble was more," Domenico stared blankly, "than a child's death."

"*Piu della morte di un bambino? Sei bastardo bassotto. Era la morte di nostra figlia!*" Bianca spat in his face.

Domenico pulled a handkerchief from his pocket and wiped her spittle from his face. He turned to Vincenzo. "And, you? Did you know this was going on?" Vincenzo stared, as if his mother's words had turned him to stone. "Did you?" Domenico said. Vincenzo's eyes flickered. His mouth turned up in a sneer.

Her business concluded, Bianca started to walk away. Domenico grabbed her arm.

"Let go of me!" She jerked her arm free. "The touch of Sciorri men makes my skin crawl."

"Wait. Please," he spoke quickly. "There's something you don't know, something that I didn't think mattered at the time, but now ..." His eyes watered.

"What could you say that I'd give a damn about?" she whispered harshly. She turned, and the crowd parted.

"This boy cannot be my father's son."

Bianca turned, her eyes sizzling hatred. "After what I've suffered, you dare to call me a liar?"

"Dear God, Bianca. No. If I had told you years ago, perhaps none of this would have," his voice trailed off. Tongue-tied with some enormity only he seemed to perceive, he waved his hand and rubbed his watering eyes.

"Bianca," his voice cracked. "My real father, Domenico Sciorri, died of pneumonia when I was a baby. His brother, Vincenzo Sciorri, married my mother. I called him Papa because he was the only father I ever knew. Your child," he looked at Vincenzo, "he is my uncle Vincenzo's son and my nephew."

Ana clamped her hand over her mouth as the crowd gasped in unison. Overcome, Bianca collapsed. Domenico caught her before she fell.

Suddenly, Vincenzo laughed at the widened eyes and the stunned gasps of those standing around them. Realizing this was a mystery that only Christ Himself could unravel, he laughed until his tears washed him clean of any illusions he may have harbored. He saw the truth as he'd always known it. Life was a mockery, a sham, a betrayal. A cruel, heartless joke. Vincenzo realized he'd never hated anyone more than he hated his family. If there had been a dust mote of hope for a new life with his new wife, his *family* had just blown it away.

Chapter 21

Ana
New York City
May 1906

The moment they set foot on crowded American soil, a disheartened but alert Ana began realizing that most immigrants had nowhere to go. If they stayed in New York City, finding a place to live would be a nightmare, she thought, until she remembered what Tonio had said.

Vincenzo has some ideas of his own. The truth is he doesn't really know his father, so he'd rather make his own way in America. He claims he has friends, contacts there ... people in the old country have already referred him to their associates in New York.

To everyone's surprise but Ana's, Vincenzo had sent their trunks to a building on Sullivan Street in lower Manhattan to a place called Greenwich Village. And after he'd mentioned some names referred by his friends in *Sicilia,* Georgio Bacci, the landlord, had tripped over himself helping them to move in. In a conversation with a new neighbor, Ana learned that the building in which they now lived used to be the old Mills Hotel. Although each apartment had a small washroom with a toilet and sink, there was a larger, common washroom with a tub and toilet on the second floor. One of the few pieces of information Vincenzo had shared was when the city put the building up for sale for back taxes, his new *friends* had hastily bought it and converted the hotel into apartments.

Ana sat in her kitchen elbows on the table, chin in her upturned palms. The same sadness that dulled her eyes for the turn her life had taken now weighed heavily on her heart. Sighing, she glanced around her apartment.

The door opened from the hallway into a small foyer and a small washroom to the right. The largest of three rooms, serving as kitchen and parlor, had a porcelain icebox with two doors and three shelves. Having stored 'cold' food in a metal box in a stream behind her house in *Sicilia,* Ana had been amazed to see how this new icebox worked. A cake of melting ice sat on a metal tray. Water flowed through a drip tube into a tray that had to be emptied as well.

A mirror hung over the sink and washtub. Two long wooden shelves held tins of flour, sugar, salt, coffee and tea. Two windows overlooked narrow yards that cut through the brick and mortar canyon the buildings formed. There was a metered gas stove with four tiny jets and a coal stove that was used for cooking and heating the apartment. A third wooden shelf above the stove held an assortment of mismatched chipped mugs, plates and bowls. Next to the stove she had stacked pots and pans, most of which Vincenzo's new 'friends' had provided. There were two smaller rooms. One was hers and Vincenzo's bedroom, the other was a spare.

She rubbed her belly, and her eyes welled with wanting the unthinkable, to give the empty room to her baby. She hadn't dared ask Vincenzo yet, for fear of *feeling* his answer. But when she'd asked Mama, Mama's reaction had stung so badly, Ana's face still burned with shame and humiliation. Mama had grabbed her arm, stopped walking and said, 'A room for a child?' loud enough for passers-by to slow down and glower.

'But,' Ana had stammered, 'I had my own room in the old country.'

'That was then. This is now. Where are your eyes?' Mama had said. 'When you walk down the street, surely they must be open! How can you not see the filth, the desperation, the squalor in front of your eyes!'

Truthfully, since moving into their apartment, Ana had not wandered very far, which was not like her at all. Her terror-filled life with Vincenzo had dulled her natural curiosity.

Visiting Mama and Papa on a block north of Houston Street where they lived was as far as she'd gone.

Her fear of Vincenzo had dulled her powers as well. No matter how she tried, she could no longer move a thing.

She couldn't do anything about her gift, but she could take a long walk. If she'd heard Mama say once, she'd heard Mama say dozens of times how blessed she was to be living in her lap-of-luxury apartment instead of a small, suffocating tenement. And Ana resented the snide comments and scathing looks from neighborhood women she'd passed on the street since that day. Did they resent her because they thought she was spoiled, or because they thought she was like Vincenzo? How could she know for sure when no one would speak to her? Determined to see these tenements for herself, one day she ventured into the world beyond Sullivan Street.

The further away she wandered, the more quickly the buildings devolved from bad to worse. Her heart churned in disgust at the tons of garbage piled in front of neglected buildings in the slums the city called immigrant housing. Those on the street she'd dared to ask said that no matter the size of immigrant families, they were crammed into two rooms, one of which might have a window or two, but most of these rooms had none.

Having stepped into one building, Ana knew it must be stifling in summer and freezing in winter. The hallways were narrow and dark. The only light in this one had come from skylights or transoms above hallway doors. Out on the street again she'd asked and learned that a law for better ventilation and one backyard outhouse per twenty people had been passed nearly forty years earlier. But even those dire changes had yet to take place. When she learned that lack of running water for bathing and laundering created conditions for typhoid, smallpox, tuberculosis, and the most dreaded of all, cholera she'd backed away, clutched her stomach, turned and ran home.

Ana blinked. Sitting in her lap-of-luxury apartment, she scuttled out from under the memory. Realizing that Mama had told the truth still weighed on her heart.

Heavy with child, she pressed her swollen hands, palms down on the table and pushed. Grunting herself up and out of her chair, she made her way to the icebox. She turned the handle, pulled the door open and sighed. Except for half a bottle of milk and some butter, the shelves were empty. Her stomach rumbled. As soon as she pulled the cap from the bottle, its smell turned the air sour. She grimaced, dumped the milk into the sink and rinsed the bottle.

The tins on the shelves and the breadbox on top of the ice box were empty, too. The meager sum Papa had given them as a wedding gift was almost gone. The grocery list in her head swam before her eyes making her dizzy with fright. The letters marched in a blur. Five pounds of flour, twelve cents, one dozen eggs, twenty-one cents, a pound of butter, twenty-six cents, half-gallon of milk, fourteen cents, five pounds of sugar, thirty-one cents, ten pounds of potatoes, fourteen cents, a pound of coffee, thirty-five cents. Crashing into each other, the letters and numbers collapsed in unreadable piles. And where would she find ten dollars a week for the rent? She desperately needed money, but fearing Vincenzo's wrath, she'd declined to ask. What would he do when he got home and found they had nothing to eat?

Blocking the thought from her mind, she walked into the empty bedroom and peered out the window onto Sullivan Street. It was getting dark. Vincenzo was due home from work any time now. Work was another subject she'd learned the hard way to avoid. When she'd asked about the job Vincenzo's new friends had gotten him … her lips trembled. A tear rolled down her cheek. Wincing, she wiped it away. The bruise had faded, but her cheekbone still hurt.

In addition to finding his mystery job, Vincenzo's friends had found decent housing for Mama and Papa. But Vincenzo made it painfully clear that kindness and consideration for her family had nothing to do with it. Papa still owed him money, and he wanted to keep Papa close to protect his financial interest.

Ana shivered and rubbed her arms. She opened the coal stove door and fed the last lumps into its hungry mouth. The pail was as black as her life and as empty as her heart. She slid into her chair. Holding her head in her hands, she wondered, how in God's name would she and her baby survive? Despite that terrible day on the New York harbor dock, when the Sciorri snakes had scattered from their scandalous nests, Ana still wondered, who was the man she'd married? Had there been one kind caring person among his people? Before docking in New York, no one had seen enough of Bianca Sciorri to draw any conclusions. Ana had sensed that Bianca and Vincenzo were not like other mothers and sons. Onboard ship, to everyone's knowledge, they'd hardly spoken. Despite Papa's invitation, *Signora* Sciorri didn't attend the wedding. The next day when Ana had passed her on deck, she hadn't bothered to look at her son's new wife!

Ana touched her face and winced, wondering how to keep the truth from her parents. Papa's adjustment to America would be hard enough without having to worry about her. But, Jesus, God she needed them now more than ever. Tonio and Rosa had warned her about Vincenzo. Why hadn't she listened? The state of her raw, ragged nerves must be bad for her baby. She took a deep breath knowing she had to relax whenever she had the chance. Forcing her mind to focus on something else, she decided to unpack the bundle she'd left for last. She untied the twine and touched the dress Mama had altered for her wedding. Despite slamming her heart and mind shut on her wedding night, now more than ever she must use her God-given brain to survive.

Desperately needing to understand her husband's behavior, she wondered if perhaps Vincenzo felt trapped. Maybe that's why he took his anger out on her. Even though they were strangers, the vows they took onboard ship had bound them as surely as if they'd been married in St. Peter's Basilica. She thought she had already tried, but perhaps, starting tonight, if she tried as hard as she could, perhaps she could turn her life around.

She patted her stomach and closed her eyes. No matter what happens, my sweet, adorable baby, you are a blessing. And you and I will be fine. She put her thoughts of Vincenzo away with her dress, when she heard laughter in the hallway. Before she could get to the door, Vincenzo opened it. He hugged a red-haired American woman to his chest, and they staggered in.

"What are you staring at?" he said in Italian, slurring his words.

"Oh no," the woman said, gaping at Ana's big belly. She squirmed out of his arms. "Listen, Vinny, I don't go with no married men." She tossed her curly mane over her shoulders.

"No, a please," he begged in bad English. "You no unnerstan. She's a notta my wife. She's a, how you say, mah seesta. Her *esposo,* her husband, he leave a-her for other woman in *Sicilia.* She's a here because she hadda no place else to go, because a ..." Vincenzo laced his fingers and starting at his chest, mimed a large protruding circle in the air. The woman giggled and nodded her understanding.

"Now," he said to Ana in soft-loving Italian tones, "you get in there," smiling, he pointed to the empty bedroom, "and you close the door and don't come out, or I'll take you in that bedroom and make you watch how a real woman satisfies a man." Dumbfounded, Ana froze. "Did you understand or are you as stupid as you look? *Uscire da qui!*

Ana stumbled into the empty room. She closed the door and sank down on her haunches behind it. Hearing Vincenzo laugh and the American woman giggle, Ana pressed her lips together and muffled a cry. When the sounds through the walls turned dark, but before the woman screamed, Ana shut her eyes tight and clamped her hands over her ears.

Chapter 22

Luisa is born
May 1906

Even though Ana lived a few blocks from her parents, for all the contact Vincenzo allowed them to have, she might as well have lived on the other side of the ocean. The larger her belly grew, the gaunter and more withdrawn she became, and over the months, when she'd managed to sneak in a visit, she'd fretted for days at the looks on her parents' faces. She blamed her appearance on her nausea, claiming the pregnancy did not agree with her, but she knew that her parents didn't believe her.

One night under the cover of darkness, Ana knocked at her parents' door. Her eye was black and swollen shut. Her bruised lip ballooned. She whimpered and clutched her stomach.

"Luisa!" Giani yelled, his voice cracked with a sob, "Ana's going into labor! Quickly, who is the midwife?"

"I don't—"

Ana screamed, cutting her mother off. Pain exploded doubling her over, racking her body with sobs and spasms,

"Go find her. Now!" Giani screamed.

Luisa tightened her robe around her, ran a hand through her tangled hair and rushed into the hallway. She beat her fists on doors until a neighbor-woman who knew the midwife, Felicia M'adore answered. After giving Giani Felicia M'adore's address, the neighbor promised Giani she would stay and help Luisa care for Ana.

Ana lay on the sweat soaked mattress drawing short panting yelps as a rusty-knife of a pain punctured her back and sawed its way around her waist through her stomach, blotting the world out. In between spasms she puffed out little cries, and then bit her lip against pain that sliced through her belly, grabbed her gut and twisted hard, making her want to die.

Eight hours later Felicia M'adore handed Ana a perfect little girl, the picture of Carlos. Smiling through her tears, Ana named her daughter, Luisa after her mother.

Ana closed her eyes, amazed that only nine months had passed when it felt more like nine years. The memories of the fire and passion she and Carlos had shared were as distant and faint as two stars in some remote constellation. It was so long ago—Ana wondered if the love she tried to recall had been real or the product of her weary imagination. But Carlos was gone, and in a flash of gut-twisting insight, Ana sensed that the romantic love she had felt for Carlos was the only one she would ever feel. As if on cue, the warm, fragrant bundle squirmed in her arms in protest.

Luisa and Giani frowned at Ana's bruises and never mentioned her black eye and her swollen lip, but Ana knew that her battered face had confirmed their worst fears. They begged Ana to let them take care of her and the baby for a month at least. Ana, who was too weak and fatigued to refuse, accepted gratefully.

The morning Vincenzo knocked at Giani's door, Ana lifted her delicate bundle into her arms and kissed her mother and father goodbye.

"We can't let her go back there to live with him, Luisa," Giani said, closing the door behind them.

"We can't interfere in their marriage. The custom—"

"How can you still talk of customs? To hell with your empty customs and foolish traditions! I die more each day knowing that it is my fault that Ana and now her sweet, innocent baby are forced to live at the mercy of that—"

He stopped talking and clutched the left side of his chest. He grimaced and stumbled as if someone had stabbed him. His face reddened and swelled, and his breathing was shallow and labored. He made his way to his bed and lay there panting and sweating, not daring to move or to speak.

Luisa stayed by his side. Her eyes never left his. Alone on this strange block in this strange country, she realized how isolated they were. Tonio was with Rosa, and God knew where they had gone or when they'd be back. Their relationship was another evil offshoot of this voyage. Onboard ship for some reason she still couldn't understand, the closeness between Rosa and Ana had seemed to dissipate. When Rosa replaced Ana with Tonio, Luisa had feared the worst. How could her Tonio not know what everyone else knew, that Rosa was a tramp? Now they were talking marriage. She prayed he'd grow tired of her and find someone more suited to him and their family.

If this were the old country, friends and neighbors would put their lives aside to support her family in their hour of need. But they were in America now, and with crystal clear hindsight Luisa realized that their lives had taken an irrevocable turn the moment they'd boarded the ship. Giani exhaled a sigh and his features relaxed and Luisa assumed his pain had subsided.

"Giani?"

"Luisa," he said, lifting himself up on his elbows. His voice sounded strangely calm. "Today you must go to the post office."

"The post office, but—"

He clutched his chest and Luisa stopped talking. "Go to the post office. See if we have mail from the Italian Consulate. If not, you must take the subway and go there in person."

"To the Italian Consulate? Me? But—"

"Yes, Luisa, please. You can do it."

"But my English is bad. And I know nothing about—"

He saw the look on his wife's face. He breathed in short, painful spurts and said, "Luisa. I must tell you something I—"

"Please rest! You need to conserve your strength." She touched his forehead. It was cold and clammy.

"There's no time to rest." He grasped her hand. "Luisa, I never told you the whole truth about the bargain I struck with Vincenzo when he agreed to marry Ana."

"My God Almighty what could you have left out?" The room was spinning.

"I wanted to protect you, but I'm afraid I can no longer afford that luxury."

Luisa grew paler and weaker with each word he spoke.

"For the past several months Vincenzo has been pressuring me for the money I promised to give him after he married Ana."

"Oh, Giani."

"I tried to tell him I was doing everything possible to keep my part of the bargain, but he wouldn't accept it. I repeated what the authorities had told me. That between unification and trouble with organized crime, Italy was in a state of upheaval. And that in such a state sometimes records get lost or destroyed. I swore I was working with the consulate to expedite release of my funds. I told him that as soon as they arrived, I would place them in his hands, personally.

"My God, Luisa, the night Ana came to us bruised and in labor I knew her life, her marriage, everything was worse than we could have imagined. Vincenzo thinks I'm lying about the money, and he's taking it out on Ana. What have I done to my Ana?"

"But Giani, what if the consulate won't—"

"They will help us, Luisa. *Gesu Cristo* up in heaven they must! Go! Go now, please!"

After Luisa had closed the door behind her, he struggled to get to his feet. Desperate and racked with pain, he ran his hands through his hair and wiped his sweaty forehead.

"God forgive me. I've failed as a father and a husband. I failed to make the best life for my wife. And I gave the child of my heart and her child to a madman.

"Only a monster would blacken the eye and cut the lip of a pregnant woman regardless of who her child's father is. Ana would have been better off unwed. We could have raised her child here, together. And to hell with what everyone else thought!"

He dried his tears. It was too late. Or was it?

In his panic he'd forgotten to tell Luisa to check the mailbox before going to the Post Office. Normally she'd do that on her own, but in their state of mind these days...

A flicker of hope burned, illuminating an idea. If the Italian Consulate had sent their money, he would not give it to his pig-dog of a son-in-law. He could book passage back to Italy. And if they passed judgment on his Ana, he'd claw out their eyes with his bare hands.

Lighter of heart, he grabbed the mailbox key and inched his way along the wall down three flights of stairs to his mailbox. His sweating fingers trembled. On the third try he slipped the key in the hole, turned it and opened the mailbox door. Beads of sweat dripped from his chin and nose staining the return address of the Italian Consulate. The ink ran. He wiped the envelope on his shirt. His heart throbbed like a stab wound. He leaned on the wall taking measured breaths.

"Thank you, God." He kissed the envelope, trying to smile, but grimaced in pain instead. "Ana and her baby will be fine now. I'll give Vincenzo a little cash to throw him off. Then one day while he's at work, Ana, her baby, Luisa and I will board a ship back to Italy. That coward bastard will never dare to follow."

Relieved he'd found a way out, Giani ripped open the envelope, unfolded the letter and began to read: Dear Mr. Testadura. We regret to inform you...

Searing pain cut its way down his left arm and sawed through his heart. Giani slid down the wall onto the floor. His face white, his chin dropped to his chest. The letter tight in his grasp, his hand hit the tile floor.

The horse's hooves echoed through dew-laden cobblestone streets. Draped in dark purple, the horse pulled the black hearse past Giani's home in Greenwich Village for the third and last time. The small band that followed behind played a dirge, accentuating every few notes with a clash of brass cymbals.

Ana sobbed and stuffed the crumpled letter into her pocket. Domenico Nucciarone, the funeral director and provincial acquaintance, promised he'd never tell Luisa that they had to break Giani's fingers to pry the letter from his hands.

Chapter 23

Ana and Rosa
March 1911

Her Papa died five years ago, but every time Ana pictured his loving face, the pain of his death ripped through her heart as if it happened yesterday. Her jaw clenched tight and hands trembling, Ana set a cup of *demitasse* in front of Rosa, who sat opposite her at the kitchen table.

Rosa gasped, draping her sweater over the back of her chair. "My God, Ana, what did that *bastardo senza cuore* do to you this time?"

"Nothing. This time. I was thinking of … of … something and someone else." Knowing that her parents and Rosa had never seen eye to eye, Ana thought it best not to mention Papa to Rosa. Instead, she gathered her resolve, straightened her spine, cleared her throat, reached across the table and took Rosa's hand. "I need help, and you're the only one who can give it."

Eyes wide, Rosa shook her head slowly. "I know that look. How many times must I tell you? I can't help you get a job," she said, squeezing and then releasing Ana's hand.

"Can't?" Ana whispered hoarsely, "or won't?"

"Either. Both," Rosa said. "If you suddenly get a job with me at the Triangle Shirtwaist factory, Vincenzo will blame me. He already smells a rat and has made veiled threats."

"What?"

"After you asked his 'permission,'" Rosa spat out the word, "he pulled me into an alley, grabbed my wrist, twisted my arm and said, 'I'm the man. I earn the money. Ana's work is cooking my meals and keeping my house clean.' He threatened to kill you and make Luisa an orphan if I helped get you a job at the factory or anywhere for that matter."

"He won't know it was you, Rosa. I swear it."

Rosa grasped and squeezed Ana's hand "And how would you keep it from him?"

"He knows that some women in the neighborhood already work there. I'll say that one of them helped me. If he dared threaten them, he would have to answer to the men in their families. He's a coward who only bullies the weak and the vulnerable, like me and my poor Luisa."

"Ana, he may be a coward and a bully, but he's not stupid. He knows those women still remember the way you were in the old country and would never help you. Besides, everyone knows that you're not as desperate for cash as the rest of us."

A, there-I-said-it look crossed Rosa's eyes, surprising and wounding Ana.

"We've all heard talk on the street about the 'bonuses' Vincenzo gets from his job on the docks," Rosa said.

Anger usurping hurt, Ana said, "Do the talkers on the street know that his 'bonuses' rarely come in cash?" Her voice dripped with contempt. "And when they do, he makes it painfully clear that the cash is his, not mine. I take what he gives if he gives it, and I keep my mouth shut for Luisa's sake. Even so," she said, her contempt tinged with triumph, "I've managed to hoard every penny I could without raising a ripple of suspicion." She stared blankly and said, "The possibility of running short of money puts me at great risk." The look on Rosa's face confirmed what Ana sensed: that her eyes betrayed her fright. "Rosa," she pleaded, "I'm twenty-three years old. I've had three baby girls, two by Vincenzo. You've seen how he torments Luisa," she said, clenching her fist. Her guilt for conceiving Luisa in sin had grown on her heart like a tumor. Watching her daughter forfeit a normal healthy life for the sins of her mother had choked Ana so, there were times she could hardly breathe.

"There's something wrong with Luisa," Ana said averting her eyes. "She's not growing the way she should."

"What are you talking about? How do you know that?"

"I compare her to other five-year-old children who play with each other at the park. They know words my Luisa doesn't. She doesn't know the alphabet. She doesn't recognize the letters in her name. She can't count past seven. She's underweight for her age."

"That doesn't mean anything. She's just growing more slowly. She'll catch up."

"I don't know, Rosa, and it scares me."

"Ana—"

"Vincenzo forbids me to call for a doctor," Ana said, cutting Rosa off. "So one day, I confided in Felicia M'dore the midwife. She asked me a lot of questions. The last one disturbed me so much, I couldn't sleep that night."

"What was it?" Rosa said, looking worried.

"She said, 'I know your history with Vincenzo., Ana. Tell me, did Luisa cry a lot when she was an infant?' When I nodded, she said, 'Did Vincenzo ever get angry enough to shake her or hit her?'" Ana's lips trembled.

"Well, did he?" Rosa asked, sounding appalled.

"I don't know. There were times that I had to leave her alone with him."

"What did Felicia say?"

"She said that if he did those things, he could have damaged her brain." Ana grabbed Rosa's hand. "Do you see why I am desperate for work? I am desperate to get her away from him.

"You were with me two years ago when Siena died of influenza. You were at my bedside a few months ago when Caterina was born dead. My heart is strangling in vines of guilt and rage that are so thick it can barely beat. I want to claw the flesh off his face and tear the eyes from his skull, but I'm terrified that he will kill me before I succeed, and then who will care for and protect Luisa? And the irony?" she said, unclenching her fist. "It is by the grace of God and Vincenzo's lust for other women that I've not gotten pregnant again. And then, my rage ebbs into a suffocating impotence. Rosa, I'm desperate. I can't bring another child into this world to live under his roof," she said, clenching her jaw. "Luisa is five years old, and she is so terrified of him, she barely eats, hardly utters a word and rarely comes out of her room when he's home. She's retreating deeper and deeper inside herself. Vincenzo hates children, but he hates her most of all because she is another man's child. I'm her mother. I am the only one who can save her. If it's the last thing I ever do, I will take her far away from him, but I can't do it without money."

"Think, Ana. Even if you had money, where would you go?" Rosa asked, unaware that each question she asked was a stake she drove into Ana's heart.

"And when the money runs out, what would you do? Where would you live? How would you care for yourself and Luisa? You're very smart, but you're an unskilled, immigrant woman with a child to clothe and feed. There is no one out there who can help you, Ana. Not your mother, not even your poor father, had he lived."

Ana's eyes welled, and suddenly Rosa's eyes widened as if something had just occurred to her. "I have an idea. Becoming a citizen might help you a lot. Have you tried? I haven't yet," she said not waiting for Ana to answer, "but I've asked and found out that the law changed in nineteen-oh-six, the year we arrived. Now the government wants more detailed information. But that shouldn't be a problem."

"Becoming a citizen would take too long. I need a job now with you at the factory today."

Rosa shook her head. "I don't mean to seem harsh and uncaring, but you must open your mind and hear me." She grasped Ana's hand and squeezed hard while emphasizing each word.

"You don't want to work with me, Ana. Hundreds of immigrant women and girls sit at row upon row of sewing machines twelve hours a day every day for twelve dollars a week in that cramped, rat-infested firetrap. Even though we don't speak or understand English very well, we aren't stupid, and we're not blind. The shirtwaist factory is a sweat shop. No light. No air. Those of us who dared to point this out are told to shut up and get back to work. That we're lucky we have jobs. Others get fired right on the spot."

"Yet you've worked there for one year and you continue to do so," Ana said, sniffling. She wiped a tear from her cheek. "You are fearless and so full of life. I envy your boldness."

"You're mistaken, Ana." I'm not fearless or bold. I hate that job. I work because I have no choice."

"I'm desperate," Ana said. She squeezed Rosa's hand so tight that Rosa grimaced. "For my Luisa's sake, I must get a job at the factory now. I beg you, Rosa, put in a word for me."

Ana let Rosa's hand go. Rosa flexed her fingers and frowned. "Wait a minute," she said, her eyes widening. "I'm not sure, but there might be a way for you to earn money without working at the factory or anywhere outside this room."

"How?" A faint ripple of real hope lapped at the shore of Ana's heart for the first time since the she'd married Vincenzo.

"It's called 'piecework.'" She saw Ana frown and said, "Tonio was at Punziano's grocery store and he overheard Punziano mention it to a couple of women."

"What does 'piecework' mean?"

"Well, instead of having immigrants come to a factory to assemble their product, a factory delivers its unassembled products to immigrants' homes. Then someone comes to pick up the finished product. The more products you assemble, the more you get paid."

"Oh my God, Rosa, that sounds perfect. I could do that," she said, smiling. Suddenly, the smile slipped from her face. "What kinds of products do they send? Are they complicated? Do I need to follow instructions in English?"

"No, silly," Rosa said laughing. "They're like feather tassels that you fasten to men's hat bands. Or powder puffs that you sew and then stuff inside paper envelopes."

"But how many do they send?"

"As many as you can handle."

Ana looked around her nervously, thinking. She could do that while Vincenzo was at work, but what would she do with the feathers and powder puffs when he came home?

As if reading Ana's mind Rosa said, "Before Vincenzo comes home, you could stick everything back in the factory box and shove it under your very high bed behind your trunk. He never looks under the bed, so he'll never see the box."

"Rosa, you're brilliant. You've helped me solve a big problem."

"I wish I could help Tonio," Rosa said.

"Why? What's wrong with him? Is it that he can't find work? Why doesn't he do this piecework? He could finish many more products than I, and he would make lots of money."

"The problem with Tonio, Ana, is that he's never really adjusted to life in America."

The sound of disgust and regret in Rosa's voice weighed heavily on Ana's heart.

"He's so depressed he can't find and hold a steady job. Ever since your father died he's gotten worse. He keeps saying that he wants to go back to the old country. He heard the new immigrant men saying how Italy is at war with Turkey and now wants to invade Libya. Yet he refuses to face the truth, Ana, that there is nothing in Italy for us to go back to."

"I'm sorry, Rosa. Is there anything I can do to help? Perhaps I can talk to him."

"I've lost my voice trying." Rosa jumped up suddenly. "I must go," she said, grabbing her sweater. "They lock the Washington Street door. If I'm late I won't get inside. They'll dock my pay for lost time or they'll fire me, and I can't afford to lose my job."

Chapter 24

Rosa
The Triangle Shirtwaist Factory
March 25, 1911

"Damn you, Tonio," Rosa mumbled, cursing him for the hundredth time for her late start this morning. She'd kept her head down and her foot working the sewing machine's pedal as hard as she could all day long. Thank God she'd arrived at work seconds before the foremen had locked the factory doors. Blinded by her fury with him for almost being locked out, Rosa had slammed into Mr. Isaac Harris, the owner and her foreman's boss, almost knocking him down.

"*Signor Harris, mio Dio, mi dispiace,*" she'd stammered, while tears had welled in her eyes.

Sewing machine wheels stopped whirring. Foot pedals had stopped thumping. The clamber from eight long wooden tables crammed with women sewing and cutting—stopped. Eyes looked up. Mouths gaped. Hands, feet and heads froze in position. The air grew heavy with silence. It pressed on Rosa's chest and kept the sob fighting to be free locked in her lungs.

Mr. Harris had stared down his nose. Under the force of his burning contempt Rosa shrank inside herself. After a few interminable seconds, he'd straightened his shoulders, stuck his chin out, raised his hand, brushed their encounter from his lapels and walked out the door.

"*Testadura!*" her boss, Mr. Dooley, shouted. His fists clenched and unclenched as though they'd wanted to grab her and fling her out the window. "*Arrivare al lavoro.* Get to work," he snarled. He looked at the others, a frozen tableau. "*O ti licenzio tutti.* Or I'll fire the lot of you."

Her face hot with humiliation, Rosa kept her chin to her chest, darted her glance right and counted. "*Uno, due, tre.*" At table four she slid past the third machine to her cutting station.

Hours later with her heart still pounding, Rosa glanced at the clock on the factory wall. 4:40 pm. In three hours and twenty minutes she'd be done. She was still madder than hell at Tonio, but she was grateful she had not lost her job. Tomorrow was Sunday. Having worked last

Sunday, she decided to take tomorrow off. She'd asked Tonio to stop at Punziano's for some onions and garlic and greens and beans. She grimaced, hoping he would remember. Being more depressed than usual lately, he'd forget to put on his shoes if she didn't remind him.

In between cutting Rosa stole glances at Dooley who sat at his desk, puffing on a cigarette and staring blankly, thinking about when to fire her, no doubt. He lifted one leg over the other, crushed the butt on the bottom of his shoe and got to his feet. Under the tables were scores of large wooden bins overflowing with months of cotton scraps. Looking distracted, he tossed the butt into a bin, crossed the room, opened the door to the stairwell and closed it behind him. He knew that smoking was banned, but how could she fault him when others had sneaked cigarettes, blowing the smoke into their shirts to avoid being caught.

Rosa sniffed, wrinkled her nose. Her eyes widening at the unthinkable, she got to her feet. Wisps of gray smoke curled into the air from the bin like exotic snakes from a charmer's basket.

"My God," she whispered, not believing her eyes. She made her way past her coworkers, but by the time she got to the door the bin was in flames and women were on their feet, screaming and pushing their way toward her and the door.

"Mr. Dooley," she screamed. Pounding her fist on the door with one hand, she tried the knob with the other, but the door had either jammed or was locked.

"Mr. Dooley," Rosa screamed, pounding the door harder. By this time a wave of women yelling, "Fire!" rose up and surged to the front of the room.

The room was getting hot. Fire was stealing their air. Rosa fought hard not to breathe and harder not to panic. "Mr. Dooley, please," she said, banging the door so hard, her fists began throbbing. Surrounding her, a crowd of women pounded with her, shouting, "Open the door!"

Suddenly, the women froze. Their eyes wide with horror as they watched the flames jump from bin to bin to the blouses impaled on their machines. Desperate to move away from the fire, they stampeded toward the wall, crushing those before them against it.

"Fire! Fire!" they sobbed, pounding the walls.

The door opened a crack.

"Get back! Get back!" Those near the door shouted. "Get back! Make room!"

Mr. Dooley forced his way into the room carrying a hose. He tried the nozzle, but the hose valve was rusted shut and the rotted hose fell apart in his hands.

"Turn on the sprinklers," a woman screamed.

Averting his eyes, Dooley silently shook his head.

On the tail of stunned silence, women wailed, pushed and shoved. Someone shouted, "Look!"

Flames were eating their way through the long wooden tables. Those trapped by bulky machines wailed in horror.

"There's a fire escape outside that window," a woman shouted, pointing in its direction. Those closest to it, pushed, shoved and clawed their way out the window. It must have been rusted or poorly anchored to the wall, because it collapsed under their weight, plunging those women to their deaths. Those left behind looked stunned beyond screaming.

"Wait! This building has four freight elevators, and two of them are on this floor," Rosa said. Dooley grabbed her arm. "Let go of me, damn you," she screamed. "I saw you start this fire."

Twitching nervously, he clamped his hands over Rosa's mouth and darted his eyes furtively around him. "Shut up and listen, you little wop. There's only one that works," he said, "Even if it were on this floor, it won't hold more than twelve."

"God damn you and Blanck and Harris to hell," Rosa shouted.

"Let me out," another woman screamed. "I don't believe him. I want to see for myself."

The coworkers-turned-mob raised their fists and shouted in agreement. With the women's attention diverted, Rosa saw Dooley push his way out the door. While the mob shoved its way to the elevators, some tripped and got trampled, only to find that Dooley had told the truth.

Their faces portraits in desperation, some pried the elevator doors open and jumped into the empty shaft, trying to slide down the cables and land on top of the cars.

"The stairs!" someone shouted. "They lead to the street."

"Don't!" Rosa shouted, hanging back. "I don't know about the Greene Street exit, but you know as well as I that the Washington Place exit opens inward. And they always keep it locked to prevent theft and keep the union out. If you try, you may be trapped like rats."

"Would you rather stay here and burn to death?" a woman with crazed eyes shouted. "I say it's worth taking the chance."

"Andiamo!" the woman shouted louder, and a crowd followed.

Suddenly, they heard the fire truck sirens. "We're going to be all right," Rosa said.

And looking hopeful for the first time since the fire had started, the women smiled through their tears.

"Staying here is our best bet," Rosa said.

"But the fire," they said, sounding anxious.

"It's our only chance to be rescued," Rosa said, softly.

And the women stayed behind.

Chapter 25

Ana, Tonio and Luisa
March 25, 1911

Knock! Knock! Knock!

"Just a minute!" Ana said. She swept the sewn and unsewn tassels and powder puffs into the factory box and shoved them under her bed. "I'll be right there," she said, shoving the trunk in last.

"Ana. It's us, Tonio and Mama."

Breathing a sigh of relief, she wiped the sweat from her brow with her apron, abandoned the trunk and opened the door.

"I'm sorry, Ana," Tonio said, standing in the doorway, cap in hand.

"Sorry? For what?" Ana said, pasting her brightest smile on her face, something she seemed to do a lot since coming to America.

"For dropping in unannounced," Tonio said.

"Don't be silly. Come in. You know I'm always happy to see both of you."

Tonio had been coming to visit her regularly since the day Rosa had told her about piecework, most likely at Rosa's behest. She owed Rosa for that. Talking with Tonio and trying to muster strength in her own heart to help him muster strength in his was the least she could do. And now that Papa had died, Mama came to visit more often, too. Both seemed to know when Vincenzo was not at home. She loved Tonio and despite the rocky road that had defined their relationship, she loved Mama, too. They were all she had from a past that no longer seemed real.

"Are we interrupting something?" Mama said.

"Of course not. Sit," Ana said, pointing to the kitchen table and chairs. She looked out the window. It's a little late for lunch, can I fix you a cup of coffee?"

"Not for me," Mama said.

"Or me. I gotta leave in about fifteen minutes," Tonio said. "I gotta walk over to the factory to meet Rosa. What were you shuffling around in here? It sounded like something heavy."

"Oh," Ana smiled. She knelt on the floor and pulled the cardboard box from under the bed. "Piecework," she said, smiling proudly. "I'm so good at assembling tassels, sewing powder puffs and stuffing them into envelopes. I make more money than I thought possible." Her smile faded. Her gaze wandered. "I still don't have what I need to take Luisa and I away from Vincenzo, but it feels good to be doing something," she said more for her own benefit than theirs.

"Ana, have you thought about what Vincenzo will do if he finds these powder puffs?"

"He won't find them, Mama."

The usual 'glance' passed between Tonio and Mama rankling Ana. It was obvious they thought she was foolish to think she could ever escape him. They could think what they like. She ignored them and looked in the box. But Mama was right. When she increased her quota, she would need a better hiding place. If Vincenzo found out she was working behind his back, losing every cent she had worked her fingers numb to earn would be the least of her worries.

"So," she said, "I know why Tonio is here, but what brings you here, Mama?"

A bedroom door creaked open and Luisa peeked out. "There is my sweetheart and my answer," she said, smiling. "Come to Nana, *bedda mama*."

A rare smile etched its way onto little Luisa's face. She eased out of her bedroom across the kitchen and into her grandmother's arms.

"There's my girl," Luisa said, pressing the child to her heart.

"I hope you can see how your visits brighten her day, Mama," Ana said, smiling.

"Of course, I brighten her day," Luisa said, kissing the child noisily on her cheek.

Knock! Knock! Knock!

"Ana, open up. Quick."

"It's Georgio Bacci, my landlord," Ana said, sounding worried. She saw little Luisa stiffen in Mama's arms and she could have kicked herself for her knee-jerk reaction. She got to her feet and opened the door. "Georgio? What is it? What happened?"

"Fire," he said, sweating profusely.

"What?" Ana gasped and headed for Luisa.

"No." He grabbed her arm. "Not here in our building. I smelled smoke. I ran into the street, and someone said it was the factory where Rosa works. When I met Tonio and your mother on the stairs a short while ago, I thought I would run up here and—"

"Rosa?" Tonio jumped up and ran out the door.

"Tonio. Wait!" Ana yelled. She turned to her mother. "Mama?"

"Go after your brother," Luisa said, holding her granddaughter closer. "I'll stay with her."

"Tonio!" Ana shouted, tearing after him.

She followed him down the stairs through the hallway and out the door onto Sullivan Street. They turned onto Houston. The eight or so blocks to Greene Street and Washington Place stretched out before them like the vanishing point on an unreachable horizon. A block shy of the factory they merged with a crowd shrouded in thin, grey smoke.

"I gotta get through!" Tonio cried, coughing. "My wife is …" His voice trailed off.

Vhummph. The explosion hit like a fist of heat and light. Beneath them the ground rolled. Above them smoke billowed into the sky, twisting in the wind like a giant gray kite.

"NOOOOO!" Tonio screamed, coughing harder.

Seeing the fire mirrored in Tonio's eyes, Ana looked at the building.

Their faces portraits in horror, several young girls huddled behind an eighth-floor window.

"Rosa!" Ana screamed.

"Let me through, damn it!" Tonio shouted. The crowd parted like a biblical river.

"Tonio!" Ana grabbed his arm. "There's nothing you can—"

Tonio jerked free and ran toward to the cordoned off trucks.

Her eyes and nose running, Ana coughed and ran after him.

"Please," he sobbed, grabbing a fireman's arm. "You gotta let me through. My wife, she's—."

"Sorry sir," a firefighter said, "you gotta step back."

"No. You don't understand my wife—"

"No. *You* don't understand. *You* cannot get through," the fireman said, and then shouted at the crowd, "will somebody, please get him outta here?"

Two strapping men stepped out of the crowd. Jaw muscles twitching, eyes burning and lips tight with obvious pity, they grabbed and held him.

Her heart breaking, Ana watched the veins in Tonio's neck bulge with impotence.

"Rosaaaaa!!!!" he screamed, coughing and straining to get free.

Pale, anxious faces drifted away from the window. A hush fell over the crowd.

Tonio stared at the building and suddenly stopped struggling. His eyes ran. Tears streaked his cheeks and chin. He seemed not to notice. His shoulders sagged. His arms fell to his sides.

"Tonio?" Ana said, coughing. Frowning, she turned toward the building, looked up and gasped. The eighth and ninth floors were ablaze. A chair flew through the window. Splinters and shards rained down on firetrucks and the crowd below.

The girls drifted back into view. they watched firemen inch the ladder upward. The crowd held its collective breath. Tears cutting dirty tracks in the soot on her face, Ana praised God, thanking Him for His mercy—until—the ladder ran out at the seventh-floor.

The crowd gasped. Arms flailing, the girls' faces were twisted in screams the stunned crowd could hear. Below them the firemen spread out a net. Hands clasped and in three sets of two, six girls jumped. The net ripped under their weight. Their bodies lay in a bloody heap of heads, arms and legs bent in ways that God had never intended. The crowd wailed. Ana's eyes burned with tears.

Girls stood at the windows, the room ablaze behind them, they paused for a moment and then jumped, hitting a pile of the mangled, bloody bodies that had gone before them.

Rosa stepped into the window, a hellish charred mouth with flaming jaws devoured ceilings and walls around her. The world paused. A sentient ripple passed through the crowd.

"No, God. No. Rosa. Please. NO!" Tonio screamed.

Rosa's hair and clothes burst into flame. Her mouth contorted in agonized shock, she shrieked. The shriek thinned to a shrill. She flailed her arms, teetered and fell eight floors to her death.

"Rosaaaa!" Tonio sank to his knees, rocked his head in his hands and sobbed, "Rosaaa!"

"Tonio," Ana sobbed, hugging her brother to her.

Tonio looked up. Eyes glazed and unseeing, he pushed Ana away and jumped to his feet. Fighting his way through the crowd, he ran down Greene toward Houston.

Her heart, an empty throbbing hole, Ana jumped up and followed, screaming for him to wait. Closing the distance between them, she reached out and grabbed his shirt. He jerked loose and dove through a sea of people. The human tide turned and swept her back and onto the sidewalk. She elbowed her way to the curb, looked down the street and frowned.

A lone horse galloped down Houston toward them. Horses got spooked and broke loose often, but this one was on a collision course with her brother.

"No!" she screamed, rushing into the street.

The men in the crowd followed, shouting and flailing their arms. The skittish horse stopped. Its eyes wide with fright, it reared up on its hind legs. The crowd scattered. Tonio fell. The horse reared up again, came down on Tonio's cheek and crushed his skull.

Numb with shock, Ana sank to her knees.

Rosa and Tonio—gone on the same day? In the same hour? It could not be possible. What would she tell Mama? Racked with unbearable pain, she sobbed. Lungs bursting, she tried catching her breath but immeasurable, suffocating loss, doubled her over.

A month after Tonio's wake and the memorial service for Rosa, Ana summoned the strength to pick up the paper a neighbor had left. It recounted the horror that was the Triangle Shirtwaist Factory Fire. Choosing to die rather than relive it, she crumbled the page and opened the coal stove door. Sobbing, she put the paper in the stove but closed the door before it caught fire.

Chapter 26

Ana
May 1918

Chin to her chest and a thick black curtain of hair hiding her face, twelve-year-old Luisa sat at the kitchen table in her nightgown opposite Ana. "Luisa?" Ana said, gently grasping Luisa's shoulder. "Look up sweetheart. Come on," Ana prompted, separating the curtain of hair in two and hooking each behind Luisa's ears. "Please?" she said softly, and Luisa looked up slowly. "There's my beautiful girl," Ana said, caressing Luisa's cheek.

A bedroom door opened, and four-year-old Lia ran across the room with three-year-old Giana in tow and tugged on Ana's apron. "Mama, we're hungry." Her thumb in her mouth, Giana nodded in agreement.

"I know, and that's good because it's almost time for supper. You must wait. If you eat something now," she said, patting their heads, "you'll spoil your appetite."

"No," Lia said, stomping her foot. We want something to eat now, don't we, Giana?"

Giana nodded more vigorously, and Ana smiled.

Knock! Knock! Knock! "Ana? It's me."

"Nana!" Lia and Giana cried in unison.

"The door's open, Mama," Ana smiled and sighed, watching Lia and Giana trip over each other to be first at the door to let their Nana in.

Ana looked at Luisa's downcast eyes, and the smile slipped from her face.

"Nana! Nana!" Lia and Giana cried, hugging their Nana around her thighs. "Did you bring us something to eat?"

"It's almost supper time isn't it?" Luisa said, smiling and bending to kiss the tops of their heads.

Ana got to her feet. "Give Nana a chance to catch her breath from climbing the stairs." She reached up and grabbed an apple from a dish on top of the icebox and cut it in half. "Okay. I'll let you break the no-eating-before supper rule just this once, if you promise to take this apple and eat it in your room while Nana and I visit." Lia grabbed the apple and they both ran into their room.

Ana smiled. "Hello, Mama," she said, kissing her mother's cheek. "Can I get you some coffee? Tea?"

"No, thank you," Luisa said, taking her seat. She looked at her namesake and smiled. "And how is my first-born granddaughter today?"

Luisa looked at her grandmother and a faint smile crossed her lips.

"Luisa, can you tell Nana how you feel today?" Ana said.

Luisa sighed. "Fine."

"There's my good, good girl," Luisa said, smiling. She looked at Ana and her gaze slipped to Ana's stomach. "My God, Ana," she said, "I came here to see for myself if Conchetta, that fat snake of a friend of yours, was lying to everyone in the neighborhood, but she was telling the truth. Oh Ana," Mama lamented, "you're pregnant. Again."

Mama's words struck like a slap in the face. "You say it as though it's my fault," Ana whispered harshly through gritted teeth. She saw young Luisa flinch and heard her whimper "Are you happy now, Mama?" she said. "See what you've done?"

"I'm sorry, Ana, I—"

"It's all right, sweetheart," Ana said, cutting her mother off. She reached into Luisa's lap and grasped her hand and sat. "Nana and I are not angry with one another," she said, glaring at her mother. "Are we, Nana?"

"No, of course not."

Ana cleared her throat, pasted the brightest smile she could on her face. "Guess what, Mama? Luisa has a brand-new pink dress!" she said, not giving her mother time to respond.

"Pink?" Luisa said. She looked at Ana with a half-frown, half-smile but wholly puzzled look on her face.

"Yes," Ana said, animatedly. "Would you like to see it?"

"Oh my," Luisa said. "I can't think of another thing in this world that I would like more than seeing my little Luisa's pink dress."

"Did you hear that," Ana prompted. A tremulous smile crossed Luisa's lips. "I have an idea. Why don't you go into the bathroom and wash your hands and face and then you can put your new dress on and model it for Nana. Would you like that?" Luisa nodded, and Ana said, "Of course you would, and Nana would love it."

Luisa slid off her chair, shuffled across the kitchen to the bathroom and closed the door behind her.

"A new pink dress? Have you lost your mind? What will Vincenzo do when he finds out? And why is that child still in her nightgown? It's almost time for supper. You must make her dress up early in the morning, like a normal person."

Mama's barbed comment stung, but Ana ignored it. "Vincenzo won't find out, Mama," she said, refusing to respond to the nightgown part of her mother's query. "At least he hasn't, yet."

"What do you mean, 'yet', and how do you intend to keep it from him? What about Lia and Giana? You know what they say about things that come out of the mouths of babies."

"I've told them not to say a word and they won't, Mama, because he terrifies them. And as far as the dress is concerned, Luisa has had it for a while, and every time she tries it on, she beams, Mama, and her eyes and smile confirm that I made the right decision. And second, Vincenzo never goes into her room, and when she knows he's home, she never comes out except to eat, if you can call forcing small amounts of food down your throat eating."

"A new dress. My God, Ana. Why?"

"Mama. If you had been there with us in front of the dry goods store window and saw the look on her face when she saw that dress," Ana said, choking up. She rubbed her stomach and then reached behind her and rubbed the small of her back.

"My God, Ana," Luisa said, shaking her head. "I can't believe you're pregnant again."

"Please don't, Mama. I can't take fighting with you today."

"Why doesn't that animal leave you alone? When is this one due?"

"The end of October."

Luisa blew out a breath. "Tell me how you decided to do the most dangerous thing you could by buying Luisa a new dress?"

The bathroom door opened. Her face washed, and her hair finger combed into place, Luisa slipped past Ana and her mother.

"Go on, sweetheart," Luisa said. "And hurry. I can't bear to wait a moment longer to see you in your new dress."

Luisa smiled, hurried into her room and closed the door behind her.

Ana smiled and said, "See what I mean? About the dress, Mama, you've raised seven girls, so I don't have to tell you that at Luisa's age most young girls start wanting pretty clothes and perhaps they even have a crush on a special boy, but not my Luisa. She is a joyless, depressed child, and I spend every waking moment worrying about what will happen to her.

"Do you remember the day a few weeks ago when I asked you to watch Lia and Giana because I wanted to spend some special time with alone with Luisa?"

"Yes."

"Well, we went for a walk. Luisa was holding my hand, and when we passed that dry goods store on the corner of Houston and MacDougal, she stopped so abruptly, I almost tripped over my feet. The pink dress was in the window. The way she'd looked at it, my God, Mama, her face lit up like just like it did now, and that's when I knew that I must buy that dress for her." Ana's eyes welled with tears. "I arranged to give the shopkeeper a little money each week," she smiled through her tears, proud of her defiance.

"But where did you get the money?"

"I scraped every penny I could from the pittance Vincenzo gave me. And you know that I've been working at home sewing tassels and powder puffs."

"But you had plans for that money, Ana. You were saving it to take Luisa and the little ones away from—"

"My plans have not changed, Mama," she said, cutting her mother off. "They've just been delayed."

"And now that you're pregnant again, I'd say your plans have been more than delayed."

"Mama, you wanted to hear how I bought the dress. Will you let me finish?"

"Go on," Luisa said, blowing out a breath in disgust, Ana thought.

"Anyway, I asked the factory to double my quota. I worked every moment that Vincenzo was out of the house, and I managed to save the two dollars and ninety-eight cents that I needed to buy the dress.

"Oh, Mama, how I wish you could have seen Luisa's face when I handed it to her."

As if on cue Luisa's bedroom door opened, and Luisa stepped into the kitchen, beaming and wearing a pink dress that was shirred at the neckline and waist. A thin black belt around her waist was tied into two bows, one at each hip.

"My goodness," her grandmother said, standing up, "that must be the most beautiful dress I have ever seen," she said, pausing and then she smiled. "I know why it looks familiar. I've seen a picture of this very dress in a magazine!"

Luisa had positively glowed, basking in her grandmother's words, and at that very moment the remnants of rancor Ana felt toward her mother melted away.

Lia and Giana opened their bedroom door. "Mama, we're *hungry!*" they wailed.

Ana rushed around the kitchen getting dinner ready, tripping over the toys the little ones had dragged into the kitchen and glancing now and then at Luisa, who stood before the mirror, primping and smiling at her reflection. Dear God, she seemed so normal. Instead of giving into fretting about Luisa, Ana decided to enjoy the moment while preparing supper. She'd learned early on that Vincenzo hated surprises. He insisted that she prepare a specific meal for specific nights of the week. Today was Wednesday. On Wednesdays she made spaghetti and meatballs.

Suddenly, she heard heavy footfalls on the steps. The girls must have heard them too, because all movement stopped. Vincenzo had made it perfectly clear to her children from the moment they were born that he hated messes. He loved to say, 'Cleanliness is next to godliness,' and secretly Ana had scoffed. That a man like Vincenzo could use 'godliness' in any context was a sacrilege.

Her mouth pinched with worry, Luisa checked the little ones for dirty hands and faces, and they all took their seats. Vincenzo demanded that Luisa sit at his righthand side. Ana used to wonder why, but now she suspected he did it because he knew that their fear would kill their appetites.

Vincenzo came in took off his boots and coat and put them under the wooden chair to the left of the doorway. Ana stood at the stove stirring the pasta. He went to the bedroom closet, changed his clothes and joined them at the supper table.

She drained the pasta and put it into a large, pre-heated bowl, and then ladled the sauce and meat over the pasta, sprinkled it with grated cheese and set it on the table next to a bowl of green salad. The salt, pepper, extra grated cheese, and the oil and vinegar cruets were already on the table alongside a basket of hot Italian bread. She always left the butter in the icebox, because Vincenzo believed that butter was *cosa Americana* and had no place on an Italian table.

By the looks on their faces Ana could see that her daughters were ravenous, but they wouldn't dare touch a crumb before he did. And no one talked during supper but if Vincenzo talked, they all knew that things would go from bad to worse.

He sat in his seat, and Luisa placed a glass of red wine to the left of his plate. With a racing heart, Ana checked the table to make sure she had forgotten nothing. When Vincenzo nodded, she served him. He took a mouthful of food and she waited, knowing that if the meal didn't meet with his approval, they would all know within seconds. He tasted, swallowed and grunted and she filled her children's plates, filling her own plate last.

He took a second forkful, chewed, swallowed and frowned. He held the third forkful in mid-air and then scowled at Luisa. The cruelest smile Ana had ever seen began forming on his lips. Ana trembled at the glee she saw in his eyes. She knew he was dying to tell Luisa he wasn't her father. Was he smiling because he had planned on doing it now? Her sin was the guillotine blade that Vincenzo held over her head from the day they were married. A chill as cold and as hard as that guillotine blade now scraped along her spine.

He looked away and frowned harder, clearly trying to pinpoint what it was that seemed different. He looked at her again, and a light went on in his eyes. Ana kept watching Luisa pick at her food. She seemed more listless than usual.

Vincenzo put his fork down. And the longer he stared at Luisa, the harder the terror churned in Ana's heart. His face turned deep red, and his mouth turned down in disgust as if his food had turned rancid on his tongue. Ana's heart was pounding so hard her eyes watered and blurred his face. Then his mouth relaxed, and his color returned, making her tremble harder. He looked at Ana, and she felt his rage which was hot enough to burn her face. He took a deep breath and smiled at Luisa. "Well, well, well," he said softly. "Don't we look pretty tonight!"

The dress! Ana wanted to scream. Luisa had been so caught up at primping in the mirror, she'd forgotten to take it off and hide it before Vincenzo came home. Her haste to be seated on time and to draw the least attention to herself had backfired.

Luisa's lips turned as white as her cheeks. She put her fork beside her plate and folded her shaking hands in her lap. Watching her eyes go blank, Ana put her fork down, too. How could she eat when she could barely swallow her own saliva? She cursed herself for the horror that was her innocent child's life. Her guilt for conceiving a child in love was consuming her heart like fire consumed dry wood, Watching

Luisa pay for her sins, there were times she could not function. Be that as it may none of this ever was Luisa's fault.

"What have we here? What is this?" Vincenzo said, touching Luisa's sleeve. Luisa cringed. Her eyes welled with tears, and Ana wondered if that well would ever run dry.

"My what a beautiful dress!" His silky tones were deadlier than the harsh ones could ever be. "I am getting old. My mind is playing tricks on me. I don't remember seeing this dress," he said as he touched the shirred neckline. "Why, it looks brand new."

"I can explain," Ana said, trying to direct his anger toward her.

He shifted his gaze. "*Silencio!*" he said, and she froze. "I don't want your explanation. I want hers!"

The entire scene stopped, as if the camera projecting the horror that was their lives had just jammed, forks poised at various heights between mouths and plates.

"You dumb bitch. Do you think I'm so stupid that I don't realize what you've done?" he said. "You dared to buy Luisa a dress behind my back with my money." His smile was as cold as the dark side of the moon. "If I don't punish *her* now, God knows what *you* will do next!"

He looked at Luisa and grinned. Clearly excited by the fright in her eyes he said, "Now tell me, Luisa, where did your mother buy such a beautiful dress?"

Luisa shivered. She clamped her lips tight, muting her sobs. Tears streamed down her cheeks.

"There, there now. Don't cry. Your tears will stain your new dress. You wouldn't want that, would you?" He picked up his napkin and patted her cheeks dry.

The softer his voice, the louder the alarm bells went off in Ana's head. On legs weak with fear, she got to her feet. "What are you going to do?"

He ignored her and stared at Luisa. "Come now, pick up your fork and eat before your supper gets cold. Go on." He glared at Lia and Giana and yelled, "Eat!"

No one moved. He twirled the pasta around his fork and shoved the fork into his mouth. "I said *eat!*"

Tomato and pasta bits fell from his lips onto his plate. Lia and Giana looked at their food. They wound pasta around their forks and shoveled them into their mouths.

"You," he commanded. "Eat!"

Ana picked up her fork. Twirling another forkful of pasta, he turned to his right and matter-of-factly smeared the food on the front of Luisa's dress. Gasping, Luisa looked down. Her mouth and her eyes soundless and wide with fear, she looked at Vincenzo.

"Oh, my goodness," he said, feigning regret. "What have I done? Can you forgive me for being so clumsy?" He balled his napkin in his hand. "Here. Let me fix it." He rubbed hard, grinding the stain in so deeply that no amount of scrubbing or bleaching would ever remove it.

Suddenly, something inside Ana's heart woke, as if from a coma. Her heart pumped with fury she'd forgotten to how feel. She jumped up and banged her fist on the table. "Stop!" she shouted, toppling his wineglass.

His jaw dropped, and his eyes blazed as though his brain was unable to process what his eyes just saw. He pointed at the wine-soaked tablecloth. "*Putana!* You spilled my wine! How dare you interfere when a father disciplines a daughter?" He jumped up, his chair fell back. He growled like a beast and lunged toward her.

Little Lia screamed, jumped up and pummeled him with her little fists trying to protect her mother.

His jaw tightened. He clenched and unclenched his fists. His eyes bulging, he curled his fingers around Lia's throat and squeezed. He'd done it so many times Ana was terrified that this time he really would kill her. Lia's face was red. Her eyes bulged with tears.

"Vincenzo!" Ana shouted.

He glared at her and cast Lia aside. Lia coughed and pawed at her throat. Fighting to breathe, she fell into the icebox. Vincenzo lunged for Ana.

"*Stop!*" she screamed and held out her arm. Vincenzo froze.

Lights flickered. Faucets gushed. Drawers shook, rattling utensils. Icebox's doors flew open. Eggs, milk and butter sailed through the air, smashing into the shelf above the coal stove. Mugs, plates, bowls, cracked eggs, milk and blobs of butter splattered the coal stove. Tins fell. Lids popped. Flour, sugar and salt poured onto the icebox.

Looking stunned, as Vincenzo leaned forward and looked into Ana's eyes, she imagined a thin line of pain eating its way through his skull. Wracked with dry heaves, Vincenzo hunched over the table. Moments later he straightened up and turned. His arms jerking wildly, he clawed the air blindly. Stumbling past toppled chairs and bumping into the icebox, he felt his way to the bathroom.

Chapter 27

Ana
Greenwich Village
October 31, 1918

Ana sat on her bed rubbing the palms of her hands over her belly in a circular motion until the baby stopped kicking. She tied her robe closed, got up and checked the stove. The fire was almost out. She scooped coal from the bin and stoked the embers. When the coals burned red, she banked the stove for the night.

She tiptoed across the room and peeked in on Lia and Giana. Their little mouths were open and drooling on their pillows. After kissing their sweet foreheads, she pulled their quilts up to their necks and left their door open hoping the heat from the stove would warm their room quickly. Hearing Luisa cry out in her sleep, she closed her eyes tight. Swallowing past the lump in her throat, she opened her eyes and Luisa's door, tucked her in, kissed her cheek and tiptoed out of the room.

She looked at the old black trunk on the kitchen floor and yawned. The little ones had wanted to play under the bed and begged her to move it out of their way. She asked Luisa to put it back, but apparently Luisa had forgotten. Ana pushed it under the bed and sighed. Had it really been thirteen years since she'd packed her hopes and dreams in that trunk and sailed for America? Refusing to dwell on the past, she thanked God her chores were done for the night. She pulled back the quilts, turned out the light, and sandwiched herself between the cold sheets. She yanked the covers up over her mouth and blew her breath on her hands. The stove would warm the room in a little while, but nothing could chase the cold from her heart. She lay in bed. Her seventh child was due any day now.

She peered through the darkness at familiar shapes. The icebox, the coal stove, the metered gas stove with its small oven and tiny jets. A ration of gas cost a quarter. "In the old country Mama had cooked for free," she'd made the mistake of complaining to a neighbor one day. Her neighbor frowned and said, 'You're lucky that you have a quarter.' Ana wondered what her neighbor would say if she knew that Ana's so called 'luck' had begun and ended with that quarter?

In winter when the icebox was full, Ana used a small metal box on the fire escape outside the kitchen windows for extra cold storage. The fire escape overlooked tenement houses darkened with years of soot and grime that were connected by a cat's cradle of clotheslines. The iceman delivered a block of ice daily. Winter or summer the ice melted far too quickly. The whole family saw to the drip pan. God forbid Vincenzo came home to a kitchen floor dappled with puddles.

When the summer days sizzled, and humidity thickened the air, the women crammed plump tomatoes on large wooden trays and plunked the trays on rooftops to simmer under the scorching sun. By nightfall the smell of sun-dried tomatoes spilled over rooftops and drenched the streets and alleys. In times like those Ana ached for the old country. She longed for her sisters and the nieces and nephews she'd never know. Mama and she had written them several times. They answered Mama, and although she could never prove it, Ana suspected Vincenzo had taken her letters. Comparing life in her father's house to life in her husband's, Ana often wondered what kind of home and hearth had shaped Vincenzo Sciorri.

She thanked God for Luisa's sake that Vincenzo was working late tonight. Luisa, who sensed the moment Vincenzo entered the building, would stop playing, and rush around the rooms to clean up the mess the younger ones had made. That's what had distracted her from taking her new pink dress off and hiding it before he'd come through the door that terrible May night. The louder Vincenzo's footfalls in the hall, the quieter her daughters became. She could almost hear the beat of their terrified hearts. She cursed herself for placing her children at his mercy. Although she'd never had enough money to take them and flee, buying Luisa the dress had badly depleted her funds. And she'd learned that she could no longer depend on her power. Her terror made it spotty. Illusive. Unpredictable. The best she could do was place herself between him and them. She vowed to free them from the monster they called 'papa' even if it cost her her life.

Vincenzo had not physically abused her in front of her children, yet. Terrified that he would, she drew every breath doing his bidding. She buried her terror, begging God to give her the strength to keep her fear from infecting her children more than their fear of Vincenzo already had. She remembered that terrible night a few weeks ago when she had been forced to take matters into her hands to shield Luisa, the one who needed her most …

Luisa, Lia and Giana slipped into their seats at the kitchen table, their spines as stiff and as straight as wooden poles. Ana could not believe that in the last ten years she had borne Vincenzo five daughters. Siena, her first by him, had died of influenza at two, Caterina the second, was stillborn, Adriana, the third, had died from bacterial meningitis. God rest their souls. And now she had Lia and Giana. Knowing how they'd brightened Luisa's life, she thanked God for them every day.

Luisa's luminous coal black eyes, so like Carlos's, shimmered in fear. Ana knew by the look on Luisa's face that she had forgotten to do something that Vincenzo expected but she could not remember what it was.

Quickly, Ana sized up the table. His knife and fork to the right of his plate the way that he liked them. His napkin, the wineglass—dear God was—*empty!* She clasped her hands on her lap to keep them steady and stared at her bare-chested husband.

Vincenzo put his fork down and looked at Luisa. Hot tears spilled from Luisa's horrified eyes, while her bladder emptied fear that pooled in yellow under her chair. He scraped his chair back and stood up. He towered over Luisa, and when he lifted her chair away from the table and turned it toward him, terror knitted Ana's intestines, adding another row to the twisted emotional stitches, a nightmare-pattern, years in the making. She had to do something.

He leaned forward, and cupping Luisa's head in his hands, he lifted her thin, frail body from her seat and carried her to the stool in front of the kitchen window. When her delicate fingers encircled his wrists, the pitiful sight wrenched Ana's heart.

"Up," he said, motioning for her to climb through the open window.

No, God, please! Ana's heart stopped.

Luisa's rank fear filled the room, and Ana wondered if her poor child was even aware what Vincenzo was asking. Her blank eyes seemed to mirror her fragile mind, but her fear of Vincenzo was beyond reason, and Luisa obeyed.

She looked at Giana and Lia who gaped at their father, looking too scared to move. What in God's name could they be thinking? Forcing thoughts of her little ones out of her mind, she stared at Luisa. She placed her hand over her womb, grateful that the innocence stirring inside her would not witness this torture.

Vincenzo dangled Luisa from outside the fourth-floor window.

Her eyes rolled back. A pitiful mewling escaped her lips, and suddenly … Ana snapped.

Her vision blurred.

"Do you know what you've done?" he said.

Ana's heart hammered slow and hard, waking a slumbering force.

"I'm asking you a question. Hasn't your mother taught you my questions deserve answers?" he whispered.

Ana's vision cleared.

Luisa's mouth hung open and her lips moved, but no sound emerged.

With crystal clarity, Ana saw she must stop him before he shattered more than her child's fragile mind.

"That empty wine glass has ruined the dinner that gives strength to the hands that feed you!"

Ana knew that the total concentration of his insane obsession with Luisa, another man's child, provided one, slim chance. She begged God to help Luisa hold on.

A vice-like pressure mounted between her temples.

She kept her eyes on Vincenzo, felt for the drawer under the table and pried it open, praying it wouldn't creak and give her away. She slid her fingers over familiar objects, terrified. Had she put it away? The moment her hand felt the butcher knife's blade, anger slammed through her.

A vessel too small to contain its force, her heart pumped harder.

She drew a breath and curled her fingers around the hilt.

Hard. Cold. Detached. She and the knife were one.

The force surged through her, guiding her hand from the drawer.

She slid her chair back and in one soundless fluid movement she stood up, thanking God that Vincenzo was still too involved to notice. She hid the knife behind her back, praying the others would not make a sound.

Luisa whimpered. Loose feces oozed down her legs soiling her shoes and socks. The stench filled their nostrils.

"You shit your pants?" He wrinkled his nose in disgust. "You little pig! People are at their windows watching you. You dare to embarrass me in front of my neighbors?"

Ana moved toward him, the knife in her hand.

"I ought to drop—"

Ana stuck the tip of the knife in the small of his back.

"Bring her inside, you son of a bitch or I'll kill you where you stand!" It pinched his skin, sprouting a bright dot, the size of a black widow's venom. Ana was shocked to see that blood really flowed through his veins. Vincenzo turned white and perspired. Had she surprised him?

"And after I do as you ask, what makes you think I won't grab that knife and stab you?"

"Go ahead. I'd welcome my own death to spare this child, who through no fault of her own is condemned to live with you." She twisted the tip of the knife in his flesh with each word she spoke.

And when Vincenzo didn't budge she said, "Do as I say, or as Christ is my judge I will joyfully kill you where you stand, Vincenzo, because either way my child, my children win!"

He attempted to turn, but Ana twisted the point of the knife and he cried out. He pulled Luisa to his chest, rested her on the sill, grabbed her under her shoulder and hoisted her into the room. He set her limp, rag-doll body on the stool and tried to turn around.

"'You fu—'"

"Shut up!" Ana jabbed him. Vincenzo stiffened his spine and grimaced. "Swear before God and His blessed mother, you will never touch her or any of my children again. If you refuse, remember, Vincenzo, even the devil himself must sleep some time!"

Ana knew she'd humiliated him in front of his children, and that he'd never forget. She smelled his fear, and for the first time in their lives together, it was stronger than hers. His clammy skin and sweat-stained shirt told her he'd cooperate. The courage of her conviction had saved her Luisa's life. She gained meager consolation in an act of salvation that she prayed was not too little too late ...

That moment reinforced a truth she had suspected: that anger fueled her power, but terror smothered it.

And Vincenzo terrified her.

Since she'd married Vincenzo the only times she could summon her power were if or when her anger was greater than her terror, and those times were rooted in extreme danger to her children.

The sound of his heavy, erratic footsteps on the hallway stairs brought Ana back to the present. Focused, she gasped. It sounded as though he was drunk. She lifted herself up on her elbows and tilted her ear toward the door. She heard another set of footsteps, lighter, less erratic. A pause. A thud. Two layers of laughter echoed up the stairwell. The bottom one shrill and brittle. The top one harsh and thick. Vincenzo and a woman stumbled. She heard them regain their footing and continue to climb. She closed her eyes. Counting each step, she and her panic climbed with them. When they reached the landing below they stopped, and Ana knew that in his condition, Vincenzo couldn't go on without relieving himself. The second-floor washroom toilet flushed confirming her suspicion. And the next time they stopped they were outside her door.

Vincenzo's keys jangled. She heard him fumble and swear. If he failed to find the lock, he'd yell and bang on the door. He'd wake the neighbors and they'd complain, and the next day after he left for work, the landlord would rap on her door. He'd tell her that if Vincenzo disturbed his tenants again, he'd throw her and her family out. What made him think she could influence Vincenzo Sciorri? She pushed back the covers. Wondering if she should get up and let him in, she heard the key meet its mark, and the decision was out of her hands.

The open door cast a coffin of light over her bed. Buried alive she shivered, watching the doorway frame his teetering shadow. He whispered into the woman's ear. He laughed. She giggled. He left the woman behind him and staggered toward the bed. He lifted the covers. Ana lay as still as a corpse.

"Get outta bed you lazy son of a bitch, before I kick you from here back to the old country."

He spoke Italian in soft, loving tones. His breath reeked of wine. The woman tittered and squealed. God knows what he told these American women who understood the man even less than the language he spoke. Knowing what lay ahead, Ana pitied the woman. She climbed out of bed and stumbled across the room. The baby kicked, and she laced her fingers under her belly. She felt the woman's eyes on her back. They burned through her nightgown. The woman giggled again. Ana blushed, ashamed of herself and her life, and any compassion she'd mustered for the drunken woman vanished. Any woman who laughed when a big strong man abused his pregnant wife didn't deserve her pity. That woman deserved her husband. She closed the door behind her and found her way to Luisa's bed, praying that her angels were sleeping. When the new baby came she'd put it in with Luisa. Perhaps it would bring Luisa some joy. She pulled the covers back and climbed into Luisa's bed. When Luisa stiffened, Ana knew her terrified child was awake.

The baby kicked hard, and Ana cried out. Luisa looked over her shoulder at her mother, breaking Ana's heart. Would this child's eyes be huge with anything other than terror? She pulled Luisa to her and covered her ears, praying Luisa wouldn't hear them.

The woman stopped giggling. Ana stopped breathing. She closed her eyes. Thank God for her own sake that the woman in bed with her husband was drunk. The woman moaned, and Ana shivered. What a fool she'd been to think she'd ever known fear before life with Vincenzo Scorri.

My God, she could not go on like this. How much longer must she atone for her sins? Ten years ago her sins had cost Papa his life. The pain cut her as deeply now as if it had then. Would death be the only way those she loved escaped Vincenzo Sciorri?

She stopped shaking and faced a truth. She was thirty years old and pregnant for the seventh time. She swore on the graves of Papa and Tonio again that this was the last child she would bear that monster. Maybe it was not too late to learn how to prevent another

One day while walking through Washington Square Park, Ana had overheard the neighborhood women talking about an article in *Il Progresso Italo-Americano*. Apparently, two years earlier on October 16, 1916 a woman named Margaret Sanger and her sister, Ethel Byrne had opened the first birth control clinic in America on 46 South Amboy Street in Brownsville, Brooklyn. That address and the conversation she'd overheard that day still burned in her mind …

"They say she is deeply moved by the helpless suffering among women brought on by unwanted pregnancies," Valentina, a neighborhood woman said. She had a captive audience, and she seemed to love it. The expressions in the women's eyes clearly showed that this was one subject these women knew all too well.

"It is her radical conviction—"

"My, my. It is her radical conviction?" Angie Leone said.

Ana recognized Angie, another neighborhood woman, who stood on the periphery of the crowd.

"Where did someone like you learn such words?" Angie said in a sarcastic voice.

Her eyes on the leaflet, Valentina continued reading as if no one had spoken. "That women be empowered to take charge of their lives by providing themselves with the necessary information to make a choice regarding the number of children they may have." Margaret

Sanger calls the advocating of these contraceptive measures, 'birth control.' My husband says her philosophy places her in the center of controversy." Valentina looked at her fingernails. "Especially now that she's advocated it in a booklet called *Woman Rebel*. She published specific information on preventive measures in a publication called—"

"*Family Limitation,*" Angie Leone cut her off. "Did your husband tell you that Margaret Sanger is practically our neighbor? She lives with her husband and family on Fourteenth Street and works on the Lower East Side."

Judging by the shock Ana saw on their faces, they knew no such thing. Angie looked pleased and smiled.

"How—"

"Did I know?'" Angie said, glaring at Valentina's belly. "Unlike the way your husband pays attention to you, my husband talks to me!"

Valentina gasped, but Angie ignored her.

"I can't believe your husband would share this with you!" Constancia Appollonia, Valentina's friend, said to Angie.

"Believe it," Valentina said. "Angie's husband has nothing to fear. No one knows better than he that Angie is a barren vessel who need not concern herself with birth control!"

A heavy, stunned silence fell over the women, broken only by rustling dresses and shifting feet. They lowered their eyes as if studying their shoes.

It was no secret that Valentina's husband couldn't keep his eyes off Angie Leone. Valentina had struck with obvious relish and attacked Angie where it clearly hurt most.

Angie flung her chestnut brown waves of hair away from her face. She put her hands on her tiny waist and stuck her nose in Valentina's face. "You'd better think long and hard about the apology you will make to me in public. As soon as you are no longer as big as a sow, I intend to collect it!"

Angie's words cut through the circle of women, splitting it in half. Angie passed walked past Ana, gaped at Ana's huge belly and whispered, "You poor little bastard." Then she turned and walked out of the park.

Burrowed deeply inside herself Ana had been too overjoyed about this birth control for Angie's callous remark to sting. Birth control, she smiled. For the first time since she'd set foot in America, she began to believe that perhaps its bounty and freedom existed for her as well. She must see this Margaret Sanger, or at least hear her speak. Margaret

Sanger's information might be a lifeline, perhaps a path to some small freedom she could carve within her life ...

The moans of the woman in bed with her husband dragged her back to the hell that was her life. His groans still sounded normal. Soon the woman's excitement would turn Vincenzo ugly.

As an avid reader, Ana deduced that normal, healthy men viewed the signs of a woman's pleasure as a testament to their skill. But a woman's pleasure twisted Vincenzo's urges into something dark. Through painful trial and error, she'd learned that the less she responded the more quickly his madness would abate.

The woman screamed.

Luisa whimpered and squirmed. Ana loosened her grip and petted Luisa's face. She pressed her lips together, shut her eyes, struggling close her mind to the torture the woman insisted she share.

The woman stopped screaming, and Ana knew that Vincenzo had clamped his hand over her mouth. Remembering its taste, she fought not to retch. Perhaps the woman blacked out, or maybe she died. She was surprised he hadn't killed anyone yet. Perhaps if he had, he'd be rotting in jail and her children would be free. When the bed's violent thrusts stopped, Ana knew Vincenzo was done.

Just before dawn the woman would slip out of bed, terrified she would wake him. But she had nothing to fear, because after he was done, Vincenzo slept like the dead. The lucky woman would sneak out the door and disappear into the city; a luxury Ana would never enjoy.

Certain the woman had gone, Ana rose from Luisa's bed. She held her breath and opened the door. Mindful of loose floorboards, she tiptoed across the room. Loathing the part she shared in his sin, she slipped her pillow out of its bloody case, made her way to the sink and scrubbed it until her hands and arms ached. She thought of her honeymoon night. Her lips trembled. She had to work quickly. There was always the chance Vincenzo could wake up, but she'd rather risk his temper than look in her children's eyes and lie about the blood on the pillowcase and how it had gotten there.

Watching the blood-stained water sluice down the drain, Ana made up her mind. After her seventh was born, and as soon as she was strong enough, she'd find Margaret Sanger and her clinic and learn about birth control. She twisted the pillowcases and squeezed out the excess water. Even if God had blessed her with a saint for a husband, she had too many childbearing years ahead. She loved her children, but how many more could she birth and lose to Vincenzo or diphtheria or cholera or influenza? My God, she thought, pressing her palms to her cheeks. She almost laughed realizing the order she'd listed the perils her children faced. She needed help. But who among them could or would help her? The women in the village who remembered her from the old country barely spoke to her.

Angie Leone. Maybe. Angie was brave and strong and knew about things like birth control. But why would Angie help her? Angie seemed to avoid her even more than the neighborhood women she knew. These women who *thought* they knew her. She swallowed her sadness. What was the use? Even if they were her friends, they couldn't stop Vincenzo from making her pregnant. She'd waited two years too long. She must get to the Brownsville clinic and talk to Margaret Sanger.

She squeezed the pillowcase harder, and when she turned around and bumped into Vincenzo, the blood drained from her face. She never heard him wake up.

"What are you doing?" he whispered.

He leaned against her swollen belly and pressed the small of her back into the porcelain sink. Her fingers went limp. The pillowcase hit the floor with a plop, and her mouth formed a horrified O. She moved her head from side to side. Her lips fought to form words, but her paralyzed tongue could not speak. Her bladder threatened to empty itself, and Ana tensed.

"I said," Vincenzo breathed into her face "what are you doing?" He bent her back over the sink and his lips grazed hers. She pressed her lips together to muffle a whimper, terrified she might wake her babies. She thrust her hands behind her, flattened her palms in the sink and locked her elbows. She bit her lip and the taste of blood mixed with fear, warm and metallic, dissolved on her tongue. She prayed for the strength to keep him from spraining her back.

"I was just rinsing the pillow—"

"Is this the time to do laundry and make noise while I'm sleeping?" When his hot fetid breath filled her nostrils, she closed her nose and breathed through her mouth. "Do you know how hard I work to feed you and your bastard daughter and your other little bastards?" He pressed harder against her. "I'm shocked that I haven't died an early death with the toll it takes on me."

She prayed that her children were sleeping deeply. Whatever he planned to do, she would bear it in silence. He smiled and her bladder let go. Hot urine streamed down her thighs and puddled around her feet. Vincenzo frowned in disgust. "You filthy pig. You don't deserve to live under my roof." His smile broadened, and Ana felt her sphincter quiver. "I know what to do! What a fool I was not to realized it sooner. Living with you all these years has dulled my senses." He placed his hands on her shoulders. He slid them down her arms and unlocked her elbows. "I'll never sleep, unless you get out."

"What?" she said, her face wet with tears she hadn't realize she'd shed until they'd dampened the front of her nightgown.

He grabbed her arm and lifting her up on her toes as though she weighed nothing, he swept her across the floor, opened the door and motioned for her to step out.

Ana stood mute and peered into the cold damp hallway. Her arms cradled her belly in a sad futile attempt to protect it. He threw his head back and when he laughed, Ana hunched her shoulders.

"Look at you. So small and pathetic. Whatever had ever possessed your brother to think you were strong and smart? The fool should have lived to see you now. You can't even follow a simple order." He shoved her through the doorway onto the landing. She stood at the top of the stairs. He stepped directly behind her. "Oh no, this will not do," he whispered. "I said you have to get *out!*"

On the last word he pushed her down the stairs. "God damn you to hell, you lousy stinking whore!" Were the last words Ana heard him speak before her head hit the concrete wall on the landing below and knocked her unconscious.

Chapter 28

Luisa and Ana

The moment Vincenzo slammed his door, one by one, doors on every floor creaked open. Tenants flowed up and down stairwells and puddled in hallways. When men and women saw her lying on the landing as twisted and limp as a broken toy, tears filled their eyes, and they all shook men shook their heads in disbelief.

Georgio Bacci, the landlord and first to reach her, lived on the same floor. A single man, he knew nothing about pregnant women, but this one, pregnant or not, was unconscious and in bad trouble. Lena Scala, a tenant from the third floor, pushed her way passed him.

"Oh my God. Look!" she said, pointing to the liquid pooling beneath Ana's body. "Her nightgown is wet." She sniffed, wrinkling her nose. "I think her water broke, but it smells like she's lying in something else."

The gaggle of neighbors faced one another, trading angry comments. Georgio Bacci raised his hand. "Lower your voices. Please! The last thing this poor woman needs is for that animal to open his door again. Lorenzo, go get the midwife and hurry!"

"Shouldn't we call the police too?" Lorenzo said through clenched teeth. "Someone has to do something about him."

"I can't stand it any longer," Juliana Zita said. "I can't stand how I feel when I hear her crying at night. He's a monster," she said, jutting her jaw toward Ana's apartment. "Someone should do his wife and his children a favor and kill him. Our silence helps that monster. How long must this poor woman and her children suffer? What will it take for us to stop letting him get away with it?" Lorenzo put his arm around his wife. She cried softly into his chest.

"You're right," Georgio said. "But the police would never answer a call from us. They think we're *mafioso*. Those officers of law and order who are not on the take are scared.

"We don't need cops, Juliana. We'll take care of our problems in our own way." He looked at Lena Scala. "Lena, get word to Ana's mother, Luisa Testadura. She lives a few blocks from here."

"Tell her to get a place ready for Ana and her child. Juliana, go into my room and pull the sheets and blanket off my bed. While we make Ana as comfortable as possible, let's pray that the baby waits for Felicia to get here."

The baby, a little girl, cried and the men swallowed tightly while the women dabbed their eyes. Georgio Bacci wrapped Ana in his blanket and carried her down the stairs and through the streets to Luisa's apartment. Several neighbors followed. Felicia M'dore wrapped Ana's baby in another blanket that one of the neighbors had given her. She handed Luisa the bundle, assuring her that Ana and her infant daughter were fine. "Tell Ana not to worry. There are enough of us to care for Luisa, Lia and Giana until she's well enough to come home." Juliana Zita looked at the others, and they nodded.

After Luisa had settled Ana down for the night, she cradled the newborn and choked back her tears. "My poor Ana. Can you ever forgive the blind, arrogant fool of a mother God gave you? For the years she wasted resenting your intelligence and your courage," she whispered. She reached for the handkerchief in her apron pocket and wiped her eyes and nose. "If only I could take your pain and suffering. I'm sorry my wisdom and penance have come too late." Luisa kissed the infant. "I've got to be strong for you, Ana, for your daughters, and for this precious, little dark-eyed beauty, as pure and as sweet as a lump of sugar."

She buried her nose between the baby's neck and cheek, and forcing a smile, she put the infant beside her mother. After covering Ana and her baby, she took her tears to the kitchen. She pictured Giani, Tonio and even Rosa. Not a day went by without something reminding her of their tragic deaths. She draped the rosary beads around her fingers. She knelt, made the sign of the cross and said, "My darling, Giani, I miss you and Tonio more than my life. But I thank God every day that both of you cannot see the nightmare Vincenzo Sciorri forces our Ana to live. He can't be human. Human beings treat stray dogs and alley cats better than he treats our daughter and her children. "Please, Giani, can you tell me why we decided to leave *Sicilia?* I'm such a foolish old woman, I can't seem to remember."

After returning to Vincenzo Sciorri's house, Ana had stumbled across an article in *Il Progresso Italo-Americano* announcing the advent of the second anniversary of the opening of Margaret Sanger's birth control clinic. The shock of Ana's ordeal of giving birth to Sugar, still fresh on everyone's lips had reached Angie Leone. Hearing that Angie had been outraged at the brutality Ana had suffered the night Sugar was born, Ana summoned the courage to knock at her door.

Angie's eyes glistened at seeing Ana in the hallway. Angie hugged her new friend and said, "If you hadn't come to me, I would've come to you."

Since its opening, the controversial clinic had drawn crowds of women and men both outraged and supportive from all over the city. Terrified that Vincenzo would kill her if he knew, Ana followed Angie through the crowd to the front door of the clinic. When they stepped inside, they saw Margaret Sanger. What she lacked in height she seemed to make up for in courage and strength. Dressed in black, Margaret Sanger stood among groups of nervous, anxious women. Her words had clearly mesmerized them. Margaret Sanger smiled and answered their questions while handing out pamphlets that restated her views and advice about birth control in several languages. Angie and Ana stood by and waited. When their turn came, she offered a warm hand and smiled.

"Hello," she said. "I'm Margaret Sanger. How can I help you?"

Chapter 29

Ana
Greenwich Village, New York
1930

Ana gasped at her image in the cracked mirror hanging over the kitchen sink and the rag she had wrung dry slipped from her fingers into the cold water. She was forty-two but the fragmented image she saw in the mirror looked sixty-two. She dried her chapped hands on her apron, leaned toward the mirror and traced the lines around her eyes and mouth. Ana knew she had never been a great beauty, but someone she'd loved long-ago said that her smile and the sparkle in her eyes more than made up for that. But her eyes had since dulled. They'd overlooked so much, they'd forgotten how to see.

When had she last smiled or laughed, but why would she? She was married to a monster. She'd learned long ago not to count on her power. The night she'd held the knife to Vincenzo was the last time she'd felt it. With or without her power, she'd never lost sight of her goal. She lived for the day she would set her family free. Of the eight children she bore him, five had died. An infected appendix and pneumonia had taken the Lia and Giana in 1921 and 1923. She missed all five every day. Luisa, Sugar and Johnny were all she had left.

Ana remembered the night that Johnny, her only son, was conceived. Vincenzo had come home drunk. His eyes had glowed like two hot coals. He staggered in, grabbed her arm, and lifting her off her feet he said, "The men on the docks make fun of me, because every time *you* get pregnant *you* make girls!"

Ana gloated inwardly now, as she had then at a truth Vincenzo would never know. If he'd fathered a hundred sons, he'd never earn the respect he craved from the men on the docks, men whose power he'd envied and feared, because those men held one basic value that Vincenzo Sciorri lacked.

Those men valued family.

That night his rants had rendered her speechless. After thanking God for taking the daughters he'd fathered, he'd damned God for sparing Luisa.

He let her arm go and kicked a chair aside. Lips pulled back in a sneer, exposing yellow teeth, he raised his hand, and seeing Ana flinch, he grabbed her wrist. "You know what those men say? They say, 'what kind of a man can only have girls?'" He twisted her arm. "Tonight, you and me? We're gonna show 'em."

After locking Luisa and Sugar in their bedroom, he shoved her onto the bed. "You better make a boy," he whispered in her ear. Crushed by his weight and barely able to breathe, Ana wondered if Margaret Sanger realized it took two to practice birth control.

On November 21, 1919, Johnny was born.

After giving Vincenzo his son, Ana had wondered if life would change. It had. For the worse. Vincenzo told her repeatedly that he married her for the money her father had promised, but her father died before keeping that promise. When the pitiful sum her papa had paid him ran out, Vincenzo threatened to leave her and her 'bastards.'

"But you cook. And you keep them," he said, nodding at the children, "out of my way." He pinched her breast. She bit her lip hard to keep from yelping. "And I take what I want when I want it. It's the least you can do to keep the roof over your head and to keep your belly full."

Ana ran her finger down the crack in the mirror, mimicking the tear running down her cheek. The reasons why Vincenzo had cracked the mirror were long forgotten. The lessons she'd learned, however, were not. Surviving life with Vincenzo Sciorri meant keeping her head down and her words locked behind her lips.

She picked up the rag and squeezed it dry again. She glanced at a half-filled mug of weak tea and scraps of dry toast, remnants of the breakfast she'd tried to coax Sugar into eating. She frowned hard, thinking, she must remember to clean up before Vincenzo got home.

She stepped into Sugar's room. Sugar's eyes were closed. She looked at her child and namesake, whom Mama had callede 'Sugar' the night little Ana was born. She smiled, happy the nickname had stuck. Each shallow, rapid breath made Sugar's chest rise and fall with a jagged rattle. Her features contorted in pain when she swallowed. But she was sleeping, and that was good. Mama always said that sleep healed better and more quickly than any medicine. Ana folded the rag and held it above Sugar's forehead. A cold compress would bring Sugar's fever down, but what if it chilled her? She put the compress on a small wooden table near Sugar's bed and frowned.

Was it the scant light of day filtering through the grimy window, or did Sugar's face seem paler? Her glands were so swollen her neck seemed to disappear. She felt Sugar's cheek, terrified there was more going on than a fever and sore throat. Ana's head ached with worry. She frowned and rubbed her temples. Where was the doctor? He should've been here by now. She smoothed her faded housedress under her thighs, and sat on the lumpy bed, chastising herself for not stuffing the mattress with more cotton rags when she'd had the chance.

When Sugar's chest rattled again, Ana swore under her breath. Fearing it was diphtheria, she should have sent for the doctor sooner, but Vincenzo said if she did, he'd hurt Sugar worse than the sickness. She swallowed and closed her eyes, refusing to cry. Vincenzo said that crying served no purpose. This time perhaps he was right.

She heard a knock. Thanking God, she tiptoed out of Sugar's room, cleared her throat, patted her hair into place and opened the door. Her lips curled into a self-conscious smile. "Dr. Robilatto. Thank you for coming."

The doctor walked through the door carrying his black leather bag. His cheeks looked sunken and hollow. His yellowed, rumpled shirt hung loosely on his frame. She saw him wrinkle his nose. Embarrassed, she lowered her eyes. The airless room smelled stale with sickness, but she dared not open the window for fear of making Sugar's condition worse.

"Where is she?" he said, avoiding her eyes. He seemed ruder and more impatient than usual. Feeling rebuked, Ana nodded toward Sugar's room.

The doctor sat on the bed. He put his leather bag on the floor and pulled out a tongue depressor and stethoscope. He placed the stethoscope on Sugar's chest and listened. After feeling her glands, he opened her mouth, flattened her tongue with the depressor and peered in and frowned.

Startled awake, Sugar pushed his hand away from her mouth. A deep coughing spasm seemed to grip her chest like an iron vise.

"Mama!" she cried, in a hoarse, phlegmy voice. She winced when she swallowed.

Ana bunched a fistful of apron in her hand. She didn't have to ask. She saw her answer in the doctor's eyes. He reached in his bag for a syringe, a vial of medicine, and some flexible tubing.

"Diphtheria."

The word suctioned the breath from Ana's lungs. The disease had reached epidemic proportions; the city had closed schools, but up until a few days ago Sugar had seemed fine. Ana let go of the apron and wrung her hands. What if Luisa and Johnny—

"What's that?" Sugar whispered, uncoupling Ana's train of thought. Her eyes widened at the needle.

"It's medicine, Sugar," the doctor sighed, smiling and patting her head. "You need it to get better."

He looked at Ana. "There's no time to test for an allergic reaction." He turned the vial upside down, inserted the needle, and drew the medicine into the syringe.

"Will it hurt?" Sugar's lip trembled.

"A little pinch. Now, turn on your stomach."

Sugar's eyes shimmered with fear. "Mama!"

Sugar held out her hand, and Ana took it. Compared to her hand, Sugar's was slender and hot. She knelt and kissed it. "Do as the doctor says."

Sugar cried and turned over. Ana lifted Sugar's nightgown to her waist and slipped her panties below her buttocks. The doctor doused a ball of cotton in alcohol, rubbed a spot on her buttocks and gave her the shot. Sugar cried out and Ana closed her eyes.

"Now comes the hard part," he said, cleaning up.

The hard part? Ana shuddered, wondering what that could be.

"You have to hold her down," he said, straightening the tube. "Look in her mouth. You see that black fuzzy membrane? We've got to keep it from growing over her throat."

"No, Mama!" Sugar tried to lift herself up, but collapsed in a deeper, phlegmier coughing spasm.

"Please, sweetheart. He has to do this, or you won't be able to breathe."

"Hold her down, Ana," the doctor said impatiently.

"No. Mama, please," Sugar screamed.

Sugar squirmed, coughing and retching. "For God's sake, keep her still!" the doctor said. His face turned red.

Completing the intubation, he wiped the sweat from his brow with a forearm. Sugar's breathing eased, she stopped fighting, and the doctor exhaled with what seemed like relief. His eyes looked puffy and bloodshot, as if he hadn't slept in a week.

Sugar's frown melted, and she breathed rhythmically.

"I've done all I can, Ana. It's up to God now."

He pressed the bridge of his nose between his thumb and forefinger and sighed. "There's always hope." His voice was raspy and flat with fatigue. He shook his head and whispered. "But I suggest you pray very hard."

Several tears broke free and rolled down Ana's cheeks. She sniffled and tucked Sugar in.

He packed up his bag. Ana followed him to the kitchen sink. He put his bag on the kitchen table, ran the water and grabbed a bar of Kirkman's brown soap from the sink ledge. He nodded at a kettle of steaming water on the coal stove. Ana filled the sink and he scrubbed his hands, frowning as if he had more to say.

She put the kettle down and glanced at her hands. Years of scrubbing grime from Vincenzo's shirts had made them rough and dry and aged before their time. They matched the face of the woman in the mirror. Suddenly ashamed, she clasped them behind her back.

The doctor dried his hand with a dishrag. His features slowly hardened. He tossed the dishrag on the drain board. "Why didn't you call me sooner?" It was not a question. It was an indictment.

She felt her cheeks burn with humiliation. It was a fair question, one she would ask in his shoes. The answer? She was a coward who'd waited until her husband left for work before asking a neighbor to call. Ana raised her trembling hand to her mouth knowing what would happen when Vincenzo found out.

She thanked God Vincenzo had no friends. A neighborhood acquaintance passing by might nod but would never stop and chat. People not only ignored Vincenzo, they avoided him. The only way he'd know the doctor was here was if Sugar or she told him.

Ana's tears ran down her cheeks. The doctor retrieved the dishrag and gestured for her to take it. She dabbed at her eyes. He pulled a fresh tongue depressor from his bag.

"What are you doing?" She dropped the dishrag on the table.

He felt her forehead. "You're cool. Open your mouth." He stuck the long flat stick into her mouth and depressed her tongue. She gagged, and he pulled it out. "No sign of infection, yet, but you could be contagious." He nodded at the closed door next to Sugar's room. "Johnny and Luisa?"

"Fine so far," she said, terrified that they might get infected, too.

"I'll look in on you and them after Vincenzo gets home from work. I have to examine him too."

Ana sat on a kitchen chair, dejected and resigned to the inevitable. Vincenzo would find out. She closed her mind against the consequences for calling the doctor to save Sugar's life.

"When I file my report with the Board of Health, they'll quarantine your home and family."

Her eyes widened. "Quarantine? But—"

"Whether you show symptoms or not. It's the law, Ana."

"But my husband must work, and I must shop for food."

"Ask a neighbor to leave what you need by the door." He picked up his bag. "Obey the quarantine, if you don't you'll be fined or worse. Do you understand, Ana?"

She nodded and then said, "Doctor?" She was terrified to ask, but she must for Sugar's sake. "Do you know the healer, Candela, the woman they call Keeper of the Keys? Conchetta says—"Pausing, Ana recoiled under his glare.

"Candela is an old woman of questionable sanity, complicated by her drinking. I know you're desperate, Ana," his eyes softened, "but if you turn to Candela, you will condemn Sugar to death."

She buried her face in her hands. He touched her shoulder and said, "I'll see you tonight." He snapped his bag and let himself out.

"Mama?"

Ana heard Sugar gagging. She wiped her tears on her apron. "Just a minute, sweetheart. Mama will make something to help ease the pain when you breathe."

Along with a large tin box she pulled out from under the dresser next to her bed was a copy of a book, *Tales of Greek Gods & Men*. Its cover and pages were tattered and yellow with age.

She traced the name of Apollo, Greek god of healing, feared by all gods, and she remembered how Apollo and the book had enthralled her. What an arrogant, foolish child she was to believe that some 'power' she had might be a sign that she was a goddess, too.

Sighing, she tossed the book on her bed. She rummaged through the tin box's meager supply of buttons, needles and threads. She moved bits of material aside until she found cheesecloth. She cut it into four pieces. After mixing a paste of hot water, dry mustard and flour, she spread it on the cheesecloth and sandwiched the pieces together. She placed one poultice on Sugar's chest and the other under her back.

Sugar's lips were so pale they blended in with her cheeks. Her waxy skin glistened with sweat. Ana felt the stench of death filling the room. It lurked, waiting to snatch her baby.

"Get back, damn you, and go straight to hell!" she sobbed, waving her arms at the invisible demon. She lay next to Sugar and closed her eyes. If Sugar died tonight, Ana had no one to blame but herself.

Chapter 30

Ana

Bang! Bang! Bang!

Torn from sleep, Ana bolted upright. She swept her hair from her eyes. What was she doing in Sugar's bed? She frowned deeply and remembered. Last night while lying next to Sugar, apparently, she'd fallen asleep. She placed her ear next to Sugar's mouth. Grateful her baby was still alive, Ana slid off the bed. The floor was as cold as a block of ice and absorbed the warmth from her feet. Her nightgown had ridden up past her thighs. She shivered, pulled it down, fumbled for her robe and then remembered. She'd left it on the bed in the parlor where Vincenzo and she slept. She suddenly winced. Her right arm above the elbow hurt. A purple bruise throbbed where Vincenzo had grabbed and twisted her arm yesterday morning, a reminder that he liked his coffee hot. She didn't remember hearing him come in last night, but he must be asleep in their bed. She slipped out of Sugar's room into the parlor. Terrified of waking him, she decided not to look for her robe.

She heard fumbling outside the door. Holding her breath, she tiptoed through the dark room avoiding the creaky boards, leaned against the door and listened. Her heart thundered in her ears. She cracked the door and peeked into a dark, empty hallway. She opened the door wider and the paper attached to it fluttered.

"Diph-the-ri-a," Ana read.

The Board of Health had issued the quarantine.

She closed the door softly, leaned her forehead against the frame and exhaled a ragged breath. How would she explain this to Vincenzo? Wait, something was off. Vincenzo never would have slept through such racket. She switched on the light. Except for her book *Tales of Greek Gods & Men,* her bed was empty.

Relieved, she put the book on the kitchen table, slid onto her chair. Vincenzo hadn't come home last night. The doctor hadn't come back either. God knows the doctor had had his hands full. As for Vincenzo, she didn't know where he was and would never ask, even if she cared.

She must check Luisa and Johnny, asleep in the other bedroom. She squeezed the knob, turned it gently and tiptoed into their room, terrified they'd be sick too. Thank God their foreheads were cool. She closed their door and looked in on Sugar who was still asleep. She removed the mustard plasters gently and closed Sugar's door behind her. She set the poultices on the table. Suddenly, the room spun. She needed to make a cold compress for Sugar's head, but first she needed to eat. She brewed a pot of coffee and was toasting bread when someone knocked at the door.

"Just a minute." She turned the flame under the coffee down. She hurriedly pushed the tangle of sheets and blankets aside and found her robe. She slipped it on and answered the door.

"Conchetta?" Ana peered into the dark hallway behind her friend. "If the Board of Health finds you here they'll—"

Conchetta put her hands on her ample hips. "Are you going to let me in?"

"Sugar has diphtheria. The doctor says it's catching."

"Piss on him and on the Board of Health."

Conchetta took off her coat and draped it over a kitchen chair. Conchetta was brave, even braver than Ana had been in another life. She tossed her soft wavy hair over her broad shoulders, peeked into Sugar's room and frowned at the tubing. She turned toward Ana who stood by the stove, frowned harder and asked, "How is she?"

On the shelf above the stove was a bottle of Vincenzo's red wine. Ana moved it aside and grabbed a mug. She put the pot on the stove and the filled mug on the kitchen table and shook her head.

"I told you so," Conchetta said, pointedly. She took her seat at the table.

"Please, Conchetta," Ana said. "I can't take anymore guilt."

Conchetta sipped her coffee. "Is Vincenzo gone?"

"He never came home."

Conchetta set the mug on the table and looked over her shoulder at Sugar asleep in her bedroom. "How will you explain the quarantine and the tubes down your daughter's throat?"

"I'll say the Board of Health did it."

Conchetta nodded and faced Ana. Ana sank into her chair. She felt her despair dim her eyes. She took the mustard plasters from the table and tossed them into the sink.

"It's not the doctor's fault," Ana said, addressing the clear accusation in Conchetta's eyes. "You and I both know who's to blame."

Conchetta leaned over the table. She pushed Ana's hair away from her face. "Ana, look at me." Ana kept her eyes averted. "Damn it, Ana," Conchetta said. She grasped Ana's chin, forcing Ana to look into her eyes. "First, you are not to blame. Second, Sugar does *not* have to die! Not if you send for Candela."

Ana pushed Conchetta's hand away. "That's out of the question. Dr. Robilatto says—"

"Ana, listen. Candela—"

Ana shook her head vehemently and stood. "No. *You* listen." She darted a furtive glance at Sugar through the bedroom doorway. "First, keep your voice down. Sugar needs to sleep more than we need to argue."

Looking chastised, Conchetta nodded.

"Second, what do we really know about this Candela? Have you forgotten all the strange things people say about that old woman and her keys? She seems to have appeared one day in Washington Square Park, but no one can remember how or when. And Dr. Robilatto says she drinks."

"Rumors. You can't afford to believe them," Conchetta said, frowning at *Tales of Greek Gods & Men* as if she'd never seen a book before. She moved it aside. "You've heard what the people say. She carries a set of priceless keys and heals immigrants who are too poor to afford a doctor."

"Yes. I've also heard she's an old woman who walks the streets alone day and night, carrying those keys, yet no thug dares to steal them. She sits and stares at Hangman's Elm as if possessed by it. You choose to hear only the good. Some people say her healing powers, if indeed she has them, have a dark side and come from Satan himself."

"Ana," Conchetta drummed her fingers on the book, "you're being ridicu—"

"No. You're being ridiculous. Think! How can keys have the power to heal? And if by some miracle she healed Sugar, I would live in fear of the dark power that helped her do it."

"Ana. For God's sake!" Conchetta whispered. She got to her feet and grabbed Ana's arms. When Ana cried out, Conchetta slipped the robe off her arm saw the bruise. "That son of a bitch!"

Feeling her face turn red, Ana pulled her robe closed.

"Sugar is dying, and you sit here talking nonsense when you could be saving her life." Conchetta eased Ana into the chair. "Do you remember how sick my Matteo was a few months ago? Who do you think saved my Matteo? The good doctor?"

Ana nodded. How could she forget? Matteo had had pneumonia. After the doctor left, Conchetta had gone to Candela and begged her to save Matteo's life. Word spread fast. Conchetta had been so grateful since that day, when people fell ill, Conchetta would find Candela and bring her to them. The more lives Candela saved, the greater Conchetta's esteem in the eyes of her friends and neighbors. Conchetta mentioned the strange woman in such intimate terms one would believe that she and the *keeper of the healing keys* broke bread on a regular basis.

How could she fault Conchetta for believing in Candela's 'power?' Matteo was alive and well, but having had power herself … Her thought trailed off and Ana shivered. "But Candela's ways are strange and dark. And Vincenzo—"

"To hell with Vincenzo. You have another chance to save Sugar's life. Are you going to stand there and argue, or are you going to take it!"

Feeling the bruise on her arm, she took a breath and then nodded."

Ana reached across the table and squeezed Conchetta's hand. "You must promise me on Matteo's life that you won't tell a soul. Not even Frank." Ana looked at Sugar, small and frail in her bed. "If Vincenzo finds out … "

Conchetta stood and picked up her coat "I know. I promise. But before I go I need that." She grabbed Vincenzo's wine from the shelf, kissed Ana's forehead and hurried out the door.

BOOK TWO
CANDELA

Chapter 31

Candela
Washington Square Park
Autumn 1930

Candela sat on a bench in Washington Square Park watching the earth stir dawn into day. She wrapped her shawl tightly around her. She looked at her aching hands and sighed. Arthritis had swelled her knuckles and twisted her fingers into brittle twigs. Once sleek instruments of flawless precision and beauty, they lay in her lap, spotted and crippled with age, clinging together like two old frightened people. She watched the wind spin brown leaves into crunchy funnels and sweep them across the path through an iron fence that corralled a tree. A bronze plaque, green with age, affixed to the fence read, "Hangman's Elm." Candela frowned at a tattered scarf of a mist that draped the elm's seven branches. For some reason it mystified and intrigued her.

She shrugged the mist off and stared at the elm. In times of stress and profound fatigue the tree gave her strength. It replaced doubt with trust, confusion with order and restored her faith in her instincts. The elm was as wise and just as it was old, but ancient Greeks believed the elm had a dark side; that it stood at the door between life and death; that witches shunned it, but demons embraced it. A shadow roosted on each of its seven boughs like a murder of slumbering crows. On certain afternoons in thinning daylight, the shadows swooped down and taunted, "We know a secret."

On those nights Candela dreams of a dark shadow that rises from the roots of Hangman's Elm. It drifts through the streets past crowds that fall back and scatter. Streetlamps flicker in its wake. It passes through her street level window and presses down around her. Its skeletal fingers graze her cheek. Pressing shrunken lips against her ear, on plumes of rotting breath it whispers, "The past never stays buried."

In the morning she'd wake bathed in a cold sweat with her nerves raw and jagged.

The anemic autumn sun shed light without warmth. Candela shifted in her seat and watched passersby, their heads down and their collars up. When some glanced her way and smiled, she felt their warmth ripple through her briefly, growing cold as they moved away. She was lonely, and as much as she longed to be close to the people she healed, the instinct to keep her distance overruled. She gathered her shawl and started to rise, when pain skewered her joints. Wincing, she eased herself down on the bench. She exhaled slowly, and her shawl parted, exposing two keys that hung on a gold ring attached to a chain at her waist. Through eyes welling with pain, the keys shimmered, mirage-like and fluid. How ironic, she thought. In her hands the keys had the power to heal, but they would not or could not heal *her.*

"That's the twist that's turned this life and others I've led into nightmares." Her eyes widened at the sound of her words.

I led other lives?

Candela shook her head. That scattered thought, like so many others these days came out of a new darkness, a blind spot, an intermittent forgetfulness that scared her more than the shadow in her nightmare. Her jaw set, she shook her head in denial again. "Ordinary people might forget they'd led other lives," she muttered. People passing by frowned and gave her a wide berth. "But I am not ordinary. You know it's true," she said to a young couple that frowned and moved away quickly.

But she was special. Gifted. A gifted healer. If she'd led other lives, she would remember. Of that there was no doubt.

Satisfied, she shut her eyes tight and folded her arms across her chest. But the thought of past lives intrigued and teased her. It came and went, playing hide and seek in her mind. Suddenly, it grabbed her and dragged back further and further through the maze in her mind, a maze that twisted and turned like the roots of Hangman's Elm. It ended with …

"Breanna," Candela said, opening her eyes. The strange and beautiful name conjured …

A bouquet of black curls. Dark round eyes. A broad smile. Dimpled cheeks. Wild tendrils.

And then there was nothing.

Sister? She had no sister. What she had was a rational explanation. She was exhausted enough to dream while awake. That was it. A dream. She looked at a man passing by. "I have no sister," she said, "now or ever. If I had a sister I would remember."

Like she remembered her 'other lives'?

"If I have a sister, where is she now? Have we led one or more of these lives together?" Candela sighed. "I have no sister. I've been alone ever since—

A sister. Past lives. She bit her lip hard enough to taste blood and frowned. Were these the elm's secrets? Was it Breanna's mouth in her dream that pressed itself to her ear, insisting *the past never stays buried?*

Candela grasped the keys and sighed with relief. They were solid and real. She could trust them. She caressed the translucent gems embedded in both, gems of color and light that healed. A wafer-thin solid gold disk etched with an intricate maze floated freely inside the ring. She traced the maze with her finger and stopped short of its bottomless center. The longer it held her gaze, the harder it was to pull back. She was tempted to give in, but the time was not right ... Not right for what? She couldn't remember. Her spotty memory was beginning to worry her. Her finger poised on the rim, she teetered.

"Pardon me." A hand touched her shoulder.

Candela gasped and pulled her hand back from the rim.

"I'm sorry. I didn't mean to frighten you," he said.

She ignored him. What had she almost done? If she couldn't remember to steer clear of the rim ... She closed her eyes and the rest of the thought scattered like tickertape in a parade.

"Ma'am?"

Candela opened her eyes. She looked up into the eyes of a tall young man who seemed genuinely concerned and frowned. She tucked the keys in her lap under the shawl.

"I'm Eric Van Broc, and this," he said, pointing behind him to a brood of gangling boys and girls of various shapes and sizes, "is my fifth-grade class."

She gazed from Van Broc to his students and back to him again. Struggling to focus, she cleared her throat. "It's nice to meet you." Extending her hand to him, she looked at the children. "All of you." Surprised to find out she meant it, she managed a hesitant smile.

His students giggled, and Van Broc smiled. He grasped Candela's hand. Heat flared through her fingers. She froze the smile on her face, determined to hide her distress.

"We're studying the history of Washington Square Park, and I thought I'd bring it to life by teaching it right here," Van Broc looked at Hangman's Elm, "where it all happened." He gently released her fingers. "That is, if we're not disturbing you."

"You're kind to ask, Mr. Van Broc," she said, feeling better as his hand slid from hers. "Of course, you may teach, that is, if I may listen," she said, surprising herself again.

"I'd be honored," Van Broc said. His warm, broad smile lit up his eyes.

Candela watched a blue-eyed boy with black curly hair wander toward the plaque on the iron fence. She looked beyond the fence at the elm. Its branches were bare. The mist was gone.

"Hey, Mr. Van Broc!" he said. "Hangman's Elm." His eyes widened with fascination. "Does that sign mean they hung people here?"

The boy's excitement rippled through his classmates. Several students broke away from Van Broc, crossed the path and crowded around the sign.

"They did hang people here! Look!" Another boy yelled, raising his arm, pointing to a sturdy branch where a bracelet of bark had been worn away. "I'll bet that's where they tied the rope!"

Van Broc excused himself and joined his class. "That's exactly what it means," she heard him say. "Newgate prison stood a few blocks away over there on Christopher Street. The city needed a hanging tree and a graveyard close by." The kids looked at Hangman's Elm. Van Broc sat cross-legged on the grass, his back to the tree and plaque. His students scrunched down around him. "At three hundred years plus," he patted the ground, "Hangman's Elm may be the oldest elm in Manhattan, but the city stopped the hangings in eighteen-nineteen."

"Gosh," a buck-toothed girl said, looking at Van Broc. "If they hung people on that tree and buried them here, does that mean we're sitting on dead people?"

"Yes." The kids buzzed, and Van Broc said, "Not all of the people here died swinging from Hangman's Elm. From the late eighteenth century to the early nineteenth century, cholera and yellow fever swept through New York, killing people by the thousands. It's rumored that some ten to twenty thousand bodies are still buried under this park."

Looking worried, two boys and a girl jumped up. Van Broc chuckled and waved them down. "Believe it or not, this was such a beautiful place, that when people came here to escape sickness they ended up staying, despite its gruesome history. In fact, so many people ended up staying, that the city had to hire builders to divide the farms and level the hills. With families moving in, they retired Hangman's Elm and made the graveyard into a village green. But all that digging for so many years had weakened the earth, and when the army paraded their canons across the grass, the ground collapsed and exposed the graves."

The children stared at Hangman's Elm clearly in awe. "Wow," they cried in unison.

"But before the hangings and the disease, my great grandfather, Wilhelm Van Broc," he paused and counted, "seven times back—"

"*Seven?*" said a small, slender girl with big brown eyes and a mop of tight, bouncy ringlets.

"Yep. He was Director General of New Amsterdam, which was?"

"What New York City used to be called," said the blue-eyed boy who'd first read the plaque.

"Now back in the sixteen thirties my grandfather looked at all this land," Van Broc swept his arm wide to indicate the park and beyond. "He knew it would be perfect for growing tobacco. So, he claimed it and named his plantation *Bossen Bouwerie*. That's Dutch for farm in the woods.

"Hey! I know the Bowery." A thin, wiry dark-eyed boy jumped up and poked his chest with his thumb. In his excitement a pink gumball fell from his mouth. "*My* grandpa lives there. But it ain't no farm no more," he said, beaming with obvious pride.

Candela watched Van Broc frown at the pink gum in the grass. He pushed it behind the fence with the tip of his shoe, leaving it in plain sight, and Candela smiled. Eric Van Broc was obviously a very good teacher. The class was obviously enthralled. Better to have the boy pluck his gum from the ground when the lesson was over than stop the momentum.

"Did you know," he said, patting the ground again, "that we're sitting on an ancient creek bed?"

"We are?" they answered in unison.

"Yes. And do you know what else?" He paused and looked over their heads. Their gaze swept the park with his. "The ancient creek that ran through here under Hangman's Elm was," he paused, and when every child's eye was glued to his, he breathed out, "was haunted."

Candela frowned at the word which made her uneasy. She shifted in her seat. She hadn't heard that word in connection with the park, but judging by the children's reaction, 'haunted' seemed to work. He clearly had their attention. She watched Van Broc's words lead the children's astonished eyes to Hangman's Elm.

"Mr. Van Broc?" The thin girl with the big round eyes raised her hand and shook her head. "My mother says there's no such thing as ghosts." Her ringlets bobbed in negation.

The others watched Van Broc, as if waiting for him to say that this was another one of his tall tales, when a small boy with bangs that met his eyebrows said, "So, who said the creek was haunted?"

Van Broc said, "The Canarsee, the native people who'd lived here a long time ago, were first to claim the stream was haunted. Back in their day, *Manata*, that's what they called it."

Manata. Candela frowned. A strange word, so why did it seem familiar?

"*Manata* flowed right through the whole park." He raised his arm and cut a swath through the air, charting *Manata's* course on the invisible map of their imaginations.

"What does *manata* mean?" Tommy asked.

"It's the Canarsee word for devil water. It was renamed Minetta," he said, looking toward Minetta Lane.

A smile played on Tommy's lips. "Devil water?"

Riveted, Candela leaned forward.

"That's right," Van Broc said. "Imagine," he jerked his head back, and in one synchronized movement they gazed at the elm, "hundreds of years ago, sitting under the elm in the arms of a haunted mist?"

Candela followed their gaze and drew in a sharp breath. She stared at the children who gawked at the elm. The mist draped its boughs in plain view, but instead of screaming and pointing, *they seemed not to see it.* She closed her eyes, massaged her temples to the drumbeat of her heart and opened her eyes.

The mist was gone.

Was it a figment of her imagination? Or was it real, and was she the only one who could see it? That sounded crazy. Was she losing her mind? Or did she hear Van Broc say it? She sized him up: he was a good teacher who embellished an amusing tale to keep his children spellbound so they would pass some test and he'd keep his job. That was it. Plain and simple.

The children fidgeted. Van Broc cleared his throat, focusing their attention. "I'm going to tell you a story about Hangman's Elm, the Canarsee, and how *Minetta* Creek or Brook got its name that you won't find in any history book." He wagged his finger. "And do you

174

know why?" They shook their heads. "Because Wilhelm Van Broc told it to my great grandfathers, who told it to my grandfather, who told it to my father, who told it to my sister and me."

Tommy Repepe asked, "You have a sister?

"I do indeed."

"Is she a teacher too?"

"No. She's a social worker." They frowned, looking confused, and Van Broc said, "You all know how Dr. Robilatto fixes people's bodies and Father Andretti fixes their souls, right? Well, some people's lives need fixing, too. Well, my sister Roberta helps to fix lives. As a matter of fact, my sister works with Dr. Robilatto and Father Andretti."

Candela didn't know Van Broc's sister but she knew the doctor and the priest.

"Once upon a time," Van Broc began, "before there was a New York City, a Greenwich Village, or even a Washington Square Park, the Canarsee lived here. One summer morning three braves were hunting near *Manata*, when they looked up and saw a little girl." Van Broc rubbed his chin and looked at each student. "About seven years old, so the story goes."

Candela got to her feet when a mild breeze scampered across the path, carrying Van Broc's tale with it. Curious, she paused.

"She was barefoot with reed-like arms and spindly legs," he pointed, "she was sitting under the elm alone." Their glance followed Van Broc's finger to Hangman's Elm. "Her face was badly sunburnt and peeling. Her dress was torn and faded. She looked as if she had gone for days without food or water.

"One brave cupped water in his hands and held it to her lips while the others scouted the brush along the stream looking for clues. There were none. No footprints, no doused fires, no wagon tracks, no sign of her people. It seemed that the little girl had appeared out of nowhere as if by magic. But that wasn't the only spooky thing. She had the fairest skin ever and her hair, a tangled mass of red, a color they'd never seen on a human head, glowed in the sun like fire. And her eyes! They were gray with vertical pupils that seemed more catlike than human."

Candela's head throbbed. Had Van Broc described her eyes?

"Appearing dazed, the girl pointed at Hangman's Elm, saying—"

I followed the mist to the tree. Candela mouthed Van Broc's words.

"The braves mumbled that there was no mist or rain. The skies had been clear for days."

Tommy raised his hand and pushed his horn-rimmed glasses against the bridge of his nose. "How did she know their language?"

"That's what the braves asked their chief when they took her back to camp. But the chief, a kind, wise man reminded them that hunger and thirst made people see things.

"The girl had been with them less than a week when strange things began happening." Candela moved to the edge of her seat, and Van Broc looked up. His gaze locked with hers. He frowned and stopped talking.

"Mr. Van Broc?" Tommy tugged on Van Broc's shirt.

"What?" Van Broc's said, blinking.

"What strange things?" Tommy asked.

"Things started disappearing."

A girl with braids stopped biting her nails. "What kinds of things?"

"Animals." Van Broc glanced at Candela. He looked ill at ease. "Dogs and..."

Curiosity seemed to break out on Tommy's face like measles. He tugged Van Broc's shirt harder. "Dogs and what else, Mr. Van Broc?"

Van Broc swallowed and frowned. "Children," he said, looking as if he might choke on the word. They sucked in their breath.

"Then what happened, Mr. Van Broc?" Tommy asked.

"After an investigation," Van Broc said in a hesitant voice, "the Canarsee discovered the disappearances had one thread in common."

"What's 'one thread in common'?" they asked.

Van Broc seemed not to hear them.

"Mr. Van Broc?" Little Miss Ringlets glanced around. "Where's the stream now? Did it disappear, too?"

Tiny flashes erupted behind Candela's eyes ... And the teacher, the class, the elm and the park shrunk to the size of an Alice-In-Wonderland doorway. The doorway began receding into a vastness devoid of heat and light where time and space could not be measured even by gods.

"Mr. Van Broc!" Little Miss Ringlets yelled and ...

Candela gasped. The doorway disappeared, and the park and everything in it returned to normal.

"I said," hands on her hips, Miss Ringlets sounded annoyed, almost angry. "Where is the stream? Did it disappear, too?"

"*Manata*, devil water didn't disappear. The builders changed its course." He locked eyes with Candela's. "Now devil water flows directly under Hangman's Elm."

"Devil water." The curly-haired boy grinned, looking proud.

"Yes, but today it's called Minetta Brook. By the late eighteen hundreds the city had to drain Minetta. "In eighteen twenty-seven the city had built Washington Square Park and buried the past once and for all, we hope. But you know what they say," Van Broc paused and looked at Candela. "The past never stays buried."

Candela froze. Eyes wide, she looked at Van Broc.

The boy with the horn rimmed glasses asked, "What did you mean when you said that the Canarsee believed the disappearances had one common thread?"

"The thread was the red-haired girl. After the animals vanished and the crops withered…"

…people were starving. They called the stream manata. *Terrified by events they could not explain, they turned on the red-haired girl with the strange eyes and yelled, "witch." The first stone they hurled shattered her temple.*

Stars burst behind the little girl's eyes, and then there was darkness.

Chapter 32

Candela
1930

Candela awoke with a start, turned right and left and noticed the park was empty. Van Broc and his class were gone. She took a deep breath and closed her eyes. Did she dream them? They seemed so vivid. So real. She opened her eyes and glanced at the elm. The mist was gone. A pain, sudden and sharp, pierced her skull.

The first stone they hurled shattered her temple.

Raising a shaky hand to her head, she touched the spot on her scalp where the stone in Van Broc's story had hit the red-haired girl. She glanced at the keys.

In her hands the keys had the power to heal others, but they would not or could not heal her...that's the twist that's turned this life and others I've led into nightmares.

She bit her lip. Other lives she'd led? She vaguely remembered thinking that, and then? Nothing. With its blurred highways and faded byways, the map of her memory got harder and harder to read. Was she losing her memory? Would her mind follow? Being old and alone she depended on her memory more than ever.

Breanna.

Perhaps she was not alone, she didn't know. Right now she knew that she was cold, hungry and so thirsty her throat was closing. She remembered Van Broc and smiled, slowly, feeling more at ease. He was a fifth-grade teacher with a mesmerizing, generational tale. Something in his story, for which she had no rational explanation, had pried a door in her mind loose, freeing a memory. She must avoid jumping to conclusions. Van Broc could be a figment of her exhausted imagination as well. She folded her hands in her lap and focused on the crowd. A knot of tourists stopped, read the plaque, stared at the elm, made their predictable comments and moved on.

The sun set sail. Under the braids of watery light in its wake, Candela got to her feet. An impudent breeze sniffed her hair and toyed with the fringe of her shawl. She shivered and crossed the path to the crunch and crackle of fall's remains under her feet. As trash and twigs funneled around her ankles, she paused in front of the elm, pleased that she and the elm were connected. Heading toward the Sullivan Street exit, she looked down and frowned. A bright pink nub caught her eye. She bent slowly, picked it up and smiled, relieved. She wasn't losing her mind. Van Broc and his class were as real as this wad of gum. And his story really had triggered the memory of a past life.

The thought swirled round and round in her head like a leaf in an autumn breeze. She looked at the park as though seeing it for the first time and realized she was certain she had lived here in another, shorter life, a life that had ended badly. Had her other lives ended badly, too?

She put the gum in her pocket and wandered toward the wading pool at the heart of the park. Soon the city would turn off the water for winter. She sat on the pool's concrete edge, and after watching the water loop from fountain to pool and back, she pictured the elm, sat on the bench and wondered. Was she like the water, caught in an infinite loop, doomed to lead life after life?

She tipped her head back and frowned. She must've lost track of time. The stars had stapled night to the clear sky like millions of shiny rivets, but on the ground a mist draped the elm like moldy batting on abandoned and rotting rafters. The gauzy mist mummified trees, bushes and benches, yet people moved through it, talking and laughing as if it wasn't there.

The mist draped its boughs in plain view, but the children ... seemed not to see it ....

She shut her eyes tight, took a breath and opened them slowly. She looked up and saw the moon clearly. Mist came from oceans, rivers and streams, didn't it?

Manata, devil water didn't disappear. The builders changed its course. He locked eyes with Candela and frowned. Now devil water flows directly under Hangman's Elm.

Candela had strange eyes. Her hair was gray and had dulled from coppery to muted red. She had to be the girl the native Canarsee had found. *She* had followed the mist to the tree. The builders had buried *Manata,* but her recurring nightmare warned that the past never stayed buried. Did the people in the park not see the mist because it was buried in a past that had nothing to do with them, and everything to do with her?

A chill skittered along her spine. She'd give the world to confide in someone. Anyone. Disembodied faces drifted in and out of the mist. Even if a friendly one surfaced, what would she say? That in addition to this life, she'd lived another very short life as a scrawny red-haired girl with strange, catlike eyes among the Canarsee near Hangman's Elm? That a stream was called *Manata,* a Canarsee word meaning devil water, because the Canarsee believed the stream was haunted? And did the people she was talking to notice that they were walking in a fog? She stifled the urge to laugh. If Dr. Robilatto, Father Andretti and the others that doubted her sanity saw her laughing out loud for no reason, it would not end well for her. Her doubts subsiding, she tucked the keys under her shawl and took stock. She'd lived for decades among the immigrants in Greenwich Village. At least that's what she'd always believed. Now she wasn't sure.

"Candela?" he said.

She looked up. "Dr. Robilatto."

Next to Dr. Robilatto stood a plump, sweet looking young woman with fine features, fair skin and freckles. She wore a green coat that matched the widest, greenest eyes Candela had ever seen. Dr. Robilatto said, "It's dark and cold and you're shivering." Candela nodded, but kept her eyes on the young woman, who returned her gaze. There was something familiar about her.

"Candela, this is Bertie O'Donnell. She's a … a friend." Candela noticed Bertie O'Donnell frown at the word 'friend.' Dr. Robilatto took Candela's hands. "You're freezing," he said, rubbing them in his. "I don't know if you are aware, but we are in the middle of a diphtheria epidemic. You look fatigued. Go home and rest by the fire or you'll catch your death. Then where would the *immigrants* be?"

Candela frowned at the sarcastic emphasis on that word. Bertie O'Donnell's frown seemed to deepen as well.

"I'll walk you," he said.

"Thank you, but no." Candela shook her head.

"I insist," he said.

She patted his hand. "I'm fine. Nice to have met you," she smiled at Bertie O'Donnell and walked away.

"Very well," he mumbled to himself, tipping his hat. Before he ran off in the opposite direction, Bertie O'Donnell grabbed his arm.

"Doctor?" she said, and he turned and looked down his nose at her hand on his arm. She let him go. "What was that all about?"

"What?" he said abruptly.

"The barb about the immigrants. And why did you introduce me as a friend instead of a social worker?"

He stared at her, looking genuinely perplexed. "First of all, I doubt Candela would even know what a social worker is," he said, impatiently. Seeing the look on Bertie's face, he sighed. Pressing the bridge of his nose between his thumb and forefinger, he said, "I apologize, Bertie. I guess this epidemic is taking more of a toll on me than I realized.

"Look, you're young, idealistic and new at this, so I'll save you the trouble of learning the hard way. If you're gonna work with neighborhood people, you need to understand first that Candela is delusional. She showed up one day decades ago."

Bertie frowned. "From where?"

Dr. Robilatto shrugged. "She never said and as far as I know nobody has ever asked. She sits by Hangman's Elm day and night mumbling God knows what to God knows who. She believes she heals people with these keys she wears. The problem, no, the *danger* is that the immigrants believe it, too. And when they turn to her instead of me, especially during an epidemic?" He spread his arms and raised his eyebrows. "You see where I'm going with this." He exhaled his frustration. "At least *my* concerns are based in legitimate fear. If you talk to Father Andretti—" he mumbled. His hand hitting the air with a never-mind slap, he turned and began walking away.

Bertie grabbed his arm again. "What does Father Andretti say?"

"Uh. It's nothing." He shook his head. "I shouldn't ..." His voice trailed off.

"Please. You're their doctor. Father Andretti is their priest. If we're going to work on their behalf, I need to know everything I can about them. How they feel. What they value. What and whom they believe in and trust."

Chin to chest, Dr. Robilatto sighed. "Father Andretti thinks ..." He raised his head and looked into her eyes. "Let me first say that Candela wields a lot of influence with these people. They're very protective of her."

"Understood," Bertie said. "She's obviously helping them. So, what's Father Andretti's problem?"

"He thinks she practices black magic."

"What?"

The incredulity in her voice seemed to rock the doctor back on his heels. "I know it sounds crazy, but ..."

"Did Father Andretti actually *say* that?"

"Not in so many words, but, tell me, Bertie, did you notice her eyes?" He shivered.

"I didn't look long enough."

"Her pupils are vertical, like a cat's." He shivered and rubbed his arms.

"Well," Bertie cleared her throat, "although rare, there are recorded cases of humans with vertical pupils."

"And," he added, ignoring her remark, "there are a few instances where Candela, oh, I don't know. Let me put it this way. There were *very* few instances where some people had actually improved after she saw them."

"Whatever her eyes look like, how can Father Andretti jump to a she-worships-Satan conclusion?" She shook her head in disgust. "Where does Candela go, I mean, when she's not sitting on a bench mumbling at Hangman's Elm?"

"She lives in a basement apartment north of Houston on Thompson. Why?"

"Have you ever visited her or seen her keys?"

"Of course not," he scoffed and straightened his coat, indignantly. "Nor do I intend to, unless it's for medical reasons. She's a crazy old woman," he blurted, surprising Bertie. He shook his head, and the moment he turned his back, Bertie, who bristled at his lack of professionalism and compassion, scanned the park, spotted Candela and hurried down the path toward her.

Eyes downcast, Candela walked through the park alone, as usual, but perhaps not for much longer. Her frown gave way to a hesitant smile which broadened with each step she took. *The past never stays buried.* In her past there was a sister. Breanna. Candela shivered and sneezed. Perhaps she should listen to Robilatto and go home.

"Excuse me, Candela?" a voice behind her said, panting.

Candela stopped and turned, surprised to see the doctor's young friend. "May I talk to you?"

"Bertie?" Bertie's full, red lips parted in a dazzling smile showing remarkably white teeth.

"You remembered." Bertie said, looking surprised.

"Of course. *I did, didn't I?*" Beaming with confidence, Candela walked to a bench by the side of the path and motioned for Bertie to join her. She sat, and her shawl parted, exposing the keys. Bertie's eyes widened. Candela tucked the keys under her shawl. "You look familiar," she frowned. "Have we met before?"

Bertie frowned. "A few moments ago. Dr. Robilatto introduced us." She stared at the shawl hard, as if trying to see through it to the keys.

"I know," Candela said, relieved that she really did know. "I mean before that."

"I live uptown, but you may have seen my big brother, Eric Van Broc. He lives in the neighborhood. He's a grade school teacher at PS 3. We're a year apart but people mistake us for twins."

... some people's lives need fixing up, too, and my sister Roberta helps them do that. Sometimes she works with Dr. Robilatto and Father Andretti.

"Yes. I saw him in the park with his class." Her gaze wandered. "Was it yesterday?" she said, more to herself. "His students seemed to like him very much."

Bertie, who hadn't seemed to notice the minor confusion, smiled and held out her hand. Candela did likewise. "I'm Roberta, Bertie Van Broc. O'Donnell's my married name." She shook Candela's hand gently. "Dr. Robilatto tells me you're a healer. Is that how you support yourself?"

Candela nodded. "My physical needs are few. In exchange for healing those who can't afford the doctor or whom the doctor has not helped, I accept their humble respect and any meager donations." She neglected to mention those who pooled their resources and replenished her wine. Dr. Robilatto had introduced Bertie not as a social worker, but as a friend. Dr. Robilatto had also warned Candela to stop drinking. She had to watch what she said. She couldn't risk the doctor or the meddlesome priest finding out that she'd decided to drink as much as she pleased. "Your brother mentioned you to the children. He said you were a social worker."

"Yes, that's right," Bertie said. "Now that I've answered a question for you, may I ask you one?"

"Fair enough," Candela warmed to Bertie's smile.

"Dr. Robilatto said something unusual about you."

Candela scoffed. "He doesn't like me, and why should he? I'm his competition. What was your question, and what was his answer?"

"That makes two questions. If I answer both, you owe me another answer."

"Fine," Candela smiled.

"Where did you live before coming to Greenwich Village? When I asked Dr. Robilatto, he said he didn't know, and to his knowledge, neither did anyone else."

The question was simple enough, but it hit like a wrecking ball on a condemned building. Sweat beaded on her skin despite the autumn chill, and she felt her face go pale beneath it. There was tightness in her chest. She ran her hand over her lips. How could she forget where she came from? Her head hurt with trying to remember.

"Candela?" She felt Bertie's hand on her forearm. "Are you okay?"

"Of course," she said, forcing a smile. Hoping to deflect, she said, "Did you know that we have something in common?"

"Oh?" Bertie frowned.

"Yes." Candela placed her hand over Bertie's. "Neither of us were only children. You have a brother, Eric. I have a sister, Breanna." Patting Bertie's hand, she rose unsteadily to her feet. "I'm sorry, Bertie, but I must go now. One of my people needs my help. I was on my way to see him before you stopped me."

"Of course," Bertie said, rising with her. "Is there anything I can do to help him or you?"

"No, thank you."

Moving as fast as she could, Candela followed the lamplit path to the street. What was she running from? Her past lives? Her sister? She stopped at Hangman's Elm and gasped. Three of its seven branches glowed with their own light. Four remained draped in shadows. Suddenly she knew she would lead seven lives. She'd led two lives close to the elm. Would she live the next one here as well?

The past never stays buried.

Her heart pounded, and suddenly Candela was afraid.

Chapter 33

Candela

By the time Candela entered the street door to her basement room, she realized that the shock of learning about her lives was nothing compared to not knowing where she had come from.

She breathed in and wrinkled her nose, welcoming the distraction. The hall reeked of onions, garlic, and abject neglect. Her stomach churned. She'd been in the park since sunrise in a thin dress and shawl with nothing to eat or drink. A fifteen-watt bulb cast shadows that added a layer of dinge to walls thick with greasy soot. She looked up and squinted at a ceiling splotched with years of leaks. Paint chips littered the tile floor. She swept them into a corner with the side of her shoe, pulled her house key from her pocket and let herself in.

Her room was small with one street level window that gave little air and less light. She unhooked the healing keys from the chain around her waist and put them on a small rough-hewn table. She draped her shawl over a wooden chair. There was a clock on top of her small wooden dresser on the opposite wall. Both clock and dresser were payments from a grateful neighbor for healing his sister. The clock read 8:00 am. Her heart thrummed. She couldn't remember being gone all night. She frowned at the blue velvet box on top of the dresser in which she stored the keys. She always kept it locked behind a panel under her window. Her frown deepened. Had she forgotten to squirrel the box away before leaving this morning, or was it yesterday morning? "You old fool! You must hide the box away whether the keys are in it or not!"

The dresser had four warped drawers, and the mahogany stain was worn in spots where countless hands had struggled to pry the drawers open. Life was hard enough without her arthritic hands in a tug-of-war with a dresser. She kept the drawers opened wide enough to reach inside.

She slipped out of her clothes and into a white cotton nightgown she'd pulled from the top drawer. She turned the gas on. She should eat, or at least brew some tea. Instead, she reached for a cup and filled it with wine from a bottle she kept on the table. She stoked the coal in the stove, blew on her hands and rubbed them together. She lifted the cup and toasted. "To Van Broc. To my lives and last but not least, to my sister, Breanna, wherever you are." She upended the cup.

Where did you live before coming to Greenwich Village?

With shaky hands she refilled the cup, looked at the bottle and frowned. It was almost empty.

The past never stays buried. The words staggered past her in a drunken parade. Next to her dresser was a small closet where she kept her bottles of wine. She stood up quickly, bumped the table and tipped the cup, but she couldn't work her fingers quickly enough to grab it. She massaged her hand, cursing her arthritis and the empty bottle. She took a dishrag from a hook above the sink and sopped up the spilled wine. Her shoulders stooped in confused frustration. She plopped the dishrag down, sank into her chair and took in her cramped little room with its chipped porcelain sink. The splotched ceiling pressed down, and the yellowed walls closed in, making it hard to breathe. She pictured Hangman's Elm, the conundrum that both comforted and disturbed her. Shadows roosting on its branches spawned nightmares claiming the past never stays buried. Had they opened a portal to another world? Hers and Breanna's? But where was that world? Where had they come from?

She looked at the keys. Breanna and she were sisters, who'd shared a life or lives in the past. If only she could remember. Were they destined to share another? Perhaps this one? Was it her imagination or was Breanna here now? She sensed it. Her heart pounded. She grabbed the keys and smiled. She may hold the healing keys, but Breanna held the keys to the past. She ran her hand across her mouth and reached for the empty bottle, sighed and put it down. Her eyelids drooped.

Someone rapped softly on her door. Candela woke with a start. She got to her feet and cracked the door and peered into the hallway. "Conchetta?" she said, mildly surprised.

"Candela, thank goodness I finally found you. Forgive me. I know it's very early, but I have a friend, Ana." She handed Candela Vincenzo's wine. "Her daughter is dying, and she needs your help."

Chapter 34

Ana and Candela
1930

Ana sat at her kitchen table, flipping through *Tales of Greek Gods & Men* distractedly, praying she'd made the right decision.

Knockknockknockknock.

She got to her feet her and rushed to the door. "Conchetta! My God, where have you been?"

Panting, Conchetta raised her hand in a hold-on-a-minute gesture. She stepped inside and slipped out of her coat while Ana peered into the empty hallway. She closed the door. "Where's Candela? Sugar is worse. Vincenzo just left. He gets home from work in a few hours." She gazed around the room shuddering at the price she'd pay if she failed to clean up before he arrived. But fear of losing Sugar outweighed her fear of anything he could do.

"When I didn't see her on her bench near the elm, I spent hours looking until I found her." Conchetta's face was flushed and sweaty. She pulled out a blue and white kerchief she had tucked between her ample breasts, wiped her brow and collapsed into a kitchen chair that groaned under her weight. Her breathing slowed. "Candela will be here soon," she said, bunching the kerchief in her hand.

Knock. Knock.

Pasting a smile to her face, Conchetta jumped to her feet, bumped Ana, knocking her off balance, opened the door and gasped, "*Signora Testadura?*"

Ana could feel the fake smile slip from Conchetta's face.

"Mama!" Ana clasped her hands. "*Entra. Entra. Per favore.*"

Eyeing Conchetta with clear disdain, Luisa stiffened, lifted her chin in the air, scowled at Conchetta and said, "*Con il tuo permesso.*"

"*Naturalmente, Signora, perdonami,*" Conchetta said. Tripping over her own feet, she stepped aside, wiped her forehead nervously and closed the door behind Luisa Testadura.

"Mama, why are you here?" Ana kissed Luisa's cheek.

"Why am I here? How can you ask such a question? Must I spell it out for you? I am here to see my granddaughter, of course," she sniffed. "I waited next door in Nucciarone's doorway until your animal of a husband walked down the block and out of my sight. Is he working days now?"

"You waited in the funeral parlor for Vincenzo to pass?" Ana giggled.

"Then I saw her," Luisa said, jutting her jaw at Conchetta, "running down the street *come se fosse il diavolo stasso* was chasing her. I followed her into the building right to your door. Instead of you asking me why I am here, I should be asking you why is *she* here? What's going on?"

Knock. Knock.

"Perdonami, Signora," Conchetta said, tripping over herself again to open the door.

A small woman of undetermined age stood in the poorly lit hallway. Bowing her head in the customary show of respect, Conchetta whispered, "Candela. Thank you so much for coming."

Luisa's eyes widened. "Candela?" she whispered. "Are you crazy? Send her away. If your husband finds out—"

"I know, Mama, please," Ana said, feeling the blush to the roots of her hair. She lowered her head and whispered, "Sugar will die if I don't do something."

"But—"

"Please, Mama. Let's not fight. Not now."

"Fine," Luisa said, straightening her shoulders. "I want very much to stay, but I'll leave you and you, she cleared her throat, to your 'guests.' Promise you will send for me if Sugar's condition changes. She nodded at Candela, who did likewise and then left Ana's apartment.

Ana, who had no preconceived notion of the keeper of the keys, did not expect the woman she saw. Candela's pale face seemed etched in lines of concern. Her red, peppered-with-gray hair was pulled back from her face and neatly fastened in a bun at the back of her neck. Most disarming of all were her slate gray eyes with black vertical cracks for pupils—more other worldly than human. Her badly arthritic fingers clutched her black shawl tightly around her slender, arthritic body.

Conchetta extended her hand. Candela reached for it, and her shawl slipped from her shoulders, exposing two large solid gold keys on a solid gold ring.

Gasping, Ana glanced at Candela, whose disarming eyes seemed to widen at her reaction. Her gaze drifting toward the keys, Ana slipped into her chair.

The key ring was hooked to a gold chain around Candela's waist. She gasped at the gold, wafer-thin disk that appeared to hang suspended inside a ring, the size of a silver dollar. The disk was etched with an intricate maze. She followed the maze to its center, sensing that if she stared into it too long, something irrevocable would happen. A mysterious gem in each key seemed to fuse the luster of diamonds, rubies, sapphires and emeralds and disperse it in versions of light and color Ana had never seen. At that moment Ana knew, as well as she knew her name that Conchetta was right. Candela had the power to heal. Candela grasped the keys, and Ana blinked. She frowned at the keeper's fingers. "How can these miracle keys heal everything but the hands that hold them?" she mumbled, distractedly.

"Ana!" Conchetta stammered, "How could you be so ru—" Conchetta stopped abruptly and looked at Candela. "Thank you for coming," she said, wringing her hands, clearly humiliated. "Forgive my friend. She's distraught."

Candela raised her hand. Conchetta's frown eased but her eyes became dull with confusion.

"Conchetta?" Ana frowned, reaching for her friend's hand, but Ana's hand stopped in mid-air, and her puzzled gaze drifted toward Candela. Their eyes met, and Ana fell silent.

There was something unusual about this immigrant woman. Despite perceiving the keys like no other, Ana seemed to regret seeking Candela's help. Of whom or what was she afraid?

Candela took in the small, cramped flat. An unusually high brass bed, a dresser, an icebox, a coal stove. On a shelf above the coal stove stood a framed picture of a handsome man whose dark eyes were devoid of compassion. There was a mound of soiled laundry in the washtub. Dishes piled in the sink were caked with bits of dried, discolored food. She stared at the bedroom doors. Behind one, a young girl of perhaps twelve lay sleeping and burning with fever. Behind the second, a healthy son lay asleep in his bed. Another daughter, the eldest, who did not seem quite right, crouched behind the bedroom door, listening.

"What's the sick child's name?"

Candela spoke in perfect Italian, thinking if she spoke in Ana's tongue she would put Ana at ease.

Ana stood, clasped her hands and tilted her head toward the sick child's room. "We call her Sugar." Candela noted Ana's eyes brighten when she said this child's name. "She has diphtheria. The doctor says..." Her voice trailed off. She blinked back tears and turned her face away.

Candela brushed past Conchetta. "Take me to her."

Conchetta blinked, shook the fog from her eyes and joined them in Sugar's room.

Candela asked, "Where is the child's father?" And the handsome man with cold, cruel eyes in the photo above the coal stove swam past her mind's eye. Ana did not answer. Grazed by a menacing chill, Candela asked, "Where did you say he is?"

Ana frowned, averting her eyes. She grasped her apron and picked at its frayed edges. She dropped her apron and wrung her hands. "No one said Vincenzo had to be here." She smoothed her apron over, folded her arms across her waist and cleared her throat. "He works on the docks in East New York They switch him from nights to days at their whim." She looked into Candela's eyes. "Sugar is Vincenzo's favorite child, but we must eat, so he must work whenever they want."

Conchetta scoffed. Apparently, Ana had lied. No time to ponder why now. Death hovered. Candela needed to act. "You must step outside now," Candela said without looking at Ana.

Ana's eyes glistened, and her shoulders slumped, but she showed no signs of moving. Draping her arm around Ana, Conchetta nudged her out of the room and closed the door behind them. Ana collapsed in Conchetta's arms.

"Candela is Sugar's last chance," Conchetta said, guiding Ana into a kitchen chair.

Dazed, Ana nodded and stared. "I know I'm to blame for every terrible turn my life has taken, but I pray to God that Sugar does not pay the price."

"Nonsense! You've done nothing wrong. You are a good wife and a good mother," Conchetta said. "Candela will heal Sugar. You'll see."

The small, stuffy room was dimly lit. To avoid undue distraction, Candela locked the door behind her and sat by Sugar's side.

The sight of the child alarmed her. Watery blood drained from her nose. She drew back the covers. Sugar was small and fragile. Sweat plastered her nightshirt to her distressingly thin body. Her face was a pale oval with delicate features under a crown of tight, black curls that had been hastily swept upon her head. On each pale cheek was a red dot.

Death's rouge. The end was near.

Out of time, Candela removed the tubing. Sugar gagged and clawed weakly at Candela's hands. Gently restraining the child, she touched Sugar's forehead. Fever raged under her palm. With unwavering confidence in herself and the keys, she unhooked the ring from her belt. "Don't worry," she whispered, "you'll be, as they say, right as rain."

No matter how many times Candela had watched the keys heal, the process continued to excite and amaze her. Standing over Sugar, she took a deep breath, knitted her brow in concentration, grasped the keyring's edge and held the keys inches above Sugar's chest.

The disk began spinning. The gems' mixture of light and color coalesced. The disk picked up speed; the gems burned white and bathed the room in a soft glow.

Sugar's chest began rapidly rising and falling. Candela took Sugar's pulse. The gems pulsed in sync with the runaway beat of the child's heart. Deep in her chest a phlegmy cough rumbled. Her muscles contracted, curling her into a ball. She opened her eyes. "Mama!" she croaked, convulsing with sobs. She coughed up ropy phlegm. Candela sat her up and patted her back hard, dislodging mucous. Through chattering teeth Sugar screamed, *"Mama!"*

A fist *pounded* the door. The knob *twisted.* A ragged voice pleaded, "Open this door." *Pound.* "Now!" *Pound. Pound. Pound.* "Now, damn you!" *Pound. Twist. Twist.*

Candela struggled to stay focused.

"Ana! Stop!" Conchetta whispered, harshly.

Sob. Pound. "Stop, Ana!" *Twist.* "Damn it, Ana! She's the one and only chance we have to save Sugar's life!" Shoes scuffled away from the door. Muffled sobs followed.

The apartment grew eerily silent. The bed began trembling and rose one foot in the air. Candela gasped, watching the normal healing process turn *abnormal.* Her arm weakened, and her fingers trembled. Her eyes widened in disbelief as the keys guided her hand over Sugar's mouth.

The bed set itself down. Her chest and hips arched, Sugar floated in mid-air as if possessed by a marauding, malevolent spirit. Her chin tipped to the ceiling and her mouth was opened wide. In an upward cascade, disease flowed from Sugar's mouth into the keys. The gems turned blood red, painting the room in a red glow.

Sugar's breathing slowed. Her frown relaxed. The disk stopped spinning. Death's rouge began fading from her cheeks. The gems cooled. The red glow ebbed.

Dazed, Candela laid the keys beside Sugar and pressed her ear to her chest. Her lungs sounded clear. Speechless, Candela stared at the keys. Who was this child for the keys to heal her in such a radical and strange manner? Sugar moaned. "You'll be fine now." Candela took the damp compress Ana had left on the small table next to the bed. She wiped the dried blood from Sugar's nose and mouth. Sugar suddenly opened her eyes. They were large, dark and round. Their intense gaze, strangely intimate, held Candela captive.

Sugar raised herself up on her elbows. "Mama?"

The sound of Sugar's voice broke the spell, and Candela blinked. "She's in the kitchen." She moved Sugar's curls away from her forehead. "Lie down, close your eyes. You need rest."

Looking exhausted, Sugar slid back. The moment her head touched the pillow, her lips parted, and her breathing slowed. She licked her lips, revealing one deep dimple in each cheek. Her lashes were thick and black. Her cheeks were as translucent as fine china. Candela's mouth froze in mid-smile seeing…

…a bouquet of black curls, deep, dark round eyes, a broad smile, dimpled cheeks, wild tendrils.

Her heart raced. Dizzy with joy, she blew out a breath as the oddities clicked into place. The resemblance! The bed rising. The keys drawing death from Sugar's body… the room bathed in blood-red.

She did not have to find Breanna—

Breanna had found her!

Elated, her heart soared until pricked like a pin to a balloon. Something phissed from its shredded remains, something she must remember to do upon finding Breanna. Her brows furrowed in concentration, she fastened the key ring to the chain around her waist and got to her feet. The room spun. She staggered toward the door. Taking short ragged breaths, she pressed her head to the jamb and closed her eyes giving thanks that her search had ended before it began: Breanna had been reborn in Ana's daughter.

Knock! Knock! Knock! Twist. Twist.

"Is everything all right?" Ana asked, anxiously.

Candela opened the door. Everything was almost perfect except for the looming question: What was it she needed to do when she found Breanna? Conchetta, who sat at the kitchen table, drinking coffee, put her cup down and looked at Candela who said, "She's out of danger. Food and sleep will do the rest."

Ana stumbled past Candela into Sugar's room. She pressed her lips to Sugar's cheeks. "It's a miracle!" she cried, giggling as though she'd drunk too much wine. She tiptoed out but left Sugar's door open behind her. She sniffled and wiped her eyes on her apron. Clasping her hands, she knelt in front of Candela.

"Thank you so much. How can I repay you?" She looked around the room at her meager belongings. "Take anything you want. Take it all. It's yours."

"There is one thing."

"Anything."

When Conchetta opened her mouth, Candela pressed her finger to her own lips. Conchetta fell silent. Her shoulders slumped, and her eyelids fluttered until her eyes went blank and ceased to perceive.

Candela grasped Ana's hands, and lifted her to her feet. She was far too young for her dark hair to be streaked with so much gray. Her face would be pleasant if it wasn't so tight with worry. A veil of sadness clouded her eyes. The floral print dress, faded from too many scrubbings, failed to hide the bruise on her upper arm. Her hands must feel exactly as they and she looked – rough and warn beyond her years. Candela refused to leave Breanna in Ana's care without knowing her well.

Ana gazed into the cool, slate gray of Candela's eyes. Her arms slackened. Her breathing slowed.

Candela closed her eyes and saw …

Ana's soul riddled with potholes, gouged of memories too painful to bear. A dark, oppressive force coiled her heart like a snake. The picture above the coal stove swam into view again.

Vincenzo.

She must purge the terror from this good woman's soul that this man evoked. She must purge him from Ana's life. But she knows she must never go beyond healing. If she interferes in the lives she touches, she would change the course of their fates, and they would pay dearly.

Change the course of whose fate? Hers? Breanna's? Ana's? She opened her eyes and looked in Ana's. Behind the sadness were kind, honest eyes. "Do you have other children?".

"Eight," Ana said. "I mean I gave birth to eight. Seven girls and one boy. I lost five girls. One was stillborn. Four died from sickness. Luisa, my oldest, Sugar, and Johnny, my youngest are all I have left.

"I've tried to make peace with their loss, but my own children are not the only loved ones I've lost. I'm one of eight," Ana volunteered, appearing to smile a little too brightly. "Three of my sisters died young." Her smile faded, aging her face. "Three stayed in *Sicilia* with their husbands and children. My brother Tonio and I came to America with Mama and Papa." Her eyes shimmered. "Mama and I write to them, I check the mail every day, but they never answer me."

Candela saw *Vincenzo pull a letter from his pocket and toss it into the coal stove behind Ana's back.*

Ana smiled weakly, "My mother was a seventh daughter, and I am my mother's seventh daughter."

"You were the seventh daughter of a ..." Her voice fading, Candela ransacked the remote corners of her mind where she harbored old memories. Thank goodness the oldest memories were the last to go.

"Whenever I felt sad as a child, Papa would say that as the seventh daughter of a seventh," her voice trailed off. "Is something wrong?" Ana said, looking worried.

"Of course not," Candela said distractedly.

"Papa used to say that as the seventh of a seventh, I was special and blessed in more ways than I could imagine." Smiling, Ana glanced over her shoulder at Sugar.

Seven. Candela frowned hard. That number continued to surface. It meant something important. Beneath the din of Ana's voice, Candela tore through the archives in her mind, desperate to retrieve all they stored about sevens. Seven colors in the rainbow. Seven notes in a diatonic scale. Seven deadly Roman Catholic sins. Seven numbers in the Roman ... numeral ... system. Seven hills of Rome. Seven branches on Hangman's Elm.

Two ... glowed with their own light. Five remained draped in shadows

"Ironically, Sugar is my seventh daughter as well ..."

Seventh daughters are not a common occurrence. But Septissima, a third generation of sevenths with power that might rival your power?

194

For that little miracle, Breanna," Candela scoffed, *you'd need help from father.*

Help from father? Whose father? *Their ...* father?

Candela's mind reeled, and her tongue swelled with such thirst, she would hock the keys for a bottle of wine. "Ana?" The word croaked out in a dusty rasp. She rubbed a shaky hand across her mouth. "When was Sugar born?"

"Midnight, October thirty-first nineteen eighteen."

Eve of All Hallows.

Shaken, Candela bumped into the kitchen table, knocking a book to the floor. *Tales of Greek Gods & Men.* On the cover a Greek God was holding a lyre. Slung over his shoulder were a bow and a quiver of arrows. Around his waist two gold keys hanging on a gold chain. *Her keys.*

Were there keys on her own book cover? She'd looked at that cover hundreds of times. Why couldn't she remember?

"That was my favorite book," Ana said, bending to pick up the book. "Apollo is my favorite Greek God." She hugged the book to her. "As a child on our farm in Sicily, I would sit by a stream under a big elm in our backyard and read this book every chance I got."

Apollo. God of Light, Music, Archery, Poetry. Prophecy and the art of ... *healing.*

For that little miracle ... you'd need father's help.

Apollo. Their father, Candela's and Breanna's, was Apollo. Greek God of Healing?

Her eyes welled with shock. This was not possible. From the bottom of a long dark tunnel, she heard Ana say, "Candela, what's wrong?"

Conchetta's eyes fluttered. She shook her head, and she yawned as if waking from a fitful sleep.

Thirst raging, Candela mumbled, "My work here is done," and made her way out of Ana's apartment.

Chapter 35

Candela

Drowning in a flood of confusion, Candela hugged the wall and made her way shakily down the stairs and out the door. She leaned against Ana's building, gulping in mouthfuls of night air. In a few short hours a bizarre turn of events had blown what she thought was her life to bits. She licked her lips, rubbed her hand over her mouth, and headed for home as quickly as her arthritic legs allowed, but her mind had beaten her to it. She envisioned the empty bottle on her table and stopped.

Damn prohibition. Damn the eighteenth amendment and the Volstead Act. She hoped that by her next life people would come to their senses and repeal both. Craving a drink, she remembered that Conchetta had brought her a bottle as payment in advance for healing Sugar. It was on her table where she'd left it. Her composure regained, she took a step.

In vino veritas, in aqua sanitas.

In wine there is truth, in water there is health. What were those words supposed to mean? She limped down Sullivan Street, muttering in disgust. "Words are merely sounds men make by forcing air from the lungs through the voice box. Once spat out they are gone, dissipated into nothingness."

In vino veritas, in aqua sanitas refused to be spat out, and they wouldn't wash down without wine. They spoke to her in Latin. A dead language. Dead or alive, if she'd never learned Latin, why did she understand it? Another word whose Latin letters floated like dandelion wisps tangled in the wind. She frowned hard collecting them. "Damn it! What did they spell?"

Septissima. A superlative of seven.

Of course, a Septissima would be the most desirable, strongest, most potent vessel of all.

Desirable? Strongest? According to whom and why?

Ironically ... Sugar ... my seventh daughter ... was born at the stroke of midnight October thirty-first nineteen eighteen.

That afternoon the elm's shadows had danced in such excitation, making Candela more anxious than usual. Exhausted, she'd fallen onto her bed and into an odd dream.

The wind howled like a pack of wolves rattling some trash cans and knocking over others. It whipped through trees and streets, sweeping debris from alleys and smashing them into a familiar doorway. On the third landing in a dirty hallway, bathed in sweat and tears Ana cried out in pain, and ...

Breanna was born.

Candela stood in her doorway unable to move as pieces of the unknown moved into place. *Tales of Greek Gods & Men* was Ana's favorite book. She'd read it under an elm by a stream in the same way Candela had read hers under Hangman's Elm. Only the streams differed. Ana's flowed by her elm. *Manata,* devil water, flowed under Candela's elm. Her head throbbed. Perhaps most of this made no sense because key pieces were missing.

... Never taking her eyes from the keys, Ana slipped into her chair.

Ana and Sugar were the keys. Relieved, Candela giggled at the pun, surprising herself. Sugar was too sick and too young to question. She must speak to Ana. The sooner the better.

Hungrier than she'd been in days, Candela slammed her door behind her, opened her icebox and grabbed a wedge of parmesan cheese. She tore a hunk of bread from a loaf on top of the icebox and put the bread and cheese next to a knife on a cutting board on the table. She slipped into her chair and picked up the knife. Ignoring the pain in her hand, she cut off a piece of cheese and popped the cheese and bread in her mouth. Chewing contemplatively, she reached for the wine. Frowning hard, she put the bottle to her lips, took a large swallow and wiped her lips on the back of her hand.

The past ... never stays buried. Reincarnation.

Heady with wine and revelation, she took another swig. Pooled in her lap were the keys and chain. She'd often wondered why there were two. Did one belong to her sister, Breanna? She smiled and sliced another hunk of cheese, winced and dropped the knife. Her eyes welled with a sharp pain accompanied by a sharper revelation. If the keys were in Breanna's hands, could Breanna heal her?

She got to her feet, slowly. The room started spinning. On her way to her dresser for a nightgown, she saw herself in the mirror on the wall opposite her bed. Old eyes in a face seamed with lines and mottled with age stared back. She frowned at this woman, this bag of crippled-with-pain bones.

How can these miracle keys heal everything but the hands that hold them?

Ana had seen the irony. More proof that Ana, Sugar and she were inextricably bound in some great mystery from which one indisputable fact had emerged: She and her sister, Breanna, had come together again in this life. Why now? Sugar was a child. And goddess or not, Candela was a very old woman. Had they been brought together again only to be ripped apart?

Frustrated, she lifted the mirror off the wall, flung it across the room, cried out in pain and sank to her knees. Tracks of tears crisscrossing the lines in her face, she pounded the floor with her fists. Pain shot past her elbow and shoulder into her jaw. Broken glass bit into her hand like hundreds of crystal teeth. Panting, she grabbed the edge of her bed, got to her feet and stumbled to the sink. She rinsed her hands, gently extracting glass.

The keys clanged against the sink. She turned off the faucet. It was early, but she was exhausted. She slipped out of her clothes and into her nightgown. Before going to bed, she usually put the keys in the box and stored the box in the vault under her window. Tonight she would sleep with the keys close to her heart. She pictured Sugar and frowned. Whatever deed she must do when she found Breanna nagged like a toothache. Images rolled through her mind. One froze on the shelf above Ana's coal stove. Her heart raced. Vincenzo was clearly a monster whose path she was destined to cross.

Of course a Septissima would be the most desirable, strongest, most potent vessel of all.

Her body was beyond exhaustion. Her eyes fluttered with fatigue, but one thought kept her eyes wide and her mind on high alert. She knew from *Tales of Greek Gods & Men* that while sevenths of sevenths had great power, the third generation, *Septissima,* had the greatest power of all. Yet, she'd sensed no power great or small in Ana or Sugar. And, if they had this power, why hadn't they used it against Vincenzo?

Chapter 36

Conchetta Juliani
1932

"I know it seems like it happened a long time ago, but I can't stop thinking about it. You had to be there, Frank. The moment Candela set foot in Ana's apartment that morning, Ana ignored me completely." Conchetta set a piping hot bowl of lentil soup in front of her husband, who sighed and shook his head. "And after all that I've done for Candela she ignored me, too." Conchetta murmured.

"*Gesu Cristo,* Conchetta. It doesn't *seem* like it happened a long time ago, it *did* happen a long time ago, two years to be exact. Will you please stop harping on it?" Frank said, annoyed.

"That's just the thing, Frank. I can't." Her eyes darkening with the memory, Conchetta set one bowl of soup at her place and another in front of her son, Matteo. She swept her housedress under her voluminous thighs and sat. She placed a napkin on her lap, dipped her spoon into her soup and blew.

"And besides, that's not the way it was supposed to happen, Frank" Conchetta sipped her soup and frowned. Instead of paying attention to her, Frank was watching their son whose dark eyes grew darker with every word she spoke, but she could not stop. "I had to bite my tongue to keep from reminding them." She felt her cheeks heat up with the anger that forever burned behind her eyes. "If Ana had slapped my face, she could not have been more disrespectful."

Conchetta put her spoon down. "Did they realize what I risked defying Dr. Robilatto and the American Board of Health to convince Ana to send for Candela? Do you even realize it? *I,*" she poked her chest, "was the broker. *I* spoke for Ana. *I,*" she poked harder, "got Candela to agree to see Sugar. If it wasn't for *me,*" she poked hardest of all and coughed, "Sugar would be dead."

Frank sighed louder, picked up his spoon, looked the table over and said, "Where's the grated cheese?"

Conchetta got to her feet. "I pour out my heart, and you ask for grated cheese? Have you not heard a word I said?"

"What I heard two years ago and what I've heard twice a week since is a woman who insists on acting like a spoiled child." Frank dipped his spoon into his soup and shoveled lentils into his mouth.

Conchetta slipped into her seat. "You're wrong, Frank. As far as I'm concerned, Ana's insulting behavior that day in front of Candela changed something between us forever."

"Do you know what I wish?" Matteo blurted. "I wish Sugar was sick again, but this time I wish she would die."

Choking on his soup, Frank jumped to his feet, grabbed his napkin and coughed into it.

"Matteo, how could you say such a thing?" Conchetta gasped.

"How?" Frank yelled between coughing and clearing his throat. "You must be joking." His eyes watered, and he coughed hard into his napkin. "It's as plain as the moon in the sky. He gets it from you."

"Me?" Completely astounded, Conchetta stood up.

"Stop it, both of you!" Matteo said, slamming his fist on the table and squeezing his eyes shut. He opened his eyes and glared at Conchetta. "Mama, I keep hearing you say the same thing over and over again!" He stood up fast enough to knock his chair over. He picked it up, set it in place and then walked out of the kitchen.

"Matteo!"

Unaccustomed to hearing his father raise his voice, Matteo stopped, turned and faced them.

"Get back here and tell your mother and me what made you say that terrible thing about Sugar."

The muscle in Matt's cheek twitched. "I'm sorry, Papa," he said, choking the words out. "I need some fresh air." He grabbed his coat from a hook on the wall and shut the door behind him.

"Matteo!" Frank yelled louder, and then glared at Conchetta.

"It's Matt," Conchetta said.

"What?" Frank said, sounding aggravated. "What are you talking about?" he said, looking bewildered.

Conchetta grabbed her napkin. "It's Matt," she repeated, squeezing the napkin in her fist. "Sugar told Matteo that we live in America and that he should start telling people to call him Matt." She threw the wadded napkin on the table.

By the wave of Frank's hand, Conchetta knew that he had abandoned the subject of what Matteo called himself for the present.

"Are you going after him?"

"I don't need to go after him," Frank said. "You're the reason Matteo said what he did about Sugar."

"What? How dare you." She was appalled.

"For God's sake, Conchetta, listen to how you talk about Ana and Sugar. Every day for two years and counting, you've been setting a terrible example. For once in your life would you stop and think before you open your mouth. You are his mother, and what you say influences him far more than you think. You should be protecting him and guiding his thinking."

Conchetta sat and closed her eyes. A tear squeezed through her lashes and rolled down her cheek. She opened her eyes and picked up Matteo's napkin. "Frank, can't you see that I *am* trying to protect him." She sniffled and dabbed her cheek and then threw her napkin on the table.

"By getting him to wish the same thing you do, that Sugar was dead?"

"You know that I don't really wish she was dead, it's just ..." Conchetta's voice trailed off. She picked up her napkin and dabbed at another tear.

"It's just ... what? Finish your thought. Get it out or it will fester."

"Frank. You go to work every day. You don't know or see half of what goes on here."

"Well, tell me the half I don't know."

"Fine. You see the way he acted tonight? Matteo comes home from school every day, either depressed or elated, depending on how Sugar has treated him or whether she's thrown him over for another boy, which happens about twice a month."

Frank sighed. "They're children, Conchetta. Being a child means being fickle. It won't be the first time some girl breaks his heart, and it won't be the last."

"That's not all, Frank. There's something else. Ever since Candela healed her, Sugar," she frowned, "is different."

"Different?" Frank said, frowning. "What do you mean?"

"In addition to breaking his heart every other week, she's bossy. She orders him around like a servant or a slave. She's moody and she takes her moods out on him. And what makes him unhappy makes me unhappy. You know what they say, Frank, you're only as happy as your unhappiest child."

Frank exhaled an I-give-up sigh and said, "From where I sit, what you are saying sounds exactly like the same complaint all your friends with daughters Sugar's age have." He looked at the table. "And where the hell is my grated cheese?"

Conchetta got to her feet, yanked the icebox door open, grabbed a wedge of cheese and slammed the door shut. She grabbed the grater from a drawer next to the sink, dug her nails into the wedge and grated the cheese into Frank's soup. She suddenly stopped grating, stared blankly at the melting cheese and frowned hard. Something had happened at Ana's that day. She lost time that she could not account for. The harder she tried to remember, the bigger the blank spot became, and it still drove her crazy.

"Conchetta," Frank said pointing at his plate. "Are you finished grating yet?"

She blinked, shrugged, tapped the wedge against the grater and shook the remaining shreds into Frank's bowl.

"Well, what you said completely contradicts what Matteo told me," Frank paused and looked at the ceiling. "I believe it was yesterday." He looked at Conchetta. "Yesterday Matt said that Sugar and he loved each other and that when they grow up they're getting married."

The cheese and grater slipped from Conchetta's hands into Frank's bowl. Soup spattered. Brown stars dotted Frank's shirt. A brown puddle seeped through the white tablecloth.

"This is your fault," Conchetta said.

Clearly perplexed, Frank said, "What are you talking about?"

"He wouldn't get ideas about marrying Sugar if you didn't encourage him."

"What ideas? So, he's got a crush on a girl. What healthy, normal fourteen-year-old doesn't?"

Conchetta's eyes widened and Frank cleared his throat.

"And how did you respond to him?" Conchetta said, bristling.

"I said, Matteo, this is America. Your mother and I came here so that you could step outside that door and make your dreams come true. I only wish my parents, God rest their souls," he made the sign of the cross, "had been able to do the same for me. Now this is the plan. You go to school. Get an education, a good job and then you get married. And then I said ... "

Frank droned on, and Conchetta closed her eyes as the seed of a headache germinated in the caverns of her mind. Frank's advice, although well-intentioned was pitiful, and of course, he never mentioned Sugar. Didn't Frank realize that this wasn't a crush? Couldn't he see that Ana's daughter had cast a spell on her son? And

Sugar? She has her clutches too deeply into Matteo, and Conchetta vowed to change that very soon. Someday Sugar was going to steal the fruit of her womb, fruit as precious as the Blessed Mother's unless, her eyes narrowed. "Unless I stop her."

"Did you say something?" Frank said.

"Eat, before your soup gets cold."

Later that night after Matteo came home, apologized and went to bed, Conchetta tiptoed to his door and listened. Hearing his rhythmic breathing, she clicked his bedroom door closed. "The thought of my son marrying Ana's daughter eats at my guts," she said, joining Frank on the couch.

Frank held the newspaper in front of his face. "You have to calm down," he said, scanning the front page. "You're making too much of this. They're just children. This is America—"

"Yes, and because this is America," she whispered, cutting him off, "Sugar has decided that my Matteo, named for my papa, should call himself Matt, to fit in."

Frank sighed, heavily. "Conchetta, this is America, and these are modern times. Kids grow up here doing things we never did in the old country." He turned the page.

Frank's words chafed her heart like flint against stone. "You can't talk me out of my feelings. I bore him. I'm connected to him in a way you never were and never will be. I know what's best for him. Better than you or anyone ever will."

Frank put the paper down, massaged the bridge of his nose and stared at his wife through bleary eyes. "For God's sake, Conchetta, can't you see that even with our approval, they couldn't get married for years. They may think they're in love now, but five years from now?"

"Frank—"

He held up his hand, and she stopped talking. "You should be on your knees thanking God that it's Sugar he thinks he loves. It could be worse."

"Tell me how. Please. I'm dying to know."

"If he married an outsider instead, he'd forget the old ways. He'd forget customs and language. And their children won't know where they came from, where they belong or who they belong to."

He was right, damn him. In the old country there were no outsiders. Only people from different parts of the same place. In the old country children were buried in the same place they were born. In America the outside world was a train ride away and there was a station every few blocks.

"Conchetta." He put his arm around her. "There are good and bad sides to everything. Ana comes from good, decent people, one of the best families in the old country," he smiled.

"But—"

"But nothing!" Frank raised his hand, silencing his wife. "Ana does not come from people who are mixed up with the criminal element either here or in the old country."

Conchetta wiped her cheeks. "You forget about Vincenzo." She looked into Frank's eyes. "He's a crazy, brutal man. People who live in their building hear things. What affect does Vincenzo have on the girl my son wants to marry?"

Frank opened his mouth, but nothing came out. For once it appeared that her wise, forgiving man had no answer.

"Remember when we moved into this neighborhood," she said, rolling the newspaper into a core, "and Mariana Triani introduced herself to me at the market?"

"Yes." Frank sighed and closed his eyes.

"Remember I told you how she'd warned me about Vincenzo?" Conchetta twisted the newspaper in her hands. "The way she described him chills me to this day." She looked into Frank's eyes. "Mariana said, 'He's strange and dark, that one. He traveled with us on the ship. To this day our men have nothing to do with him.' But she never said why. I wanted to know, but I never asked, Frank. I swear. I felt that if Ana needed to tell me about her life, she would." Conchetta twisted the newspaper tighter. "But, she didn't have to say a word. Her bruises and her eyes said it all." Conchetta's chin trembled and she closed her eyes.

Frank took the paper from her hands and stuffed it between the pillow and the arm of the couch and hugged her.

Nestling against him, she felt his heart beating under her hand. "How could I turn my back on Ana and still look myself in the mirror each day?" Conchetta said. Frank sighed and pressed his cheek against her forehead. "Damn! If only I'd met Mariana and the other women before I met Ana that day in the park, none of this would be happening!"

"And so we find ourselves on familiar ground," he said softly. "You must forget about 'if only.' I believe Matteo and Sugar would have met no matter who had befriended you first. They go to the same school."

Conchetta closed her ears to him. What in God's name made her convince Ana to send for Candela that day? If she'd kept her mouth shut, Sugar would be dead. Conchetta shivered and closed her eyes. Dear God. Conchetta wondered how she could be so hateful! Her eyes narrowed, because she was a mother whose first instinct was to protect her son.

Damn Ana! This thing between Matteo and Sugar was all her fault. All of it! Conchetta vowed to make it her business to see Ana tomorrow, and when she did, she would give Ana a piece of her mind.

Chapter 37

Ana and Conchetta
1932

"It's getting late, Luisa," Ana said as she and Luisa turned the corner from Houston onto Sullivan Street. "If we get to Punziano's and pick up the groceries I need for supper now, I will have enough time to get back and have dinner ready before Papa gets home."

Halfway down the block Ana saw Mr. Punziano under his store awning adding potatoes and onions to wooden bins. Picking up their pace, Luisa and she hurried past two vacant store fronts, Nania's Bakery and Capiello's Shoe Repair, and stopped in front of the grocery store.

"Good afternoon, Mr. Punziano," Ana said, joining him under the grocery story awning.

"Good afternoon, Ana, and good afternoon to you, too, Luisa," Mr. Punziano said, smiling. "My goodness," he said, "you look lovelier every time I see you."

Luisa blushed, and smiling shyly, she averted her eyes.

Ana cleared her throat and took two brown paper bags from a shelf near the stalls. "Luisa, sweetheart, would you take this and fill it with five nice potatoes and three onions?"

Luisa nodded, took the bags, turned on her heel and did as she was told.

"She is such a beautiful girl," Mr. Punziano said, as always.

The implication being, what a pity she's not ... normal. Ana watched him watching Luisa. Continuing to smile he turned and faced her, and for one second, she wanted to claw that smile off his face, but the second passed taking her harsh reaction with it. She smiled and said, "Thank you." He was a good man and she knew he meant well. Those in the neighborhood who smiled at her with pity in their eyes meant well, too. But after twenty-six years of seeing the neighborhood people look at Luisa in 'that way' and being forced fed their pity she wanted to scream. Ticking off the items she needed, she followed Mr. Punziano into the store and said, "I'll take a pound of coffee, two pounds of sugar and—"

"I'm sorry, Ana," Mr. Punziano said, glancing out the store window at Luisa who was examining each potato diligently before placing it into the paper bag. "I'm afraid I can't extend your credit until you settle your bill."

"What?" Ana said, turning whiter than the flour she'd planned to ask for next. Her temples pounded. "I don't understand. You know my credit is good."

"Well," he sighed, shifting his stance uncomfortably, "it was. I mean it is, but if you can't pay me what you owe me now," he said. His voice trailing off, he held his arms out with his palms turned upward and slowly shook his head.

"Please, Mr. Punziano, would you reconsider? As soon as my husband gets paid, I swear I will pay you what I owe."

"You said that last time, Ana."

"I know, but something came up and I ran short." Her mind raced down every possible avenue, but none led to the kind of money she needed to settle her bill. "Vincenzo gets paid next Friday. I'll settle with you on Saturday."

If Vincenzo found out she was working behind his back, losing every cent that she had worked her fingers numb earning would be the least of her worries.

Her heart raced harder. If she used the money she had left from the pittance Vincenzo gave her, it still wouldn't be enough. If she borrowed from Mama and tightened her belt as well, she might make it. "Mr. Punziano," Ana said, as the pounding in her temples subsided, "I'll be back this afternoon with some of the money, and I will bring you the rest tomorrow."

Ignoring the heat she felt in her cheeks, Ana hurried out the door. "Luisa, put the bags down. We must leave now." She turned and bumped into Conchetta.

"Well, well, Ana. I'm glad I ran into you. There's something we need to talk about."

"I'm sorry, Conchetta. I can't talk now. I'm in a hurry. I forgot my money at home." The lie turned the taste on her tongue rancid. "By the time I get my money, come to pick up what I need for supper and get home again Vincenzo will—"

Conchetta grabbed Ana's arm. "I'm sorry, Ana, but today, Vincenzo's supper will have to wait. I need to talk to you about Sugar and Matteo. I have no time to waste, so I'll get right to the point. Ever since Candela healed Sugar, Sugar has changed. She's … just … different," Conchetta said, letting Ana go.

"What do you mean, different?" Ana said, feeling beads of sweat pearl at her hairline.

"Don't be coy with me. You know very well what I mean," Conchetta spat. "I see it in your eyes. My son's moods rise and fall like a roller coaster at the World's Fair. Do you know why? Because Sugar picks fights with him every other day. I bet you didn't know, that besides dressing like the little … the little …" Conchetta held her hand horizontal to her mouth and bit down index finger, "that she really is, your precious daughter skips school. And I don't give a care about her or that, but Matteo cuts school with her. His grades are poor and…"

Luisa clutched Ana's arm. With every charge Conchetta leveled, Luisa squeezed Ana's arm tighter. Ana looked at Luisa and gasped. She looked as sick at heart as Ana felt. As much as it pained her to hear, Conchetta was saying what Ana had known for years but was too scared to face: Sugar *had* changed. She was not the same girl she had been before Candela healed her.

There were periods of time that Sugar seemed like her old self. But the duration and frequency of those periods were unpredictable. At first the changes were gradual. Sugar seemed restless and dissatisfied. She no longer enjoyed the things she used to. Her moods were erratic. They swung from even-tempered to argumentative. As much as Ana hated to admit it, Conchetta was right about Matteo. The more Sugar changed, the more Matteo, who had been good natured and forgiving like Frank, had changed along with her. Sugar may have fought with Matteo, but she fought with Johnny, too. Generous to a fault before the healing, she became selfish to a flaw after. She'd made it painfully clear that she wanted Luisa out of her bedroom. From the few conversations Ana had had with other women, she'd learned that these changes were "juvenile storms" of sorts that simply needed to run their course. But Sugar's storms seemed to grow in number and intensity, and they seemed to sweep across boundaries that, at Sugar's age, the headstrong Ana could never have imagined. She stopped seeing her old friends, including her best friend, Chiara Triani, and she showed no interest in finding new friends.

"But worst of all," Conchetta said, panting with emotion, "she carries on with other boys right in front of my poor," she sobbed, choking out, "Matteo."

"That is a lie. Sugar would never do that," Ana said. "She has loved him from the moment they met." Ana loved Matteo as if he were her own. She was happy and almost relieved that Matteo and Sugar were 'friends.'

"You've got to do something," Conchetta said, grabbing Ana's other arm. "Have you talked to Candela?"

"Of course I have," Ana said, pulling her arm free.

"Ah. So you admit that I'm speaking the truth!"

Ignoring the comment, Ana said, "I risk my life visiting Candela every chance I got for the longest time, begging her to help me."

"And?"

"I know Candela wants to help. I see it in her eyes, but she keeps insisting that if she interferes, she will set very bad things in motion that she will not have the power to stop."

"That is crazy talk. What does it even mean?

"Damn it, Ana! Sugar is your daughter. You must control her before she breaks my Matteo's heart for good." Conchetta frowned and stopped abruptly. "What about Vincenzo?"

Those three words struck like bullets. Luisa gasped. Ana froze.

"What about him?" Ana said harshly.

By the surprised look in Conchetta's eyes it was obvious that Conchetta realized she'd shot off her mouth without thinking, as usual.

"I mean," Conchetta stammered, "has he noticed the change in Sugar, too?"

"And if he hasn't," Ana said, tears welling in her eyes, "are you asking me to tell him so that he will punish her? Is that what you're saying?"

Conchetta gasped and took a step back.

"How dare you!" Ana said, feeling Luisa stiffen beside her. "You know what Vincenzo is capable of," Ana said, nose to nose with Conchetta. "I have bruises in places you can't see, yet you would want this brutal, monster to do to my child what he does to me to protect your son?" Ana pried Luisa's fingers from her forearm and grasped her hand. Her mind racing, she said, "You can go straight to hell, Conchetta Juliani!" She turned and hurried down the street dragging Luisa behind her.

Struggling to keep up with her mother, Luisa tripped and fell. Ana slowed down. Her temper cooled, and she helped Luisa to her feet. "I'm sorry, Luisa. Sometimes that woman makes me so angry I can't see straight." Suddenly, Ana realized that as vile and as outrageous as

Conchetta's suggestions were, Conchetta had raised a valid point. Very little got past Vincenzo. She could tell by the way he looked at Sugar, he knew she was different. He'd punished the others for less, yet he chose to ignore her. Why?

And then she realized that however much Vincenzo hated his children, he hated his wife more. What better way to worsen the hell that was her life than by watching Ana watch Sugar ruin her life?

"That bastard!" Ana said, panting as she ran up the steps to her apartment. She took the key out of her purse and opened the door. "Luisa," she said, as she pulled the box of powder puffs and tassels out from under her bed in the parlor and retrieved a tin can containing some bills and some coins.

"Go to your room and don't open that door until you hear my voice," she said, shoving the box back under the bed.

"No, Mama, please," Luisa begged, clearly terrified. "Don't leave me alone. What if Papa comes home?"

"I'll be back before that, I promise you," Ana said, her heart breaking in two. "Do what I say."

Thanking Mr. Punziano for his generosity and understanding, Ana took one shopping bag in each hand, hurried out of the grocery store and started down Houston Street when she saw Matteo exit from the vacant store front next to Nania's Bakery. She stopped and put her shopping bags down.

"Matteo. Wait. Can you help ..." she said. Her voice trailing off, Ana frowned.

Head down, hands jammed deep in his pockets, and shoulders hunched. Matt looked more upset than she'd ever seen. He obviously didn't hear her. He hurried up Houston Street and turned onto Sullivan. Wondering what could have troubled him so, she picked up her bags, walked to the store front and peered in. Gasping, she dropped her bags, not believing her eyes.

Sugar stood in the doorway, dressed in clothes that Ana had never seen before, kissing a boy Ana did not recognize. Their hands were all over each other.

"Sugar!" Ana cried.

Sugar gasped and pushed the boy away. In a face caked with makeup her eyes widened in surprise, and for an instant she looked as if she might cry. Instead, the look in her eyes ... *changed.*

"Hello, Mama," she said. On lips smeared in red her smile grew as distant and cold as the remotest star in the sky.

"'Mama?" The boy said, smirking. He glanced from Ana to Sugar, and the smirk slipped from his face. "No shit, Sugar. She's your mother?"

His confusion must have struck Sugar as funny, because she laughed hard. The boy rushed past Ana, and Sugar began laughing so hard, she clearly could not catch her breath.

"My God," Ana said, "Conchetta was right about you. Look at you! *Sei vestito come una prostituta!* Why? How could you hurt Matteo or your family like this?" she said, her chin trembling with anger. "You make me feel so ashamed I could die."

Sugar straightened up. Her eyes wide with tears that streaked her makeup, she staggered into Ana's arms sobbing, "I'm sorry, Mama. I'm sorry. I'm sorry, I'm sorry," she cried, again and again like a phonograph needle stuck in a nightmare groove.

Chapter 38

Ana
1935

Ana sat on Luisa's bed watching her sleep and thinking. Three years had passed, and she still could not obliterate the image of Sugar and that boy from her mind. But on that day another strange wrinkle appeared in the fabric of Sugar's life. Sugar had insisted to the point of hysteria that she wasn't the one who'd kissed that boy in the storefront that day. She kept begging and pleading with Ana to believe her. The sincerity in her voice had broken Ana's heart, but as much as Ana had wanted, she couldn't deny what she'd seen with her own eyes. As the days rolled into weeks and months the incident faded, and except for an occasional bump in the road, Sugar had returned to a normal state of mind.

A normal ... state of mind? Was that it? Was Sugar mentally ill? God forgive her, but one mentally disturbed child had been more than enough to bear.

A new layer of terror shrouding her heart, Ana conjured visions of Bellevue, the oldest hospital in the country and the last resort of the poor, especially poor immigrants. There were rumors that Bellevue had never turned anyone away. God knows what went on behind its doors.

"Mama?" Luisa whimpered.

Shivering the image of Bellevue off, Ana cursed the demons that continued to haunt Luisa's dreams. She kissed her gently and coaxed her back to sleep. She slipped out of the room, eased the door closed, closed her eyes and leaned on the door frame. Luisa was twenty-nine years old with the mind of a fourteen-year old. "Who would take care of her after I die?" Ana wondered.

She sighed, turned up the gas under the coffee pot and refilled her cup. She sat at the table and watched the morning sun scour light through the grimy window. Mornings were hardest of all. Each day forged another link in the chain of days she bore to atone for her sins. She cooked Vincenzo's meals, cleaned his house, and when he forced himself on her, she retreated to a place beyond revulsion. A place where she'd carved her goal in stone. Somehow, someday, no matter how long it took, she would set herself and her children free. She owed it to them and to herself.

Her heart ached for Johnny, her only son. She put her cup down and closed her eyes. Vincenzo had denigrated Johnny and had beaten him into submission as a young child. The older and angrier Johnny got, the more withdrawn he became and the further he strayed. He was only sixteen and when there was talk on the street about those who had given him a 'job,' knowing what that meant, she realized that she had failed him, too. If her children had grown up with parents like Papa and Mama, how different their lives would be. The pain of losing Papa still pulsed with every beat of her heart. When Mama contracted diphtheria two years ago, Ana relived the terror she'd faced with Sugar. She'd sent for Candela and then prayed until her head throbbed. Candela did everything she could, but she could not save Mama.

Missing Mama, Papa and *Sicilia* today more than usual, Ana reached under the dresser next to her bed and pulled out a large tin box. She set it on the table and lifted the lid. *Tales of Greek Gods & Men* swam before her eyes, her silly, beloved book that once upon an eon had almost convinced a foolish, arrogant girl she might be a goddess. She'd last felt her 'power' the night she'd saved Luisa's life.

Life in *Sicilia* belonged to a past that no longer existed. For her. But the chains of the past that bound her had bound her *paisano* as well. These women looked at Ana Sciorri, but they still saw Ana Testadura. And she couldn't blame them. She should be thankful. She still had one friend, Conchetta, whose friendship she'd almost lost three years ago.

That night, after lying awake sick at heart and desperate to make amends, the next day Ana had searched every street and alley until she'd found Conchetta. After Ana had humiliated herself by apologizing publicly, Conchetta agreed to forgive her if and only if Ana swore that Conchetta had told the truth about Sugar. Reluctantly, Ana agreed.

On one hand, as a mother, Ana understood that Conchetta worshipped the ground Matteo walked on and would go to any length to protect him. On the other, Conchetta was a spoiled childish, silly, selfish woman who took Frank's generous nature for granted. But to be fair, hadn't Sugar treated Matteo the same way? Unlike Conchetta, who'd spent every waking hour scheming to split their children apart, Ana had spent that time praying that they would marry sooner rather than later. Ana used to believe that Sugar and Matteo were meant to be, but ever since the healing, she wasn't as sure. Doubts and conflict aside, one thing was clear: Matteo and Sugar were children with adult temptations. If history repeated, Sugar would be permanently stained with shame and disgrace. Ana set her cup down wondering if what the Bible said was so. Would the sins of the mother be visited upon the hearts and souls of her children, and would those sins cost them their friends? Before the incident Ana had been able to get past Conchetta's cold eyes and forced smile. But after? Friends, she scoffed. Perhaps she was not meant to have them. Her first and best friend's betrayal had ripped out her heart. She'd forgiven Rosa long ago, God rest her soul, but try as she might, Ana could not forget.

Another fear that kept her awake nights surfaced. Had Mama, Papa and Rosa lived, they would never have breathed one word of truth about Luisa. But Vincenzo would relish confessing her sins to Sugar and Johnny. She could see it in his eyes. It was just a matter of time.

Closing the lid on the book and the past, she slid the box under the dresser and said, "I ache with failing Luisa and Johnny, but I cannot," she clenched her jaws and her fist, "I cannot, I will not fail Sugar."

Knock! Knock!

Pulled from her thoughts, Ana gasped.

"Ana? It's me, Bertie."

Knock! Knock!

"Ana, please, I know you're in there. I heard you moving around. Open the door. I need to speak to you about Candela."

Ana opened the door and frowned at Bertie. "Is Candela all right?"

"For the moment," Bertie said, brushing past Ana. "I'm worried about her safety."

Ana frowned as if she hadn't heard correctly. She closed the door and said, "Sit down, Bertie. Can I get you something? Tea? Coffee?"

Bertie waved the offer away.

"How is she in danger?" Ana asked.

"Father Andretti and Doctor Robilatto. They've been complaining about her since I met them. Candela has a bad heart, and she may be forgetful and perhaps a tad not right in her mind, but she's not a danger to herself or anyone else. In fact, from what I've witnessed, it's quite the opposite. Candela helps almost everyone that crosses her path."

"I know that better than most. Candela is the reason Sugar is alive."

"That's right, isn't it? I know for a fact that Andretti and Robilatto are itching to swear under oath that Candela's drinking is a danger to her mental and physical health. They want to commit her, which, in my opinion, has always been their ulterior motive. Andretti still believes that Candela worships the devil, but Robilatto?" Bernie scoffed, "He's just plain jealous."

"I agree, but I still don't know what you want from me."

"You've known Candela for years. You can help me protect her by testifying to her character and your perception of her state of mind."

Ana felt the color drain from her face. "I can't do that," she said, shifting uncomfortably in her seat.

"Why not?" Bernie said, sounding appalled. "You just said that she saved Sugar's life."

"Exactly," Ana said, and Bertie frowned. "Even when Sugar got so sick, Vincenzo refused to spend money on doctors. When I told him there was an old woman in the park who healed people with her keys practically for free, he said he heard. And that if I ever sent for the old hag, he'd break both my arms and hers, too. But at that time I had no choice. I had to send for Candela. To this day, I am terrified that if he found out Candela healed her or that I have anything to do with her at all, he would kill her and me."

Bertie sighed deeply and said, "I know your history with him, and I understand your fear," she said, shaking her head. "I work with Andretti and Robilatto, so you may not believe me when I say this, but despite the frustration I feel with Candela, I worry about her. I see how lonely she is. Loneliness is bad for anyone's mental and physical health."

Ana nodded. "I know how much she cares for and perhaps even loves the people she heals. I know they love her, so I don't understand why she insists on keeping her distance."

"I've wondered about that, too," Bertie said.

Ana reached across the table and grasped Bertie's hand. "You are kind and patient with people, and especially so with Candela. I used to see you walking through the park or sitting beside her near Hangman's Elm deep in conversation, and that made me happy for her. I also know you can't really be her friend, because you are a social worker, which is a doctor of sorts."

"Thank you," she said, getting to her feet. She walked around the table and patted Ana's arm. "I must leave, but if you decide to testify in Candela's behalf ..." she said, squeezing Ana's arm.

Ana winced. Bertie frowned. She held Ana's wrist and carefully moved Ana's sleeve above her elbow. She gasped at the greenish purple bruise on Ana's upper arm.

"My God. I'm reporting him now," she said, heading for the door.

"No, Bertie, please," Ana said, grabbing her arm. "If you do, Vincenzo will kill me."

"No, Ana, he won't. You and your children will be safe, I promise," she said. "What that man has done to you and your family is unspeakable. He's a criminal. He belongs in jail."

"No, Bertie," Ana said. Tears streamed down her cheeks.

"You don't know him like I do." She wiped her cheeks with her hand.

"Ana, for the hundredth time, you must let me help you."

"And for the hundredth time, Bertie, you and I know there is no help for women like me."

"Ana—"

Her face set in grim determination, Ana opened the door. "Bertie, you must leave, now and please don't come back," she said, with finality.

"But—"

Ana stood silent and resolute.

Bertie's eyes glistened. Looking too shocked to speak, she brushed past Ana. Tears pooling in her eyes, Ana closed the door and pressed her cheek against it, realizing too late, that she did have another good friend for years, but now that friend was gone.

You've known Candela for years. You can help me protect her by testifying to her character and your perception of her state of mind.

"My God," Ana whispered. She turned and flattened her back against the door. She darted her eyes furtively. "What kind of person am I? How can I forsake Candela in her hour of need? She saved my child's life! And how could I chase Bertie away?"

The answer was simple. Fear of Vincenzo.

Suddenly, a windstorm of images whirled through her mind … Sugar … in the store front with that boy … the cold distant smile … Sugar swearing that girl wasn't her.

Three years had passed …Sugar had returned to a normal state of mind.

Three years of relative calm. The calm before the storm? A jittery terror writhed in the shadows of Ana's mind, chilling her to the marrow of her bones. *I cannot, I will not fail Sugar.*

Vincenzo be damned. Something terrible was going to happen to Sugar. Ana felt it in her bones.

Ana changed her mind. She would do what Bertie asked. She would testify on Candela's behalf, but first she had to protect Sugar. And to do that she had to talk to Candela. Candela had the answers Ana needed. She could not protect Sugar without knowing the truth. She tiptoed across the room and eased Luisa's bedroom door open. Her breathing was steady. Ana closed Luisa's door. Praying that Luisa stay asleep and knowing that Vincenzo would not be home for hours, Ana grabbed her purse and her shawl and locked her apartment door behind her.

Chapter 39

Candela, Ana and Bertie
1935

Candela sat at her kitchen table opposite Ana, pleased but surprised by her visit. As far as Candela knew, Vincenzo Sciorri was still a bully and a coward, who'd forbidden Ana to have anything to do with her. Candela felt her face grow warm with anger. Her heart ached for Ana, and she suddenly realized that she hated Vincenzo as much if not more than *she hated ... Breanna?* Her head swimming with confusion, Candela closed her eyes.

"Candela?" Ana reached for her hand. "Are you all right? You look pale."

"I'm fine," she said. She opened her eyes and breathed deeply. "Nothing a good night's sleep wouldn't cure." Forcing her face into a smile, she offered Ana wine, and when Ana politely refused, Candela brewed tea. She poured, and her hand shook, rattling the teapot's cover.

"Something to eat?"

Ana frowned. "No, thank you."

Her nerves in check, Candela returned the teapot to the stove, took a deep breath and cleared her throat. "I know you risked a lot to come here, so is anyone sick?"

"Sugar, but you know that, don't you? You said that if you could fix her, you would have done it a long time ago."

Candela sighed. She grabbed the bottle of wine and began filling her cup. Ana touched her arm gently and nodded at the cup.

"It's early. Do you think you should?"

Candela ran her hand over her mouth, pushed the cup away and clasped her shaking hands.

Ana shifted in her seat and cleared her throat. "You know I will be grateful to you till the day I die for saving Sugar's life," she said, wincing. "But can you tell me why Sugar must pay such a steep price, while you save other lives for free?"

"I don't understand," Candela said.

"I think you understand very well. But I'll spell it out for you, again. Sugar is not the same girl she was before you healed her."

"Please, Ana, not again. I've told you a hundred times there's nothing I can do—"

"Can't or won't," Ana said, her voice laced with anger.

Candela eyed her bottle of wine.

"I came here for answers," Ana said, glancing around the room, "and I'm not leaving without them.

"What is that?" she said, eyeing *Tales of Greek Gods & Men* next to the clock on Candela's dresser. Frowning, she got to her feet, went straight for the dresser, picked the book up and carried it to the table.

Looking confused, she set the book down. "You've known this is my favorite book for years. You saw it in my apartment." Her voice rose, surprising Candela. "Why didn't you tell me you had a copy, too?"

Candela grabbed the cup to steady her hands. Wine spilled over the side, streaking her fingers with purple tears. Avoiding Ana's eyes, she drained the cup and then refilled it. "I was waiting for the right time."

Ana slid into her seat and clasped her hands on the book. "The right time? For what?"

Ana heard Candela speak in a breathless, unholy litany. She rambled on about an old and powerful secret they shared that Ana was unaware of until now. The longer Candela talked the thicker the air got and the dimmer the room became. The weight of Candela's words settled on Ana's chest like a wool blanket in August, making it hard to breathe.

Candela's gaze never relented. The more she spoke the wider her eyes grew. They glowed with excitement, and suddenly Ana wondered why she'd never noticed how strange and catlike Candela's pupils were. But now she understood what the doctor, the priest and others meant when they said Candela's eyes were strange and made them uneasy. Growing more ill at ease herself, Ana realized that Bertie was mistaken. Her observation of Candela being 'a tad not right in her mind' didn't begin to describe what appeared to be wrong. Candela grabbed her hand just as Ana had felt the urge to jump up and run out the door screaming.

"Now do you understand, dear Ana, how fate has brought us together?"

Forcing herself to be gentle, Ana freed her hand from Candela's grasp. "*Si.* Yes. Of course, of course, but now I must go." She grabbed her purse, mumbling, "I need to find Bertie."

"Bertie? She has nothing to do with us. Has she been talking to you? What did she say?"

"Nothing. I mean," she said, squeaking the words out. "I need to go. If Vincenzo finds out I was here today ..." She averted her eyes, saw *Tales of Greek Gods & Men*, and she backed away from the table. The book she loved had suddenly changed into a strange and terrible omen. Ana felt her way to the door and turned the knob.

Candela got to her feet. "Ana! What's wrong? Don't go. Wait."

Ana opened the door and ran.

There was only one explanation for Ana's strange behavior. Bertie O'Donnell had lied to Ana. Candela had to find Ana and make things right. She wrapped her shawl around her, locked her door, and made her way to the street step-by-painful step.

Ana rushed up the stairs in Candela's hallway facing the naked truth. If her intuition was right and Sugar was in danger, whatever the future held, Ana could no longer count on Candela to help. She had to face it alone. She burst onto the street from the dark hallway, and thousands of little black dots floated before her eyes. She swooned, about to pass out, when fingers like steel clamps tightened around her wrist.

"Vincenzo!"

She darted furtive gazes up and down the street, knowing that even if the street had been jammed with people, no one would help her. He bent her arm back and slammed her into the door until it opened. He shoved her into the hallway and against the wall. His breath grazed her cheek. She grimaced in disgust. He'd been drinking. Fear turned her saliva acidic and her breath ragged. His mouth to her ear, he rasped, "I been watching you. I knew sooner or later you'd come here for help. You shoulda gone to Conchetta instead."

"I don't know what—"

"You shut up when I talk. Remember?"

"But I—"

"Did I give you permission to talk?" He grabbed a fistful of hair and banged her head into the wall. Her teeth rattled in her jaw, and she felt her brain bump against her skull. The pain hurt so bad, but she dared not cry. Crying would end in more pain.

"Let her go."

Vincenzo turned. "Who the f—" He squinted and said, "Well, well. After all the the years and all the things I've heard about you, you must be Candela."

"I … said … let … her … go."

Gesu Cristo! The old bitch's voice made his blood run cold. He rubbed his bleary eyes. They stared into her eyes and widened in shock. What was wrong with her eyes, or was he drunker than he thought? Deciding on the latter, he grinned, slurring, "Izzat so? Well, you gotta do better than that."

"NOW!"

Her voice shrilled through his skull, slamming him into the wall. Before the pain hit, he heard *crack*. His skull throbbed past the roots of his hair to the roots of his eyebrows. Nausea sloshed in his gut. The stain in his crotch spreading, he slid down the wall, retched and passed out in urine and vomit.

Shaken, Ana backed away from Vincenzo and Candela. She stumbled out of the building onto the sidewalk and bumped into Bertie O'Donnell.

"Ana?"

"My God, Bertie. I'm sorry for being such a coward. Can you forgive me?"

Bertie caught Ana before she collapsed. She, ran her hand over Ana's hair and gasped at her bloodied palm. "What happened?"

Bertie's face swam before Ana's throbbing head. "Please, I must go home."

"I'll walk you there, after you see Dr. Robilatto."

"No. I need to go home. Luisa is there alone."

"Not until you tell me what happened," Bertie said, shoring Ana up by her arm. She looked at the building and frowned. "Did you just … did Candela do this?"

"God no," Ana cried, "she'd never … "

Ana's knees buckled, and Bertie slipped her arm around Ana's waist. "That does it! I'm taking you to see Robilatto."

"Wait," Ana cried. Bertie loosened her grip. Her heart churning, Ana looked down at Candela's street level window. Her fierce loyalty shaken, she weighed the facts. She knew Bertie was a good person who cared about Candela. Whatever the outcome, Ana trusted that

Bertie would do whatever it took to protect Candela, like she had for the past five years. But after hearing what Candela had said, Ana's world had shifted, changing her priorities. She must do whatever it took to protect Sugar.

"Vincenzo is in the hallway, drunk. He banged his head on the wall and passed out," she said, still bending the truth to protect Candela. "If he wakes up—" she said, shivering. "Take me home, and I'll tell you everything that I should have told you years ago, but only under two conditions: No priest and no doctor. And your solemn oath that no matter what you hear, you will not move against Candela without consulting me first."

Frowning at Bertie, Luisa came out of her room and sat at the table next to Ana, who smiled and caressed her cheek. Deciding to omit the parts that the priest and the doctor could use against Candela, Ana gave Bertie a detailed account of Candela's conversation.

Looking dazed, Bertie slowly shook her head and stared past Ana. "I had no idea … I mean, Candela really believes she lived among the Canarsee?" Ana nodded. "My God. The day Robilatto introduced us in the park, I asked her where she'd come from before moving to the Village, and she deflected by saying that we had something in common. I had a brother, Eric. She had a sister, Breanna, and then she left, claiming there was someone in the neighborhood that needed her help.

"I never pressed her on it, because I figured she had a perfect right not to tell me, or that maybe she really had forgotten, and I didn't want to embarrass or upset her. But *everything* else? My God, Ana, she's delusional. I mean I'm not qualified to give her the help she needs. I know what I promised, but I've got to tell—"

Ana grabbed and squeezed Bertie's arm, hard. Looking stunned, Bertie winced. "I don't believe for one minute you would ever do anything to harm Candela. But you will cause her great harm and pain if you tell the priest or the doctor what I told you."

"But …"

"But nothing. In the years you've known Candela, has she or have her beliefs ever caused harm to herself or anyone else?"

"No."

"Exactly. If you tell the doctor and the priest what I said, they will commit her to Bellevue. I can't even imagine the deplorable conditions at Bellevue, but I bet you can. How long do you think it will take the immigrants to turn against the three of you? They love and believe in Candela. We lead wretched lives with little hope. Don't take her away from us or us away from her."

"What should we do, then?"

"Leave her be for now," Ana sighed, crossing her fingers, "until she gives you reason to act."

After more coaxing, Bertie finally agreed.

Of all the bizarre tales Candela had told, there was one Ana feared most. If Bertie found out that Candela believed Sugar was her sister Breanna, reincarnated, she would bypass the doctor and priest and haul Candela off to Bellevue herself.

Chapter 40

Conchetta
October 1939

Conchetta stood at the kitchen sink, soaking the dishes. Seething over Matteo and Sugar, she banged a soapy glass in the sink and yelped. Jagged glass sliced a tiny mouth in her palm. The tiny mouth spit up blood. She held it under the faucet and rinsed. Gritting her teeth, she squeezed a dishrag against it and winced. She picked the last of the broken glass from her hand, sucked blood from her cut and cursed herself for the thousandth time for making the biggest, the worst mistake of her life on the day she'd begged Candela to heal Sugar. She'd told Ana years ago that Sugar was no longer Sugar, but somebody worse. Finally, that afternoon she'd confronted Ana at Punziano's, something had happened to make Ana see Sugar as the little tramp she really was.

Truthfully, Conchetta never gave a good goddamn about any of it except for the parts that affected her son. There were days when things seemed to quiet down but she knew from experience that it was only a matter of time before they'd start up again. And Conchetta had a sinking feeling they were due for another bout.

There was something else that she'd been stewing over for years. After healing Sugar, Candela seemed to forget that Conchetta, the keeper's broker, even existed, that is, until or unless Candela wanted news about Ana and Sugar. Sluicing blood tinged suds down the drain, Conchetta fished in a drawer next to the sink for a clean rag and wrapped it around her palm. Feeling spurned, she muttered, "What do they have that I don't?"

She turned off the faucet, dried her hands and slid into a kitchen chair. Her palm throbbed. She closed her eyes and focused on the crossroad where her life had taken a turn for the worse. She remembered sitting in church day and night, clutching her rosary beads and promising God everything if he would free Matteo from Sugar's cheating clutches. Then one afternoon while she sat at home sinking in a black pool of despair, God's help had come with a knock on the door.

"Chi e?" Conchetta grunted, annoyed. Hoisting her considerable hulk out of her chair, she lumbered across the room and opened the door. Mariana Triani stood in the doorway, looking distressed and wringing her hands.

"Mariana? *Che cosa c e? Entra. Entra.* What's happened?"

Mariana lowered her eyes and wrung her hands, worrying Conchetta. "I don't know how to tell you this, but," Mariana raised her eyes. "Never mind." She shook her head emphatically. "I shouldn't have come."

"Nonsense! You know you can tell me anything." Conchetta took Mariana's hand, led her inside and sat her on the couch. "Now talk," she said, sitting opposite her.

"Well," Mariana said, clenching her hands until her knuckles turned white. "I don't how to—"

"For God's sake. Talk!" Conchetta snarled, and Mariana's lips turned white.

"Well, you know my daughter, Hillaria?"

"Of course. Oh my God, Mariana. Is she all right?"

"Yes, yes. She's fine. That's not it." Mariana bit her lip and said, "Well, a few days ago Hillaria said she heard a rumor that Sugar *e* Matteo *sono fuggiti,*" she frowned, searching for the English word. "Eloped," Mariana nodded vigorously. *"Si.* Sugar e Matteo eloped *nel mese di settembre."*

"September? *Gesu Cristo,* we are in October!" Frowning, Conchetta asked, *"Qal'e la data di oggi?"*

"Oggi? Today is Monday, October nine," Mariana said.

Realizing why Matteo had not been able to look his mother straight in the eye for weeks, Conchetta rushed Mariana up off the couch and out the door.

Her throat choked with fury, Conchetta took to the streets, walking as fast as her legs could move her. Sweaty armpits and ample breasts heaving, she glanced up and down the streets, alleys and into doorways and storefront windows. She spotted Sugar on Sullivan Street walking by Nucciarone's Funeral Parlor. She caught up, grabbed her arm and spun her around.

"What the— " The blood drained from Sugar's face. The crowd parted like oil drops on water.

"Is it true?" Conchetta yelled, panting.

"Is what true?"

"You. Matteo. Did you—?" She couldn't bear to say it.

Sugar jerked free. "Elope?" Sugar said, smiling broadly. "As of September first, *I* am Mrs. Matthew Juliani," she said, her voice dripping with arrogance.

"When did you—"

"Matt met me on my lunch hour one day during the last week in August. We pooled our money, got the license—"

Conchetta frowned, trying to remember where she was and what she was doing the day that her son had gotten married. "But when *exactly* did you ...?"

"You remember that new movie we wanted to see? *The Wizard of Oz?*"

Frowning harder, Conchetta shook her head, too dumbfounded to speak.

"Well, we heard it would be at the Capitol Theater on Fifty-first and Broadway through September sixth. On September first we bought the tickets and got married at City Hall by a Justice of the Peace."

Pale-faced and sweating, Conchetta made the sign of the cross.

Sugar flashed a slow smile. "After a very *intimate* dinner," she said, fluttering her eyes, "we went to see *The Wizard of Oz* to celebrate. It was a great film. Some guy named Frank Baum from Chitten," she frowned, "Chitten-something or other in upstate New York wrote the—"

Conchetta slapped Sugar's face.

Sugar's face hardened. Her eyes went so cold and dead, that the not-too-easily-frightened Conchetta stepped back from eyes that were no longer eyes, but anger, lust and triumph wrapped in evil. Smirking, Sugar turned and sauntered down the street.

Hating Ana's daughter more than she'd thought possible, Conchetta fought hard, reined in her unruly temper, and with unaccustomed but resolved calm, she followed Sugar with just enough distance between them to go undetected, down the subway steps and onto an uptown train. Sugar got off on Forty-second and Sixth. Huffing and puffing, Conchetta followed Sugar crosstown to the Commodore Hotel. Surprised and completely baffled, Conchetta ducked into a nearby doorway and caught her breath. She peeked out and watched Sugar glance up and down the street. The moment Sugar stepped into the hotel's revolving door, Conchetta made her way toward the entrance. Teeth chattering and arms growing goose bumps but determined to find out what her son's *wife* was up to, Conchetta sidled up to the hotel window, pressed her face to the glass and saw Sugar snake through a crowded lobby to a doorway, over which a sign read, The Grill.

"Matteo's a machinist," she muttered. "Unless he makes guns for the mob, he couldn't afford this hotel in a million years. So, who is that little tramp he's married to sleeping with?"

Her mind bubbling with savory suspicions, Conchetta waited in the cold and damp. With no sign of Sugar by dark, Conchetta thanked God that Frank worked so hard he practically died when he slept. If he woke up to an empty bed, he would automatically assume that she'd gone to early Mass. With no sign of Sugar for hours, Conchetta's suspicions had simmered into a 'stew' too thick and delicious to eat alone. To smother her guilt and to rehearse for the main event, she imagined serving the stew to Frank first. She imagined him sniffing and grimacing in disapproval.

Without proof your suspicions are nothing but lies, Frank's voice echoed through her mind.

Damn Frank. One thing that Conchetta knew as well as her own name was that Jesus hated liars. Hadn't her sainted Mama said so a million times? The faces of her blessed mama and her ethical husband had thrown up a brick wall that stopped her dead. She had to think. She had to devise a foolproof plan.

Matteo knew how much she hated Sugar. Conchetta knew that if she told Matteo what she saw, he'd side with Sugar even if his own mother had irrefutable proof. But if Frank and Matteo heard it from *someone else*...She turned up the flame under the stew and stirred, convinced that what she'd cooked up was...her right...her just...desserts, for...for...for the pain that...that would shatter her poor son's heart...and retribution, for the pain of...a mother...losing her only son to a lying, cheating tramp. Surely, the Virgin Mother, having a Blessed Son of her own, would understand. Conchetta closed her eyes and stirred harder. After sharing the 'stew' with a good friend, she would make it very clear that she had *no proof*. She would make her friend swear not to breathe a word. Doing that would – *lei avrebbe perlustrato*, Conchetta searched for the English word...scrub...scrub away *her* guilt while *her friend* inevitably but joyfully betrayed her.

How her pulse had raced to the beat of her buoyant heart! Feeling lighter on her feet than she'd felt in years, Conchetta had barely felt the cobblestones beneath her feet as she headed crosstown to the subway and home.

Chapter 41

Sugar
The Commodore Hotel
October 9, 1939

Hate smoldered through Sugar in waves that left her knees folding like rubber and her head feeling lighter than a helium balloon. How dare Conchetta attack her in the street in front of the whole neighborhood! A train screeched. Sugar gasped and looked around as if she'd just awakened from a nightmare. She found herself standing on the far end of a deserted subway platform with no memory of how she had gotten there. She fixed her sights on the oncoming train to avoid losing her balance or getting dizzy.

The train stopped. Its doors slid open. Dazed, Sugar got on but...

... *she* ... got off at Forty-second Street. She walked crosstown for fifteen minutes before stopping abruptly in front of a building and its revolving door. The big block letters above the entrance said: Commodore Hotel. She frowned, and then smiled. This place had probably caught her eye because Sugar's coworkers, those empty-headed dolts, kept insisting that The Grill, the Commodore's cocktail lounge, was *the* watering hole in Midtown. Perfect! Her smile broadened. Right about now she could use a drink.

The empty wedges of glass that made up the door began to revolve slowly. The smile slipped from her face. Was this a joke? Maybe it was a promotional stunt for a magazine, a newspaper, or maybe for the hotel itself? Looking east and west for a tangible hook upon which to hang her suspicion, she netted more than she'd bargained for. For some inexplicable reason, Forty-second and Lexington Avenue, second only to Times Square known for being the most crowded part of the city, was completely deserted. She froze, ear cocked. Some silence soothed. This one was deadly. It stretched out over the city, long and unbroken, dull and heavy.

A breeze picked up, and she shivered and zipped up. Rethinking that drink, she jammed her purse under her arm and started walking away, when the smell of steak and fries made her stomach rumble.

Needing something to eat, she stepped into the revolving door which spun fast, making her dizzy. The door stopped so quickly her shoulder hit the glass. She lost her balance and teetered into an empty, dimly lit lobby. She glanced over her shoulder and frowned. Except for a vaguely familiar-looking woman standing on the sidewalk and peering through the hotel window, the street still appeared to be deserted. She frowned harder trying to place the woman, when piano notes, barely audible, rippled through the lobby. *Stardust.* She recognized the haunting melody; and mouthed the heart-tugging lyrics, all the rage about ten years earlier. She drifted along on the lyrics and notes to the lounge, as the woman at the hotel window faded from her mind. The closer she got to the lounge, the louder the music and laughter. No wonder the street was deserted. Everyone supposed to be out there seemed to be in here.

She crossed the threshold into The Grill and shivered. A glint of light on metal and mirrors distorted her vision but heightened her awareness.

The air was erotic with scents, and her mouth watered, igniting her hunger for something beyond food. Despite a blue wispy veil of cigarette smoke and the clanging of plates and forks, she heard every word everyone spoke. She smirked, and ignoring the impulse to eavesdrop, she looked across the crowded room. On the opposite side were two doors. Each time a waiter pushed in and out of the kitchen, she could hear the rattle of pots and pans and the *phisss* of soups and sauces boiling onto stovetops as clearly as if she were standing there.

The cracking of ice cubes in drinks on the tables and bar was as loud and clear as the crack of a mountain lake in a spring thaw. Drawn to the loudest, she turned and saw … him.

He stood at the bar laughing and talking with friends, and she knew if she stared long enough he'd look her way. He turned, and when he smiled and raised his drink, she tried to avert her eyes, but the look in his—

The heart she had kidnapped, beat with such fury, she thought it might burst.

You know what it's like to live at the whim of a heartless man. It pounded. You have a husband who worships you. Why would you cheat and risk losing him?

She ran her hand over her lips. This wasn't cheating. She was … just … curious.

Despite the crowd, there was an empty stool at the bar. Knowing that nature hated vacuums, she ignored the pesky heart and slid onto the stool, filling the void. She put her purse on the bar and swiveled. Her gaze swept the room, and to her amazement he'd dropped out of sight. She shrugged and faced the bar.

The piano struck a discordant note. The hair on the back of her neck rose. She sensed his nearness. She looked up and saw his reflection in the mirror. He was standing behind her. She averted her eyes for a moment and when she raised them, he was gone. Again. She twisted around in her seat, scanning the bar when she heard, "What'll it be, ma'am?"

"'Ma'am?'" the barkeep repeated, sounding annoyed. "Pink lady," she said and then scoffed. That sounded like something Sugar had heard an actress say in one of those wastes of time she loved called the movies. She was hot and thirsty and to her surprise the drink was sweet, cold and smooth going down. The bartender set down another. She waved it away, but the bartender pointed. She saw *him* and smiled. He raised his glass and smiled a seductive, intimate smile that reached into Sugar's heart which pounded so hard it hurt.

He emptied his glass. She did the same.

He slipped off his barstool, clearly amazing his friends. They followed his gaze and grinning at her, they raised their hands in an 'atta-boy' slap on his back.

Average height, bronze skin, angular jaw. His eyes were dark and hypnotic. He leaned on the bar. His face was inches from hers. The pink ladies perched on her shoulders dared her to touch the cleft in his chin. She did, and he laughed. The sparkle in his eyes, his smile and the tilt of his head dared her to rise to the challenge. He grinned. She laughed, showing her dimples. She'd played this game so many times before, she'd lost count.

He held up her empty glass. The bartender filled it. Smiling, she held out her right hand. "I'm Ann," she said. Anglicizing her name rebuked her like heartburn. And somewhere in its core, the heart she'd abducted suddenly knew how Conchetta had felt when Sugar made Matt do the same. She squashed the thought like an ant at a picnic and said, "My friends call me Sugar."

He held her right hand to his lips. His kiss lingered. His energy surged through her. She hadn't felt this alive since the gods knew when. He grasped her left hand. He turned her wedding ring counterclockwise, and this poor heart galloped like a runaway horse. She disengaged gently.

"I don't usually come here," she said, giggling at how deliciously numb her tongue and lips felt and how hard they struggled to form her words.

"Barkeep?" he smiled and held up two fingers. "I've probably come here enough to make up for the both of us. I work on Wall Street at the stock exchange. And you?'

"Sears, Roebuck. Comptometer operator."

"Impressive," he said.

He kissed her hand again. Her heart raced harder. Somewhere inside it a tiny voice begged her to leave. The room spun. Deciding the voice might be right she slipped off the barstool. She stumbled. He caught her. Feeling her face redden, she mumbled that she was Italian, meaning she only drank homemade red wine with dinner and not very often.

It was hard to talk, but harder to keep from falling. She shook her head trying to free the cloud from her brain. "I'm sorry. I feel like such a—"

His lips stopped hers with a kiss. He whispered in her ear, "Say yes."

Her ear felt warm and moist; every inch of her tingled.

He saw her frown and he said, "To having dinner with me."

He let her go but caught her before she slipped to the floor. She tried to apologize again, but he waved it away saying, "Trust me. If you have something to eat you'll feel better."

He reached for his wallet and signaled the headwaiter. After a smile and a handshake, the headwaiter led them past the restrooms to an empty candle-lit table in an out-of-the-way corner. He took the menus from the waiter and handed her one. She needed to pee. She glanced at the restrooms and frowned. Funny, she hadn't noticed the phone booth between them before. A tiny annoying voice whispered, "Call Matt. It's late, and he'll be worried. "

She stood. He stood, and as if he had read her mind, he walked her through the maze of tables and stopped at the phone booth. He slid his fingers between hers and turning her wedding ring counterclockwise again, he said, "Go ahead, call him." His eyes and smile dared her. "If that's what you really want."

He brushed his lips against hers, and her occupied heart fluttered. She stepped into the phone booth, and he closed the door behind her.

She dumped her purse on the ledge under the phone and searched for coins. She lifted the phone off the hook. Her head ached. She hung up the phone, rested her head in her hands, took a deep breath and then picked up the phone again. She slid a dime into the slot and frowned hard trying to picture Matt and her together, but the image was as weak as a paired response that hadn't been reinforced lately. She hung up and shrugged. He opened the door and took her hand. His touch seemed to make her move forward without touching the ground. Barely getting through dinner, they went straight to his room for dessert.

Sugar woke up, groggy and nauseous in a room she didn't recognize. She sat up and groaned. The clock on a nightstand said 4:00 a.m. Had she been here almost all night? What would she tell Matt? Her head felt like she'd slept with it wedged between two steel pillows. She closed her eyes and massaged her temples, trying to retrace her steps. After the run-in with Conchetta she'd been so blind with rage that she'd ended up in the subway with no recollection of how she'd gotten there. She remembered getting off the train at Forty-second Street and walking crosstown. She remembered stopping at a sign over a doorway that said Commodore Hotel but everything that followed was either blank or fuzzy. Was she still in the Commodore?

The bed moved. She turned, saw … him … remembered what happened … and … her stomach churned with disgust.

He smiled. He began to … *change* ... and the room smelled like something dead had decomposed in it.

Sugar froze. The thing staring into her eyes was small, and it looked dead. Its hair was gone. Whatever covered its skull was black and withered. Instead of eyes, two small voids in its skull housed tiny infernos. It crushed her to its chest. In a puff of putrid air its dead mouth sighed, *"Breeeannnnaaaah. The past never stays buried."*

And then *it* … grabbed her shoulders, clamped *its* lips over hers, and began to suck as if trying to drain her of everything she was.

Movement registered in the corner of her eye.

It …stopped sucking and let her go.

Candela stood by her bed. She took a deep breath and cried, "Candela! Thank God!" She leaned over the side of the bed and vomited. She looked up and gasped. Candela was gone. She was alone.

She shut her eyes tight. "Candela!" she screamed until she ran out of breath.

She opened her eyes and found herself standing *outside* the Commodore Hotel on a crowded Forty-second Street. People walking by fanned out, to give one of New York City's 'crazies' plenty of room.

Feeling so ashamed she could die, she hurried down the street hovering close to the buildings. Needing time to think, she opted to walk to the village from midtown. Wading through what had happened in the Commodore last night, a wild theory began forming in her mind. The more she rejected it, the harder it persisted. It was so insane that even Mama, her strongest advocate, would be hard pressed to believe it. Yet, looking back on her life, this crazy, insane theory made perfect sense. Sugar stopped walking.

The train stopped. Its doors slid open. Sugar got on ... but... she ... got off.

"*She* was the one who went into the Commodore Hotel. *She* was one who'd cheated on Matt. It was *she* who'd done all those disgusting, hurtful horrible things to the people I love.

"And now I have a name to go with all those deeds."

Breanna.

"Who the hell is Breanna? What is she to Candela, or me," Sugar said, frowning. "And what does she have to do with Mama?"

Chapter 42

Candela
1939

Knock! Knock! Knock!

Longing for the half cup of wine and hunk of bread on the table, Candela rose and opened her door.

"Candela, I'm sorry." Hat in his bruised, soiled hands, Lorenzo Zita stood in the dark, shabby hallway. Gangling and awkward, he shifted from foot to foot. His eyes were pinched, and his lips were puckered, two features that aged most immigrants beyond their years. "My wife, Violeta, she insist," Lorenzo said, lowering his eyes. He ran his fingers over his frayed cap and picked at some stray threads. "I come to you about my Eliana, Candela. My baby. The doctor, he justa leave," Lorenzo paused. He shook his head. "We hear from Ana. She say when Sugar was twelve, you save a Sugar's life. My wife she," Lorenzo looked in her eyes. He sobbed like a wounded creature. "Please, I do anything."

Candela touched his hand. "Go home to your wife and daughter. Wait with them for me."

"*Grazie*, Candela." He exhaled his fear in one long and wavering breath. Candela saw the relief in his eyes.

Lorenzo ran a grimy sleeve across his eyes and nose and managed to smile. He squeezed her hand and lifted it to his lips. He bent forward to kiss her hand and his head hit the bulb dangling from the ceiling in the hall. She hoped the light's dancing shadows masked the agony in her eyes. He let her hand go.

"I'm Lorenzo Zita, and I live in—"

"Ana's building on Ana's floor."

"*Si. Grazie mille,* Candela."

She closed the door behind him, went to her window and slid back the small panel door beneath the sill. She saw *Tales of Greek Gods & Men.* She stared at the book, surprised. This is not where it belonged, and she didn't remember putting it there. She frowned harder.

Her hands shook. She bypassed the blue velvet box, reached for the book, hugged it to her chest and closed her eyes. Had she really seen the keys fastened to Apollo's waist on Ana's copy that day, or had she been so distraught, she'd imagined them? How long ago had that happened? She couldn't remember. She opened her eyes, looked at the book and saw Apollo, wearing her keys around his waist. Weak with relief, she put the book down, reached for the blue velvet box, lifted its cover and took the keys. She traced the maze on the disk, careful to avoid touching the center. Lorenzo's eyes loomed large in her mind. Candela sighed, grabbed her shawl and closed the door behind her.

It seemed like yesterday that Eric Van Broc had pulled back the curtain on one of her lives. The following day she'd found Breanna in Sugar. She was so sure that these extraordinary events were part of a greater mystery that would unfold in time. She paused at the door to Ana's building and stared at her reflection. Four years ago, when Ana had come to see her, instead of keeping her distance, Candela ignored her instinct and told Ana exactly what she wanted to know. Ana, her only friend in this world, had paid a brutal price at Vincenzo's hands. From that day to this, Candela had had no choice but to stand silently by while Vincenzo's abuse had taken its toll on his family.

Regretting that day every day that followed, she grasped the door knob. She stepped inside and gagged in disgust. Vincenzo's stench filled the hallway. Candela paused and raised her eyes toward Ana's floor. Luisa had grown into a woman with a child's mind, Johnny had fallen prey to the criminal element, and then there was Sugar. Against Conchetta's wishes, Sugar and Matteo had married.

The good news was that despite the startling changes, Sugar had survived. Candela frowned wondering which one had really survived? Sugar or Breanna? She shook her head and frowned. Did Breanna even exist? Had any of those strange events really happened or were they, like Bertie had hinted so many times, the product of a lonely old woman's wine-soaked imagination? The menacing feeling that had taken root in Candela's heart the night she'd found Breanna in Sugar had all but faded. A trace of a thought still nibbled around the edge of her memory. What was it that she must do upon finding Breanna? Sighing, she put the thought aside and knocked on Lorenzo Zita's door …

Locking her door behind her, Candela put Lorenzo's stipend, a bottle of red wine, on her kitchen table. She placed the keys in the blue velvet box and grabbed *Tales of Greek Gods & Men* from the shelf. She closed the panel door and tossed the book on her bed. She draped her shawl over her chair, reached into the icebox for milk, poured it into a pot on the stove and lit the gas. The hot milk might soothe her stomach, but it did nothing for her nerves. She turned off the gas, grabbed the wine, grimaced and pulled the cork. A pervasive chill made her shiver. She upended the bottle and peered out her window. A gust of wind swept candy wrappers, cigarette butts and newspapers along the sidewalk and street like a giant invisible broom. After taking a longer swig, she rummaged through her dresser and slipped into her nightgown and into bed. Sliding the book under her pillow, she peered out the window.

A huge pearl moon hung in the sky. An oblong of cold, dead light poured through her window. Her eyes grew milky with moonlight. The smell of rot filled her nostrils, a reminder of what lay deep beneath the ground. Her eyes rolled under her eyelids, and she whimpered, searching the gaps in her mind for the secrets that someone had whispered in her ear, long, long ago.

Chapter 43

Breanna
Goddess of Heaven and Earth
October Rome 49 AD

A huge pearl moon hung in the sky, lighting the Appian Way and all lesser roads leading to Rome. Breanna, goddess of earth, stood in her temple courtyard on Palatine Hill, the center of the universe. A braid of gold fastened the tunic across her breasts. The fluted garment fell to her feet in soft, white pleats. Entwined with white gardenias, her thick, luxurious hair fell to her waist in coal black ringlets. A temperate breeze parted the curls framing her face, exposing her pale, slender throat.

Breanna closed her dark eyes and breathed deeply, shivered and then opened them quickly. A torrent of moonlight rained down a smell of rot that filled her nostrils, a reminder of what lay deep beneath the ground. Primeval and decomposing, yet present and *alive,* it clung to her face and hair. She tipped her face to the sky and frowned. Tattered clouds sutured together and bandaged the scar-faced moon. And suddenly the night was darker and more silent than death, much like she imagined the rift to be, except for the eyes. She felt them roam her cheeks, lips and throat, stirring her terror. Rabid, hungry, flatter and more feral than a snake's. Eyes of a predator poised to strike. She rubbed her arms trying to wipe away the cold, clammy trail in their wake. The wind picked up, sweeping the clouds and darkness away.

Her heart slowing, Breanna sniffed the air, exhaling relief. The air smelled fresh, and the eyes were gone. Regaining her composure, she chastised her foolish self. The smell, if indeed there had been one, was most likely an inept slave concocting some odious mortal victuals for their equally odious feast. She'd find him and have him flogged – tomorrow. Tonight she must deal with more pressing matters. She gripped the stone railing until her fingers turned bloodless.

It was Autumn. The season Breanna hated and feared most. The ill winds of fall ushered in days when time lost all meaning, when past, present and future fused into one. But during that time, there was one day that life hinged on death, twixt twilight and dawn, the day fraught with danger for men and gods.

Eve of All Hallows.

On Eve of All Hallows, the diaphanous veil between life and death parted and the dead walked among the living. On the Eve of All Hallows, Mania, the loathsome goddess of rage and madness, whom Hades had banned to the dregs of the River Styx, roamed earth, harvesting food, little creatures and children to please him. A human soul was a better offering, but the soul of a goddess and Apollo's keys were priceless tributes, certain to undo the ban and reward Mania with the thing she coveted most: a place of distinction in Hades' vile court.

It was also the time of year that the power of gods over men was at its weakest. To retain control through this dreadful time, the gods turned a blind eye to the deeds of man by grudgingly granting favors more generous than usual. And, most terrifying of all: on Eve of All Hallows every god on Mount Olympus must grant any request a mortal made, but few mortals had dared ask because they knew the season was short, and the gods had long memories.

Breanna turned east toward Circus Maximus. She let the stone railing go and flexed her aching fingers. She knew that men prized good health and heaven's protection. Good health be damned, she scoffed. To be free of heaven's 'protection' had consumed the willful Breanna from the first beat of her tiny, cruel heart.

It was on that very eve centuries ago, in a flash of desperate brilliance, Breanna had devised a way to dominate men and free herself from heaven's 'protection' in one clever maneuver. She offered her father Apollo, god of healing, an irresistible bargain: In exchange for his keys, Breanna vowed under pain of *death by her own hand,* to relinquish all ties with him and heaven forever.

Apollo let it be known to all gods that his feelings for his cherished but incorrigible daughter had bound him to warn her that if he accepted her terms, the perils of All Hallows Eve notwithstanding, the bargain was set in stone. And neither god nor man could undo it.

Drunk on unbridled freedom, the wayward Breanna had cajoled and bullied her timid half-mortal sister, Candela, into abandoning heaven with her. After the irrevocable break, as a slap in the face to their father, Breanna had turned her back on Olympus and defected to Rome. But the price of freedom soon became painfully clear: The chance of losing her life, the keys and her kingdom grew riskier every year.

At the outset, much to Breanna's amazement, mortals had made an audacious demand: If she failed to suspend all laws and provide an opulent feast to ring in the end of harvest, men would abandon their faith. Gods had one fear above all: If their memory grew cold in the hearts of men, their kingdom and heaven would vanish forever.

So, every October tens of thousands jammed the city to gorge themselves with the food and drink that Breanna grudgingly provided. Waves of people pressed through the maze of crooked alleys and narrow streets that emptied into the forum. The heart of the city teemed with Breanna's slaves, who toiled day and night, setting up stalls alongside public shops that opened onto the sidewalks. They seasoned assorted meats with exotic spices and herbs from distant, mysterious lands, braised them in huge vats of bubbling oil and placed them in cauldrons to simmer in gravies and sauces. Scores of cooks and maids baked crusty loaves of golden brown bread. Hundreds of weary hands broke the loaves into hot steaming chunks and piled them in large woven baskets alongside tables laden with light, flaky pastries, delicate cakes, plump, ripe berries, and glazed fruits. The aroma permeated every crack and crevice both god and man- made. Clouds of rich, spicy vapors wafted up from the valley, over the hills into a night that crouched like a giant cat waiting to lap them up. Plied with excessive wine and their goddess's tacit approval, men and women wiped sugar and grease from their chins, traded spouses and lovers for strangers or friends and wandered into the growth that covered the hills to couple until they were spent.

Enraged at being coerced to provide yet another feast for mortals, Breanna turned her back on Rome and crossed the courtyard to her quarters. Two silent guards, one on each side of the entrance, stood at attention. With the slight nod of her head, the guard on her left stepped to his left and opened her door. When the door closed gently behind her, she pressed her forehead against the frame and squeezed her eyes shut, struggling to lock out her fear.

Failing miserably, she opened her eyes and took in her quarters. The frescoes on the temple walls done in creamy beiges and deep warm rusts captured Greeks, Latins and Etruscans performing quotidian tasks. After stopping to stroke their delicate faces, she knelt and caressed the floor where her cousin Diana, goddess of nature, memorialized in mosaic tiles and determination, was portrayed leading a hunt. She looked past her bed to a bronze ladder back chair with soft matching cushions to a pedestal stand displaying a blue velvet box. The box held the healing keys.

She glanced at Candela, the miserable ingrate, who refused to bow before her, in thanks for her freedom from the shackles of heaven's 'protection.' Sprawled out by the hearth on a pair of blue cushions, Candela engaged in her favorite, worrisome pastime. She raised a diamond-encrusted goblet of red wine to her lips.

Breanna picked up the blue velvet box and sat in front of the fire. Watching the fire's porous wood spit burning sparks, protesting its flaming fate, she set the blue velvet box in front of the hearth. Candela picked up a bejeweled decanter and filled an empty goblet.

"Here. Drink. You look like you need it."

Breanna raised the ruby-encrusted chalice to her lips. Before drinking she said, "*In vino veritas, in aqua sanitas.*" Candela shot her a, what's-that-supposed-to-mean glare, and Breanna grinned. "Heed my words, before it's too late." Draining the goblet, she licked the blood-red drops from her lips. She set the cup in front of the hearth and gazed into the fire. Its flames danced in her eyes.

"Before we review our escape plan—"

Sighing, Candela refilled her goblet. "*The* escape plan?" she slurred, glancing sideways through lidded eyes. "Again?"

Breanna glared at her. Her dark, narrowed eyes grew darker. Her lips curved into an icy smile that could wipe the marble smile from a statue's face.

"I mean we do that every year." Candela's hand shook. Wine sloshed over the goblet's rim. Red tear-like drops sluiced through diamond clusters, dribbling down the goblet's stem. "And nothing ever happens," she said. She steadied her goblet on a flat stone in front of the hearth and licked the wine from her fingers.

Breanna stared blankly. "This year I caught a foul, rancid scent in the air."

In a please-spare-me gesture, Candela waved Breanna off and reached for her goblet. She drained it and gazed at the fire.

Breanna took a calming breath. "As I was saying," she stressed each word and then paused for effect, "before we review our escape plan, we must decide where to hide the keys." She opened the box and held up two large solid gold keys on a solid gold ring that captivated her eye.

A mysterious gem in each key fused the luster of diamonds, rubies, sapphires and emeralds and dispersed it in versions of light and color like none that existed on earth. The key ring was hooked to a gold chain. A solid gold, wafer-thin disk appeared to hang suspended inside the ring. The disk was etched with a dazzling maze, hypnotic in its intricacy. Breanna's eyes glazed over. Her fingers followed the maze dangerously close to its center – gateway to the rift, a place without heat or light, a place so vast that time and space could not be measured. Even by gods.

"What are you doing?" Candela cried, yanking the keys from Breanna's hands. "Portal to eternal damnation the rift is," she mocked, but her face was whiter than marble. Exhaling, she gently placed the keys in the box, picked up the decanter and emptied wine into the goblet.

A hair shy of grateful to her half-mortal sister, Breanna frowned. The moon, the odiferous smell, the rabid, feral eyes, real or imagined, had thrown her off balance. If Candela hadn't … Closing her mind to what could have happened, Breanna reined in her racing heart, collected the keys and caressed the disk with great caution. "I'll agree that while the rift is a vast nothingness, it is not quite eternal damnation either. It's more like damnation's," she paused, frowning, 'foyer.' Her frown melted into a cold smile. "From which you and I can and will return."

"It's never been done." Candela closed her eyes and rubbed her temples, looking weary of Breanna's obsession.

"Because it never *had* to be done," Breanna said, losing what miniscule patience she had. "We'll be the first."

Candela opened her strange, cat-like eyes, and Breanna wondered where in heaven or on earth had those eyes come from?

"You're mad." Candela stumbled to her feet. Her slate gray cat's eyes glistened. She pinned her arms defiantly to her side. "I would never enter the rift, willingly or otherwise." Her flaming red hair shimmered in waves of firelight and indignation.

Amused, Breanna stored Candela's fear of the rift along with her weakness for mortals – two powerful tools she vowed she would use against her sister one day. "The maze and the rift play an integral part in making my plan foolproof," she smiled, enjoying Candela's discomfort.

"No plan is foolproof." Candela shrugged her off. "Besides, I've no time to feed your obsession with rifts and plans." She made her unsteady way toward the door.

"You're not going anywhere," Breanna whispered.

Candela grabbed the latch. Blinking hard, Breanna ran her hands down her own thighs.

Candela's legs vanished. Her torso hit the marble floor, hard. She cried out, and Breanna smiled, wondering if Candela's mortal lovers would find their legless half-goddess appealing.

Candela's astonished eyes bulged and watered with shock. Tears streamed down her cheeks. Amused, Breanna sneered and folded her arms over her breasts.

"I pulled you back from the rift!" Candela cried.

Breanna scoffed. "You came perilously close to disappearing completely." Sighing, she blinked hard and rubbed her hands down her own thighs. Candela's legs appeared whole and curled beneath her. Breanna clenched her teeth. "By Jove, Candela, if your legs so much as twitch, that is the least of what will happen!"

Turning toward the fire, Breanna propped up two pillows beneath her. Curled up near the hearth, she lifted the keys from the box and stared at the maze. Mindful of avoiding the center, she contemplated the Eve of All Hallows' most dangerous threat – Mania.

"If Mania attacks, we'll escape through the disk on the key ring and hide in the rift."

"And how will we return?" a subdued Candela asked.

Breanna stared more deeply into the fire. "It's common knowledge that the mortal seventh daughter of a seventh daughter is a suitable and susceptible vessel for the reincarnation of a goddess."

"Reincarnation?" Candela repeated, as if hearing the word for the first time.

Breanna scowled, annoyed at how slowly Candela's wine-sodden brain responded. Staring intensely into the fire, she enunciated each word as if speaking to a child. "Of course a *Septissima* would be the most desirable, strongest, most potent vessel of all.

"Seventh daughters are not a common occurrence. But *Septissima*, a third generation of sevenths with power that might rival your power? For that little miracle, Breanna," Candela scoffed, "you'd need help from father."

"I'd sooner stick needles in my eyeballs," Breanna snapped. "No matter." Her flaming eyes dimmed. "The seventh of a seventh will do. When one is conceived anywhere in the world, I will enter her soul and sleep."

"Until?"

Breanna gazed at the large stones bordering the hearth. She got to her feet, reached for the poker alongside the fireplace and prodded two stones. One gave. She jammed the poker between them and pried the looser one free. She dropped the poker, knelt to pick up the box that held the keys and slipped it into the hollow. "If you are reborn before me, you must find the keys." Breanna replaced the stone. "Then you must find the host-child in whom I am sleeping and protect her at all costs. Remember, Candela, you must never go beyond healing. If you interfere in the lives you touch, you will set events in motion you will not be able to stop. Those events will change the course of our fate, and you will pay the price."

"Protect at all costs, yet don't interfere? How?"

Breanna ignored that pesky detail and said, "When my host turns twenty-one, I will emerge, and she will fade."

"Is that an arbitrary age?'

Breanna rolled her eyes. "If you had paid attention you'd know that mortal-to-goddess transformation takes twenty-one mortal years to complete.

"Candela, you must remember at all costs that when I emerge, it is essential that I successfully integrate during the twenty-four hours of my host's twenty-first birthday."

"And if you fail?"

Breanna frowned. "Fail?" she whispered, shaking her head imperceptibly. Her cheeks paled. Her deep, dark eyes glistened. Her gaze became hollow. She shut them tight to shield them from what she saw.

Suddenly, her spine stiffened. She opened darker, colder eyes. Beneath them her lush mouth formed a bitter smile. Focused, she rose. Her breasts swayed under the folds of her fluted tunic. She narrowed her eyes.

"I will not fail. Nothing," she panted, "can or will stop me. And when I am fully integrated, we will return with the keys and reclaim our kingdom."

"What if your *host* refuses to fade?"

"Sanctified gods in heaven!" Breanna's hand curled into a raised fist. Candela shrank back. "Why did I choose a fool to rule beside me?" Her fist unclenched and dropped slowly to her side. "Refusal is not an option."

"Except on the Eve of All Hallows when she is free to reject you." Candela said, just a hair shy of arrogant, Breanna thought.

"Yes, but my mortal host won't know that, will she?"

Her eyes narrowed under a scowl. Her head aching, and nerves wound tighter than a hundred springs, Breanna arched her back and rolled her shoulders.

"When you say the woman will fade, what you mean is for you to live, the woman must die."

"Well done," Breanna clapped slowly. Her cold smile fell short of eyes that sparkled with comprehension. "I'd be careful if I were you. Your mortal half is showing." Her smile faded. "Your weakness for mortals will be your downfall." Candela blushed like a common maiden standing naked before a god. "Relax," Breanna said, reining in her impatience. "Nothing will happen to her body."

"And her soul?"

Breanna sighed. "Her soul will fade, and she will merely observe life through my eyes, so to speak."

"What if we live and die without finding each other?"

Yawning, Breanna examined her nails. "We repeat the process until we do." She picked at her cuticles.

"How many innocents—"

Candela froze. Breanna's razor-edged glare could slit a pig's throat.

"Refusing to obey to save a few mortal lives is treason," she whispered, clearly dousing Candela's passion. Breanna scoffed. "I knew you'd see it my way."

"I think you've overlooked something."

"I doubt that but enlighten me." Breanna said, frowning at Candela.

"There's more than one way into the rift. If Mania follows—"

"She'll find us and kill us, steal our souls and the keys, and leave the kingdom to be plundered by savages. Damn!" Breanna said.

"There is a way we may be able to hide in the rift," Candela said, getting Breanna's attention.

"How?" Breanna said, frowning.

"By maintaining silence."

"That's surprisingly brilliant!" Breanna cried, relieved but surprised and annoyed that Candela had upstaged her.

Candela beamed, then Candela frowned, and the beam in her eyes dimmed.

"What are you thinking now?" Breanna said, impatiently.

"How long do we maintain silence? From what I've heard the longer we stay in the rift, the weaker we become."

"The length of our stay would not be a factor if we could communicate." Breanna placed the keys in the box and slid the box into the hollow under the stone. She kept her hand firmly on the stone and squeezed. She was certain there was a way to communicate. She felt it, just beyond her grasp. She let go of the stone and clasped her hands on her lap. Deep in thought, she frowned. "You know when we are reborn Mania will find us. And on *that* Eve of All Hallows, when we are most vulnerable, she will attack." Breanna stared into the fire.

Candela touched the stone that covered the keys. Her eyes grew large and luminous. "If one of us returns before the other, the keys will preserve us until we reclaim the kingdom."

"It might not work that way, exactly." Breanna shut her eyes tight and rubbed her forehead, hard. Sighing, she opened her eyes and looked at Candela. "If we're forced into exile, the keys may not heal us when we're reborn.*"*

"What?" Candela shivered despite the flaming hearth.

Breanna stared distractedly. "Sickness. Aging. Death may be the price we pay for escaping into the rift."

"Perhaps for a half-mortal, but surely not for you. You're a goddess—

Breanna cut in. "The thought of losing the keys, the kingdom ..." Her voice trailing off, Breanna broke free. She ran into the courtyard to the stone railing. Absorbed in thought, she watched as Rome blurred before her eyes. Having followed her sister, Candela touched her shoulder. Breanna turned. Her tears fell. In a very rare show of affection, she hugged Candela close.

Stunned, Candela whispered. "You're colder than marble. I'll get you a wrap."

"Mania won't wait for the Eve of All Hallows this year. Breanna squeezed Candela's hands. "She'll rise up from the River Styx, the devil water, and strike tonight!"

A fleet of silvery clouds sailed overhead, obscuring the moon. Torches burned on either side of Breanna's quarters, providing little warmth and less light.

Candela shook her head. "She wouldn't dare. Not while we're strong, on guard and can defeat her."

"A goddess and a *half* and the keys in one swoop is a tempting motive," Breanna smirked. She could see the hurt in Candela's eyes. Annoyed, but needing an ally, she grasped Candela's arm and softened her tone. "What if she foments revolution?"

Candela cleared her throat and nodded at Rome. "Unrest foments revolution. The men I hear sound happy."

"Thanks to you, their healer," Breanna said, wistfully. Suddenly, she narrowed her eyes. "If I didn't know better, I'd say you care for them more than you care for me or the gods."

Candela's eyes flashed. "How can you say that?"

The way Candela's lips trembled, the way she lowered her eyes, Breanna knew she had touched a nerve. Candela stared at Rome, pretending to be unruffled, but pretending and lying were things she did not do well.

"Only fools care for men, Candela. They're fickle and will betray you when it suits them."

"I'm trying to stay on their good side till the season ends."

Breanna let go. They walked across the courtyard. The guard opened their door, and her eyes widened with sudden glee. "I know a way we might be able to communicate." She smiled at Candela. "Once a year in a dream on the Eve of All Hallows. A date we would never forget." Breanna's eyes darkened. "The night of the beast is nigh. I felt it in the wind."

"Perhaps what you felt was merely the wind."

"The die is cast," she mumbled, and then looked directly into Candela's eyes. "Don't you see, Candela? The dye has always been cast. The problem is we've never noticed."

"We'll follow your plan. We'll," Candela grimaced as if pushing words past the lump in her throat, "escape through the rift."

"If we stay too long in the rift, we may never return." Breanna said.

"But you said we could stay as long as it takes."

"Yes, and you reminded me that no one has ever done it." Frowning Breanna said, "Remember, Candela, you must never go beyond healing. If you interfere in the lives you touch, you will set events in motion you will not be able to stop. Those events will change the course of our fate, and you will pay the price.

"Before we part, Candela, you must remember at all costs that when I emerge, I must—"

Chapter 44

Candela
1939

Candela groaned in her sleep. The smell of rot filled her nostrils, a reminder of what lay deep beneath the ground. Primeval and decomposing, yet present and *alive,* it clung to her face and hair.

Candela coughed herself awake. Hammer-to-anvil blows pounded hatred for Breanna so deeply into her soul and the dream so deeply into her heart nothing could pry them loose. But it wasn't a dream. Was it? Her life in 49 AD had been her first ... her original life.

Where did you live before coming to Greenwich Village?

"Rome. I am Candela, half-sister to the goddess Breanna and daughter of the Greek God Apollo!" she cried, giddy. Everyone but she had been mistaken! She was neither senile nor insane. She'd been reincarnated, twice that she knew of, and this life made three.

Except for an oblong of moonlight, her room was dark. She held her throbbing head in her hands and wobbled out of bed toward her closet. She grabbed a bottle of wine, stood it on the table and slipped into her chair. Hunger gnawed. Thirst raged, darkening her eyes. She caressed the bottle.

In vino veritas, in aqua sanitas.

Heed my words before it's too late.

"Damn you to Hades, Breanna," Candela shuddered and pounded her arthritic fist on the table. Pain seared her eyes. Hot, bitter tears burned her cheeks. Her dream of a loving sister had been a sham. The reality was a nightmare. She pushed the bottle aside, got to her feet and opened the icebox. She pulled out a bowl of chicken soup, poured it into a pot on the stove and turned up the flame. She grabbed a hunk of bread and a wedge of cheese. The smell of soup, sweat and terror swelled the air. She stared at the chicken soup in the pot and visions of Rome, the temple, the keys and the hateful, frigid Breanna bubbled up. She looked down and gasped. Her terrified hands had kneaded the bread back into dough.

Despite her terror or perhaps because of it, her ravenous stomach rumbled. She needed to eat. She needed strength for whatever lay ahead. She grabbed the cheese grater and a spoon from the drain board, returned hot soup to the bowl and topped it with mounds of cheese. She dipped her spoon through the melting cheese into the soup and ate. Swooning, she scooped up another spoonful. She looked at the empty bowl and leaned back in her chair. Her dream had yielded more than she'd bargained for. The cowardice in herself and the bully in Breanna filled her with disgust. While resolving some questions, the dream had spawned others. She pivoted, slowly and deliberately, taking in the room. Her forehead creased into a frown. "*How* had their lives in that world ended? Breanna was terrified that Mania would strike before the Eve of All Hallows. Her frown tightened. She'd bet this life that Breanna *had* plunged Mania into the rift, but she needed proof. Acting without proof might set wheels in motion that she could not stop.

Two facts were painfully clear. Phase one of Breanna's insane plan had worked. For phase two to work, that is, for Breanna to live … Sugar … must … She squeezed her eyes shut.

… Sugar's changed … She's not the same girl she was before you healed her. At first, I thought the changes were normal but now …

"Twenty-one mortal years to complete the transformation." Ana was right. Sugar had been changing all along. Into Breanna. If all went according to plan, Breanna would emerge on Sugar's twenty-first birthday—Eve of All Hallows.

Emotions roiling, she hurried to the bathroom, stuck her head in the bowl and heaved. Thanking goodness that toilet tissue had replaced the Sears Roebuck catalog, she ripped some from the roll and wiped her mouth, raised herself up and stumbled into bed. Knowing the number of lives she had already led or would lead, be they seven or not, suddenly became irrelevant. The crucible, the gauntlet she must undergo was clear. She must protect Sugar without arousing Breanna's suspicion. But how, when goddess and mortal lived in the same body? She would follow phase two to the brink. "And then what?"

She yanked *Tales of Greek Gods & Men* from under her pillow and got out of bed. She lifted the keys from the blue velvet box. Teeth chattering, she stoked the coals in the stove, sat at her table, filled her cup with wine and drank. Holding the keys, she traced the maze to the rift, a place devoid of heat and light, a vast nothingness, where time and space could not be measured.

"Even by gods."

She drained the cup, shut her eyes and waited. Wine normally warmed her, but times were no longer normal, nor had they ever been. She moved her chair, but the closer she sat to the fire, the colder she felt. She hugged the keys to her floundering heart. They stole her warmth, slipped through her hands and clanged on the floor. Confused, she shivered and stumbled into bed.

Hours later despite bone-deadening cold, she willed her feet to the cold floor, blew her breath into her hands and rubbed her arms. She opened the stove door and peered inside. The fire was almost dead. She grabbed a small shovel she kept in the bin, stoked the embers and fed it. She emptied the wine bottle into her cup and sniffed. Her eyes welled with tears. She'd never felt more alone. She envied Atlas whose shoulders merely had to bear the weight of the world. She moved through her dream looking for clues that she must have missed. A weapon to wield in the battle that loomed ahead. Closing her eyes, she lifted her cup and drank.

In vino et veritas.

She opened her eyes, wide.

Ironically ... Sugar ... my seventh ...

"Was a *Septissima,*" Candela whispered.

Seventh daughters are not a common occurrence. But a Septissima, a third generation of sevenths with power that might rival your power? For that little miracle... you'd need help from father.

Frustrated, she cried out, "If Ana is the seventh of a seventh, and Sugar is a *Septissima,* why haven't I, Candela, a gifted healer and half-goddess, sensed their power? And, if mother and daughter have such power, why haven't they used it against Vincenzo?"

Candela frowned. She remembered having wondered about that before. Almost word-for-word. So what if she forgot to remember it? People forgot thoughts until the need to remember brought them back. But ... she was not like other people.

She dressed as quickly as she could. Time was running out. She must find Ana or Sugar before the unholy 'transformation' was complete. She fastened the keys to her waist and, staring blankly, she broke out in a cold sweat. "There was another task. A crucial task having to do with the transformation. If only she could remember what it was.

Knock! Knock! Knock!

She gasped.

"Candela? It's Bertie. Are you all right? Open up."

Bang! "Come on, Candela. I know you're in there. I've been out here for ten minutes. Who are you talking to? Who's in there with you?"

Candela shuffled across the room and opened the door.

Bertie stood in the hall, one hand on her hip and the other curled around the handle of a briefcase. "Nobody's seen you for days." Frowning at the empty wine bottle on the table, she walked past Candela, placed her briefcase on the floor and pulled the kitchen chair under her. She glanced at Candela's bed. Eyebrows raised, she said, "*Tales of Greek Gods & Men?* Interesting reading." She frowned at Candela. "I had no idea. And, you missed our last three sessions."

What in Hades was she talking about? She had last seen Bertie on the day she'd confided in Ana. The day Vincenzo had tried to kill Ana in the hallway. How long ago was that?

"Today's visit would have been four. I'm not leaving until we talk." Bertie took a breath and glanced around the small apartment. "You're alone."

"Of course I'm alone," Candela said, struggling to bring Bertie's runaway train to a screeching halt. Bertie meant well, but she didn't know what was at stake, and telling her was out of the question. Consumed with finding Ana or Sugar, Candela stood by her door, hoping that Bertie would take the hint. Bertie sat at the table.

Glancing at *Tales of Greek Gods & Men* she said, "Who were you talking to?" She rummaged through her briefcase and pulled out a file.

"Who was I ... *what?*" Candela held the door knob.

Holding a file in mid-air, Bertie faced her. "Pardon me. What I meant to say was who were you yelling at?" Candela slammed the door. "I practically heard you from the street." Bertie put the file on the table and looked at Candela, who stood beside her. "Honest to God, Candela. Do you know how many times I've come to your defense, excuse me, your rescue? Don't you realize that if Doctor Robillato and Father Andretti were here in this room right now, you'd be on your way to Bellevue for psychiatric evaluation? They've spent the past nine years looking for a reason to put you away."

Nine years? Put me away? Robilatto had just introduced them a few months ago. "Why would they—?"

"Want to put you away? For God's sake Candela, how many times must I tell you? Andretti believes you worship the devil and practice black magic, and Robilatto believes you pretend to heal people."

Pretend? Candela stared at Bertie as if she were crazy.

"Candela, let me be clear. I agree with them only on one point. You abuse alcohol." She looked down her nose at the bottle. *"In vino veritas, in aqua sanitas."* Stunned, Candela froze. "In wine there is truth, in water health. In other words, if you drank water instead of wine, you would have remembered that I scheduled today's meeting last week. You promised, I mean you swore that you would remember. Wine and old age make a deadly cocktail. If it took such a toll on your mind, God knows what it's done to your body."

Candela grasped the back of her chair to steady herself. Bertie was either confused or lying. She wouldn't lie unless, Candela's eyes narrowed, she was working with them! Compared to what was at stake, Robilatto, Andretti and even Bertie were three cockroaches not worth the time it would take to crush under her heel. Candela closed her eyes and breathed deeply.

"I'm sorry, Candela. You must know how fond I am of you. I'm on your side, have been for years. Why do you make it so hard for me to help you?"

Candela opened her eyes as Bertie opened her file labeled: **Candela: October 1930.** A fake file designed to fool her. Bertie *was* working with *them to* lock her up. *For Breanna to live ... Sugar ... must ...*

She was out of time. She must warn Sugar that her life was in danger before ... A pincher of pain clawed her heart. Panting, she clutched her chest.

"Candela?" Bertie frowned, "Are you all right?"

Masking her pain, Candela backed away. Her arms fell to her sides. Her shawl parted, exposing the keys whose color and light caught Bertie's eye. The file slipped from Bertie's fingers, and when Bertie's eyes glazed over, Candela gathered her shawl and made her way out the door.

Chapter 45

Sugar
October 30, 1939

Steel columns labeled West 4th Street rifled past the subway train window like a shuffled deck of playing cards. The train jerked to a stop, the doors slid open, and Sugar stepped out of the half empty car onto the platform. She ran her tongue on the roof of her mouth. Tasting metal and grime, she wrinkled her nose. Her legs felt like lead. She put one in front of the other and forced them to move, swinging her arms with each stride. The tick-tock of her high heels echoed through the cavernous subway station, an ominous clock marking ominous time. Her head throbbed. She stopped, rubbed her temples, and checked her watch.

"Three o'clock." She pushed through the metal turnstile and headed for the West 4th exit. She had less than ten minutes to come up with a reason why Matt would not be at her twenty-first-birthday dinner tomorrow night. Less than ten minutes to decide whether to tell Mama that Matt had asked her for a divorce.

A gust of wind blew down the stairwell. Strafed with gum wrappers, paper napkins and grit. Sugar kicked the debris away and rubbed her eyes. "Damn," she said, sneezing. Her eyes watered and stung. She shut them tight, sniffled and fished in her purse for a Kleenex. She held the tissue over her nose and blew. Tripping up the last step, she rubbed her eye and stumbled into someone. It was an old woman holding a brown paper bag. She grasped the woman's arm to keep her from falling. The woman looked at Sugar and dropped her bag.

Sugar frowned. "I'm so sorry. Are you okay?" The woman looked familiar, but those eyes removed all doubt.

Candela, the healer who'd supposedly saved her life years ago, looked smaller and frailer than Sugar remembered. She wore her dulled red and peppered with gray hair parted in the middle, pulled tight at the sides and coiled in a bun at the back of her neck. The immigrants called her Keeper of the Keys, because they believed the keys she wore had the power to heal. How many times had Sugar been told she was living proof of that? Sugar knew she should feel warmer and more grateful—but—that wasn't gonna happen now or ever. Candela's eyes gave Sugar the creeps. Her pupils were cat-like and bottomless, and Sugar had the most irrational fear. She was terrified she might get sucked in if she stared at them too long. The older she got the more she realized that regardless of what Mama said, Bertie O'Donnell was right. There must be a rational explanation for Candela's 'miracle' powers. More curious still, Sugar recalled that for as long as she could remember, Mama had sung Candela's praises. Then, something must have happened because a few years back Mama had refused to mention Candela's name..

"Candela. Are you … "

Their eyes locked, and the city began retreating like a vague dream. In the muffled, opaque distance to the tune of fading horns, a flurry of vaguely familiar images shuffled through Sugar's mind like a slick deck of cards in a high-rollers' game. Candela … by her sick bed … outside school … behind her in St. Anthony's church … in the park … in the background … at her wedding ... at …

The Commodore Hotel.

The horror of that night had ripped her from uneasy sleep with recurring nightmares in which she starred as a horrific figment of her own imagination. Behind the tattered curtain lurked a shadowy image. Breanna. And a nagging question. Who was Breanna, and what did she have to do with Candela?

Sugar's terrified heart thrummed. She'd put off finding out long enough. Now was her chance, if Candela would let her.

She let go of Candela's arm, grabbed the railing corralling the subway stairwell and steadied herself. Her face felt hot with confusion. She glanced down and saw Candela's bag lying on the ground. It had split open. Bread fanned out in a doughy deck of oversized cards. Grated cheese sprinkled the sidewalk.

"I'll get it," she said, grateful for a chance to delay the inevitable and turn away from those creepy eyes. She dropped down to her knees, gathered the slices of bread and wrapped them in the torn paper bag. She scraped the cheese off the curb with the side of her shoe, and steeling herself, she handed them to Candela who'd reached so deeply into Sugar's mind, she could not feel the cobblestones under her feet.

Their hands touched, and spaces and lines between street, people and buildings blurred. Her arms dropped to her sides. Her purse slipped through her fingers and hit the ground, spitting up lipstick, tissues and wallet. Coins rolled toward the curb. A passerby picked them up and tapped Sugar's arm, breaking the spell, and the world shimmered into focus.

Ashen-faced, Sugar mumbled, "Thank you." The stranger nodded. Sugar sank to her knees. As she scooped up her wallet, lipstick and tissues, a glint of sunlight-on-metal winked, catching her eye. She looked up and froze. Two gems embedded in two gold rings hung from a chain at Candela's waist. The keys. The gems. The maze. Sugar gasped. Mama's descriptions of Candela's keys had failed, miserably. The disk began spinning. Spellbound, Sugar watched, and a ghost of a smile touched her lips. Suddenly, she needed to feel the keys, the chain and the disk in her hands. She dropped her purse and reached out, but Candela backed away. Flinching as if slapped, Sugar looked up and into those eyes. Frowning distractedly, she closed her purse, got to her feet and to her senses.

"I hope I didn't hurt you. I'm on my way to Mama's. I've got a lot of things on my mind," she said, frowning. The harder she tried not to ramble, the less she succeeded. "That's no excuse for not watching where I was going, but I, um, have questions that only you can answer," she said, and suddenly she felt foolish. Damn it. What was wrong with her? Trying hard to focus she said, "Would you mind if I..."

Sugar's voice faded as Candela's eyes widened in surprise. She'd searched the streets for two days and nights, compelled to warn Sugar that her life was in danger on two fronts: Breanna and Mania. Of the former there was no doubt. Of the latter she needed proof.

Sugar, who'd mostly avoided contact, was here now, talking to her. This was nothing short of a miracle. Candela smiled at the beautiful young woman standing before her. Sugar's eyes were so like Breanna's, deep, dark, huge and flashing with conviction. Her lashes were as thick as sable and brushed the tops of her cheeks when she blinked. Her lips were full and red. Her hair was swept up in a bouquet of black curls with several stubborn and defiant tendrils. Candela's smile faded as the critical juncture at which Sugar, the mortal, ended and Breanna, the goddess, began. Unlike Sugar, Breanna was cunning and ruthless. In matters of state she ruled with an iron fist. She masked treachery in kindness, and in the blink of her eye, she would sacrifice anything or anyone to protect the keys, the kingdom and most of all— herself.

How many years ago had she dreamt of Breanna? Nine? Seven? She frowned. Why did the number seven seem so significant? She rubbed her hand over parched lips. She was so thirsty, she couldn't swallow. Is Bertie right? Do I abuse alcohol? Do I drink as much now as I did in forty-nine AD?

Remember, Candela, you must never go beyond healing. If you interfere in the lives you touch, you will set events in motion you will not be able to stop. Those events will change the course of our fate, and you will pay the price.

That was then, and this is now. If Breanna knew that one night, after following Sugar into The Commodore, Candela had to intervene, her life would be worth less than an empty wine bottle.

She saw Breanna behind Sugar's eyes, squirming like a caterpillar struggling to break free of its cocoon. Be that as it may, circumstances had changed, meaning Breanna must not awake or emerge prematurely, if at all. Praying that the gods in heaven were deaf to her blasphemy, Candela began to abort, when she suddenly realized that the reason their world had ended was right in front of her—locked in Breanna's mind. If she missed this chance to probe, she might not get another. On one hand she should wait, on the other, Sugar would turn twenty-one tomorrow, on the Eve of All Hallows. Breanna would be uncontrollable whether or not she awoke prematurely. The task Candela could not remember but needed to perform when Breanna awoke was locked in Breanna's mind as well. There was only one way to smash those locks. She must return to 49 AD by tapping into Breanna's mind. Candela dropped the bread, grasped Sugar's wrists and—

The world around them turned opaque. Blaring horns, screeching brakes and hissing busses went mute.

Let go of me.

Don't be afraid. Candela's voice soothed, *like a rich, thick unguent.*

What? How are you ...?

Pain knifing through her chest, Candela winced, breaking the spell, and Sugar found her voice. "Let me go now or I'll—"

Ignoring her pain, Candela tightened her grip and—

Suddenly, Sugar stood in the center of a large room. Pivoting slowly, she stared at the frescoed walls. She knelt and caressed the figure of Diana, goddess of the hunt, in tiny black mosaic tiles that spanned the entire room. It was crazy. Insane. Impossible. Everything in this room and in this mosaic looked familiar, because … *she'd seen them in Mama's book!*

Drawn toward a pedestal table, she tiptoed across the floor. A crackling log sputtered. Sugar walked toward the hearth and frowned at the pale blue pillows lying on either side. She picked one up, pressed it against her nose, sniffed it and sank to her knees. She ran her hands over the stones that bordered the hearth, settled on one and lifted it up. The space was empty. She dropped the stone and ran through the door onto the balcony like she'd done hundreds of times before. Millions of stars pricked the sky. Their cold, distant light gave no warmth.

A slender woman of medium height stepped out of the shadows. Her eyes, steel gray and feline, glittered like starlight. Her fiery red hair fell to her waist in a luxurious cape. A braid of gold fastened the tunic across her breasts. The fluted garment fell to her feet in soft, white pleats. Her magnetic smile met Sugar's gaze with beautiful, strange, but familiar eyes.

"Candela," Sugar said feeling the heat and color drain from her face. She stumbled toward the balcony on wobbling knees leaned on the railing and looked over the city. "Rome," Sugar said, and Candela nodded. "Ancient Rome, but how do I know it?" Sugar rubbed her arms, looked down and gasped. The garment she wore resembled Candela's.

Candela lifted the gold chain attached to her waist. Two gold keys jangled against one another, and Sugar said, "They should be under the stone by the hearth. I put them there the last time we—" Her head swam. She stumbled. Candela eased her onto a stone bench by the railing and then pointed to the center of the terrace where the moon showered light on silver roses. Drawn, Sugar giggled. She buried her nose in their velvet-like petals and breathed in. The sweet scent of spring melons and sweeter wines made her head light and her mouth water.

Suddenly, Sugar *turned.*

Eyes narrowed, she scowled. Candela's heart shrank from Breanna's antennae. She knew she must abort now while she still had control. But if she aborted now, she would lose the chance to find out the task she must perform when Breanna awoke. She would lose the chance to learn how their world ended. She grasped Sugar's arms, overrode caution and passed through Sugar's eyes into Breanna's.

Breanna rarely scolded herself, but tonight she made an exception. How could she have been so careless and allow the rift to seduce her? She mustn't think of that now. To forget, she would lose herself in her mortal lovers, a drug she could never resist.

Grasping a handful of silver rose petals, the miracle blossom that bound time's hands, she sprinkled them into her bath. She slipped out of her tunic and lowered herself into the water. She breathed in their fragrance and licked her lips. Molded to her body, the wilted petals reversed aging. Following a luxurious soak, Breanna summoned a young female slave who toweled her dry and massaged her with oils. Ignoring the stubborn tendrils, the slave fastened her hair in curls on the crown of her head, bowed, then slipped into the shadows.

Breanna slid between silky sheets. Her deep, dark eyes fluttered closed. In a tug of war with sleep, she hesitantly surrendered. Her breathing slowed, and then she frowned at a spidery chill skittering up her spine.

A dark shadow drifts past crowds. Flaming torches die in its wake, revelers fall back and scatter. It floats up Palatine hill through the temple and past the guards, who, paralyzed, stare in confusion. It passes through her bedroom door. It presses down around her. Skeletal fingers graze her cheek. Skeletal hands lift her. Pressing shrunken lips against her ear, on plumes of rotten breath it whispers, "Breeeannnnaaaah."

Breanna woke screaming.

The thing staring into her eyes was small and dead. Its hair was gone. Whatever covered its face was black and withered. Instead of eyes, two small voids in its skull housed tiny infernos. It crushed her to its chest. In a puff of putrid air its dead mouth sighed, "The past never stays buried."

Candela froze. Breanna and she shared the same nightmare, proof positive that Mania, the grave danger in 49 AD was a clear and present danger in 1939.

The keys! In her haste to be with her lovers, Breanna had forgotten them by the hearth.

There's more than one way into the rift.

Breanna blinked hard and plunged herself into the rift ...

... despite no longer existing, the body with which Breanna had lived and loved glistened with icy tears that flowed from eyes without substance. Trembling with phantom chills, her essence curled into a ball. Thank heaven for the plan. *Thank heaven?* On the brink of madness, Breanna laughed, cried, swore. Why had the vacuum that was the rift failed to smother her torment?

... had she taken Candela with her? How many times had she almost cried out? Instead, she'd heeded Candela's warning:

No matter the outcome, we must maintain silence. Communicate in the rift. Once a year, in a dream on the eve of All Hallows, a date we will never forget.

Those words were tiny flames that had kept Breanna from cursing the darkness. But, had they ever communicated? Had she pulled Mania into the rift with them? Desperate, she clung to the plan. Once reborn, find Candela, the keys and reclaim their kingdom ...

... had she really been a goddess, or had it all been a dream? Did she have a sister, or had she dreamed that, too? If she had a sister, she should know her name. It all seemed so vague...more like a dream...had it ever been...real...?

Shaking uncontrollably, the normally unshakeable Candela reeled and receded.

"Don't go!" The eyes behind Sugar's begged.

Candela faltered. A pinpoint of light sped toward her.

... for you to live, the woman must die.

Candela aborted.

Candela's sleeve bunched firmly in her hand, Sugar said, "Candela."

Under the frown Candela's eyes looked clouded with sadness. The lines around her mouth seemed deeper. Sugar glanced down and frowned at her purse and the bread and cheese strewn around it. She knelt, scooped the bread and bag up and handed them to Candela. Candela smiled, and Sugar frowned. Suddenly, the eyes that had scared her most of her life seemed to soothe rather than frighten.

"Thank you," Candela said. Her mouth seemed to sag with unspoken words that Sugar suddenly realized how vital it was that she hear. Looking worried, Candela backed away.

"Wait. Please. Don't go!" Sugar's plea was foreign to her ears yet as deeply rooted in her as the roots of the three hundred-year-old elm. On the coattails of that thought came a solid image of something that ... could ... not ... be ... possible.

Chapter 46

Sugar
October 30, 1939

Candela had been in the room with her at the Commodore Hotel that night, but more to the point, Candela had the answers she needed. She craned her neck and ran a few feet, but the crowd had swallowed Candela up. She looked at her watch and gasped. Four o'clock? She was late. She had to get to Mama's. How in God's name did she lose an hour?

Candela.

Shifting gears, she balled her hands into fists and picked up her pace. Images depicting the horror at the Commodore wavered before her eyes. Parts that made her tingle fused with parts of strangulating terror, from which one clear image emerged: the person who'd told Matt about the Commodore was the one person in the entire world with the most to gain if Matt and she divorced.

Conchetta.

Sugar would never forget the look on Matt's face the night he confronted her. His eyes had mirrored his heart. The heart that, through no fault of her own, she'd shattered.

As a comptometer operator for Sears, Roebuck, working pre-Christmas overtime had been a godsend. She needed to tell Matt about the Commodore but while their unforgiving schedules kept them from crossing paths, they gave her the time and space she needed to find the words.

She stood outside her apartment door rifling through tissues and makeup in her purse, searching for her key. Heart pounding, she held her breath and fit the key into the lock. Acutely aware of every click in the lock, she squeezed the knob, eased the door open and paused to listen. Scant light from streetlamps played tricks on her eyes. She tiptoed past the kitchen. Her eyes adjusting, she peered into the darkness. Their bedroom door was closed which meant that Matt was asleep. Breathing a sigh of relief, she felt her way to the sofa, sat on the edge and closed her eyes. That night at the Commodore was a dagger, poised to cut her marriage to shreds. She knew that to minimize the impact, Matt had to hear it from her first, but how could she explain what seemed insane and what she fully did not understand. Terrified she'd lose Matt for good, she'd put it off.

A *click* reverberated through her as light filled the room. She jumped up. "Matt!"

He crossed the room. "Where were you?"

"You know where I was."

His face less than an inch from hers, he put it to her. "Did you ever stay the night at the Commodore?"

How could she put her crazy theory into words? "That night … wasn't what you think."

"Then, you admit it?" He grabbed the sweater she wore, twisted it under her chin and had her up on her toes. "Who is he? Does he work with you? How long have you been sleeping with him?" Curling his free hand into a fist, he drew his arm back. "I oughtta— "

Eyes brimming, she gagged, "No. Matt. Please."

Matt flinched, loosened his grip and pounded an end-table with his fist, knocking the lamp to the floor. She coughed and rubbed her throat. He slumped onto the couch and held his head in his hands. His voice cracked, and she wanted to cry.

He rubbed his eyes. "My mother was right about you, about everything." He grabbed her, and holding her tight to his chest, he breathed into her hair, "I can't do this anymore. I want a divorce."

"Conchetta was wrong," Sugar sobbed. "Trust me."

"*Trust* you? Really?" He threw his head back and laughed through emerging tears, breaking her heart.

"It's not what you think."

"No?" He sniffled and wiped his eyes. "Convince me."

She slid into his arms. He didn't push her away. That meant something. Didn't it? *Say something. Anything. Or you'll lose him for good.* "I love you. I always have, I always will. Please don't leave me. I need your help. My life is in danger."

After swearing that everything she said was true, Matt never said a word. He just stood there white-lipped with glassy, unreadable eyes under a tight frown. She'd never felt so alone. Her life had jumped the rails in nineteen thirty, the year Candela healed her, but Conchetta wasn't the only one who'd gotten things wrong. Sugar jammed her hands more deeply into her pockets and walked faster. Her black leather handbag hung from her hand, hitting her hip with each step.

Matt and she were meant to be, but after the "healing" things had changed, slowly at first and then at speeds that still made her head spin. Her appetites had run the gamut from beef so rare and nauseating it mooed on her plate, to cravings she'd been too embarrassed to admit even to herself. She'd go to bed exhausted and wake in a cold sweat. She was plagued by mood swings which, thank God, would even out. It was during one such reprieve that, swearing she loved him and would never hurt him again, she'd begged Matt to elope.

Lost in thought, Sugar bumped into a very pregnant woman, who scowled, put her hand on her stomach and said, "Watch where the hell you're going!"

Watching the pregnant woman move on, something dark and undefined began taking root in the fertile soil of her mind. Something was growing inside her. Something that had been fighting her for control. If it won, she would disappear forever, and no one would be the wiser. Not Matt. Not Mama. If not for that night at the Commodore—

The weight of the truth bent her knees. She wasn't the one who'd hurt Matt so badly at times she wanted to die. She wasn't the one Conchetta had slapped – if she hadn't gone into The Commodore that night, who had? Seeing her in the flesh that night, Conchetta had unwittingly jumped to the wrong conclusions.

It seemed that all roads did not lead to Rome." They led to Candela. The thought made her heart race with anticipation.

More curious still ... for as long as she could remember, Mama had sung Candela's praises. Then, something must have happened, because a few years back Mama had refused to mention Candela's name..

On that note, finding Candela would have to wait. Finding out why Mama had stopped singing her praises had just taken precedence.

Chapter 47

Sugar
October 30, 1939

Sugar broke into a run. By the time she reached Mama's she was glad she'd followed her gut and asked Matt for help, but there was still one snag in her stocking: He never said he would help her.

Pushing the thought aside, she pushed through the street door and into the hall and started to climb the stairs, when the past flooded the stairwell in a jumble of flashes and echoes. The higher she climbed the faster and harder they hit. Her vision blurred. Her head throbbed with an ache that skittered along her brow to her temple.

Luisa, a cowering little bird ... Mama wringing her hands, begging her and her siblings to pick up their toys before Papa got home.

Sugar stopped climbing and leaned against the wall. Why had Papa treated Mama so badly? She was gentle and kind and always found good in people. She found it in Candela and Aunt Rosa, God rest her soul. Despite their contentious history, she even found good in Conchetta. But she never found it in Papa, because it didn't exist.

Sugar reached the landing where she was born. After she'd heard the story, she said to Johnny, "Now I know why Mama lost God knows how many other babies."

Johnny's cheek twitched. His eyes burned, and his features became as hard as stone. He pounded the wall. "However bad Papa bullied me and you, it was nothing compared to what he did to Luisa. When I was a little kid, Sugar, I cried myself to sleep every night because I was too weak and too scared to stop him."

Johnny was right. Poor Luisa had gotten so nervous, she wouldn't go to school. Her world had become so small, she seemed to stop growing. One day Dr. Robilatto told Mama that Luisa would never be older than twelve. Mama had cried, kissed Luisa's face and blamed herself. That was another mystery Johnny and she couldn't unravel. Why would Mama beat herself up, when the world knew that Papa was to blame for everything bad that happened in their lives? One day, when Johnny and she had asked Mama why Papa picked on Luisa,

Mama would sigh, close her eyes and say, "Everyone handles life differently. He handles it badly and at the expense of others."

Sugar reached their landing and paused. She remembered the night Papa had locked Luisa out of the apartment for some imagined transgression. Sugar, who'd shared a bed in a room with her big sister since birth, woke up that night hearing Mama, fighting to catch her breath in between deep, strangling sobs. Trembling, Sugar reached out, but the bed was empty. Luisa was gone. No matter how long and hard Mama dragged in breath after breath begging, he refused to unlock the door. Sugar dared not move till she could almost hear a leaf fall from the Elm in Washington Square Park. And then, holding her breath, she tiptoed through the kitchen and front door into the hallway. Luisa sat on the cold floor under a dim hall light, staring at nothing. Her legs curled beneath her, her nightgown tucked under her knees. Sugar slid down next to her sister, patted her tangled hair, wiped the tears from Luisa's cheek and whispered, "Why does he treat you this way?" Luisa looked at Sugar and whispered, "Pink dress."

Pink dress? It made no sense. Most times the words Luisa spoke rarely made any sense. Growing up, Sugar had never seen a pink dress in their apartment. And she didn't know anyone who owned a pink dress.

One night, while Mama and she were making sauce, Papa stumbled through the door. His eyes were bruised and black, his cheek was cut, and bleeding and his nose looked broken. When Mama cried out and tried to help, Papa shoved her into the sink and shouted, "Get the hell outta here!" As he stumbled into a bedroom and slammed the door behind him, Johnny burst in from the hallway. Her face ghost-white, Mama screamed, "Johnny, thank God you're here. Papa's in the bedroom. He—"

"I know, Ma." He hugged Mama and whispered against her cheek, "I'm moving out."

"Out?" Her lips trembled. Her eyes pooled with tears. She reached out and stroked his face. "Why? Where?"

"Close by, and don't you worry, Ma, please. Okay?" He clasped her hands and kissed them.

"Of course I'll worry. What will people say?"

Johnny had smiled and stroked her cheek. "It's better this way. And don't worry about anything else." Scowling, he'd thumbed at the bedroom door.

Johnny had packed what he needed in a small bag. He said to give the rest of his things to St. Anthony's.

After Johnny moved, Sugar and he had drifted apart. When Papa found out about Johnny's new friends *around the corner*, he never touched Mama again.

Why did Mama marry Papa? She didn't need him. She had parents who loved her. She was smarter than Papa. Sugar remembered how Mama had helped them with their schoolwork and wondered how Mama could know so much. Mama had laughed with them by day, but at night, when the steps groaned with his footfalls, she turned into someone else. But hadn't they done the same?

Sugar stood outside Ana's apartment. She opened her purse, reached for her compact and powdered under her eyes. She snapped her compact shut and slipped it into her purse. She straightened her shoulders and knocked twice and opened the door.

"Hi, Mom."

"Mom?" Ana stopped pulling the clothesline toward the kitchen window. "You only call me Mom when something is wrong." She unclipped the clothespins and dropped them into a drawstring pouch that hung on a nail on the window frame.

"Really?" Sugar widened her eyes, hoping to stave off the news about Matt and her awhile longer.

Ana glanced at the clock. "You're an hour late. I was getting worried," she said, tossing clothes into a bin.

Sugar hugged her mother. "Either way, aren't you happy to see me?" she teased, kissing Ana's cheek.

"I'm always happy to see you," Ana smiled, patting her cheek. She lifted her laundry bin from the floor and set it on the kitchen table, stirred the sauce bubbling in a pot on the stove and asked, "Where's Matt?"

A badly stained pink dress on the top of the heap caught Sugar's eye. She reached for it. "What's this?" She traced the stain with her fingers.

"Just old stuff," Ana grabbed the dress a little too quickly, Sugar thought. She folded it stain-side-in and tucked it under a shirt. "I'm giving these to St. Anthony's. They can throw away what they don't want."

Sugar moved the shirt aside, picked up the pink dress and frowned. "Funny thing happened on my way up. When I got to our landing, it triggered a memory about the night Papa locked Luisa out of the apartment. I never told you, but very late that night, I snuck out and asked Luisa why Papa treated her so bad, and she said, 'pink dress.' And I walk in and here's a pink dress. Quite a coincidence, if I believed in them, which I don't. Can you tell me what Luisa was talking about?"

She looked at Ana, who shot a nervous glance at Luisa's room. Following her glance, Sugar said, "Is she in there?" Ana nodded. She slid into her chair. Her shoulders sagged. She clasped her shaking hands on the table and lowered her eyes. A gulf seemed to widen between them. Teetering on the edge, Sugar whispered, "Papa treated Johnny and me bad, but he treated Luisa almost as bad as he treated you. Johnny and I tried to figure it out, but we couldn't. We used to wonder what kind of home life Papa had grown up in to make him the animal he is."

She glanced at Ana who averted eyes that looked more tired than Sugar had ever seen. Tracing the stain with her fingers Ana smiled through her tears and said, "That was the night I got so angry at him I couldn't stop shaking, and then I stood up to him. And Papa backed down."

Stunned, Sugar raised her eyebrows and Ana said, "It really happened, I swear."

"Please tell me about it, Mama," Sugar said.

Ana straightened her shoulders. Her lips seemed firmly set against opening.

"I know how talking about the past upsets you. But there are things I need to know that only you can tell me."

Ana sighed and nodded. Her eyes glimmered. "As I said, it really happened. That night, I thought, if looks could kill, our problems would be over," she said in a flat, resigned voice.

Realizing that the first piece of a puzzle she'd spent her life trying to solve had just slid into place, Sugar's heart pounded.

"You were seven, the night Papa locked Luisa out." Ana smiled mirthlessly. "A fitting age for the third generation of seventh daughters."

Mama hadn't mentioned her seventh daughters' nonsense in so long Sugar had forgotten about it.

"The times he lost control after that first incident had resulted in blinding headaches that made him retch and vomit and laid him up for hours." Mama smiled, and Sugar smiled, too.

Sugar sat opposite Ana. She flattened the dress on the table, ran her hand over the stain, pictured Candela and frowned. "Before I got here I literally ran into Candela. Hard enough to knock her groceries out of her arms." Her mother seemed to flinch at the mention of Candela's name. "It's a funny thing, but when I used to think about Papa and those sudden, strange headaches, despite all my doubts about Candela, I had this vague feeling that she had something to do with them. But the more I tried to figure it out, the less sense it made. The headaches made him less of a threat and eventually that was all that mattered, I guess." She stared at the pink dress. "Mama?" Sugar frowned. "Please, Mama, tell me what happened."

"You're right, Sugar. Candela had nothing to do with your father's headaches."

Ana's eyes welled. Sniffling, she reached into her apron pocket for a handkerchief. Seeing the pain in her mother's eyes,
Sugar took Ana's hand. "Mama, I'd rather die than cause you more pain, but I need to know about the past. I need to know what happened."

Ana brewed a pot of espresso. She put two steaming cups on the table and sat. "I knew there would come a time when the past would catch up with me," she said.

"I'm sorry, Mama."

"Don't be." Ana blew on her coffee and sipped. "You have a right to know."

Forgive me, Sugar, she thought, but I can't tell you the whole truth. Not now. Maybe not ever. Ana cleared her throat, put the tiny cup on its saucer and began.

"At the tender age of twelve most young girls start wanting pretty clothes and perhaps they even have a crush on a special boy, but not my Luisa. She was a joyless, depressed child, and I spent every waking moment worrying what would happen to her after I die"

Chapter 48

Sugar and Ana

"My God, Mama," Sugar cried. "You made lights flicker and faucets gush, and bottles fly off shelves? How did you …"

A door creaked open. "You lied, Mama," Luisa yelled from the doorway.

"Luisa?" Ana said, surprised by the outburst. She got to her feet and faced her daughter. "No. It wasn't like that."

"Yes. It was," Luisa said, closing the distance between herself and her mother. "You lied. I heard what you said just now, and I remember what you said before."

"No, sweetheart," Ana said. "I didn't exactly lie."

"You told me it was an earthquake. You made me swear not to tell anyone. Not the neighbors. Not even grandma. You said earth quakes don't happen a lot or to everyone. You said that unless people saw what happened here with their own eyes, they wouldn't believe me. They'd say I was lying." Luisa frowned. "You made me tell a lie, because there was no earthquake."

Sugar grasped Ana's arm. "You owe us the truth about what happened that night."

Ana winced and stared at Sugar's hand.

Sugar gasped at the pain in Ana's eyes. "Oh God, Mama, I'm sorry," she said letting go.

Ana looked at Luisa. "Come. Sit. Sugar is right. I owe you, all of you, the truth."

Ana patted Luisa's cheek. "Let's start with coffee," she said, stirring the simmering sauce. "By the time I'm finished, you may need something stronger." She grabbed the coffee pot, filled three cups, and, setting the pot on a hot plate, she stared into her cup. She lifted her cup, sipped, placed it in the saucer and looked into Sugar's eyes. "How many times have I told you that as the seventh daughter of a seventh—"

Sugar shifted, clearly annoyed. "Mama, please not—"

"Stop it, right now!" Ana said. "You asked me to tell you. If you want to know then you must listen." Sugar lowered her eyes. Ana patted her hand, and Sugar raised her eyes. "This will take time, and at times it will seem strange and hard to believe, but every word I am about to tell you is true. So help me God..."

"So let me get this straight," Sugar waved her hand glibly. "You had this power to move things all your life, all *our* lives, and instead of using it, you let him torture and abuse us?"

Ana's heart pounded. "I swear. It wasn't like that."

"No? Then what was it like?"

"I learned as a young girl that I had the power to *move* things, like I said, until I married your father. On our wedding night," the words burned the back of her tongue, and her eyes glazed over. "After he ... I lay as rigid as a corpse until he fell asleep. Barely breathing and in such pain, it hurt to cry, I crept into the bathroom and looked in the mirror."

Luisa's face grew pale. In contrast Sugar's dark eyes grew darker and rounder.

Ana ignored her impulse to stop. "My breasts and cheeks were purple with bruises. My lip was split. Rage I hadn't felt in years bubbled up inside me. Lights dimmed. Towels tied into knots. The medicine cabinet flew open. Bottles sailed across the room, exactly like they did right here in front of Luisa, Lia and Giana that night. Suddenly, your father was in the tiny bathroom with me. He wrapped my hair around his fist and called me a witch. He told me to clean it up, and then banged my head into the wall."

Sugar said, "I could kill that son of a bitch with my bare hands!"

"It's all right. It happened a long time ago. It's over."

"No, Mama. It's not all right no matter how long ago it happened. As long as he lives it will never be all right or over."

"I tried getting my power back," Ana said. "I swear. I was desperate. I knew our lives would be different. Better, safer. I combed my memory," Ana said, smiling mirthlessly. "And I found that back then, like everything else in my life, the advent of my power had stemmed from a fight with Mama.

"I was reading *Tales of Greek Gods & Men* by the elm and stream in our yard, when Mama opened the door and yelled for me to come in. She said they were hungry and they were sick and tired of always having to wait for me.

"Well, I got very angry, perhaps even enraged. You may think that I reacted strongly at being yelled at for such a minor thing. But you must understand that when I was a child growing up, Mama got mad at me *every day* for something I did. So, when she yelled at me for that, my anger boiled over, and things began," Ana paused, and then said, "moving. Leaves, twigs hurled through the air. The stream whipped up stones One hit my cheek. I grabbed the book before it fell into the stream. Suddenly, I felt terrified, and everything stopped.

"I remember being dazed all through dinner that night while dozens of questions passed through my mind. Did I cause it? Was it a gift? A curse? Why did I have it and not my siblings? Mama kept telling me to stop daydreaming," Ana scoffed.

"After deciding it was a gift, I began to think of the endless possibilities this gift could give. Dishes washing themselves. Beds making themselves. I could hide my siblings' toys. I could spill their ink." Ana giggled. Sugar giggled, too, and Luisa smiled.

"A similar incident happened at the home of Alberto Petruzzi, the boy to whom I was ... betrothed."

"Betrothed?" Sugar said.

"Betrothed," Ana sighed. Relaying the story, she watched Sugar's and Luisa's eyes grow wider with every detail.

"Watching Alberto shove his food into his mouth against his will until he vomited, I realized the enormity of my new-found power and that my anger fueled it."

Sugar frowned. "I don't understand, Mama. If anger fueled it, then why—"

"Fear smothered it, Sugar. And your father terrified me every day of our married life.

The smile slipped from Ana's face. "There was only one other time that my anger had turned into rage strong enough to overwhelm my terror. It happened before you and Johnny were born, Sugar. It was the night Vincenzo dangled," she swallowed hard, "Luisa out that window for the sin of forgetting to fill his wine glass."

Luisa's face went from pale to white. Her eyes welled with tears, and Sugar's eyes grew so wide she looked like she was in pain. Ana reeled, fighting her panic. Sugar had a right to know. But how could Ana tell her without herself and Luisa reliving the horror?

"Mama? Maybe you shouldn't ..."

Ana shook her head and cleared her throat. "You have a right to know the truth." She started speaking slowly, and then her words flew like arrows into Sugar's heart. Despite Ana's mouth going dry and seeing the pain of reliving the past dull Luisa's eyes, she kept talking.

"I knew I had embarrassed him badly in front of Luisa, Lia and Giana, God rest their souls. I knew he'd never forget it. But," Ana smiled, got to her feet, stood by the stove and stirred the sauce. She raised the spoon to her lips and tasted. Satisfied, she set the spoon on a saucer on the stove and turned off the gas. "But I smelled his fear, and for the first time since our wedding night, it was stronger and more rancid than mine."

Sugar got to her feet and clenched and unclenched her fists.

"Are you all right? You don't look so good." Ana turned on the faucet, ran her hands under the water, reached for a dish towel on a hook near the stove and wiped her hands.

Sugar reached for the pink dress in silence.

"Let me have that, sweetheart." Ana reached out, but Sugar held the dress close to her heart.

"So, Papa's abuse and brutality toward you and Luisa was worse *before* the pink dress and empty wine glass incident? Worse than anything Johnny and I ever experienced?"

Ana frowned. "Yes. He knew that my threshold for danger to myself was far more flexible than the threshold for danger to my children. And the headaches kept him in check."

"Mama, Matt works for Domenico Sciorri in his machine shop on West Broadway."

"Yes, I know," Ana said. "I also know that Domenico's stepson, his American wife's son, still owns it."

"That's something I never understood. Domenico Sciorri lives a few blocks away, and all these years Papa never had anything to do with him. Now and then I'd hear neighborhood people whisper about Papa's father, and how he'd brought another woman with him to the dock when he met the ship."

"Yes," Ana nodded and began filling them in.

Sugar shook her head slowly in disbelief.

"So after that strangeness on New York Harbor," Ana said, "your grandmother, Bianca Sciorri, turned around, got on the boat and sailed back to the old country," Ana looked into Sugar's eyes. "Despite how horrible that chapter in your father's life or his whole life may have been, I will never forgive him for anything he does. People suffer far worse, but they don't lose their humanity."

Ana stood, shook her head and sighed. She set a large empty pot in the sink, ran the water and looked out the window. "It's getting late. When will Matteo get here?"

Sugar ran her fingers through her hair. "He's not coming."

"Why not? Is he all right? If you listen to Conchetta ," Ana turned off the faucet and lifted the pot to the stove. "Matteo's been working himself to death. He's not getting sick, is he?"

"Oh God, Mama, there's no easy way to put this," Sugar said.

Looking troubled and confused, Ana held the pot in mid-air.

"Matt wants a divorce."

Ana dropped the pot in the sink. Water and pasta sloshed over the sides and puddled on the floor. "My God, Sugar. No one in our family has ever divorced. What are you doing? To yourself. To us. You are Roman Catholic! The church forbids divorce. If you died this minute, you'd go straight to hell for your sins."

Gasping, Luisa clamped her hands over her ears and shut her eyes tight. Her eyes glassy with unshed tears, Sugar jumped up and grasped Ana's hands. "Mama, please!"

"No!" Ana jerked free. "And what do we tell your father?"

"For God's sake, Mama, after you just spent the last two hours telling me about this?" Sugar pulled Luisa's pink dress from the laundry. "Do you honestly think I give a damn about what he thinks?" She threw it on the floor.

"Stop!" Luisa screamed, jumping up. "Stop!" she ran into her room and slammed the door.

Sugar panted. "I'm sorry," she said, regretting her harshness.

"What will people say?"

"People? Like who?" Her regret vanished. "Conchetta?"

She could fight to the death defending herself. How ironic that Papa, the cruelest most godless man and Conchetta, the most spiteful woman would have her mother, God, the pope and the Church on their side!

"Just people," Ana said. "You live with your lot in life, Sugar. You don't divorce." Ana kissed her fingers and raised her hand to her forehead.

Sugar grasped Ana's hand in mid-air. "Don't, Mama. What good did the sign of the cross ever do us?"

"Are you adding blasphemy to your list of sins?" she sighed and stroked Sugar's cheek. "I watched your face earlier. I never should have told you about the past all at once. I've had years to digest it. You've had minutes. You must be in shock. Have you eaten yet today? You shouldn't go without eating."

"There are some things food doesn't cure."

"Like divorce? My God, Sugar. I know you were married at City Hall, but you were married at Saint Anthony's, too. You vowed to be faithful forever before God and the whole neighborhood. Two months later the boy who spent his life loving you wants a divorce?" Ana said her eyes bright with tears. "I've heard rumors about you at the Commodore Hotel."

"What?"

"I defended you. I said it was a lie. But it wasn't, was it? Why else would Matt—"

"Mama! Don't you want to hear *my* side of the story? Look, I know you're not comfortable with ... with certain ... kinds of ... talk, but it's your turn to listen to me. What's fair is fair, isn't that what you always taught us?"

Ana sniffled and half-laughing, half-crying said, "And all these years I thought you weren't listening."

Chapter 49

Sugar

Ana poured two cups of coffee. Sugar sipped, shook her head slowly and set the cup down. She stared into the deep, dark liquid. "Honest, Mama. This is the hardest—"

Knock! Knock!

Sugar frowned. Ana looked at the clock. "Your papa is working, and I'm not expecting any visitors."

"Sit tight." Sugar slid off her chair and opened the door. "Matt?" she said, dumbfounded. "Does this mean—"

Matt pulled her close. "I'm in, God help me."

"Matt," Sugar breathed. "I love you." When he didn't answer, disappointment grasped her heart. One step at a time. She was grateful he was here, but she was terrified he would go through with the divorce, especially after hearing what she had to say.

"Matteo?" Looking confused and overjoyed, Ana wrapped her arms around him and kissed his cheeks. "So good to see you."

"Thank you. It's good to see you, too." He glanced from Ana to Sugar. "I'm interrupting something." Sugar looked at Ana, and Matt said, "No problem. I'll be back later."

"No, Matt. You have a right to know what happened at the Commodore that night more than anyone. Please sit."

As he sat between her and Mama, Sugar blew out a breath and said, "This is the hardest story I have ever had to tell, but what terrifies me is that neither of you will believe me."

"You won't know until you try us," Matt said.

Nodding, she lowered her eyes, took a deep breath and said, "First, I need you to believe that *I* couldn't stop what happened that night, because … it was not happening to me, it was happening to … to … her."

A thick wall of silence fell, broken only by the sound of their breathing. Matt held her gaze. Unnerved, but determined, Sugar said, "If it hadn't been for Candela—"

"Candela whom you avoided your whole life?" Ana said, breaking the silence. "I don't understand."

"I know. I have a hard time understanding it myself. But now that I know about your power, you might be the only one who can understand." Seeing the puzzled look on Matt's face, Sugar said, "I'll tell catch you up later, I promise."

Matt nodded, and Sugar breathed a sigh of cautious relief.

"When Conchetta attacked me in public on the street that day, I," Sugar said, pausing for emphasis, "I did not counterattack. *She* did."

"She?" Ana said. "Conchetta saw you go into the Commodore Hotel. Viola Triani told me. I called her a liar. But everything she said was true."

"Conchetta. Of course. She was the woman outside the Commodore window, looking in."

Matt and Ana looked at each other, perplexed, and Sugar said, "I know what it looked like to Conchetta, but she was wrong. I didn't cheat. I swear it wasn't me."

"Do you expect us to sit here and believe—"

Sugar cut her off. "Can you let me walk you through before you ask questions?"

They looked at each other and nodded, reluctantly, Sugar thought. In their shoes she might not be as generous.

"Okay," Sugar sighed. "After that blow up with Conchetta, I was so angry, I found myself on the West 4th Street subway station with no recollection of how I had gotten there.

"Anyway, the train stopped. Its doors slid open. I got on ... but, I swear, *she* ... got off ..."

While she spoke Matt watched her, clenching and unclenching his jaw. By the time she finished, he looked pale and shaken and as if he would vomit. Oddly enough, Mama looked relieved.

Ana poured herself a cup of coffee. She motioned the pot toward Sugar and Matteo. Both declined, and she set the pot on the stove.

"If you know who Breanna is, Mama, you've got to tell me."

"I've known since thirty-five."

Sugar was up out of her chair. "Four years ago?"

Matt looked as astounded as Sugar felt.

"Yes," Ana said.

"Then do you ... do you believe me?"

"I'm trying very hard to."

Sugar's eyes welled with tears. "Thank God. That's a good start," she said, slumping into her seat. She looked at Matt who looked as if he was trying hard but couldn't quite believe her either.

"That morning, Luisa had been whimpering badly. To comfort her, I started talking." Ana smiled weakly. "Hearing my voice always seemed to calm her." Her smile faded. "I told her how worried I was about the changes in you. I'd noticed them shortly after Candela healed you. I confronted Candela many times. She had the answers I needed. But she refused to tell me. She said if she interfered in the lives she touched she would set events in motion that she would not be able to stop. I refused to accept that excuse any longer. The day I confronted her, I swore I would not leave until she answered my questions."

Ana got to her feet, dragged a large tin box from under the dresser next to her bed and pulled out *Tales of Greek Gods & Men*.

"My God, I haven't seen that book in ..." Sugar paused, frowning.

"Years." Ana finished Sugar's sentence, clutching the book to her heart. "I was so afraid your father would burn it in the coal stove, so I hid it."

"Bastard," Sugar muttered. "What does it have to do with Candela?"

"She has the exact copy. I've read this book so many times I could recite it from memory, and when Candela started ... talking ... most of what she said, except for the parts about her and the keys, came straight from this book!"

Sugar touched the book lightly, and a montage of images flashed before her eyes. An ancient temple ... frescoed walls ... silver roses ... scents. Confused, she frowned.

"I listened to her, but I kept hearing Bertie O'Donnell saying that Candela may be sweet and harmless, but she was not in her right mind. Bertie was doing everything she could to protect her, but it was just a matter of time before Dr. Robilatto and Father Andretti put her away.

"Honest to God, Sugar, the things Candela said scared me half to death. And God help me, they changed the way I saw her, forever."

Frowning, Sugar rubbed her temples. "And I thought you had finally come to your senses and realized that there was a rational explanation for that key-healing nonsense." Sugar frowned at Apollo's picture. "What did she say?"

"She talked about recurring nightmares with a shadowy figure that warned, the past never stays buried. What terrifies me is that your nightmare corroborates hers and makes her craziness less crazy. She rambled on about a haunted stream flowing under Hangman's Elm that creates a mist that only she can see. Years ago, when she overheard

Eric Van Broc, Bertie's teacher-brother, tell his class that story, she swore that it triggered a past life she'd led among the Canarsee, a tribe that lived in what is now Washington Square Park," Ana said as Sugar's eyes widened. "There's more."

The longer Ana talked, the more astonished Sugar looked.

Ana grasped Sugar's hand. "She said that *you* ... my God, how do I say this? She said that *you* are her sister, Breanna, reincarnated."

Sugar felt the heat and color drain from her face. The room began receding. She bit down hard on her lip to keep from fainting. Ana squeezed her hand harder.

"The changes I saw in you, and the ones you saw in yourself, were part of an on-going transformation that would be complete on the Eve of All Hallows on your twenty-first birthday."

"Tomorrow night." Sugar wiped the sweat from her lip. "Andretti and Robilatto were right. Candela is crazy."

"She said that Breanna had laid down the law. Beyond healing, Candela must never intervene in people's lives. To do so might risk their lives and alter the course of their fate. And, there was something she needed to do when Breanna 'woke up,' something critical, but she couldn't remember what it was."

Sugar got to her feet, grabbed her purse and her jacket.

"Where are you going?"

"Candela's."

"No," Ana pleaded. "Candela believes everything she told me. If she helps Breanna complete this transformation, you will die."

"Mama, all my life you've told me that Candela loves me. What if you're right? What if she wants to help *me* and not Breanna?"

Matt's chair scraped the floor as he got to his feet. "Speaking of help, you asked for mine, remember? Well, I'm coming with you."

"Thanks, Matt, but I changed my mind. Candela has the answers I need, and I don't think she'll give them in front of you." Sugar grabbed *Tales of Greek Gods & Men*. "Mom, can I borrow this?"

"Sure, but why?"

She slipped the book into her purse. "I've got a hunch." Sugar closed the door behind her.

Matt stood and grabbed his jacket.

"Where are you going?" Ana said.

"I'm not letting her do this alone."

Ana grabbed her coat. "Me neither."

Chapter 50

Candela
October 30, 1939

On a surge of adrenalin, Candela pushed through the crowd into Washington Square Park. Beads of sweat erupted along her hairline and streamed down her cheeks. Lightheaded and panting, she reached her bench opposite Hangman's Elm and sat for hours. She was furious with herself for not warning Sugar her life was in danger. But after looking into Breanna's eyes she knew that had she done so, Sugar, like Ana, would never have believed her. She closed her eyes and faced the truth: She'd failed Sugar.

She pressed her lips together and sealed off a scream. Something clammy touched her cheek. She frowned and opened her eyes. The mist cocooning her seemed damper and thicker. She massaged her temples. Mist might cloud her vision, but her mind was clear: The probe past Sugar's mind into Breanna's had confirmed what both she and Breanna had feared most:

Mania attacked Breanna prematurely ... in her haste to escape her fate Breanna had run right into it by plunging the three of them into the rift. Mania was here now for their souls, a priceless tribute to win back her place in Hades' vile Underworld court.

It was Mania who had tried seducing Breanna that night at the Commodore Hotel, which complicated Candela's dilemma. Breanna and Sugar were in grave danger, and she could only save one. The probe had exposed another layer. Candela loved Sugar but loyalty to Breanna and the kingdom had been woven into the fabric of Candela's heart at her creation. Her impossible choice was clear: Love or Duty. Dazed and exhausted, she got to her feet and stumbled into a passerby.

"Candela, my child."

The voice set her teeth on edge. She opened her eyes. They narrowed to slits. "Father Andretti. Dr. Robilatto."

Honest to God, Candela ... if Doctor Robillato and Father Andretti were here ... now, you'd be on your way to Bellevue for psychiatric evaluation. They've spent the past nine years looking for a reason to put you away.

Father Andretti grasped her hand. "What an incredible coincidence," he smiled, squeezing her hand. "We were just talking about you. Weren't we, Doctor?" Robilatto smiled and nodded. "You're going to have your hands full with the new wave of immigrants."

"Yes," Dr. Robilatto said. Candela glanced from one to the other and kept silent. "Oh, of course," Dr. Robilatto said, broadening his smile. "I know how deeply immersed one gets in healing the sick. But, Candela," he said, leaning in, conspiratorially. "There's another coincidence, which, in a very tiny way, may link us to history."

Candela frowned. She had no time to stand here and listen to whatever obscure point he was trying to make.

"You are aware of course that Hitler invaded Poland."

Goodness! How could that get by her, she thought, but kept her eyes blank.

"No?" Dr. Robilatto said. "I'm surprised. It's been all over the radio waves for weeks. I can see by the look on your face that you're wondering what that has to do with our little community."

"May I?" Father Andretti interrupted.

"Be my guest," Robilatto smiled.

"Hitler invaded Poland on September first, the same day that Sugar and Matteo eloped. You know of course that millions of Germans migrated here in the eighteen-hundreds. I hope the coming wave will fully integrate those who are here."

"Fully integrate?" Candela said, stunned.

Integrate.

That was it! That was the piece she'd been struggling since forever to remember.

"Integrate," she uttered the word in visible relief. Relief turned to unbridled joy, and she laughed out loud. The stunned looks on the good doctor's and the sainted priest's faces almost bent her in half with laughter. She straightened up as tears streamed down her face. She did, however, manage to stop herself from throwing her arms around them in undying gratitude for the colossal favor they had unwittingly done her.

Candela, you must remember at all costs that when I emerge, it is essential that I successfully integrate *during the first twenty-four hours of my host's twenty-first birthday.*

Candela stopped laughing abruptly. "And if you fail?" she whispered, reliving the conversation with Breanna.

278

"What?" Father Andretti asked. She stared at the doctor and priest who looked at her as if she were completely insane. Two minutes ago, he would have unnerved her, but now she didn't give a damn. They were insipid, irrelevant twits whose opinions meant less than nothing.

I will not fail. Nothing ... can or will stop me.

"What if your *host* refuses to fade?"

Dr. Robilatto grasped her shoulder. "What host? Who are you talking to? What are you talking about?"

Refusal is not an option.

"Except on the Eve of All Hallows when she is free to reject you."

"Halloween?" Looking astonished, Robilatto stared at Andretti. "What in God's name does Halloween have to do with any of this?"

"Black Magic. Devil worship," Father Andretti clearly gloated, "have everything to do with Halloween."

Yes, but my mortal host won't know that, will she?

Candela's heart thrummed. Could victory be that easy? Must Sugar simply refuse to integrate? Candela couldn't waste precious time speculating. "Doctor? What is today's date?'

"October thirtieth. Why?" He looked more confused.

Sugar turns twenty-one at midnight.

I-I hope I didn't hurt you. I'm on my way to my mother's, and I've got a lot of things on my mind. That's no excuse for not watching where I was going...

"What time is it?"

The doctor checked his wristwatch. "Eleven o'clock."

One hour to the Eve of All Hallows. She had until midnight to find Sugar and tell her how to save her life. She started to walk away.

Dr. Robilatto stepped in front of her. "Where are you going?"

"Ana's."

"Are you crazy? You know Vincenzo hates you."

Gratified she'd chosen love over duty. Candela smiled. She wanted to hurry, but the mist was thicker than usual and made her slow down.

Father Andretti said, "Doctor, will you tell me what just happened?"

"The Keeper of the Keys is clearly having a mental breakdown. She's way overdue," Robilatto frowned. "Father, I'll follow Candela. Call Bertie O'Donnell and have her meet us at Ana's. Be quick about it. Candela is clearly unhinged. Vincenzo is violent. Something very bad is going to happen."

Chapter 51

Sugar and Candela
October 30, 1939

Panting heavily, Candela paused at the door of Ana's building. The fog was so thick she plunged her hand through and grabbed the doorknob. Feeling the doorknob turn in her hand, she let it go. The door opened and sucked mist into the hallway. Sugar stepped through the mist onto the sidewalk, bumped into Candela and grabbed her before she fell.

"My God. I seem to be making a habit out of assaulting you. Are you all right?" Dazed, Candela nodded. "Good, because you're just the person I want to see. Your place or mine?"

Sugar watched Candela unhook the keys from her waist and store them behind a small sliding panel under her window. Sliding the panel closed, she gazed at the clock on her dresser. Sugar followed her gaze. Eleven-thirty. Candela retrieved a bottle of wine from a small closet next to her dresser. She placed it and two glasses on the table. She uncorked the bottle and filled each glass. Sugar raised hers. "To truth."

"To truth," Candela said, and clinked Sugar's glass.

Sugar pulled *Tales of Greek Gods & Men* from her purse. She put it on the table next to the bottle of wine. "Mama told me all about your conversation the day she visited. I'm here tonight for answers of my own."

"Does that mean you and Ana believe me?" Candela picked up the bottle and refilled her glass. She tilted the bottle toward Sugar's glass. Sugar placed her palm over her glass. Candela shrugged and put the bottle on the table.

Sugar raised her glass. "What I believe will depend on you." She sipped, put the glass on the table, looked Candela directly in the eye and said, "Were you at the Commodore that night, or did I dream that?"

"It wasn't a dream." Candela drained half her glass.

"I remember what happened that night, but I need you to confirm it for me." Sugar said, sipping.

Candela upended her glass and grabbed the bottle. "Breanna had unwittingly plunged Mania into the rift with us. Every god in heaven and every creature in the Underworld, especially Mania, knew that Breanna was promiscuous. It was Mania who seduced you, or rather she seduced Breanna, at the Commodore that night."

Sugar grimaced. "That guy was a—"

"A demon. A devil. Yes. The opportunity I took to look behind your eyes and into Breanna's showed me that Mania tried the same thing in forty-nine AD. And her goals have not changed for two thousand years. She wants my soul and yours or rather, Breanna's, and the keys in exchange for her place in Hades' court.

My God, thought Sugar! Were Mama, Bertie, the doctor and the priest right? Is Candela telling the truth, or has she broken with reality?

"There's something I found out on the night I healed you," Candela said. "I know seventh daughters of seventh daughters have great power and that the third generation, *Septissima,* has the greatest power of all. So, why don't I sense any power in either of you?"

Those incredible eyes glistened, and Sugar suddenly realized how vulnerable Candela was. The truth would cause her great pain, something Sugar did not want to do. Whatever happened that night, whatever Candela had done to heal her, Sugar had survived. Mama was right. She owed Candela her life. She also owed her the truth. To deny her the truth or feed her delusions would be cruel, wrong and hurt her more in the end. She laid her hand on the book.

"Mama claims she used to be able to move things with her mind, but that was a long, long time ago. I know Mama is very smart, and she has a vivid imagination. She devoured every book she could hold in her hands, including," she patted the book, "this one. And me?" Sugar smiled. "If only I did have such power, but the truth is I don't. I am as powerless as any human.

"Look at the title of this book. It begins with the word 'tales.' And that's what it tells. Tales. As in mythology. I've thumbed through it on and off. Gods, goddesses. Sevenths. *Septissimas.* Death. Rebirth." She turned the book toward Candela. "Mama read it cover to cover many times. And everything you are saying is all here, except ..." Sugar sighed. "The Roman Empire fell in four-seventy AD, give or take. It's nineteen thirty-nine. Rome is a modern city in a modern country. You and Breanna have no kingdom to reclaim."

Candela shed one tear, breaking Sugar's heart. She turned the book toward Sugar. "You're wrong. I know it's hard to believe and it sounds insane, but the truth is Apollo is my father. My keys are around his waist. Look."

Suddenly, Candela's eyes went wide and blank. "Do you see it?"

Frowning, Sugar looked around. "See what?"

"The mist is in the room. It's so thick I can hardly see you," Candela said.

To Sugar's astonishment, Candela waved her hand as if trying to clear a mist that was not there. Not knowing how to comment, Sugar slowly turned the book around. Candela frowned, picked the book up and held it to her face. "There are no keys," Sugar said.

Candela drained her glass and set it on the table. "There's a misprint in your copy." She got to her feet and felt her way to her dresser, grabbed her copy and returned to the table. "See?" She grabbed the bottle, felt the rim of the glass and poured.

Sighing and shaking her head imperceptibly, Sugar leafed through the book. "This chapter takes place in forty-nine AD. It's about a goddess, Breanna, daughter of Apollo, but it never mentions a half mortal sister or healing keys. You told Mama that this past life came to you in a dream. Is it possible that you dreamt about this chapter and were so enthralled that you put yourself—"

Candela slammed the book closed. "You are not listening!" She winced and panted. "The Commodore. Mania. The attack … happened. It was real."

Sugar frowned and rubbed her temples. Her head suddenly throbbed as if a herd of elephants stampeded across her forehead. The crushing pain made it hard to think. "I know it was real, but the harder I try to understand, the more it slips away."

"Breanna is erasing it from your mind. If you don't remember what happened, you won't know she exists."

Squinting through her pain, Sugar saw Candela get to her feet, 'wave' her way through the fantasy mist, grab the clock from the dresser and set it on the table. She grabbed Sugar's wrist.

"Look. Eleven fifty-five. You've got to believe me. Your life depends on it. In ancient Rome Mania was banished to the bottom of the River Styx—"

Candela was hard to hear. The stampeding elephants blocked her voice.

Candela let Sugar go and said, "Where would Mania live in the here and now?" Her pupils grew round and burned like a madwoman's. "*Manata.* Of course. Devil water. She lives in the stream that flows under the elm.

The mist ... seemed to appear at will. Was it her mind or ... or was she the only one ... who ... saw it? Did the people in the park not see the mist because it was buried in a past that had nothing to do with them, and everything to do with her?

Candela's burning eyes widened. "It fits. We're all connected. You. Me. Breanna. The keys. The elm. The mist. The Ancient Greeks believed the elm had a dark side; that it stood at the door between life and death; that witches shunned it, but Demons embraced it!" Giddy, Candela laughed, and Sugar gasped.

"One shadow roosted on each of its seven boughs like a murder of slumbering crows. On certain afternoons in the thinning daylight, the shadows swooped down and taunted, 'We know a secret.'

"But there are no more secrets. Mania was my nightmare. It was she who whispered that the past never stays buried.

"One night I saw three of its branches glow with their own light. Four remained dark. You see, Sugar, they symbolized two of my past lives and this present one. When I am reborn again, a fourth branch will glow." Candela's eyes stopped burning. She held Sugar's face in her hands. "Your life is in danger."

"My God, Candela. Do you hear yourself? Mama, Bertie, the doctor and the priest are right. You need help, and you need it right away. I owe you my life. Please let me help you."

Candela grasped Sugar's sleeve. "Look at the clock. It's eleven fifty-eight.

"Listen to me. In two minutes Breanna will emerge. By midnight on the thirty-first, your twenty-first birthday, the transformation from mortal to goddess will be complete. Breanna has until midnight on the thirty-first to fully integrate. If she fails—"

Sugar frowned, feeling something familiar and frightening. Something she hadn't felt since the night at the Commodore Hotel. It was fighting her for control, and if it won, she would disappear forever. And no one would be the wiser. There was something about the Commodore she couldn't remember. Her mind reeled with confusion. Was Candela right and the rest of them wrong?

"Sugar. To defeat Breanna you must stop the integration. The moment she emerges you must shout—"

The clock struck twelve.

"*In vino et veritas.*" Breanna's lips curled into a cruel smile.

"No!" Candela cried out, clutching her chest.

"Look at you. How your eyes glitter with terror and your face contorts with pain," Breanna said, doubling over with laughter. "Behavior so unbefitting for a goddess. She straightened up and sniffled. Her features set in cold hardness. "You betrayed me!" she shouted.

"No, Breanna. It wasn't like that," Candela said, panting. Her knees collapsed and she sank to the floor.

Breanna glared down on Candela. "I warned you that wine and your weakness for mortals would be your downfall. I—"

Her senses on high alert, Breanna narrowed her eyes to slits, she frowned and leaned toward the door. "Do you hear that, Candela?" she asked, not really wanting an answer. "*Her* precious Matt, *your* precious Ana, the doctor, the priest and the social worker are on their way down the stairs," she said, sneering. "They won't save your miserable, traitorous life. I'll see to that."

Knock! Knock!

"Sugar!" Matt shouted, "Open the door!"

Breanna's features softened. Her eyes pooled with tears. She opened the door. "Matt," she cried and flew into his arms. "Thank God you're here," she said, kissing his cheek. Her eyes narrowed at the panel under the window that held the keys to her kingdom. She'd be back for them. Soon. "Candela needs help. Hurry!"

"Sweetheart," Ana said, hugging her daughter. "Are you all right?"

"Of course I am, Mama," Breanna said. "I knew Candela would never hurt me. She loves me, just like you said."

"My God," Dr. Robilatto rushed past Sugar and Ana and knelt at Candela's side. "Father Andretti, call an ambulance. We've got to get her to Bellevue."

The priest hurried out the door.

Robilatto checked Candela's pulse. Candela frowned, opened her eyes and looked at the doctor. His eyes on Candela, Robilatto said, "Sugar, what happened?"

Candela's fingers circled his wrist. "Doctor, she's not—"

"I don't know, Doctor," Breanna said, cutting Candela off. "We were talking and then she clutched her chest. Her face turned white and twisted in pain," Breanna began sobbing.

"Please," Candela panted, her fingers clasping his wrist. "She's not—"

"Candela," he said. "Don't try to talk. Please. Rest. Stay calm. Help is on the way."

Breanna sobbed harder. Matt held her closer and said, "It's okay, baby."

Breanna's mind raced. She had to get out of here. She had to kill Mania, now, while Mania thought Sugar was in control.

She lives in the stream that flows under the elm.

She had to get to the elm in Washington Square Park. "Matt," Breanna sniffled. "I feel faint. I need to step outside for some fresh air."

He held her in his arms. "I'll go with you."

"No," Breanna said, impatiently.

Matt frowned. *Damn!* Breanna knew she'd answered too harshly. "I mean. I'll be fine." She let her kiss linger and felt him respond. "I'll be right outside," she whispered in his ear. "You stay with them. The doctor may need your help. I'll wait for the ambulance and point them in the right direction."

Ana's eyes narrowed. It wasn't like Sugar to show so little concern. *The train stopped. Its doors slid open. Dazed, Sugar got on ... but... she ... got off.*

She went into the Commodore Hotel. I wasn't one who'd cheated on Matt. I wasn't the one who'd done all those hurtful things to the people I loved, she did. And now Sugar had a name to go with all those deeds. Breanna.

Ana was a believer. While the doctor put a pillow under Candela's head and Matt covered her with a blanket, Ana slipped out the door and followed Breanna.

Chapter 52

Breanna
October 31, 1939

Collar up and head bent against the wind, Breanna hurried north toward Washington Square Park. Her forehead creased into a frown Her paced slowed. Was it her imagination or was someone following her? Her breath scratched against her throat. Her frown tightened. She stopped abruptly and turned. The street was empty. Dismissing her overactive imagination, she shivered, turned north and picked up her pace.

Seeing Breanna stop, Ana gasped and ducked into a storefront. Her heart roared. She held her breath, closed her eyes and pressed herself into a corner. Waiting the longest few moments of her life and praying that it was safe, she opened her eyes. She slid along the store window and peeked out slowly. Watching Breanna hurry across the street, she slipped out of the doorway, moved down the street close to the buildings and closed the gap between them.

Breanna gagged. The wave of nausea swelling inside her could roll a steamship. Woozy, she stopped walking and gagged harder. If she didn't rest, her legs might give out and she'd be clawing her way to the park over cobblestones on her hands and knees.

Nausea, her constant companion these days, wasn't from gorging. The last time she'd gorged and purged was in Rome in forty-nine. The mere memory reached in and twisted her bowels like a fist. She leaned over the curb and retched. She walked a few steps, and pressed her forehead to the cold, soothing metal of the lamppost, wanting to die. Smells sent her reeling. Good. Bad. It made no difference. Sizzling steaks. Mildew. Savory sauces. Rotting garbage. Honey cakes. Rancid fish and oil and gas from the East and Hudson Rivers. Breanna steadied herself. Despite the onslaught of sewage and fumes, she sucked in little breaths, ferreting out oxygen. Her stomach struggled to right itself. She crossed the street to the park and hurried down the path to Hangman's Elm.

***

Ana gasped. My God. For Breanna to vomit, something was wrong with Sugar. "If you hurt my baby …" Her voice vibrated. "I'll … kill … you." Hearing the words and imagining the deed, she felt her face burn with anger. A vague but familiar feeling flexed her fingers. Her pulse throbbed. Her heart pumped energy through her veins like electricity through wire. Breaking the chains of fear it rose to the surface. Trembling with rage, Ana entered the park and moved down the path. Breanna stood by the plaque and gazed at the elm. Inching closer, Ana stepped over the iron rail and hid behind Hangman's Elm.

Breanna ran her hand over her stomach and saw …

… *Sugar in Matt's arms six weeks late and smiling. No more doubts. No more fears. No more craziness. This time was for keeps. She'd never felt better or more certain about anything in her life.*

Breanna raised her fist and snarled, "Damn you to Hades!" Did she hear someone gasp? She frowned, turned around quickly and blew out a disgusted breath. Her nerves were raw. She must integrate soon. She clenched her hands into fists and pounded them on her thighs.

"Pregnant." Having destroyed too many to count, how could she have missed this one? She relaxed her fists, grinned slowly and patted the bump. "No matter, sweetness. Whatever the outcome, you're next."

She tried to swallow, but fingers tightened around her throat. She twisted around. There was no one behind her. The path was empty. She clawed at her throat, trying to pry them loose.

Sugar.

Breanna blinked hard, and feeling the fingers fall way, she grinned. "Too bad our night at the Commodore happened before you could tell him. Poor Matt will never hear the good news."

Breanna frowned as a tattered scarf of mist formed on Hangman's Elm. Suddenly, Apollo's words echoed … *The elm has a dark side …*

Breanna grinned. "That witches shun but demons embrace. Demons like Mania." Her grin faded. She shivered and rubbed her arms. "How can I fight Mania without Candela?" Fear seeped through, weakening her courage. Despite the damp air, sweat pearled above her lip. She reached inside, fighting the urge to run. Her eyes grew as hard as her new resolve. "Win or lose, the keys are locked safely away. You may take me, but without the keys, you are damned to the River Styx for eternity. Do you hear me, Mania? And a fight could cost Sugar her

287

baby. Hmm," Breanna grinned, feeling stronger. "Is this what Daedalus meant by killing two birds with one stone?"

Breanna's words cut Ana's gut like a knife. Ana's eyes shone with rage. She must protect Sugar and her baby or die trying. She stepped away from the elm.

"Timing is everything," Breanna said, pivoting. "Do you hear me, Sugar? I will not get sucked back into a vacuum and rot, waiting to be born again. You, and I and," she spread her hand over her stomach and closed her eyes, "and whatever *this* is, will integrate. Now!"

Breanna frowned, annoyed. She opened her eyes. Someone was standing behind her. "Ana," she said without turning.

"How do they say?" Ana said.

Feeling Ana's breath on her neck, Breanna turned. Amused, she smiled.

Returning her smile, Ana said, *"Actions speak louder than words."*

Streetlights flickered.

Breanna laughed, "Is that all you've got?"

Ana blinked, and the wind sang. Dirt and leaves danced to its tune, getting caught in Breanna's hair. Breanna's mouth twisted into a grin. She threw back her head, but before she could laugh, a gust of wind tore the laugh from Breanna's mouth. Ana frowned. Seeing Breanna's eyes narrow, Ana scowled, and the wind roared, sending Breanna back on her heels. It thrashed the bare limbs of surrounding bushes and trees. Breanna raised her arms. An all-consuming anger turned each feature on Ana's face to stone. The wind roared louder and harder, rattling trash cans and whipping the elm's massive branches. One massive branch split from the trunk, striking Breanna's shoulder, weakening her hold. Her knees buckling, Breanna glared. Ana's eyes bulged. The wind stopped. A hush fell over the park.

Somewhere a clock struck...

One...

Fear slammed through Breanna. Ana stepped back. Her eyes mirrored Breanna's terror, terror she could not sustain without going mad.

Tatters of fog knitted together and thickened.

Three...

Breanna knew she must integrate now. Ignoring the swirling mist, Breanna closed her eyes.

Five...

Ana screamed. Her focus breached, Breanna opened her eyes and...

...It stood before them. Black withered skin. Eyes infernos of rage and madness. Skeletal fingers caressed Breanna's cheek. Its mouth inches from hers, in a cloud of green putrid air, it sighed, "Breeeannnnaaaah. The past never stays buried."

Seven...

Her stomach churning, Breanna gagged. While fighting the demon's grip, a faint voice rose in her throat.

To defeat Breanna you must stop the integration. The moment she emerges you must shout—

"I reject you," Sugar said, reading the words etched in fear in Breanna's mind.

Breanna froze.

Sugar felt the demon's grip tighten.

Ten...

"I reject you," Sugar cried.

Breanna's hold weakened

"I reject you," Sugar shouted. "I reject you!" she screamed. "I reject you!" Sugar shrieked and shrieked as loud and as long and as hard as she could.

Eleven...

Breanna's eyes bulged. The demon clung harder. Beyond terror, Breanna blinked hard, plunging herself and the demon into the rift. Sugar's eyes rolled back in her head. At the stroke of...

Twelve...

Sugar's body stiffened, arched and collapsed.

Chapter 53

Bellevue Hospital
November 1, 1939

Bertie stood by Candela's bed between Dr. Robilatto and Father Andretti. "She looks so frail." Her eyes glistened. Her lip trembled. "What's the prognosis?"

With a God-knows shrug, Robilatto said, "The admitting doctor confirmed my diagnosis. Candela had a massive heart attack." Bertie gasped. "Alcohol complicated her physical and mental health."

"I warned her over and over to stop drinking," Bertie pulled a tissue from her purse and dabbed her eyes.

"It's fortunate for Candela and us that Bellevue is the most modern facility for treating alcoholics," Dr. Robilatto said. "She's in the best hands."

Father Andretti folded his arms over his chest. "Uh, pardon me, doctor, but those would be God's hands," he said, looking smug.

"Yes, of course," Robilatto said, clearing his throat. "In any event, I hope she comes through this. I don't know how Ana or Sugar would take it if …" Dr. Robilatto's voice faded. He frowned and looked around. "Speaking of Ana and Sugar, where are they?"

"Right here," Ana said.

At the sound of her voice, Dr. Robilatto, Father Andretti, Bertie and Matt watched Sugar and Ana walk into Candela's room.

Sugar smiled at Matt who moved to her side. She looked at Candela and the smile slipped from her face. "How is she? What happened?"

Robilatto sighed and shook his head. "Her condition is critical." He cleared his throat and nodded at the doorway. "Why don't we gather in the waiting room where we can talk freely?"

While the others followed Robilatto, Matt held Sugar back. "What happened? Where were you? Are you okay?"

"Sugar?" Candela heard Sugar's voice, but the mist was too thick to see her. Candela leaned on her forearms and tried to sit up but collapsed from the exertion.

Sugar's face emerged from the mist. "No, Candela. You've got to rest. Your condition is—"

"Critical. I know. What time is it? What day is today?" she panted.

Sugar checked her wrist watch. "It's one thirty am. November first. All Souls Day," she smiled. "The Catholic Church's Holy Day of Obligation. Quite a fitting day to end our fantastic journey, don't you think?"

"Then you believe me?"

"Yes. I believe you. Matt and Mama believe you, too. You rest. We'll be right outside. We'll talk later, I promise."

Candela frowned. "Sugar?"

Matt had stepped out of the room. Sugar stopped, turned and gasped. The room was suddenly filled with a fog so thick Sugar couldn't see an inch in front of her.

What terrifies me is that your nightmare corroborates hers and makes her craziness less crazy. She rambled on about a haunted stream flowing under Hangman's Elm that creates a mist that only she can see. Years ago, when she overheard Eric Van Broc, Bertie's teacher-brother, tell his class that story, she swore that it triggered a past life she'd led among the Canarsee, a tribe that lived in what is now Washington Square Park.

Shaking but unafraid, Sugar moved through the mist to Candela's bed. Her heart pounding, she said, "I see it. Your mist. I see it! I see it!"

On a face ravaged with age, illness and fatigue, Candela smiled, and the mist vanished. Her smile faded. The lines in her face deepened to seams. The seams beaded with perspiration. She clutched her chest. "Breanna?" she panted.

"Gone."

As Candela met her gaze, Sugar stared into her incredible eyes, and suddenly, she stood in a large, familiar room. The Roman temple.

Yes, she had seen the room in Mama's book, but that did not change the fact that she'd stood in that room before. And she was standing there now.

The temple and its lavish decor were exactly as she remembered. The black mosaic of Diana, goddess of the hunt. Silver roses that swelled the air with the scent of spring melons and sweeter wines. The blue velvet pillows on either side of a hearth. The loose stone under which Breanna had hidden the keys. The balcony under millions of cold, distant stars that gave little light and no warmth.

At the sounding of murmuring silk, Sugar turned.

"Candela," she whispered, gaping in awe now as she had then.

Candela's amazing eyes, steel gray and feline, glittered like starlight. Her copper-red hair fell to her waist in a fiery cape. A braid of gold fastened the tunic across her breasts. The fluted garment fell to her feet in soft, white pleats. Candela's magnetic smile met Sugar's gaze, and for the second and last time, Sugar saw Candela, the breathtaking creature, half mortal daughter of Apollo, the Greek God of Healing.

Candela's smile faded. Her face turned old, pale and dead.

"Mama!" Sugar screamed.

Chapter 54

Sugar

Staring blankly, Sugar followed the others into the waiting room. Matt slid into the seat next to Sugar's. "Drink this." He handed her a cup of cold water.

"Thanks." Sugar sipped, watching Dr. Robilatto talk with a man in a lab coat. Another doctor, she presumed. The doctor kept glancing at an open file in his hand. He would occasionally peer over his glasses and glance their way. Dr. Robilatto raised his hand and said, "Bertie? Can we speak with you for a moment?"

"I know this is a bad time," Matt whispered, but while we're waiting for them to wrap it up, can you please tell me where you were and what happened?"

Promising details later, Sugar hit the high points. Fifteen minutes had passed.

"Jesus," Matt said. "So, does this mean that Candela wasn't senile or crazy? That everything she told you and your mother about Ancient Rome, this goddess-reincarnation stuff, the elm, the mist, Mania, everything was true?"

Sugar sighed. "On one hand it's crazy and hard to believe. On the other, I know what I saw. I know what I felt, and there was this horrid struggle that went on inside me for years, Matt. You know. You were the victim of my moods and my behavior. As of one a.m. this morning, whatever it was, thank God it's gone for good." Tears streaming down her face, Sugar placed her hand on her stomach.

"Are you okay?"

"Better than okay," she smiled at the question in Matt's eyes. "Oh-oh," she said and jutted her chin outward. Matt followed her gaze and saw the doctor close his file. "It looks like Bertie and the doctors are winding down."

Dr. Robilatto said, "This is Doctor Finn. He's a psychiatrist on staff. He was able to ask Candela a few questions before she passed." Dr. Robilatto addressed Dr. Finn directly. "Candela has no relatives that we know of. Everyone here can verify that Ana and Sugar were her closest friends. Father Andretti, Bertie and I knew and, uh, worked with Candela for years. I'm certain that Candela would approve if you spoke candidly about her physical and mental condition."

"Very well." Dr. Finn peered over his glasses. "I took the liberty of conferring with Mrs. O'Donnell to shed some light on my preliminary findings." He opened his file. "Although we will never reach a firm diagnosis, based upon my conversation with Candela and Mrs O'Donnell I believe Candela was delusional. What she thought of as her 'rebirth' or awakening was due to a deepening descent into dementia complicated by alcohol abuse."

"My God," Ana said.

Sugar wondered what the doctors and Andretti and Bertie would say if they knew everything that had happened a few hours ago and what had been happening for nine years since the day Candela had healed her.

"She claimed to remember things that just are not true, that cannot be true for obvious reasons. People with dementia break with reality at different rates. Candela appeared to function well on many levels until she passed. I can only speculate that her progression or deterioration, depending upon your perception, had been slow for years but became rapid with age."

For every question Sugar, Ana and Matt asked, all of them, the doctors, Father Andretti and Bertie O'Donnell had plausible explanations.

"Dementia." Ana scoffed. "If that's so, how do you explain all the people she healed and those of us who witnessed it? My Sugar would have died of diphtheria, if not for Candela," Ana said, staring blankly. "It was as if she could almost read minds."

Robilatto took the question. Matt got up and the doctor took his seat. "Think! Did Candela really heal Sugar or was it a combination of the toxin I had administered earlier, Sugar's good health and her youth and our good luck?" he said, sounding clearly ruffled He paused and looked at Father Andretti. "And God's mercy, of course." He reached for her hand, and Sugar gasped at the disgust on her mother's face. "Candela was smart and perceptive. The immigrants were poor and easy to read. Their wants and needs were basic. Most of all, she was intuitive, thus their perception that she could read minds."

"If I may add one final comment," Dr. Finn said. "You mentioned that Candela had a copy of the book *Tales of Greek Gods & Men*. Apparently, she was so enthralled with that book that the more her dementia progressed the more real her place in that story became."

Nodding in ascent, Robilatto patted Ana's hand and rose, clearly indicating the conversation and the subject were closed.

Sugar watched Ana press her lips together. She saw Ana's jaw muscle tighten and her eyes dim with false acceptance. This time she agreed with her mother's sentiments completely. There was nothing more to say to him or them or anyone here, now, or ever.

Chapter 55

Ana and Sugar
Washington Square Park
November 1, 1939

Sugar sat between Ana and Matt on Candela's bench in Washington Square Park until sunrise. The branch that nicked Sugar's shoulder lay on the grass by the plaque. It was massive. If it had hit her head, it would've killed her. She gazed at the tree and wondered if it felt the loss of its severed limb. Her shoulder throbbed like a toothache, but she suffered pain in places drugs couldn't reach. She grabbed Matt's and Ana's hands and squeezed.

"Can someone please tell me what happened and if any of it was real?"

"Candela was real, Sugar." Ana said, patting Sugar's hand.

"Yes. And she healed me, too." Matt said.

"My God. You're right," Ana said. "In all of this craziness I forgot. That was the reason Conchetta had used to convince me to send for her in the first place."

"No matter what Robilatto says, he was jealous of her. It ate him alive, because Candela succeeded where he failed in ways that had nothing to do with healing. I saw it with my own eyes."

"Robilatto was right when he said that both of you especially you, Ana, had been closer to Candela than anyone. I know that for a fact, because it drove my mother crazy."

"When I think of the years wasted when I could've gotten to know her. She wanted that. I know she did. Every time she looked at me I could see it in those eyes," Sugar said. "Those eyes scared the hell out of me until I *really* looked into them."

"I know how you feel. I asked her my questions," Ana said. "And when she finally answered them, I ran."

Intermittent conversation followed periods of silence. The autumn sun elbowed its way through clouds, leaving frosted grass on either side of its tepid footprint. When the sun set on their silence, Sugar said, "I'll never forget the look on her face when she realized that there were no keys around Apollo's waist on the cover of either book,

Mama. She imagined them like she must've imagined a lot of what happened."

"I believe that the doctors were partly right. She was ill physically and perhaps mentally ill with age. But regardless of what they said, we know the parts that were real. My God, we all know what we saw, and we'll never forget it."

"But whether the keys had power," Matt said, "they were real. Speaking of the keys, where are they?"

"I saw Candela hide them," Sugar said. Her head began aching. She closed her eyes. The harder she tried to remember, the more her head pounded.

Matt said, "If you stop trying so hard, do you think they might pop into your head?"

"Beats me. All I know is that I've been starving for pickles and ice cream for weeks."

"Pickles and ..." Matt said, "You mean you're ... you mean ... we're ...?"

"Starving." Ana said, turning white. "Oh God. We've been out all night. Vincenzo is probably home starving, oh God."

"Ana," Matt said, taking her hand. "You're not going back there alone."

Ana lingered, drew in deep breaths and squeezed the doorknob hard. "What will I say? He'll never believe ... how can I explain any of this?"

"Don't you dare worry about that," Sugar's voice cracked. She wanted to scratch her father's eyes out. "Just open the door," she said, pushing the words past the lump in her throat.

Ana opened the door into an empty kitchen. "Thank God," she whispered, and Sugar bit her lip, wanting to cry. "Matteo, Sugar, *Vieni e siediti entrambi, per favore,*" she said, sounding like a prisoner on death row who had just gotten a stay of execution. Matt pulled out a kitchen chair for Sugar and one for himself.

"*Bedda mama,*" Ana said smiling tremulously. "You must be starving, eating for two." She opened the icebox. "Let me see what I can—"

"No, Mama. If we're tired, you must be exhausted. Sit. Please. We have enough talk in us to last five consecutive lifetimes."

Footfalls echoed up the stairwell. Ana gasped, the last sound before silence entombed them. Ana's mouth tightened, and Sugar swore to end the torture that was her mother's life. The closer the footfalls, the more ragged Ana's breathing. They echoed, reechoed, stopped abruptly. The door opened.

"What's this?" Vincenzo said, slipping out of his coat.

"Papa." Pasting a smile on her face Sugar got up and stood behind Matt's chair. She wrapped her arms around his neck and pressed her cheek to his. "We have good news," she kissed Matt's cheek. "We're having a baby."

"Yeah?" Vincenzo smiled a smile that felt icy against her cheek. He hung his coat over a kitchen chair, then reached for a mug and poured a cup of coffee. "I'm not surprised," he said in a soft voice.

"You're not?"

"Of course not." He took a sip then looked at Ana. "Why is my coffee cold?" Ana opened her mouth. Sugar scowled. His hand sliced through the air. "Never mind. Tell me, Sugar, *cos e quell detto Americano, la mela non cade lontano dall'albero?*"

"The apple doesn't all far from the tree?" Sugar said, annoyed. "What are you talking about? That doesn't make any sense." How did he do it? How did he take the sweetest news and turn it sour?

"Oh, but it does," he said. He sat on the chair and pulled off his boots. "You see, you were always more like your mother than your brother and sister ever were." There was a look in his eye Sugar had never seen before.

"Vincenzo, please. Ana shifted in her seat and glanced at Sugar. "Not tonight. This is a happy time for the kids."

Vincenzo scoffed, ignoring Ana, and Sugar's simmering anger went to a boil.

"Sugar," Ana said, "Have you seen a doctor?"

Shaking her head, she folded her arms on the table and leaned toward her father. "More like my mother than my sister or brother ever were? I take that as a compliment, but my gut tells me that's not the way you mean it. So tell me, Papa, just what the hell are you talking about?"

"Please, Sugar, don't get upset. It's bad for the baby."

"Nothing really." Vincenzo put his boots next to the stove. "It's just that you truly are your mother's daughter. Isn't she, Ana?" He touched Ana's cheek.

"Please, Sugar," Ana said.

"No, Mama. I want him to tell me exactly what he means."

"Sleeping with more than one man like," Vincenzo smiled and nodded at Ana. "Like your mother did."

Matt shifted uncomfortably in his seat. Sugar stared, too stunned to speak.

"Shocked?" His mouth twisted into his cruel smile. "I never thought I'd admit this, but you are actually more respectable than your mother. She slept with one man, got pregnant and married another." Vincenzo sneered.

Ana's face turned beet red, and she whimpered.

Matt shot out of his seat. "Matt, no!" Sugar screamed, jumped up and grabbed his arm. Matt's jaw tightened. His eyes blazed. "Please," Sugar said. She felt his muscle relax under her grip. Matt blew out a breath and slid into his seat. Sugar frowned as pieces fell into place like tumblers and unlocked the secrets. She suspected Mama had gotten pregnant out of wedlock, but pregnant with another man's child?

"That explains everything," she whispered. Hatred burned like a blue flame in her eyes. "Mama never would've married you unless she had no choice." The flame turned cold with contempt. "You tortured Luisa from the day she was born, because Luisa is not your daughter."

Luisa Sciorri frowns hard. Sugar's voice leads her to the door. Sugar's words slice through the jungle of her mind. Thirty-three, and she still rarely steps out of her room when Papa is home. Luisa senses today is different. She cracks the door and peers into the kitchen. Matteo and Sugar look angry. Mama looks sad and exhausted.

"You always were too smart for your own good."

"You hated Luisa more than you hated Johnny and me because Luisa is not your daughter. You tortured Mama by torturing Luisa. Do you realize how you have destroyed her?"

Papa isn't her father and she isn't his daughter? Sugar said it, and Sugar never lies.

"How can you torture a helpless woman and her innocent child?"

Skilled at going unnoticed, Luisa slips into the kitchen and Ana's seat. She sees the slide drawer under the table, touches the handle. Images flash before her. Mama. Papa. A ... pink ... dress. Her bladder lets go and Luisa scowls.

"Do you hear me, Matt? How can I still call this animal, this sadistic son of a bitch, Papa? Sugar lunged for her father. Vincenzo slapped her face. Matt stepped in front of her and went for Vincenzo.

A scream builds. Luisa's lips tighten, trapping hatred and rage behind them. She opens the drawer, closes her eyes. Bypassing spoons and forks, she grips the knife.

"Don't even try!" Vincenzo's eyes bored into Matt's. "Whadda you think I was stupid all these years? Did you think I didn't notice how you was itchin' to fight me ever since you was a little shit?" Vincenzo's spittle sprayed Matt's cheek. "How dare you challenge Vincenzo Sciorri in his own home! I oughtta crush you like a bug, you little bastard." Matt clenched and unclenched his fists and Vincenzo sneered. "But I won't because like my daughter, you ain't worth the trouble." His colder-than-usual smile never reached his eyes. "Let me give you some advice you don't deserve. Your mother was right. You're a good boy, and she's a slut. When I married her mother," he thumbed at Ana, "at least I knew that her bastard wasn't mine. You know what she's like. Can you say the same?"

The veins in Matt's neck bulged. He reached for Vincenzo. Vincenzo grabbed his shirt. "What's the matter with you? How many ways you gotta hear it, you dumb bastard? A man's gotta know the truth about his woman. This one?" Vincenzo jutted his chin at Sugar. "She's pure *putana,* a tramp worse than her mother."

"Vincenzo, for God's sake stop!" Ana pleaded.

Vincenzo loosened his grip and patted down Matt's shirt. "You're a good boy, from a good family. You deserve much better. Ask your mother."

Luisa stood and Ana frowned. Where had she come from? Had she been she sitting there all along? Luisa got to her feet and time slowed.

Clutching the butcher knife, Luisa raises her arm, Ana screams. Luisa stabs Vincenzo's shoulder. He cries out. His eyes darken with rage. He growls, tightens his fingers around Luisa's throat and shakes her. Her head snaps back and forth. Luisa gags, drops the knife and claws at Vincenzo's fingers. Her bulging eyes water. Tears spill on purple cheeks and drip on Vincenzo's hands. Ana grabs the knife and plunges it into Vincenzo's back.

Vincenzo lets Luisa go. His eyes widen in shock. He twists his arm behind him, struggling to reach for the knife. He coughs, scratches at

300

his throat, gurgles red bubbles, falls to his knees and chokes on his blood.

Luisa coughed, struggling to breathe. His fingerprints collared her neck. Ana opened her arms. "It's all right." She looked at Vincenzo and said, "It's over. He'll never hurt us again."

Sugar stared at her father's body. "We've got serious trouble here. What are we going to do?"

"Call the police. What choice do we have?"

"No, Matt. The cops will arrest Mama and maybe Luisa." Sugar stood up. "No arrests. No trials. God knows we've suffered enough at his hands. Sugar picked up the phone.

"Who are you calling?" Matt asked.

"My brother, Johnny."

As Ana watched Matt take the blanket from her bed and cover Vincenzo, she wept for her papa. She pictured his smile. His laughing eyes. His quick sense of humor. Poor Papa. So excited and full of hope for a better life for his wife and children in America. She stared at the body that littered her kitchen floor and realized that their fates had been sealed the day she married Vincenzo.

She cried for Tonio as she saw him cross Houston Street blindly at the same time a horse had broken loose from its owner. Everyone screamed, trying to stop it but the horse reared up, knocked Tonio down. Its hoof landed on Tonio's cheek and crushed his skull. Rosa and Tonio – gone in the same day. Perhaps the same hour, minutes apart. Had Tonio lived, Ana knew he would've stopped Vincenzo from harming her family. Thank God Papa had died not knowing how her love for Carlos had condemned her family to suffer.

When Johnny's men took Vincenzo away, they all knew that no one would know how Vincenzo had died tonight. Sugar and Matt scrubbed the kitchen floor, while Ana rinsed a bloody rag into the bucket, knowing this was the last time she'd ever wash blood away because of Vincenzo. Every night for thirty-three years Ana had begged God to take Vincenzo. Tonight he died by her hand, and she felt nothing. No shame. No remorse. No gratitude. She regretted her marriage but she never regretted having Luisa. When Johnny's men buried him, Ana knew they would bury the way he died with him.Tonight she'd made good on her promise. Her children and her unborn grandchild were free.

Epilogue

Penny Mcquade
Greenwich Village, New York
October 30, 2018

Dr. Nero opened the laptop on her desk and clicked on a file labeled 'Penny McQuade.'

The office door flew open. "Finally!" The voice was young, female and agitated.

Dr. Nero looked up and watched a young and very attractive woman close the door behind her. She crossed the room in irritated strides. She tossed her purse on a brown leather chair in front of the doctor's desk and put her hands on her hips. "I've been trying to get this appointment for weeks," she said, in a shaky voice.

"I truly am sorry about that," the doctor said, kindly. She got to her feet and extended her hand. "I'm Doctor Nero."

"Penny McQuade," Penny said in a softer tone. She took the doctor's hand and squeezed. Hard. "I need help and I need it now."

"May I call you Penny?" Dr. Nero asked, trying not to flinch or pull her hand away.

Penny frowned and nodded. "Sorry," she said, releasing Doctor Nero's hand.

"Not to worry," Dr. Nero said, mindful of not flexing her aching fingers. "Have a seat."

Moving her purse aside, Penny slid onto the chair and into a shaft of sunlight that set fire to the copper red mane framing finely chiseled features in a perfectly oval face. Suddenly, Dr. Nero saw the significance in her name.

"Is something wrong?" Penny said, flashing her most unusual eyes.

They were angry-sky gray with coal-black vertical pupils. Dr. Nero recognized the symptom. A rare genetic disorder in the iris that gave the pupil a keyhole shape. She'd seen pictures in text books, never in person.

"Uveal coloboma," Penny said. "Street name, cat-eye syndrome. Nature's own guy and friend repellent."

"How did you—"

"A family doctor explained it to my mother, uh, that is, my adopted mother, and me. I understood it all right, the problem is, the rest of the world didn't."

"I'm sorry," Dr. Nero said.

Penny shrugged. "Don't be. I'm getting used to never fitting in. Anywhere."

Dr. Nero cleared her throat, slid into her seat and made a note in Penny's file to deal with that issue at a later session.

"It says here that you're twenty ... oh my goodness. I see you have a birthday coming up. Tomorrow. Halloween. You'll be twenty-one," she said, lightheartedly. She looked up at Penny. "I have an eleven-year-old daughter who would kill to trade birthdays with you."

Penny crossed her legs. "I don't have insurance. Does your file say that, too?"

The doctor's smile slowly faded. "Yes it does," she said in a neutral tone. "But the initial consult is free." A fact that did not seem to dial Penny's apparent anxiety down one notch.

Penny folded her hands on her knees and squeezed until her knuckles turned white. "I saw something in the park that ... I can't eat. I can't sleep," she paused. Her eyes glistened. She unclasped her hands and uncrossed her legs. Tears clung to her lashes like liquid diamonds. She rubbed them away with the heel of her hand. She leaned over and pulled a tissue from a box on Dr. Nero's desk.

Dr. Nero clicked out of Penny's file and closed her laptop. "Okay, Penny. You see that couch?" Dr. Nero said, glancing across the room ...

Penny sank into the soft, buttery-yellow leather couch. She clasped her hands and rested them on her stomach. Dr. Nero sat on a matching chair with her laptop and a small recorder. Penny watched Dr. Nero lean over and slide her laptop on an oak coffee table in front of the couch. She put the recorder on the end table.

Penny sat up, concerned. "I didn't know you were going to tape me."

"My ears only, Penny, I promise," Dr. Nero said, smiling. "Some first-time patients have a similar reaction. I tape for accuracy."

Frowning, Penny settled back on the couch.

Dr. Nero opened her laptop. "All right," she said, clicking on Penny McQuade's file, "I want you to close your eyes, take a deep breath and try to relax. And then, I want you to describe what you saw in the park that day in as much detail as possible. Okay?"

Penny nodded and closed her eyes. Hearing a *click* she took a deep breath and began.

"So, it happened right after I moved here. It was July. Hot but clear Big blue sky. Puffy white clouds," Penny said, squeezing her clasped hands together. "I was sitting on a bench in Washington Square Park opposite a fenced-off section of grass. There was a plaque on the fence that said, 'Hangman's Elm.' Then my eye caught the top branch of the elm." Penny frowned. "Thinking back, it was more like the branch captured my eye. Suddenly, the elm turned into a giant map. I followed the branch to the trunk, and that's when I saw them."

"Them?" Dr. Nero asked. Penny could hear the frown in her voice.

"Three people. They stood inside the fence next to the elm, and they were staring at me. Don't ask me how or why, but I knew they were a family. The father was in the middle and his daughter and son stood on either side. They didn't look real. They looked unreal, sort of faded, faint, you know, transparent. Like ghosts." Penny frowned. "Yeah. That's it," she said, nodding. "The whole scene was like something out of a movie. I used to see them every time I walked through the park past the elm."

"Used to?"

"Yeah. I figured if I avoided the park, I'd avoid them. But that didn't happen. I dreamt they were standing in my room under my window. I woke up soaking wet and on the verge of screaming. That's why I'm here. You gotta help me."

"I'll do my best," Dr. Nero said. "Do they ever speak to you?"

"No."

"Do any of them look familiar to you?"

"No. And they were dressed kind of weird."

"Weird?"

"Their clothes were old. Not torn-and-tattered old, but like a hundred-years-out-of-date old."

Penny heard the click of Dr. Nero's laptop. "Penny, you mentioned before that you were adopted. Did you grow up here, in the city?"

"I grew up on a farm in Madison County that's been in my family, my adopted family, since nineteen-ten."

"That's very rare and quite wonderful. I bet there are boxes and albums of old photos lying around in closets or in an attic." Penny nodded and Dr. Nero said, "Is there any chance that the family you saw in the park might be in one of those photos?"

"No."

"What makes you so sure?"

Penny frowned. "Their clothes. Even though they're old, they look expensive, handmade or tailored. None of the families in the boxes or albums are dressed that well at all."

"Why did you leave home?"

Penny scoffed, sat up, threw her legs over the couch and opened her eyes. "These!" she said, pointing to her eyes. "And this," she said, grabbing a fist full of hair. "I never fit in. Grade school. High school. I tried MCCC, Madison County Community College, thinking it would be different. I dropped out after a year."

"Do you miss your parents? Do you have any siblings? Do you miss them?"

"It doesn't matter. I'm never going back.

"I found this place on Thompson north of Houston. The realtor called it a 'studio,'" Penny said, putting air quotes around the word. "Which is New York City-speak for a basement room that's two times smaller than my room at home.

"Do you know that one year's rent on that place would buy a whole house in Madison County?" Penny asked, not really wanting an answer.

She pictured the sunlight struggling through her transom-like street level window in a city that she hated more each day, no matter how hard she'd tried not to. Like it or not, this was the end of the line. If she couldn't fit in in New York City with all its crazies …

"I haven't slept in weeks. I'm afraid to. I know as soon as I do, they'll … I was a server at Toloache, a Mexican bistro in midtown next to the Gershwin Theatre. I was exhausted. I kept making so many mistakes I got fired. My cards are maxed out. My iPhone is out of data, and I don't know how I'm gonna make next month's rent.

"Doctor, who are those people, and why do I keep seeing them?"

"I don't know, but we're gonna do everything we can to find out." Dr. Nero clicked off the recorder. "I want to see you again next week."

Penny stood and held out her hand. "Thank you for listening, Doctor." *But, for two hundred a pop, I don't think so.*

Penny moaned. She twisted and turned. Her eyes flew open. Bathed in sweat, she bolted upright. Despite the streetlight, it was dark out. She leaned over, switched on her nightstand lamp and gasped.

She wasn't dreaming. *They* were standing in her room under the window.

"Who are you and what do you want with me?" she screamed, feeling angry this time rather than scared. And oddly enough, intrigued.

Their eyes never left hers. Seeing them up close, their gazes were unnervingly familiar. It seemed as if they knew her. The boy and the man moved aside. The girl looked up at the window.

Penny frowned and followed her gaze. She swung her legs over the bed, feeling so enthralled, she barely felt the floor chilling the soles of her feet.

There was a small panel door under the window. Why hadn't she seen it before. Wondering what else her exhaustion had blinded her to, she moved toward the window. She stepped in between the girl and her father. And a current, sudden and swift, sizzled through her, jarring memories, that up to now she did not recall.

Shaken, she reached up and slid the panel door open. Behind it was a space and in that space was a blue velvet box, and a book, faded and yellow with age. She pulled them out of the vault. She put the box on her bed, looked at the book and frowned. Something inside her that slipped away long ago had just slipped back.

"Tales of Greek Gods & Men?" She looked up and gasped.

The family was gone.

She opened the velvet lid and stared with eyes so wide, they ached.

There in the box were the most indescribable set of keys she had ever seen.

Dumbfounded, she wondered who they belonged to, and what doors were they meant to open.

Trembling, she lifted the keys from the box.

They looked and felt like they were solid gold. They were attached to a gold keyring on a gold chain. A wafer-thin disk, twice the size of a quarter, seemed to hang suspended inside the ring. The disk was etched with an intricate maze. When Penny touched the disk, something ancient and powerful entered her bloodstream. She traced the maze with her finger. The closer she got to the center, the stronger the power became. Feeling too small to contain it, she pulled her hand back and looked at the keys.

Embedded in each key was a gem that dispersed colors and light she had never seen.

She laid the keys in the box, gently. She picked up the book. On the cover was a picture of a Greek god. The chain and the keys, disk and all, hung around his waist. Eyes wide and heart pounding, Penny opened the book and began to read.

"Epilogue. All that remained of the proud, beautiful, powerful beings that had once roamed heaven and earth were the keys to their kingdom, a thirst for their former glory and a maddening belief that one day they would return to reclaim them."

Exhausted, Penny closed the book and looked up. Her window framed an oblong of daylight. Had she read all night? She swung her legs over the bed and slipped on her socks, sneakers and jeans, a turtleneck sweater and a hoodie. It was cold. It was October 31st.

Penny froze. It all fit. The family! The keys! The book!

Her twenty-first birthday.

She slipped the key chain over her head and around her neck, zipped up her hoodie and grabbed the book. She hurried out the door, up the stairs and into the street. She ran so fast, she barely felt the sidewalk beneath her feet.

She ran through the park and got to the bench, panting. She set the book on her lap and looked at the tree. Ana, Giani and Tonio were not there. She didn't expect them to be. Suddenly, her eyes grew as wide as the smile on her face. Four elm branches glowed with their own light. A gentle breeze caressed her face, nuzzled her hair and fluttered the book's pages. She felt the keys against her heart, and for the first time in her life, Penny McQuade was exactly where she belonged.

MY VERY SPECIAL THANKS TO MY EXCELLENT READERS ...

Diane Czechowicz, my dear friend, for the hours she devoted to critiquing *Keeper of the Keys*; for her honesty and intuitive feedback and for her unwavering and continuing support.

Jan Prestopnik, my dear friend, respected teacher and critique partner for her efforts in the tedious critique process, and for possessing an understanding that helped this author to enrich the characters and their stories.

ABOUT THE AUTHOR

Rosemarie and her husband Joe, a retired school administrator, have been happily married for fifty-one years. They are blessed with a beautiful family, two sons, a daughter, a daughter-in-law, and two precious grandchildren.

Besides loving to write, Rosemarie loves to read and entertain family and friends. In addition to domestic and foreign travel, the Sheperds enjoy snowshoeing in winter and cycling the magnificent Rails to Trails along the Mohawk River on the historic Erie Canal.

Becoming an author has been a life-long dream. Thanks to family and friends that dream has become a reality.

If you had as much fun reading *Keeper of the Keys* as she had writing it, she hopes you will spread the word to relatives, friends and the rest of mankind by word-of-mouth and by posting a review on Amazon. She welcomes any comments or questions about *Keeper of the Keys*. If you would like to share, you may contact her at: rojoshep@frontiernet.net.

Other Books by this Author:

Bloodfire and the Legend of Paradox Pond

Eye of the Raven